BENEATH THE WILLOW

MICHAEL J MURPHY

Copyright © 2018 Michael J Murphy

ISBN: 978-1-925846-17-1
Published by Vivid Publishing
P.O. Box 948, Fremantle
Western Australia 6959
www.vividpublishing.com.au

 A catalogue record for this book is available from the National Library of Australia

All rights reserved. No part of this publication may be reproduced, stored in a retrieval system or transmitted in any form or by any means, electronic, mechanical, photocopying, recording or otherwise, without the prior written permission of the copyright holder.

For my wife Tracy

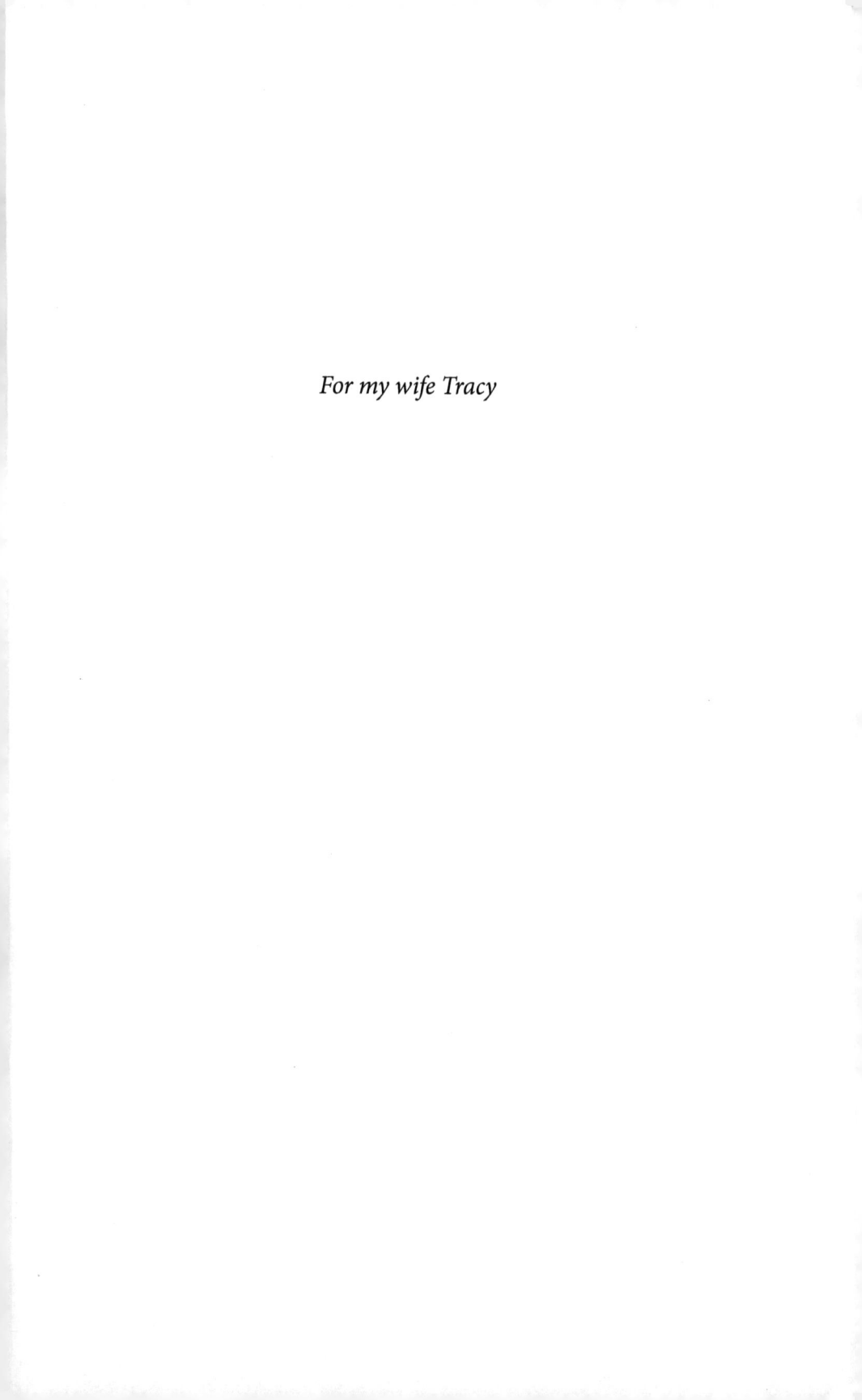

Acknowledgments

I was motivated to write this story after discovering a letter by my grandfather. He had written to my grandmother before departing for the Middle-East in 1940 with the 2nd Australian Imperial Force (AIF). While *Beneath the Willow* is a work of fiction, with historical facts interwoven into the characters' lives, I hope this story illustrates the lasting impact of war on the families of Australian men and women who served their country.

Many people and institutions helped me see this project through: not least my wife, Tracy, whose support and encouragement inspired me from day one. My parents, Rex and Jane, have been pillars of strength through the good and the tough times. I am also fortunate to have a large extended family who each played a part in the creation of this novel.

Retired Lieutenant-Colonel Gary McKay mentored me through the process of writing a book. A successful author himself, Gary's advice was much appreciated when I needed a push in the right direction.

I would also like to extend a most sincere thank you to the people at Vivid Publishing: in particular, Jason, Nicola-Jane and Christina who have worked tirelessly in the production of my book.

Although this story is fictional, the historical aspects required extensive research. I would like to acknowledge the many wonderful institutions that allow public access to archived records, including the publications by Australian author-historians that I have referred to.

The Battle of Fromelle by Roger Lee, *Fromelles* by Patrick Lindsay and *The Story of the Australian Fifth Division* by Capt. A.D. Ellis were each invaluable, both individually and collectively, in understanding the worst day in Australia's military history.

The seemingly endless amount of information that is provided by the Australian War Memorial, through its unit war diaries and various other records, is a credit to this country.

The National Library of Australia and The National Archives of Australia are great wellsprings of information. Accessing digitised newspapers through Trove allowed me to gain a sense of the public's mood in a given time.

Most importantly, I would like to acknowledge the sacrifice made by all Australians who have served in defence of their nation.

Prologue

Denman Hill, July 1953

Judith saw the headlights dance against the lounge room wall long before she heard the engine of the Ford utility. The motor roared and then subsided, as the vehicle ducked and weaved along the gravel road. She stood up and gently placed the novel she held on the sofa, and then made her way to the kitchen to boil the kettle.

Outside, the vehicle came to a sudden halt as it collided with the hardwood post of the garage. Two Kelpies barked at the intrusion to the peaceful night, while the headlights of the Ford illuminated Aunt Alice's cottage.

'What was that, Aunty?' asked Elizabeth, alarmed. She huddled closer to the much-loved woman. Alice allowed the well-worn copy of *Robinson Crusoe* to rest on the quilt that covered her lap.

'Sounded like Father's Ford,' said William.

'Wait here, children. I will go and investigate.'

Alice climbed out of her queen-sized bed. She took a deep breath, and then calmly put on her robe. David, the eldest of the children, watched his aunt leave the room as he sat on a chair at the end of the bed. He enjoyed his Aunty's stories but felt a little too old to be snuggled up under the quilt with his younger brother and sister. He silently wished his father had stayed where he was or found somewhere to sleep it off.

Alice made her way through the kitchen and opened the front door of the cottage. Instantly she took a step back and shielded her eyes from the blaze of headlights. She squinted to see her nephew Reg stumbling along the path between the house and where she stood. She sighed and then glanced to her left. She saw Judith through their kitchen window. The mother of three stood at the kitchen sink with a grim expression, prepared for the worst. Alice felt a tug on her gown and turned to see little Elizabeth, who wanted an explanation for all the commotion.

'Back to bed little one, you too, William. Your father bumped his car into the shed… that's all.' Alice tried to sound flippant, but felt exasperated.

'Bumped, sounded like an earthquake,' said William under his breath.

'David, will you continue to read while I get some more cocoa off your Mother.'

'Yes, Aunt Alice,' replied David. He had seen this scenario played out more than once, so he escorted his brother and sister back to the bedroom without any fuss so as not to cause them alarm.

'Everything all right, Reg?' Enquired Alice from her cottage doorstep, her arms wrapped around herself to ward off the cold night air.

'All right, why wouldn't it be!' replied Reg, with drunken contempt. 'Go back inside and mind your own business.'

'I have been reading to the children,' Alice said softly. She tried in vain to suggest that maybe he should act a little more dignified.

'Well good then, go and do it.'

Alice turned and made her way back to the cottage while Reginald floundered his way towards the side door of the house. Alice had just stepped through her doorway when she heard a loud crash and a pathetic yelp. She darted back outside to see Reg on the ground. He had fallen and had attempted to stand, but like a new born foal he had fallen again.

'Jesus flamin' Christ, who left the wheelbarrow here?' snarled

Reg. He clasped at his head as he eventually steadied on his feet. His mood had swung from arrogant and pigheaded to furious.

Judith heard the noise and opened the side door, while Alice watched on under a shower of light from the headlamps.

'What happened, Reg,' asked Judith, 'are you all right?'

'What happened… what happened? Stupid woman,' growled Reg, his temper white-hot. 'What happened! That lazy little bastard William left the wheelbarrow out. Could have broke me neck.'

Judith stood in the doorway, not sure what to say. She could easily say the wrong thing and escalate the situation, but she had to say something—he expected her too.

'Are you hurt, dear?'

'Where is the little brat, I'll give him what for,' snarled Reg through gritted teeth. 'In with Alice, is he?'

'Come inside and have something to eat, dear,' pleaded Judith. She moved down the step and placed a hand on her husband's arm.

Reg pushed his wife to the ground and then roared for William, as he strode towards the cottage.

'He's asleep!' cried Alice.

'William, outside now!'

In the warmth of Alice's bed, the room had abruptly turned cold with fear. William stared towards the kitchen. He expected his father to burst in at any moment, and he was ashen in colour. Hypnotised by the sounds outside, he didn't notice David stand and leave the bedroom.

'William, I'm warning you!'

'Reginald Miller, stop this craziness, you have scared the children,' shrieked Alice.

'It was me,' said a soft but resolute voice. David stood at the threshold of the cottage, scared but steadfast in the defence of his brother.

The voice didn't register with Reg, and full of anger, he continued his tirade.

'William, last chance. Outside now!'

'It wasn't William, it was me,' said David, more firmly.

'You… you left the wheelbarrow where I could fall over it,' said Reg, his intoxicated mind calculating the information. 'You should know better.'

Alice's frantic gaze darted between David and his father. Her mind was tormented by what Reg would do next; her gut wrenched, as she thought of the selflessness David had shown, trying to protect William. She took a short sharp breath and felt sickened by Reg's cowardly display.

With the taste of hard liquor in his throat, Reginald Miller's head burned with rage and confusion. Like a wild boar that charged through the low scrub, he had no compass, discretion, empathy or justification, and like a twig stepped on by that wild boar, he snapped. Reg pulled his right hand back and brought it down on his eldest son's face. The blow knocked him to the ground.

Alice screamed, and Judith stood motionless in the shadows, paralysed by shock. She loathed the man that she had exchanged vows with at the altar of St Andrews.

The act delivered, Reg continued, committed to the sin without hope of being released from its soul-destroying grip. He took off his belt and thrashed at his boy's back. Alice fell to her knees and sobbed, while David convulsed and whimpered with each violent blow. In the bedroom, with the blankets tight around his head, William cried. The father, fuelled by grog and events long ago, raised his arm again and then saw blackness. The clunk of timber on skull reverberated through the still night air.

The brave young man slowly lifted his head. He looked for confirmation that the ordeal was over. He saw his father face down in the dirt, unconscious. He appeared to be dead. David's head thumped with a pain that made him feel nauseous, and his back screamed as if burnt. The welts and cuts from his father's abuse reacted to the slightest movement. He took a moment before he rose to his feet. He glanced at his mother. Her eyes were dull and glazed over, and she swayed gently where she stood. She still held the piece of wood that had incapacitated her husband.

David looked down at his feet and was suddenly engulfed by shame. Alice rushed towards him, but he limped away into the darkness that surrounded their farm before she could reach him.

'David, come back… David!' Cried Alice. Her voice was swallowed by the cold, sombre air.

'What happened to Davo?' asked William from behind the screen door. Elizabeth clung to his side; they both stared at their unconscious father. 'What happened to Davo?' repeated William. He knew what had happened, but his innocent mind wanted the question asked so it could be denied, making it a fiction, or at least, a misunderstanding.

Lost for words, Alice opened the door and bent down to hug both children. Judith, woken from her trance, joined them. She pressed her lips hard against her babies' cheeks and stroked their hair.

Part One

ONE

Balmain, May 1915

The letter leaned on a vase full of wilted flowers perched on the mantle of the open fire. Grace Miller had not given it a second look after she placed it there; she didn't need to. Its image glared behind her eyes—as big as a silent movie screen. Its presence commanded an overbearing sense of anguish towards what may lie within the well-travelled envelope.

One of the many postmarks read Cairo in blurred ink, the writer's hand unmistakable. Her eldest son, like so many sons, had bounded off to war, full of patriotism and energies that could not be swayed. She had kissed her young Archie on the cheek, while she clung desperately to her husband's forearm—himself a veteran of the campaign in Sudan. Her son had then turned and boarded the ship for a land too foreign and distant to comprehend. Archie had been encased in a wave of masculine pride and had remained oblivious to his mother's torment.

As Grace reminisced and scrubbed pots in her kitchen, she felt a tidal wave of dread wash into Beattie Street Balmain.

* * *

Clarence Miller walked briskly along Darling Street on his way home from his job as a cadet journalist at the *Balmain Observer*. He felt good, and whistled the bouncy tune, 'Good Morning, Mr Zip Zip Zip'. He liked his job. It wasn't common in working class Sydney for a young man of eighteen to have a position like his, full of promise and potential advancement. The work excited him and appealed to his curious nature and sharp intellect. His mother, Grace, said it was the perfect job for him. If you are going to ask questions all day—she would say with a smirk—you may as well get paid for it.

A lot of Clarence's mates, as well as his father and younger brother Frank, had jobs on Cockatoo Island; his father Albert was a boilermaker, Frank a first-year apprentice. A totally decent and respectable way to make a living, Clarence would say to himself—just not for me.

Clarence noticed young George Baker on the corner of Darling Street and Birchgrove Road, a fresh bundle of afternoon edition *Observers* under his arm.

'Anzacs doing us proud at Gallipoli, read all about.'

'Hello, George.'

'G'day, Clarrie. Anzacs batter the poor old Turk,' continued George. He did not want to risk a sale on chit-chat.

The boy's exclamations immediately made him think of his older brother Archie, halfway around the world. Clarence was faced with the news of war all day in his work as a cadet journalist, but somehow, hearing it yelled out in the middle of Darling Street made it all the more real, all the more confronting.

'I'll take one of those, George.'

'It'll cost you a penny, no freebies here.'

'Naturally, wouldn't have it any other way.' Clarence smiled and handed over his penny.

'Why didn't you swipe one from work?'

'Forgot, see you tomorrow, George.'

'Yep. Anzacs, AIF do us proud,' rolled on the young salesman.

Clarence left George to ply his trade and then paused after a few steps. He leaned against the shopfront of Hickman's Butchers to look at the front page, with its scaled map of the Gallipoli peninsula, and detailed reports of the campaign so far. His thoughts drifted once again to his brother, who was amongst those George heralded. Without a letter from Archie in almost six weeks, the Miller household was in a constant state of worry. From reports filtering into his workplace, Archie's 1st Battalion was a part of the second and third waves of the initial landing.

Maybe that was good. Maybe it was safer, Clarence said to himself, though his editor, Mr Blake, had not filled him with confidence that morning, when he simply said, 'poor bastards,' as he reviewed the copy before it went to print.

Clarence folded the paper under his arm and began the walk home. Suddenly the scent of freshly baked bread invaded his senses. 'Ah, bread. Almost forgot.' He turned left and entered Reynolds's Bakery to the sound of a chattering bell.

'Can I help you, sir?' enquired a young lady from behind the counter.

Clarence forgot about the war, forgot about bread and had to remind himself to breathe. He was in love.

***

A warm loaf under his right arm, Clarence glided along Beattie Street, his newspaper, an avenue for his emotions, casually tapped the tops of the picket fence that lined the pavement. Near the front gate of his family home, Clarence paused and watched two men unload kegs of beer from a lorry into the cellar of the Exchange Hotel, a quarter of a mile down the road. His senses were heightened after his encounter at the bakery, and he could faintly make out their mumbled curses as they toiled. He could tell they yearned for knock-off time and a cool ale of their own.

Clarence gazed at the workers and pondered. *How strange it is…* his thoughts were interrupted by the bakery girl's voice inside his head, warm and soft but firm and capable, alluring yet intimidating.

How strange it is, his thoughts now clearer, *that men, living in the same environment, going to work, collecting their pay, clearing their debts, can do so, living much the same as each other. And then, by the most mundane act—like the exchange of threepence for a loaf of bread—change their lives to the point that it will never be the same.*

What could I call her? he wondered, as the man who lowered the kegs into the cellar swore at his offsider. *Beautiful, obviously, but if I were to say beautiful, then what would I say of God's other marvellous creations; the dolphin escorting a Bondi wave or a stallion patrolling a grassy plain.*

'Clarrie!' barked his father, as he stood in the open doorway of his house, at a loss as to why his son was staring into oblivion. 'If you want a job at the Exchange, I can arrange it. Come inside mate. We got a letter from Arch.'

'Oh,' replied Clarence sedately, brought back to reality. 'I have Mother's bread.'

'Come in. Mum's made a pot of tea, we'll read it together.'

Clarence followed his father into the house and allowed the sun to set on his thoughts. He ambled down the short hall, past a small sitting area, and into the kitchen. His brother Frank sat at the table and still wore the dust and grime from a hard day's work. Their nine-year-old sister Alice sat opposite Frank; she gave Clarrie a warm smile as he entered the small room.

Grace Miller turned from the cupboard fixed to the kitchen wall and gratefully accepted the loaf of bread from her second eldest. She forced a smile and then motioned for him to sit. Grace placed a tea-cup in front of Clarence and poured, as Albert Miller thumbed the envelope, as if considering his options. He stopped, picked up a knife and opened the letter while Grace took up her seat.

Beneath the Willow

1st Australian General Hospital
Heliopolis Palace Hotel
Cairo, Egypt
10 April, 1915

Dear Mum, Dad, Clarrie, Frank and Ally,
Mum, I hope the return address didn't give you a fright. I am writing to you, having had the worst of luck. Sorry it has been so long in between letters but we have been very busy with exercises and other types of training, in preparation for the front.

I am laying up in a hospital cot, twiddling my thumbs, after breaking my ankle during drills a fortnight ago. Fell over some half-buried ruins, and snap.

Grace, emotions strained to breaking point, covered her mouth as she sobbed with relief at the reprieve, confusing Frank and Alice. Albert paused to give his wife a moment. She nodded imperceptibly, and he continued.

I cannot believe how unlucky one man could be, especially after our battalion received news that we will be heading to the front soon. By the time you receive this, all outgoing mail is being held until further notice, my mates will have covered themselves in glory, while I'm lying on my back or hobbling on crutches. The Doc said I will be out of action from eight to ten weeks and there was even talk of sending me home, but I wouldn't hear of it and kicked up a big old fuss. Well as much as you can in the army. Anyway, Lieutenant Davidson, a real top bloke, played seconds for South Sydney, can't hold that against him, he spoke to the commanding officer of our battalion and convinced him to let me recuperate in Heliopolis. As long as they haven't belted the Turks already, I will be joining up with the rest of the boys as soon as the leg's right.

How is the footy going? Say g'day to everyone on Cockatoo Island. How's little Frank shaping up? Give Ally a hug and make sure Clarrie's not knocking off my good clobber. Miss your cooking, Mother.

Your Loving Son & Brother
Archie

The Millers sat in silence for a moment, as each member of the family deciphered the text in their own way.

'Well,' said Albert, 'he sounds in fine fettle, despite the broken leg.'

'Yes, very good, probably driving the doctors mad,' added Clarence, in an attempt to add weight to his father's optimism.

Grace sat silently at the table. Casually she reached out and drew the letter towards her. She gently ran her hand over the script as if it were her Archie's face. She knew these were the strangest of times, but how could a mother find relief when she had learnt that her son had broken his leg? Easily, she told herself. *Those old ruins may have saved his life.*

***

Saturdays were every working man's second-favourite day after Sunday, maybe third if you included pay day, and Clarence was no different, even though boilermakers, labourers and the like wouldn't consider a journalist as a working man. Clarence couldn't see the logic in their beliefs. Working your mind could be just as exhausting as physical work, but Clarence had given up on trying to win those arguments around the dinner table—mocking laughter always triumphed.

It was getting close to midday and knock-off time. Clarence

hurried through the jobs his boss had left him. His sole purpose for that day was to get to Reynolds's Bakery before closing. He imagined his mother's questions over his sudden love of high loaves, and then reasoned that you can never have enough bread.

With a hard cover volume of *Keats* in his hand, a birthday present from a discerning mother (Archie would receive footballs and cricket bats—as would Frank), Clarence glided along Darling Street with a smile. *Does she work on Saturdays?* he asked himself. *Surely she does.*

Clarrie entered the cramped, but neat, shop and his heart sank. A teenage boy and an older lady with dark hair, marked with flecks of grey, shuffled around each other behind the waist-high counter. Clarence went to turn and exit the bakery, but a mother accompanied by two children entered through the door. The bell announced their arrival and foiled his inconspicuous exit.

Clarence turned to take his place in the queue. He knew he was about to waste threepence on a loaf of bread he didn't really need. Slowly he made his way to the counter as the customers made small talk with the older shop assistant, while the teenager fumbled with change, bread, and anything else he laid his hands on. Clarence appeared next to be served by the young lad, when a white-aproned figure appeared at the edge of his vision. The voice was heavenly, and instantly recognisable.

'May I help you, sir?'

Clarence stood speechless. He revelled in his change of fortune.

'Sir, may I help you?' The young lady repeated.

'Ah, yes,' replied Clarence, flustered. *She must think me a fool*, he thought. 'Yes, thank you. I will have some bread.'

The child sniggered behind him. The beautiful shop assistant smiled.

'Any particular type?'

'Oh, just a loaf, I mean… a white loaf… yes, a white loaf will be fine. Thank you.' Clarence wanted to find a deep dark pit, like the one at the Colliery, and fling himself into it.

'Will the same one as yesterday be fine?' replied the young lady, having fun with her bamboozled customer.

Clarence just nodded, not game to speak.

Feeling compassion for her awkward but handsome prey, she decided to allow him some respite from his discomfort.

'May I ask what that is in your hand?'

Grateful for the distraction, Clarence looked down, then his eyes met hers, his head was giddy. 'Keats... the poet.'

'That is interesting.'

'Sorry?' replied Clarence. *Did I say something wrong?*

'It is interesting, in that I don't see many young men around here who read the Romantics. They would probably prefer to wrestle each other or something. I like Elizabeth Browning myself.'

'A very gifted poetess,' said Clarence. Then without thinking how it would sound or be perceived, as a compliment to the young lady's poetic taste, Clarence recited the first line of one of Browning's most famous poems.

'How do I love thee?'

The mother behind him gasped and the older shop assistant shot her daughter a glare that would make the fires of Hell seem soothing. Clarence, mortified at his spontaneity, placed threepence on the counter, turned and fled.

Ruth, the beautiful bakery assistant, smiled deep from within her soul. She knew she had just met the most intriguing man. *Don't be silly*, she admonished herself, *you couldn't; you don't even know his name.*

***

Under the shade of a large tree—itself under the screen of the Court House—Clarence sat on a bench. He still panted from his unplanned dash. Relieved to have escaped the glares and whispers at his flash of insanity, he was abashed yet exhilarated. Clarence chuckled softly as he recalled what had taken place in the small suburban bakery. *What were you thinking, Miller?* the young Romeo quizzed himself. *How Do I Love Thee! More like, how does the constabulary arrest thee. I should be locked up*, he continued, in his light-hearted but biting tirade; *committed or whatever they do with bumbling idiots, but I would do it again and probably more.*

He smiled, and with his eyes closed, he tilted his head back to take in the late Autumn sun that strained its way through the trees' foliage. He relaxed and released himself from self-admonishment; conjured images of his poetess entered his mind.

'Excuse me, sir.' The familiar voice found him as if it had arrived on those autumn rays.

Startled into reality, Clarence sat bolt upright. All at once he saw the beautiful young bakery assistant and the busy Balmain traffic.

Clarence shifted in his seat and fossicked for words. 'Oh, Miss. You're here.' He stood and placed a conciliatory hand in front of his body. 'Miss, let me assure you, that there was nothing inappropriate or untoward in what I said. I was meaning...'

'My name is Ruth... Ruth Reynolds,' the young lady interrupted, 'and what you said in the bakery was spontaneous and beautiful.'

She smiled and rendered Clarence helpless. Her eyes glistened, and the would-be poet toppled over a waterfall of emotions. He fell willingly into the nameless state that was now sole occupant of his very existence.

'Clarence Miller or Clarrie,' he said, as he offered his hand to shake gently. 'Would you care to sit, Miss Reynolds?'

'I would love to, and please call me Ruth,' she said in a voice that was confident yet delicate, 'but I must get back to the bakery. My mother doesn't fully comprehend impromptu acts.' She laughed, and Clarence glimpsed an independence that he hadn't seen in other girls.

'But I was wondering... and I hope you don't take this as being too forward, Clarence.' Ruth paused. She reminded herself of society's views on outspoken ladies. 'I was wondering, would you care to maybe meet for a walk one afternoon?' Ruth stopped suddenly and Clarence saw a hint of self-doubt in a woman who radiated self-belief.

'I would enjoy that very much, Ruth.' Clarence spoke her name like a groom would take his vows— maybe he was.

'Excellent,' chirped Ruth, the certainty restored in her voice. 'Sunday at two o'clock?'

'Very well, where should we meet?'

'Mr Miller!' exclaimed Ruth in jest, 'what kind of a lady do you take me for?'

' I...' choked Clarence.

'I live with my family at 20 Glassop Street. My parents would insist on meeting you before we gallop off into the sunset; they will probably send my brother along to keep us company.'

'Of course,' replied Clarence. 'Two o'clock at Glassop Street.' He smiled and then stiffened his body while he tilted forward in a mock bow.

She nodded in acknowledgement of his clumsy act. It warmed her heart, and she felt compelled to hold his gaze for a moment before she turned for the bakery.

TWO

The Miller family had never been overly religious, but they had become a regular part of the congregation since Archie departed from Circular Quay. Clarence was neither enthusiastic nor put out by the Sunday morning service. He could see that it gave his mother some comfort, and he could even admit to himself that the cold timber pews had given him time to reflect on how much he missed his brother.

Distracted by thoughts that related to how his walk with Ruth may unfold, what to say, gift, no gift, this morning's service seemed to drag on a little longer than normal. His selfish preoccupation stung Clarence with guilt when he considered where his mother's mind would be. The flock broke out into a beautiful May morning; they mingled with one another and exchanged pleasantries, and, since April 25th—concerns.

The Millers strolled home to Beattie Street and chatted cheerfully. Albert and Frank still rejoiced in Balmain's victory over Eastern Suburbs the afternoon before, which left them oblivious to Clarence's news of his impending date. His mother was more receptive and seemed pleased that her second eldest had met a nice girl from a good family. She had met Mrs Reynolds several times over the years. Alice trailed casually behind her family. She was more interested in a mangy stray dog that lingered at a comfortable distance, than her family's chatter. The dog hoped for pity, and therefore a meal or two.

The dissection of Balmain's victory continued around the kitchen table while Mrs Miller poured tea for everyone. Clarence joined in, but not having attended the game, was unable to match the others in passion. It wasn't as if Clarence was averse to Rugby League or any sport, for that matter. He attended a handful of Balmain games at Birchgrove Oval and was quite handy at water polo, without much practice. He just didn't seem to possess the primal instinct to bash into each other that most young men seemed to relish. He didn't consider himself a coward and had fought his fair share of battles as a kid alongside his big brother, but he had avoided a lot more through discretion. A trait to be admired, he thought, but not in Balmain. Barefooted dockyard workers' sons preferred knuckles. It was less complicated.

Clarence flicked through the pages of Saturday's paper. He tactfully turned the page, which contained the latest casualty lists from the Dardenelles, and settled on the advertisements. His father had pulled him aside before church and asked him to be discreet—for his mother's sake—in regard to the war. Archie was out of harm's way for now, but reading about young local boys lost, like young Perkins from Theodore Street, would do his mother's nerves no good at all.

The thought of the casualty list re-entered his mind as he stared blankly at an advert for the Sydney School of Arts. Names like Perkins and Lawson, Davis and Hayes, leapt out at him like sparks from a grindstone. Lads that had been workmates of his brother; never to be seen again, the chance to walk with a beautiful girl or belt someone on a football field—erased. Clarence had been seventeen when war broke, and his mother, aware of the countless young boys who attempted to enlist by fudging their ages, had forbidden Clarence to even consider the idea. Clarence, unlike his brother, was in no rush to join up. Archie and his mates regaled in promises of adventure, the likes never to present themselves again. Clarence's imagination needed no such promises. A hint of a southerly breeze carried across the water or the clip-clop of a Clydesdale along Darling Street would be enough to transport him away.

Now eighteen, he couldn't ignore something that nagged his consciousness. Why hadn't he enlisted? He hadn't thought about it much, not until now; was that a reflection of his character, he wondered? Was it his job? No one had said anything, but would they? Or would they whisper something long after he'd passed. *Not cut from the same cloth as his brother Archie*, they would mutter, or something to that effect. Why hadn't he joined up? The question lingered.

***

The brass door-knocker made a low thud as Clarence rapped the front door to 20 Glassop Street. A small bouquet in his left hand, he waited patiently for his call to be answered. He straightened his shoulders and adjusted his hat that matched his only suit. Heavy footsteps approached and Clarence swallowed as the door opened. A short, thickset man blocked the entrance. Intentionally or not, he emanated a defensive disposition.

'Mr Reynolds, I am Clarence Miller,' said the young suitor, hand outstretched. 'I have come to see Ruth.'

Harry Reynolds stared at the young man before him. He assessed him like a judge jaded by years of unfulfilled service, guilty until proven innocent—innocence not likely.

'Harold Reynolds,' said the baker, in his deepest voice. He took Clarence's hand and shook it firmly. 'Mrs Reynolds has prepared tea, come through.'

Mr Reynolds stepped to one side and Clarence entered. He took off his hat and placed it on the stand to his right, and waited for Ruth's father to lead the way. Clarrie glanced at his surroundings as he followed. Everything about the house was feminine, from the lace cloth beneath ornate lamps, to the oak curio cabinet that glistened with crystal against a papered wall. It was a stark contrast to his own home, which made Clarence wonder how much a bakery shop made in a year.

They passed through a narrow hall with doors on either side, and then stepped out into one end of a good-sized room bathed in sunlight. Large glass windows made up most of the opposite wall, with a mahogany bookshelf at the far end. It watched over a hand-carved coffee table, which intersected two finely upholstered armchairs. A large polished table made its presence felt in the centre of the room. It rested upon an exotic rug and could sit eight people.

At his left hand was a doorway that appeared to open into a large kitchen, while directly to his right, another doorway barred the entrance to a small yard.

'A lovely home, Mr Reynolds.'

Harry grunted and nodded. He was eager to preserve the air of authority he had tried to manufacture.

'A journalist, my daughter tells me.'

'Yes, sir, well a cadet, still learning.'

'Of course,' replied Mr Reynolds, detached, grateful for the opportunity to appear lordly.

Clarence inhaled sharply and held his breath for a moment, while he contemplated his next move. Although not sure exactly what to expect when he arrived at the Reynolds's house, he hadn't anticipated a baker to be such hard work. Whenever he had caught a glimpse of one, which was rarely, they appeared to be like every other working man, dog-tired, but covered in flour instead of soot or grease.

A moment of awkward silence passed before Clarence decided to test the conversational waters once again. To his relief, he was rescued by the sounds of clattering china and flustered female voices that approached from the kitchen. Miraculously, the frantic chatter converted into smiles as the two elegant women entered the sunroom and placed a tray on the table. One tray supported a pot of tea with matching cups and saucers; the other was filled with assorted cakes.

'Mr Miller,' said Mrs Reynolds, with a smile that was warm, but portrayed some wariness.

'Mrs Reynolds, a pleasure to meet you. You have a lovely home, and please, call me Clarence.'

'Thank you, Clarence. Some of the furniture you see was passed down from my late mother, may she rest in peace.' Ruth's eyes rolled at her mother's theatrics. 'When my brother inherited our family property near Denman, I was—either through generosity or his lack of taste—able to acquire some pieces. They hold a special place in my heart.'

'They are lovely,' replied Clarence. He marvelled how women could tear strips off a person—in this case her brother—in such a pleasant way. Mr Reynolds stood motionless to the side while his wife spoke, and Clarence realised where the real authority lay. Clarence noticed Mrs Reynolds's eyes shift downwards and was reminded of the bouquet he held.

'Ruth, these are for you,' announced Clarence, as he held the modest arrangement of flowers in Ruth's direction. She was dressed elegantly in a white blouse and long black skirt, and her dark lustrous hair, which was pulled up in a bun, highlighted her striking features. Clarence thought she was the most beautiful young lady he had ever seen.

'Thank you, Clarence,' replied Ruth. Her eyes sparkled as she stepped forward to receive the thoughtful gift. She was eager to leave the house and stroll with her new friend, but was resigned to the fact of having to continue with formalities.

'Shall we sit?' offered Mrs Reynolds, while she gestured towards the table.

'Of course, dear,' said Mr Reynolds. Harry bounded forward to offer his wife Mary a seat.

***

After she had watched Clarence answer polite but well-directed questions for close to an hour, Ruth felt it time to draw the party to a close. She discreetly tapped her own foot against her mother's shin, and waited for the message to be received.

'Well,' declared Mrs Reynolds, her daughter's Morse code acknowledged. 'Maybe Ruth and Clarence would care to take a stroll through the park.'

'If it is fine with Mr Reynolds and yourself… that would be lovely.'

'Excellent, I will fetch Thomas,' said Mrs Reynolds, adding the disclaimer. 'He would love to join you.'

Ruth's mother stood from the table and glanced at her daughter, as if to say, *What did you expect*, and disappeared to find her teenage son. Clarence rose and shook hands with Mr Reynolds, who was somewhat warmer in his demeanour, probably aware that his earlier performance had been exposed by the presence of his wife.

***

Thomas Reynolds trailed along like a government agent as Ruth and Clarence entered Elkington Park in between two large Moreton Bay Fig trees. The winter sun was determined but struggled to emit the last of the day's warmth.

'You did very well in there, Clarence.'

'Pardon?'

'At tea, with my parents—you survived.'

Clarence laughed. 'It wasn't that bad, only a couple of bumps and bruises. I must admit, I was nervous when I met your father.'

It was Ruth's turn to laugh. 'Father, oh he's just a big softy. It was all an act. I think he was more nervous than you. It was the first time he's had to meet a young man at the door of his house, asking after his daughter.'

'Really?'

Ruth spun to face her admirer. Her eyes glared and her hands were on her hips. 'Really! And what exactly do you mean by that, Mr Miller?'

Clarence recoiled. Caught off guard by Ruth's combustible response, he reacted quickly. The fire in her blood had somehow ignited his ardour.

'Nothing, nothing at all, Ruth,' pleaded Clarence, with a smirk.

'Do you think I have a little black book of gentleman callers?' she continued, clearly offended.

Thomas stood alerted in the distance. When his mother had ordered him to chaperone his sister, he obeyed; he had never thought he would be required to act.

'Ruth, I am sorry.' A broad cheeky smile formed on Clarrie's face. 'That came out wrong. It's just that… it's just that you're very beautiful and what you said surprised me a little, but what I said was silly. I'm sorry.'

Ruth took her hands off her hips and looked at Clarence through narrowed eyes. Somewhat placated, she turned to continue their walk, albeit silently for a minute or so. Her temper cooled and she suddenly felt embarrassed by her outburst. Although she was aware she possessed a fiery temperament, she was confused that it showed itself so readily in front of Clarence. Boys didn't normally get under her skin—that was her mother's job.

'Clarence,' started Ruth, as she turned to face him again. 'I apologise for my outburst, it was unacceptable.'

'Apology accepted, think nothing of it.' With a smile, Clarence held out his right arm, bent at the elbow. It was an olive branch for Ruth to take.

She returned his smile and looked into his eyes for a moment, feeling with her sight as much as seeing. *How do I love thee, let me count the ways*, Ruth said silently, every nerve in her body tingling as she took his arm.

As they walked sedately through the trees, a cool, salty breeze caressed the young couple. Warmed by emotions that exceeded his comprehension, Clarence glowed in the recognition of what was now understood; his soul entwined with another forever.

***

The following weekend, when Ruth met Clarence's mother for morning tea, it was like a reunion of sisters parted. They came together with an ease of understanding, an intuition that they had something in common; something that went far deeper than making tea. When Ruth presented a wide-eyed Alice with the gift of a small doll, she threatened to shift the natural balance in the male-dominated household of 96 Beattie Street—forever.

Ruth and Clarence spent most of their spare time with each other in the month that followed. They took walks or found a place to sit along the foreshore. They would chat or read and bask in the sun, content in their own company. A casual observation on these outings would turn into a spirited debate. The young lovers would probe each other for the answers to their newly formed universe; the events of the day often found themselves in the pages of Ruth's secret journal. Unlike the majority of girls her age, Ruth had an opinion on most matters. From politics and business to education and international relations, she would engage Clarence for thought-provoking responses. Clarence, confronted by her zeal, marvelled at her intelligence; he realised that the beauty of her features was but a clever mask for her true self. A trap for an unworthy suitor with ideas only skin deep.

On one such Saturday afternoon in early June, they sat with their backs to a tree near Birchgrove Oval. Ruth commended the state of Queensland for having followed the lead of South Australia in allowing women to stand for Parliament. She had not got the debate she had hoped for, as Clarence was in total agreement, so she suddenly changed topics.

'Clarrie, tell me about Archie. You don't say much about him and

I am reluctant to ask questions in front of your mother and father. What's he like?'

'Not as handsome as me, for starters.'

'Yes, yes, how could he be,' mocking laughter interrupted Clarence's vanity. 'No, really Clarrie, I'd like to know.'

'Well,' replied Clarence, drawing a breath, 'he is bigger than me, taller.'

'No, I mean his personality, what is he like?'

'I suppose he's more confident than me… more outgoing.'

'I wouldn't call you shy, Mr "How do I love thee",' said Ruth with a cheeky grin on her face. 'You are very gregarious.'

'Cut it out,' replied Clarence. Embarrassed, a soft pink came to his cheeks. 'More boisterous in a way, he is. If Arch is in the room you know he is there. He loves rugby league, quite a handy player too, would have pushed for First Grade with Balmain if he didn't join up.'

'So, he's not interested in Keats?'

'No,' replied Clarence, 'wouldn't know who he was.'

'Are you close?'

'Too right, we're great mates… different, but as close as brothers can be.'

Ruth studied Clarrie. His eyes dropped to the ground, so she gave him time to think, his thoughts no doubt with his brother.

'Do you miss him, Clarrie?'

'Of course,' blurted Clarence. He rose to his feet and dusted the dirt and bark from his trousers. 'Mother frets; she's aged years in weeks, I reckon.'

'Your mum is a lovely woman, I see a lot of her in you,' Ruth said with tenderness. She stood, but gave Clarence the room she felt he needed.

'I didn't know what to think when he left. They all seemed so excited, Archie and his mates; thought they were sailing off on an adventure.' Clarence paused and stared towards the small vessels moored in the bay that lined the north-eastern boundary of the park.

'The strange thing was, and I have never said this to anyone, I wasn't so convinced.'

'How do you mean?' said Ruth. She moved towards Clarence and took his hand. He lifted his eyes to meet hers. He appreciated her gesture.

'I mean, I wasn't convinced it was going to be the safari they all imagined. I know we had to go, had to help Britain, but to think that the powers of Europe—after all their chest-beating—were just going to turn tail and head home without a serious fight—ludicrous. Over before Christmas,' sighed Clarence.

Ruth had her own views on the European war, by no means subversive, but more sceptical of the political leaders who stoked the Continental furnace, so she was careful with what she said. She did not want to seem insensitive towards Clarrie's family and the young Australians risking their lives on foreign shores.

'Let's hope they all come home very soon.'

'Yes,' replied Clarence. He nodded quickly to mask the conflict that played out within him.

The young couple left the park and made their way along the terrace-lined streets. They spoke occasionally, but were mostly content with absorbing the sounds of suburban life. Alongside a wrought-iron fence, a young girl jumped rope with a rhythmic intensity that, judging by her expression, had transported her to a faraway place, somewhere with frilly dresses and painted horses, not black tar and crooked gutters. Two boys, possibly the skipping girl's siblings, made the finishing touches to a dubious looking billy-cart. A dangerous test run imminent, for barefooted lads with skinned knees and the courage for a challenge.

'I have an idea, Clarence Miller,' exclaimed Ruth. She knew it would be tough, but she did her best to bring some light back into the afternoon.

'And what might that be?' replied Clarence, with a genuine smile.

'Well… we should make our way to Father's shop and see if there is something tempting we can take back and share with your mother.'

'Sounds great, but won't it be closed?'

'The shop will be closed, but he often goes in to make everything right for Monday. Work, work, and more work for father.'

'It's settled then,' said Clarence, 'the bakery it is.'

***

Clarence waited patiently for Ruth to emerge from her father's bakery. He filled the time by peering through the glass shopfronts of the adjoining stores. He had admired some fine leather shoes in the window of Mills and Sons Boot Emporium, but turned to make his way back to Reynolds' bakery. Suddenly, a young girl—maybe fifteen—was standing directly in Clarence's path.

'Pardon me, Miss,' said Clarence, 'I didn't see you; my apologies.'

He touched the brim of his hat and stepped to one side to make his way forward, but oddly, the girl moved to be in front of him again.

'This is for you,' the young lass blurted out. She held what appeared to be a small tobacco tin in her outstretched hand.

'Thank you,' said Clarence, puzzled, 'but I'm not sure…'

Before he could finish the girl let out a suppressed giggle; she then turned and fled across Darling Street, where an older, but still young, lady waited. Totally confused by what had transpired, Clarence did the most logical thing, and prised the lid from the tin of Town Talk Tobacco. *I don't even smoke*, he thought.

Clarence pulled the lid away. He was first amused and then repulsed, as a trickle of bile rose to the back of his throat. He glanced around for the girl, but she was nowhere to be seen. He stared back at the tin's contents, and instinctively snapped the lid back on. Clarrie had hoped that the force of his act would somehow—by magic—make it disappear. Tears welled in his eyes. He saw Ruth approach from the bakery and shoved the item in his coat pocket. His head spun, but he was able remove a handkerchief from his trouser pocket and pretend to blow his nose while he wiped his damp eyes.

'Clarence, I got a passionfruit sponge to take to your parents,' announced Ruth, pleased with her efforts. 'They like sponge cake, don't they?'

'They will love it,' replied Clarence sincerely, but with an air of detachment.

'Are you all right, Clarrie?'

Clarence was confused by what had taken place but didn't know what to say to Ruth. He tried to process his emotions. He wasn't all right, he knew that; how do you react to being labelled a coward, and by a young girl. The white feather, the symbol chosen to label a man considered not to be a man in time of war, eroded his self-belief from its tin case nestled inside his coat. It was a capsule of scorn delivered by self-indulgent imbeciles, and with no charge to answer themselves, they acted with the impunity of ignorance.

'Clarrie, what's wrong, you look pale?'

'I'm fine, Ruth, sorry—just thinking about something.'

'Archie?'

'You could say that. Let's head home. That cake looks delicious.'

Not convinced, Ruth smiled and took Clarence's arm as they crossed the road.

'By the way, Clarrie, I wanted to get out of going to the church function this evening, so I told my father I had promised to help your mother with some things, so no blabbing,' the mischievous side of her personality rose again, as she peered up at Clarence through squinted eyes.

'My lips are sealed,' said Clarence. He did his best to appear cheerful but failed.

'I know, I know, I am a bad daughter.' Ruth tried to manufacture a mood change. 'But you can blame yourself and all your irresistible charm.'

THREE

Frank Miller stood in the middle of Beattie Street with his mate Jim. They passed Frank's football back and forth as Clarence and Ruth approached. A missed timed pass saw the inflated pigskin roll towards Ruth's feet. She picked the ball up and hurled it in an awkward fashion. Clarence sniggered, and Ruth replied with a slap to his arm, happy to see him in a more jovial mood.

'Hello, Frank. How are you?'

'Good,' mumbled Frank, with a shrug of his shoulders.

'Wouldn't make a footballer, would I,' continued Ruth in an attempt to make conversation.

Frank stared back at her blankly. He didn't mean to be rude; he just didn't have anything to say. It was obvious she wouldn't make much of a footballer, so if it was all the same to everyone he would just prefer to continue doing what he was doing. With a quick glance at his most prized possession, he did just that and fired off a pass to Jim.

'He doesn't like me, does he, Clarrie?'

'He doesn't dislike you at all,' replied Clarence. 'You have to understand, Frank. At fourteen, all he thinks about is sport and what's for dinner. To him, you're stranger than a mysterious creature from the deep.'

'Thanks very much!'

'A pretty one,' said Clarence, as he opened the front gate to the small front yard of the Miller residence; 'a very pretty one.'

The young couple walked into the kitchen and found Mrs Miller at the stove. Albert was seated at the table with the newspaper. He smiled as Ruth entered, not immune to her natural charm and easy-going manner. Alice sat cross-legged on the floor. She played with the doll Ruth had given her, but stopped as soon as she heard Ruth's voice.

'Ruthie,' Alice screamed. She leapt to her feet and ran the short distance across the kitchen to hug—in her eyes—a real life princess.

Clarence looked over at them and was warmed by the tender exchange. Without thought, he placed his hand in his coat pocket. He suddenly felt ill at the touch of his unwanted gift.

'Have you named your doll yet, Alice?' asked Ruth.

Alice nodded her head, but remained silent. Her eyes glistened with the unburdened happiness that children enjoy; happy, oblivious to expectations, war, and white feathers.

Alice leant towards Ruth and whispered. 'Her name is Ruthie, Princess Ruthie.'

Ruth hugged Alice and felt a joy which she knew was something beyond having a friend and companion in Clarence. It was an undeniable sense of belonging, so strong as to be preordained. Ruth had noticed Grace smile at her, and she had responded in kind. They spoke without speaking and deepened the bond that had grown between them.

Ruth joined Grace at the stove while she prepared a pot of tea. She glanced over her shoulder at Clarence, who was now seated at the kitchen table, and saw that the look of gloom had resurfaced. The same look which had come over him outside the bakery. Ruth did not want to make a scene, so she continued on, knowing the right time to talk would reveal itself.

'Excuse me, Mr Miller,' said Ruth, as she placed a cup and saucer in front of him. Albert arched backwards to make room and lifted his newspaper at the same time.

'Thanks luv, a cuppa is just what I feel like.'
'Do you like passionfruit sponge, Mr Miller?'
'Do I! You haven't?'

Ruth placed the cake in the middle of the table, but slightly closer to the head of the Miller house. She saw that Mr Miller wasn't too dissimilar to her own father; tough exteriors but soft at heart, responsive to being spoilt every now and then. Albert leant across the corner of the table to get closer to his son. 'Clarrie,' he whispered from the corner of his mouth, 'you should marry this girl. She's a gem.'

Clarence barely responded, and the reaction was not lost on his father. Although he thought it unusual, like Ruth, he reasoned it wise to wait before he enquired.

'So where have you two been today?' enquired Albert, as Ruth took a seat next to Clarence. Ruth gave Clarence a gentle tap on the leg to encourage him to respond.

'Oh,' said Clarence with a start. 'Just down to Birchgrove Oval.' He paused to accept a piece of sponge from his mother. 'Looking out at the water… not much really.'

Ruth compensated for Clarrie and interjected. 'Sometimes we will set out for a walk with no real destination in mind, Mr Miller, and talk away till we find a nice spot to relax… and then talk some more.'

'You sound like a bit of a dreamer, Ruth, just like Clarence,' said Albert with affection.

'Albert! Don't be rude,' snapped Grace. 'It's lovely that the two of them can be so at ease with each other.'

'I wasn't being rude, I was just saying…'

'It's fine, Mrs Miller. My father calls me a dreamer all the time, a romantic, as he puts it. Did Clarence tell you how we met?' Ruth smirked and showed the Millers her mischievous side.

'No, he hasn't, actually,' replied Mr Miller, grinning like a Cheshire cat.

'Now now, I am not sure we want to hear,' said Mrs Miller, taking on the role of arbiter.

'I am thinking of joining up.'

The light and pleasant mood that existed at the table up until that moment ended abruptly. Grace reacted quickly, aware of what might unfold in the coming moments, and ushered Alice into the backyard before she had time to complain. She re-joined the table and placed one hand over her brow as if to shade herself from an intense light.

'What's brought this on so suddenly?' barked Albert Miller.

Ruth sat stunned by the news. She stared straight ahead and fought a lump that had formed in her throat.

'A lot of things,' said Clarence without conviction. He knew exactly what brought it on, but shame would not allow him to reveal it. 'I should be doing my bit,' he continued hurriedly. Clarrie glared up at his father, but he felt more confused than the anger in his eyes showed.

'Doing your bit, you sound like one of those bloody posters,' his father yelled. Albert referred to the countless propaganda posters stuck to buildings all over Sydney, which encouraged young men to enlist. 'We *are* doing our bit!' Albert rose from his seat. The fear of watching another son sail away to war had set his blood to a boil 'Your brother's already over there, for Christ sake.' The decorum of tea and passionfruit sponge cake had gone, and Ruth's heart wept. She witnessed the desperation of a father trying to protect an adult son.

'Clarence, your father is right. When Archie boarded that ship… it was the hardest thing I have ever had to do.' The anxious mother sat straight-backed in her chair with her hands clasped on her lap in an effort to compose herself. 'One son is enough for any family. Please, Clarence you have a good job.'

'An excellent job,' blurted Mr Miller. 'You're doing enough for the country by being a journalist.'

'Writing about it: while men my age risk their lives protecting our way of life.'

'Protecting our way of life!' said Mr Miller, exasperated. Frank suddenly entered the kitchen, but was dismissed with the same swiftness, by a jerk of the head from his father.

'Yes,' replied Clarence, with no confidence.

'Protecting those fat little men in Europe, in three-piece suits, top hats and gold watches dangling from their pockets,' blazed Albert Miller. His words revealed thoughts that couldn't be shared with an imperialistic public, but maybe by the bar of The Exchange Hotel, where a socialist ear might be listening. 'Aristocrats and industrialists, who don't give a second thought to young working men leaping from a trench into a shower of lead, protect them!'

Grace, horrified by the images that her husband conjured, sat silently. She hoped Clarence would listen, sadly aware the dye had probably already been cast.

'I'm talking about fighting for our countrymen, fellow Australians and Englishmen that live as we do!' said Clarence more firmly. He rose from the table and removed his coat to place it on the back of his chair, as if it would relieve some of the tension that filled the small room. 'What do you expect me to do, Father, stay at home like a coward while the rest fight in my place?'

'You're not a coward, son.'

'That's not what some think,' blurted Clarence.

'Your work here is more important than you know; I don't say it, but… who says you're a coward?' Clarence's last statement eventually registered with his father.

Silence crept into the kitchen like a heavy fog into a valley; the cold damp air was intent on laying, seeping into the bones of anyone who dwelt under it, until expelled by a stronger force. Ruth sensed the time to be right and shifted in her seat.

'May I speak, Mr Miller?' Said Ruth softly, pushing the fog through the back door.

'Of course, luv, go ahead.' replied Albert, exhausted from his efforts and therefore calmer.

'Clarence, what happened outside the bakery today?'

'Nothing.'

'Nothing?'

'Yes Ruth, nothing!' Clarence looked at the women he loved, his eyes told all. He had something to say—she could see it—but the pain was too much. Ruth was mildly hurt by Clarence's unwillingness to talk, but her ego was not so big as to let it get in the way of what she knew as love for the stricken man who stood before her.

Clarence looked helplessly around the room, and then towards the floor. Without notice, he ran from the house through the front door. He broke out into the dull light and noticed Frank. He sat alone in the gutter with his football. The youngest of the Miller boy's own feelings spun inside his head, much the same as Clarrie's.

'Are you off as well?' asked Frank, with a bluntness to be expected from a working-class teenager. He peered at his older brother with dark eyes. Frank felt a hurt that came from his family's blindness towards the void that had been left in his life by Archie's absence.

Clarence stared back at his little brother without answering. Instead he held out his hands out for the ball; Frank obliged and propelled the footy by a flick of his wrists, a connection that was desperately needed at that moment.

Albert and Grace Miller, still seated at the kitchen table with Ruth, stared at each other while the fog slowly crept back in. Ruth wanted to act rather than sit, and she sprang to her feet to follow Clarence. Stiffly, she forced her way between the chair Clarrie had sat in and the kitchen wall. She dragged Clarence's coat with her as she passed. The coat fell and gave off a sound that pinged as it met the timber floor. It awakened Mr and Mrs Miller from their weary state and caused Ruth to stop and then turn.

On any other day, Grace Miller would have simply picked the coat up and draped it back over the chair, but the voice that speaks to people from the deepest recesses of their conscience begged her to investigate. She moved slowly but with focus and rose from her seat while Ruth and Albert looked on, both as intrigued as each other.

The mother of four calmly bent down to lift the coat from the ground with her left hand, while she methodically patted and squeezed different parts of the coat with her right. Grace stopped suddenly as her hand clasped a small, but solid object. She felt slightly ashamed at going through her son's coat, so she looked towards her husband. Grace realised what she wanted to do, but via a look, she sought permission.

Albert gave his wife a hurried nod. His wife, in turn, glanced at Ruth before she proceeded to extract the item from the coat pocket. Grace looked at the tobacco tin in complete bewilderment.

'Clarence doesn't smoke,' said Ruth, as she took a seat at the table. She announced what the three of them had all thought.

'Did he buy it for someone, I wonder?' said Grace. 'There's nothing in it though,' she stated, as she moved the tin from side to side, 'it's too light.'

Grace placed the item on the kitchen table. They all gawked at the tin canister until Mr Miller took the initiative, picked it up and removed the lid. Their view obscured from the lid itself, Grace and Ruth were at a loss to the look on Albert's face. You don't often see tears well in a boilermaker's eyes, but Ruth was witness to such an occurrence that day. Her hands recoiled to cover her own mouth when Mr Miller pulled the lid completely away.

'My poor boy,' whispered Grace.

'Who would do such a thing, Mr Miller?' pleaded Ruth. There was anguish in her voice and tears on her cheeks.

'Ignorant foolish people, dear,' replied Albert. He stood to face the fireplace and hide his own emotions, while he gripped the mantle hard enough to turn his knuckles white.

Grace stared blankly at the wall. 'I've seen them… walking around in their frilly white dresses, encouraged by vindictive hags or soured spinsters. They make me sick.'

Although surprised by the timbre of her voice, Ruth felt the loathing that poured from Grace's lips. She was torn between deep pity for her beloved, and unquenchable anger towards his persecutors. She was aware of a so-called 'order of the white feather', but she had never contemplated its existence, let alone as an active front in suburban Balmain.

'I must find Clarence,' cried Ruth.

'Ruth!' said Albert sharply. He stepped forward from the mantle quickly, but with the calmness of a father. 'I think it would be best if I spoke to him first.'

'Yes, Mr Miller,' replied Ruth, her cheeks flushed. 'You are quite right.'

'Give me a moment with him, dear, and then you can talk to him; a thing like this can shake a man.' Albert paused for a moment. He imagined the feeling of inadequacy injected into his son and the anger took hold again. 'So help me if I come across these wretched people, so help me.'

***

Albert took deep breaths to calm himself. Once young and once a soldier, but now a father, he prepared for a long walk as he opened his front door, not knowing in which direction or where Clarence had headed. *The walk will do him good*, he thought, *clear his head*. Grace and Ruth watched Albert leave the kitchen, and assumed he would do his best to talk Clarence around. But how could he try to prevent his son from being or feeling like a man, whatever that was, in a world turned on its head. His gut had wrenched when he watched Archie board the ship at Circular Quay. The realisation that Clarence would be embarking on one of those transports filled him with a foreboding that weakened the hardy man's legs.

As he stepped into the half-light that makes for early evenings in winter, Albert's mood was brightened to see his two sons together. It embodied what he already valued in his family.

Clarence turned to face his father. He felt like the little boy who threatened to run away but couldn't. In Clarrie's mind, that legitimised the contents of the tobacco tin.

'Son, can I have a word?'

Clarence didn't answer but moved towards his father. He knew that he would be told all the things he wanted to hear, but the words to be spoken, however logical and sincere, would make no difference to the outcome of things. He must go, he knew it. The act of a girl delivering a package in public—crude and abhorrent as it was—simply brought to light the torment that had scratched at his conscience these last weeks. Why should his brother, or any other man for that matter, fight, while he lived wrapped securely in freedom's blanket? As he walked, his thoughts turned to Ruth. How ironic to be presented with a love that was certainly fated. Its continuation was challenged by an event that could, in an instant, take life and steal love, but by staying, dissolve the spirit that created love.

***

Ruth stood in the doorway of the Miller's house. Her mind had gone over the day's events, and as she watched Clarence speak with his father, she silently began to ask questions. *Why did I suggest going to the baker; he would never have seen that stupid girl? Why did I…* Ruth stopped her mind from wandering. She was smart enough to know that these things had a way of happening, regardless of a person's intervention. Whatever they did, that girl, or a poster, or the thought of his older brother, would leap from nowhere to invade their lives, just like it had in the park that day.

The young man whom she loved with all her heart carried a burden that any man should not bear, let alone an eighteen-year-old cadet journalist, whose use of poetry wooed bakery assistants. Recent events had tested everyone, young and old, and as she watched Albert Miller shake Clarence's hand firmly, holding the grip longer than one would do normally, she felt she had grown older in one afternoon. All her social and political views, strong and unwavering, ever present and ready for battle when alerted by a chauvinistic or conservative comment, were lulled by her current concerns.

His talk with Clarence over, Albert Miller strode through his front gate towards the house, no more at ease with the situation than he had been before, but comforted that he was at least able to talk to his son. Ruth stepped from the protection of the doorway and onto the verandah. She didn't try to make eye contact with the concerned father; instead, she let him pass into the hall and into the kitchen, where a knowing embrace awaited, without the awkwardness of an unnecessary exchange.

Ruth crossed the short pathway that led to the gate and paced purposely towards Clarence with shortened breath. The need to be alongside him had overwhelmed her. She saw his eyes, dark and lost, and ran to meet him. Her arms wrapped around his waist while her face, draped in dark curls, pressed against his chest. The warmth of her body locked against his, the scent of hair, the emotion that permeated through each beat of her heart, penetrated into Clarence's pores. It intoxicated his senses and allayed his fears.

Ruth looked up at her soulmate and gazed deep into his eyes, no longer lost, but perpetually at home. Quite naturally, and without pause for thought, Ruth placed her hand on Clarence's cheek. She kissed him softly and tenderly on the lips. Ruth pulled away slowly but not entirely; she had awakened desires that surpassed what they had felt so far.

***

The cool damp air of a June evening clung to Clarence and Ruth as they strolled, arm in arm, along Glassop Street. After all the tension and emotion of the previous few hours, Clarence had felt it was best if he allowed his parents some time to themselves, not denying that the disconnection would also serve him well.

Clarence noticed the lack of light from Ruth's house as they approached. He thought that maybe the Reynolds had retired for the evening. But it was early, even for bakers.

'Looks very quiet inside, Ruthy,' Clarence remarked, as he held the front gate open for her to pass through.

'They are all out,' declared Ruth, without fanfare. She bent down and lifted a small pot to reveal a key.

'Out—you mean no one is here?'

'Yes.' She placed the key in the lock and turned it with the door knob to reveal a shadowy hallway.

'Ruth, wait! We should have stayed at...' Clarence stumbled with his speech as he was forced to follow Ruth into the house. He couldn't remain stranded on the verandah and invite a curious eye from a concerned neighbour. He bumped into the hat stand and then fell into a wall, as he fumbled his way in the dark.

'Ruth!' he called out in a hushed voice.

'Yes,' whispered Ruth. She stood directly in front of Clarrie and giggled Her voice brought him to an abrupt halt.

'What are you up to. Your parents might be home any minute!'

'They won't be, and you would know that if you paid any attention to what I say.' Ruth reprimanded Clarrie in a playful way. 'Now stop talking, I have something to say to you.'

Suddenly, the dark house seemed lighter. With his eyes adjusted, Clarrie could make out the beautiful lines of Ruth's delicate face, veiled by spirals of dark hair. Her eyes were radiant in the dull surroundings, and made Clarence feel modest, but comforted at the same time.

'Clarence,' she said leaning in closer to him.

'Yes.'

How do I love thee? Let me count the ways.
I love thee to the depth and breadth and height
My soul can reach, when feeling out of sight
For the ends of being and ideal Grace.

I love thee to the level of every day's
Most quiet need, by sun and candle-light.
I love thee freely, as men strive for right;
I love thee purely, as they turn from praise,
I love thee with the passion put to use
In my old griefs, and with my childhood's faith.
I love thee with a love I seemed to lose
With my lost saints— I love thee with the breath,
Smiles, tears, of all my life! —and, if God choose,
I shall but love thee better after death.

'I love you, Clarence Miller and I always will.' Without another word, Ruth kissed her true love. The kiss conveyed sensations and emotions so extraordinary to them both, as to fuel the flame that already existed. It ensured their love would burn resplendent through cloudless skies and darkened valleys.

Ruth opened the door to her bedroom and the sanctuary of a white-laced quilt. There, they removed themselves from the concerns of the outside world.

FOUR

Island of Lemnos, June 1915

Archibald Miller stood and overlooked the rows of white tents that made up the 3rd Australian General Hospital on the Greek Island of Lemnos. Behind the hospital lay Mudros harbour and the collection of vessels large and small. They were scattered all the way from the shoreline to the harbour entrance, which opened to the south and the Aegean Sea. He looked quizzically at the long line of sheets and other linen suspended along the foreshore to dry in the stiff breeze, and his thoughts drifted to his recent voyage and his delayed introduction to life as a fair dinkum soldier.

After being passed fit for active service, Archie had gladly said goodbye to Heliopolis, appreciative of the care the doctors and nurses had provided, but bored senseless by the dreariness of being cooped up in a ward. He had reported to headquarters in Cairo and was pleased to be re-assigned to the 1st Battalion. The young private then boarded a train for the Port of Alexandria, where the troop ship *Aquitania*, once an ocean liner of the Cunard Line, waited.

Along the wharf, a mass of people and vehicles congregated. Some carried supplies to be loaded; some, such as the horse-drawn ambulances, waited for bandaged soldiers. Archie remembered the wave of excitement that had passed through him as he forced his way through the crowd, and although he had been aware of men lying limply on stretchers, it had not entered his mind to wonder what had brought them there. His thoughts had been occupied with finally joining the fray and being with his mates.

When he had leaned against the stern rail and watched the murky water of the ancient port churn against the torment of powerful turbines, he had flicked a well-drawn smoke from his fingers, a formal declaration that his past misfortune would be laid to rest.

Although it was a warm summer's day, the wind blew hard from the northeast and ripped at Archie's clothing. It plastered the side of his face and made his ears hum and his eyes water. As the incessant gale ran over the featureless landscape, it drove the oldest Miller boy to seek shelter. He held his slouch hat securely to his head with one hand as he walked awkwardly amongst the hospital tents. He occasionally spied a nurse who tended to a patient, and once had to sidestep suddenly as a tired orderly emptied a tub of blood stained water from a tent onto the path in front of him. The orderly's action earned him a verbal tongue lashing from a middle-aged sister who appeared from the unlit recess of the makeshift ward. Her rebuke had been delivered with the aim of maintaining a certain level of sanitation in an already underequipped and understaffed facility, not out of any regard for inconvenience to a private.

Due to embark on a transport for ANZAC Cove at 16:00, Private Miller continued his search for some shelter other than a hospital tent. He felt assured that it would be frowned upon by all and sundry, in the light of the condition of the men inside. With only two hours before embarkation, Archie started to think it might be wise to make his way back to the pier and sit it out, when a familiar voice found him through the driving wind.

'Miller! Miller, you bludger.'

Archie stopped and turned to his right. He raised his hand over his brow in a tired, some would say, very Australian salute. He shielded his eyes from the harbour's glare and could make out a group of men under a tarpaulin. Its canvas flapped frantically, like everything else around him.

'It is you. Miller, you blind bastard, get over here.'

A broad smile stretched across Archie's face. 'Private Glanville, is that you?' he yelled. Archie strained his eyes to pinpoint the voice amongst the dozen or so men laid out on stretchers.

'Too right,' replied Glanville. The wounded soldier made an effort to prop himself on one elbow. 'And it's Lance Corporal, thank you very much.'

'Lance Corporal hey, things must be bad if they have promoted an Ashfield boy,' chirped Archie. He quickened his gait and then slowed it again to step carefully between bodies. He felt his jubilation fade as he peered into the wounded men's eyes. 'Sorry cobber,' he whispered to the bloke with a leg wound. 'G'day mate,' as he stepped around a soldier, his head a mass of bandages, a large patch of dried blood matted with what hair you could see. He gave a solemn nod to a young kid, no older than Clarrie. His vacant stare dealt with the pain of a jaw shattered by shrapnel.

'Bertie, good to see ya, mate,' said Archie, in a hushed but heartfelt voice. 'What the bloody hell have ya done to yourself?'

'Oh, nothing, mate, just a scratch. Got a smoke?'

'Yeah... yeah for sure.' He quickly reached for his smokes. He lit one and then placed it between his mate's lips.

Bert winced as he drew back on the cigarette. The grimace caught Archie's attention, and drew his gaze towards the wound on his mate's hip. Archie forced a smile to his lips and looked away.

'Why don't you take a load off and lay back for a while Bertie, enjoy your smoke.' Archie's voice showed concern, but not so much as to embarrass his mate in front of the other lads.

While Lance Corporal Glanville inhaled the soothing tobacco, Archie stood and quietly made his way around to the other men. He lit a smoke for those who could take one, and delivered a quiet word for those who couldn't. Beyond the makeshift shelter, a young nurse from the Melbourne suburb of St Kilda smiled for the first time in days as she watched the young Australian comfort his fellow soldiers.

Archie squatted by his mate's side once again. 'So, what are George and Alfie up to?'

Bert smiled as he removed the smoke from his mouth. 'George is doing fine, makes a bloody good jam tin.'

'Jam tin?'

'Bomb, mate, made from jam tins and anything you can get your hands on.' Bert let out a stifled cough; the contraction caused pain in his hip, which he tried to hide. Archie pretended not to notice. 'Brass didn't give us many real bombs.'

'Oh.'

'And Alfie?' asked Archie tentatively. After what he had seen around him, he wondered if he should pursue the topic.

'Alfie! He's as good as gold; he was practically running the black market.'

'Well, he is from Mascot.'

'Too right,' chuckled Bert. He regretted the emotion instantly. 'Hey, try and get him a few things before you leave, he'll appreciate it. Look after ya, when the time comes.'

'What like?' said Archie, like a real first timer.

'Anything, mate. All you'll get there is bully beef and biscuits harder than granite. Oh, and flies, I forgot the flies, plenty of them. How's the leg?'

'Yeah, all good. I was pretty embarrassed. Breaking your ankle in a drill, felt like a right fool I did.'

'Mate! After a few days clinging to the side of those bloody ridges, Alfie, George and I wished we'd done the same thing.'

'Tough, is it?' Archie's voice was reserved, but without fear.

'No walk in the park. I'd be lying if I told you otherwise, but you'll be right; tough Balmain boy like yourself.'

Both men grinned but did not attempt to speak. After all the training, myth-telling and untested bravado, crouched in a makeshift hospital without a shot being fired, a small part of Archie Miller had started to realise what this was.

The next hour-and-a-half flew by as the two mates, unknown to each other before the war, passed on what news they had. They did their best to make light of the present, neither man delving into what the future might bring.

Archie looked at his watch and declared it was time to leave. After he shook Bert's hand, he touched his mate on the shoulder. He tried, through the gesture, to say all the things he couldn't. He slowly rose to his feet and then walked away, sobered.

***

In a barge, laden mostly with supplies and a handful of other soldiers—some veterans returning to battle after being patched up on Lemnos—Archie gripped his rifle. He held it upright against his hip and upper thigh; his palms massaged the weapon with varying degrees of firmness, in an effort to control the nerves that made his muscles spasm involuntarily. His mouth was parched, so he licked his lips, but tasted only salt, as the steel barge laboured through the dark choppy sea. Their destination was illuminated in the distance by countless lamps—an enchanting sight that didn't reveal the quarrel that played out beneath the glittering canopy.

As the minutes passed, Private Miller prayed that the stress that elevated his pulse and sent trickles of sweat from his armpits along his flanks would fly away with the briny breeze, and allow him to make a good account of himself when called upon. Archie stared intently at the dazzling scene; its peaceful mask was shattered by the sound of shell-fire and the sporadic crack of a rifle being discharged. Private Miller was roused by a hand on his shoulder. He turned his head slightly and saw a large face, crinkled with exposure to the Australian sun. It hovered inches from Archie's nose and smiled. The veteran soldier produced a metal flask, already de-corked.

He held it out in front of Archie. 'Get this into ya son, it will help.'

Archie accepted the flask and downed a generous swig of the

overproof rum. He tightened his lips and instantly felt the effects of the warming spirit as it settled in his belly. He nodded in appreciation and handed the panacea back to the veteran soldier, who let out a muffled laugh as he slapped the young private between the shoulder blades.

'You'll be right, son, just keep your eyes and ears open and your head down.' The Digger reclaimed his seat and receded into the blackness. Archie was left alone with his thoughts as the sluggish craft inched closer to the shore.

Each uninitiated soldier in the small boat was in a different state of anticipation. The veterans however, felt resignation; they received and then passed on the message to disembark. The adrenalin roared through Archie's veins like fire to bushland and he was confident and ready to meet his foe. Strangely, as he leapt over the gunwale, an image of his mother filled his mind. She stood at Circular Quay, as she was the day he had boarded the troop ship. Her eyes were heavy with emotion; her message of concern had been transmitted but not acknowledged by her jubilant son. Instead it rose from his memory to jab at his heart right at this moment; instantly it conveyed the innate feelings a mother bears. As he splashed through water laced with bleached foam, Private Miller landed on the pebbled beach of the enemy, knowing what it feels like to be loved. He suddenly felt he had something to lose.

***

Balmain, July 1915
Clarence and Ruth Miller looked the perfect couple as they stood in front of St John's Anglican Church; Clarence strikingly handsome in his three-piece suit, Ruth in a white gown, as beautiful as ever. As the church bell, perched high above, rang to announce the exchange of their vows, friends and family applauded the newlyweds. Their faces glowed with pride and joy, as members of the small congregation

tossed white confetti towards them. The photographer's bulb flashed to capture their moment of bliss.

Albert Miller stood alongside Harry Reynolds, just inside the church gates. They talked politely about local issues but kept the war at arm's length on such a happy occasion. Slightly surprised but not at all concerned by Clarence's sudden declaration that he intended to marry Ruth, Harry had given the obligatory blessing to his future son-in-law. He had not made a fuss, as his wife Mary had, when Ruth disclosed the wedding date. He assumed Clarence's decision to enlist had influenced it, and being a patriotic man, felt it reason enough. In his eyes Clarence was a decent, hardworking young man, prepared to serve his country and the Empire for the greater good. Despite having to deal with Mrs Reynolds's damaged ego at not being able to plan a lavish ceremony, and her misguided fears as to what rung this would place her on, on the social ladder, things had gone smoothly enough. In the end, all that mattered to him was that Ruth was happy.

Grace Miller stepped quietly towards her new daughter in-law, as if she didn't want to intrude. She placed her hand gently on Ruth's arm and whispered something that made her eyes sparkle. Grace thought their marriage would always happen; the war, in an oddity of life, had just brought it forward. She knew Clarence loved Ruth without question, adored her in fact, and Ruth's feelings for Clarence were displayed in her every movement.

When Ruth had sat her down one rainy afternoon for a talk, Grace had no premonition of the subject. When she thought back, she would admit she was surprised but not shocked, and as the news was delivered, she had admired Ruth's assuredness. The young lady had remained respectful and calm, but glowed with contentment over her future. Grace knew Ruth was an exceptional young lady, in a time when young ladies were expected to be anything but, and she realised that she loved her like one of her own. Grace's response to the news had been everything Ruth knew it would be. It had justified Ruth's decision to tell Grace before her own mother.

Grace took a few paces back and allowed herself a moment to absorb the cheerful surrounds. She knew her son as a warm and tender person, an intelligent young man, who had promised, even from a young age, to be special, different from the crowd. Grace looked at him as he tenderly brushed confetti off his wife's cheek, and saw her son as being complete. *Damn this war,* she cursed silently. She smiled to hide her apprehension and used her fortitude to push ill-will away with the breeze.

***

Mr and Mrs Clarence Miller fought the outgoing tide of passengers who had disembarked from an earlier train. They bounced off one stranger into another; Ruth laughed and then grimaced as she desperately tried to stay with her husband on the busy Central Station platform. Their train was scheduled to depart in five minutes.

'There it is, Ruthy, I can see it. Not far now.'

'I'm surprised you can see anything. Ouch! That beastly man just stood on my toe.'

'Are you alright, dear?' asked Clarence, preoccupied with boarding the train.'

'No, I'm not actually,' replied Ruth. She realised her husband wasn't paying attention. 'Half of my foot has been sliced off.'

'That's good Ruthy, almost there. Ah! Here we are. I was getting a bit worried, Ruth, thought we might miss our own honeymoon.'

Her cheeks flushed from the effort, Ruth gave Clarence a forced smile. One part of her wanted to throttle him with the bag she carried, the other half cherished his enthusiastic but muddled way. 'Excellent, Clarrie, let's find our seats.'

The Millers stepped into the second-class carriage and found their allocated compartment. Ruth took a seat near the window, while Clarence placed their luggage in the racks above.

Clarrie let out a sigh as he dropped to the seat opposite Ruth. He was pleased that he had completed the mission of escorting his wife to a waiting train. *Women just didn't understand the pressure associated with such a task*, he thought. While it wouldn't be spoken out loud, every man worth his salt knew how important it was—especially on a honeymoon—to be able to navigate a city and arrive safe and on time, injured toe aside. Women, from his observation, didn't seem to grasp the rationale; they were likely to ask for directions.

'This is grand, isn't it,' exclaimed Clarence. He risked a public display of affection and reached over to place a hand on Ruth's leg. 'Boarding a train for the Blue Mountains… wouldn't be anywhere else.'

'It's exciting, Clarrie,' replied Ruth. She adored her husband's enthusiasm. 'I am really looking forward to seeing the Hotel Carrington, I've heard it's lovely.'

'Mr Blake has stayed there and said it is very elegant, a perfect retreat from the bustle of Balmain. It was very generous of your parents to pay for the accommodation, very generous; I must thank them when we get back.'

'You already have, a hundred times over,' laughed Ruth. 'It was very nice of them, I think it was father's idea actually, and they both know you appreciate it.'

'Apparently it was built in 1882 and is of the "Italianate style", which ironically originated in England based on Italian themes.'

'You are a wealth of information, aren't you?'

'I have been reading.'

'Obviously,' replied Ruth as she raised herself off the cushioned seat to kiss Clarence briefly on the lips. She smiled playfully, as she held her face inches from his.

'Ruth! Not here, someone will see,' his voice hushed and panicky.

Ruth gave a cheeky wink and moved back to her seat. Clarrie's face went from red to purple.

'Chicken.'

Relieved the crisis was over; Clarence shook his head and let out a controlled laugh. 'You're wicked, but I love you.'

A brief silence was interrupted by the shriek of the train whistle. Moments later the rail car jolted as the slack was taken from the couplings and the engine drew them slowly from the station.

Lulled by the gentle sway of the rail car, Clarence Miller's mind drifted away. The terrace houses and large industrial plants darted through his field of vision as the train snaked its way through outer Sydney.

Over the past weeks, Clarence's life had changed dramatically. Some of it was welcomed; some forced upon him through circumstances. Like he would watch a film in a theatre, Clarence stared blankly out the window; the view of suburbia was replaced by scenes from his recent memory. Each recollection was vivid, at times painful, but mostly warm and tender; love in its different forms. All of his thoughts linked one to the other in a maze of events that rolled to a fated conclusion.

He recalled the discussion he had with his father in front of their Beattie Street home on that Saturday in June. The feelings brought on by the white feather were still so raw at the time, and had wrenched at his soul as Albert Miller began to speak. Clarence had expected to be lectured, but instead was treated as a man by another man. Albert, a father who had himself seen what war can do, was a man who only wanted to protect his children. In the end, he was resigned to the fact that Clarence must find his own way.

The rhythmic tap-tap of wheels that crossed joins in the track drew his mind further away. He relived the instant where an outgoing but confused eighteen-year-old was left behind for a man who, presented with life's choices, had matured to know they were his to make. The following morning, after his announcement of his decision to enlist, Clarence had woken from his own bed and thought of Ruth and what they had shared. The essence of their act seemed to hover around him like a perpetual embrace.

His mind cleared of self-doubt, he had dressed and walked to Darling Street to board a tram for the city. He carried a signed letter from his father, a letter penned with a methodical calmness that masked his debilitating heartache. Clarence had made his way directly for Town Hall and the recruitment office, where he joined a line of men; it wasn't as long as the months prior to the Gallipoli landing. Eventually he had been called forward to give his details, along with the consenting letter from Albert Miller that would allow him to enlist under the age of twenty-one.

After going through a preliminary medical examination, he was passed fit for active service. His form was stamped and then handed back to the recruiting officer to be signed off. With all the paperwork out of the way, the majority of men, in their excitement or naivety, moved straight on to enlist that day. Clarence had made the decision to fight for his country, but he had a promise to fulfil before he embarked. He took note of the clause at the top of the form, which read, *I hereby offer myself for Enlistment in the Australian Imperial Force for active service abroad and undertake to enlist in the manner prescribed, if I am accepted by the Military Authorities, within one month of date hereof.* Clarence decided he would report to Victoria Barracks for enlistment on the 28th of July. It kept him inside the month by one day. He had a lot to do in just over three weeks.

Clarrie's private theatrette was interrupted by another train that passed on the track parallel to theirs. He turned his gaze towards his wife, who was engrossed in a book she had retrieved from her handbag. As the train rattled on, he pondered if he would ever fully comprehend what this woman meant to him. He smiled and turned to look back out the window; the intrusive locomotive had now passed, and he drifted into sleep.

***

The façade of the hotel was richly decorated with elegant columns that supported a large balcony. It stood guard over elegant stained-glass windows; the whole scene gave the impression of luxury, something to which Clarence wasn't accustomed. Ruth smiled and held Clarence by the arm. She nestled her cheek into her husband's shoulder as they ascended the main staircase against the chilled, Blue Mountains air. They entered a warm foyer, its pleasant climate enhanced by the thick woollen carpet and dark timbers that outlined the plastered walls, painted in soft tones.

A middle-aged man, dressed in the formal attire of the hotel staff, smiled warmly from behind a mahogany desk. He welcomed the young couple while he gestured to a porter to assist with their modest luggage.

'Welcome to the Hotel Carrington, sir. My name is George and I am the hotel's concierge; how may I be of assistance?'

'We have a room booked under Mr and Mrs Miller,' said Clarence nervously, almost like he was being interviewed.

'Certainly, sir,' replied the concierge. The man scanned something obscured from the Miller's view. 'Room 16 on the first floor.' He placed a printed card on the desk top for Clarence to sign. 'Your key, sir. One of our porters will bring your luggage up shortly.'

'Thank you,' replied Clarence. He accepted the key, pleased with being able to tick off another husbandly duty. The concierge now a distant memory, he looked at his wife, grinned and offered his arm. 'Shall we Mrs Miller?'

***

Sydney, 8 October 1915
The dark steel hull of the HMAT *Warilda* towered above the crowd. Ruth clung to her husband; her cheek was marked with tears and the woollen tunic of his AIF uniform felt harsh against her skin. With his head covered by a slouch hat, Clarence rested his cheek on Ruth's hair, while his arms were locked around her shoulders. Neither of them spoke. Both were deep in thought. Almost everything had been said over the previous weeks, while they walked among the Carrington

Hotel gardens, or at their home they shared with Clarence's parents.

An army band played, 'It's a long way to Tipperary', as hundreds of husbands and wives, mothers and fathers, and the occasional scurrying child, lined the Quay. Each said their farewells, some sombre, others more jubilant, wrapped up in the atmosphere created by the band and the countless flags and streamers that hung from every possible post or rail.

Clarence placed his hands on Ruth's wet cheeks and gently raised her chin so her eyes would meet his. The harsh voice of a middle-aged sergeant boomed above the music. He ordered soldiers to board their transport.

'Everything will be fine, my darling,' whispered Clarence. He removed one hand to gently wipe a tear that had rolled down her faultless face. 'Nothing will prevent me from being with you, nothing.'

'Please be careful, please...' Ruth's voice trailed off into muffled sobs. Her heart had experienced the exhilaration of love, now it was tortured by separation.

'Everything will be fine, I promise.'

'Clarence, I have wanted to tell you something.'

'I know how you feel Ruth and I am the luckiest man alive.'

'No, no Clarrie, I mean yes, we both love each other,' replied Ruth. She appeared confused. 'It's not that.' She paused and felt slightly ashamed that she had not shared this at a more appropriate time, but in these times of upheaval, she was uncertain when the right time was. Her thoughts were always concerned with Clarrie. 'Forgive me for not telling you sooner, I didn't want to add weight to the decisions you have made.'

'Look lively, Private, can't wait all day,' screamed the sergeant.

'Ruth, what is it?'

'We're going to have a baby Clarrie.'

For a fraction of a second Clarence was frozen. His mind danced with joy, but his body was unable to react. He stared blankly at Ruth.

'I am sorry to tell you like this but...'

'Oh, Ruth,' he cried. Clarence embraced the woman he loved like it was his last moment on Earth. He buried his head in her shoulder to hide the tears that streamed down his face. He took a minute to compose himself from his sudden outburst of emotion. It could be deciphered as fear by the other men, not as the unrivalled joy of one who is to become a father. Clarence lifted his head slightly and kissed his wife passionately on the mouth. It surprised Ruth and summoned a few whistles and cheers from his fellow infantrymen.

'Get a room, Miller,' taunted 'Sticks', Clarence's mate from the Liverpool training camp, as he passed to board the *Warilda*.

'Clarrie, I am so sorry. I should have told you days ago, please forgive me.'

'Ruth, don't be sorry, you couldn't have given me better news. We'll be a real family.'

Ruth's face let up like a beacon, overjoyed at her husband's happiness. *How foolish I was to think Clarrie would be anything but delighted.*

'We are going to be a family, Ruth.'

'Yes, my darling, a beautiful family.'

They embraced one more time, and then the two reluctantly parted. Ruth placed a white laced handkerchief, damp with tears, in Clarrie's hand as he paced backwards. He held her amulet to his face and breathed in its scent. He suddenly held it aloft, a sign to his wife that it would unite them over thousands of miles of ocean and foreign shores, till they met again. With one last nod of his head, he said goodbye and turned for the gangway.

FIVE

Ruth opened the door to 96 Beattie Street, physically and emotionally exhausted. After she had left Circular Quay, she had made her way towards the tram, impatient to get home and be with family, Grace and Alice in particular. From flags and banners to uniformed men the city was a living and breathing reminder of the war.

She placed her handbag on the table and walked out the back door, where she was certain she heard Alice.

'Hello, Grace, I'm back,' said Ruth. She saw a tiny figure dart behind a sheet Grace had hung.

'Oh, hello, dear,' said Grace, half startled. She placed a sheet she held back in the basket, and moved towards her. 'How was everything?'

'As good as I could hope,' sighed Ruth. 'Alice Miller, I can see your shoes young lady,' she added, with a bit more zest in her voice.

Alice giggled and then leaped from behind the white sheet.

'Why are you home from school?'

'I'm sick.'

'Yes,' mocked Ruth, 'you look it.'

'Go inside now, Alice,' said Grace, 'Mum would like to speak to Ruth in private.'

'Oh, do I have to?' complained Alice.

'Yes, you do, now hurry along.'

Grace gestured for Ruth to take a seat on the bench next to the lemon tree. She followed closely behind but placed one hand on her back as she eased herself down onto the bench.

'Are you alright, Grace?'

'Yes, dear, just age.' Grace looked down and fiddled with her apron. 'Was Clarence angry I didn't come to see him off?'

'No! Not at all,' replied Ruth. 'He understood that it was difficult.'

'How was he? I was worried for him, I just couldn't...' Grace stopped. She tried to hold back her emotions, but the tears fought their way out. Ruth moved quickly to put an arm around the distressed mother.

'He was fine Grace, truly he was.' Ruth's own anxieties were pushed to the side as she comforted her mother-in-law and friend. 'I decided to tell him our secret.'

Grace looked up at Ruth and wiped the tears from her eyes with the back of her hand, and then waited for Ruth to continue.

'You were right Grace,' said Ruth. 'He was overcome with joy, I felt foolish for keeping it from him.'

'You were only thinking of him, dear.'

'Oh Grace, being on that wharf was the strangest experience I have had,' sighed Ruth, 'I can't tell you how I felt, it was like I was being ripped apart. I...' Ruth paused; she had noticed Grace withdraw to a distant place. Her eyes were transfixed to a spot somewhere on her apron, while one hand wrung the other. 'I'm sorry, Grace, I am being insensitive.'

'Nonsense, Clarence is your husband, you should be able to tell me how you feel. Sometimes, Ruth,' said Grace, her eyes bloodshot and teary, 'sometimes I feel it is just too much. Too much worry. But then I thank God that my boys are alive and I thank God that Clarence brought you into our lives.'

'Grace, I feel blessed to be a part of your family. We will get through this together, I know it. Ruth rested her hands across her stomach and rubbed them gently in a circle. 'It's going to be a boy,' she stated calmly. Ruth thought of Clarence and then looked up and smiled at her mother-in-law.

***

Albert returned his timecard to its slot and walked along a narrow passage towards the exit. One side of the passage was lined with timber doors spaced evenly apart, each with a pane of frosted glass that bore the name of its department in gold letters. The other side of the corridor consisted of a blank wall, with paint that peeled off in places. As he passed the last of the timber doors, Albert was stopped in his tracks by a loud voice.

'Miller! Miller, hold up a second,' exclaimed the man. A softened sound of typewriters that clattered escaped past the clerk, who held the door-knob in his right hand and clasped the door jamb with his left. He kept his feet inside the office and only allowed the top half of his skinny body to lean out into the passageway; possibly from trepidation about mixing with the workers.

'Yes, Mr Craig,' said Albert, slightly surprised. *What does he want?*

'Got something for you, Miller; a letter.'

'A letter, what sort of letter?'

'Not sure actually,' said Mr Craig, with indifference. 'Possibly personal, came addressed to you, care of this office.' He flicked the envelope with the fingers of his right hand without releasing his grip on the door knob. It was an invitation to come forward, and sooner rather than later.

Albert stepped forward and took the envelope from Mr Craig. He thanked him with a nod and a hesitant smile, before he studied the front and back of the small parcel.

'Been here for a couple of days, sorry Miller,' said the pompous clerk, 'haven't been able to catch you.' Before Albert could answer, Craig had pulled the door shut and disappeared.

Albert remembered he had a ferry to catch, so he turned on his heel and walked briskly for the wharf. *Why would Archie send a letter to his place of work?* He broke into a jog when he saw his workmates had boarded the small vessel that would transport him to Balmain. *Can't be good*, he sighed. Albert tucked the letter into his breast pocket and then leapt onto the gangway.

A quick glance around the crowded ferry told Albert that all the seats were taken, so he took up a position against the gunwale, only a few paces from where he boarded. He stared out across the water and gently patted the envelope that lay against his chest. He decided that he would make a detour to the Exchange Hotel, where he could read whatever news Archie had for him at a secluded corner table. He was confident that fellow patrons would acknowledge this out-of-the-ordinary behaviour for what it was—a wish to be left alone.

Albert breathed in the salt air as it whipped across the harbour, and his thoughts drifted towards Clarence. Somewhere beyond Sydney Heads on a crowded troop ship, the salt air would be in his lungs as well. *How is he feeling?* he wondered. The thought churned his own stomach, and then he chuckled lightly, as out of nowhere he pictured his son on the deck of the ship with one of those bloody poetry books, while the other men played cards or stood in a circle trying to disguise a game of two-up. *He is different*, he thought, *but prouder of him I couldn't be.*

With his mind miles away on Clarence's troop ship, Albert was snapped back to reality by a tug on his elbow. He turned slowly and recognised Tom Wright, one of the leading hands in Frank's section.

'G'day, Tom.'

'Albert,' replied Tom, his tone was too serious for a Friday afternoon. 'Could I have a word, mate?'

'Yes, Tom, what can I do for you?'

Tom jerked his head to suggest that they move somewhere else. He motioned towards a fire hose that was coiled neatly beneath a hydrant. The brass fixture was situated in a small recess of the boat's main structure and provided them with a buffer from enquiring ears.

'I heard your young bloke left for Egypt today,' said Tom politely, before he broached what he wanted to say.

'Yes, mate, boarded the *Warilda* a couple of hours ago.'

'Well, I wish him all the best, my eldest is over there.'

'Thanks, Tom, I will pass it on to Grace,' replied Albert, acutely aware that Tom had something else on his mind. 'Samuel and Archie sailed on the same ship, I think.'

'Yes, I believe you're right.' Tom looked a little uncomfortable and paused for a moment. He studied two seagulls that hovered effortlessly alongside the ferry; maybe they hoped to be tossed someone's half eaten lunch. 'There was one other thing,' said Tom, his eyes still fixed on the birds.

'What's that, mate?'

'Your youngest boy, Frank,' replied Tom. He turned his attention back to his co-worker to look him in the eye.

'Frank, I hope he's pulling his weight?'

'No, it's not that, he's a good worker. Look, it's probably nothing, but he got in a dust-up today, planted one on Jimmy Taylor's chin.'

'Silly little prick,' hissed Albert. 'He'll get himself the sack.'

'Well yes, if Bob Timmins was there he would've, but luckily for Frank, Timmins was up in the office.'

'Mate, I appreciate you coming to me. I'll sort it out as soon as I get home; you have my word on that.'

Albert put out his hand to shake Tom's. He felt indebted to the leading hand for his discretion, but as he stood and waited for his act of gratitude to be accepted, he sensed there was more to come.

'Listen, Albert, this may be none of my business but in light of what happened today, I feel I should say something.'

Albert gawked at Tom with a puzzled expression, his eyebrows narrowed to form creases of toughened skin above his nose. Was this the prelude to Albert's long, but famously explosive fuse? Tom couldn't tell, so he swallowed and pressed on.

'What! Spill it out, Tom.'

'When I spoke to Frank and Taylor after their fight, I couldn't get anything out of either of them.'

'Well, that's normal. They're not going to squeal on each other.'

'Yes Albert, I realise that. I grew up on the same streets as you, but there was more to this.'

'What d'ya mean?' snapped Albert. He tried his best to stay calm as he noticed John Graham, a fellow boilermaker, cock his ear slightly.

'Easy, mate.'

'Sorry, Tom, go on.'

'I didn't expect them to say much, but I do know one thing, Jim Taylor looked very put out when he came at Frank, something had really set him off, but as soon as Frank planted one on him it was all over. Frank said something to him and he just copped it.'

'So, what! Taylor probably just shit himself.'

'Jim Taylor shit himself?' Tom looked at Albert for a second and allowed him time to think.

'You're right,' conceded Albert, 'Jimmy wouldn't cop that.'

'I thought the same thing, and then I thought, well Frank's a kid, maybe Jimmy's mellowed, you know… with age. But then I remembered something and this is why I came to you.'

Albert leaned in towards Tom, his head tilted slightly. He put his ear closer to Tom's mouth, as if he knew he didn't want to say it too loudly.

Tom glanced calmly over his left shoulder and said quietly, 'You've heard of Ron Symonds?'

Albert nodded in the affirmative, 'Scum.'

'Well that's one way of saying it. A few weeks ago,' continued Tom, 'I'm walking with the missus on the way back from the Telfords and I spot young Frank and his mate Jim outside the Dry Dock Hotel. Just passing the footy around they were.'

'The pair of 'em are always out the front of my place doing the same thing.'

'Yeh… yeh,' replied Tom, 'like most kids.'

'What's Symonds got to do with it?'

'That's the strange part. All looked normal and then Symonds appears from out the side of the pub and makes his way towards the boys. Frank jogs over to him and takes a scrap of paper from him.'

'And.'

'And that's it. Took whatever it was and that was it. Then today, Taylor comes at Frank about something, Frank plants one on him and Jimmy does nothing. Don't you think that is odd, Albert?'

Albert said nothing in reply. He rubbed his chin with his thumb and forefinger. He straightened from his slightly hunched position and gazed over Tom's shoulder toward the stern, like he was searching for an answer.

'If I had the nerve to hit Taylor, I would have swum back to Balmain before I thought about getting on this ferry, but there's Frank perched up the front of the boat like nothing's happened. Sorry to dump this on you mate, but I thought you would like to know.'

Tom waited for a reply and braced himself as the ferry brushed the buffers attached to the timbers of the Balmain wharf, . 'Well, I'll be off then, Albert, I hope it's nothing.'

Roused by the slap of heavy ropes tossed from the ferry's deck to the bollards on the wharf, Albert shook Tom's hand and thanked him. He stood with his back to the fire hydrant and deliberately waited as dozens of his co-workers shuffled past him to disembark; it gave him time to compose his thoughts.

***

Albert Miller picked up his change from the bar with one hand, and with the other, the inviting glass of ale. Some of the amber fluid spilled over its edge to trickle down his wrist as he made his way through the gathering of Friday evening drinkers. He found an empty table, placed his beer down, and then wiped his hand dry on his boiler suit before he took a seat.

His mind was still foggy from his discussion with Tom Wright. He just couldn't make sense of it. On his long walk from the wharf to the pub, he had reflected on Frank's behaviour over the past weeks. As he probed his memory for the slightest clue that would throw some sort of light on the matter, he realised how little time he had spent with Frank—apart from watching the footy—since Archie had departed, so many months before. Had he overlooked changes in Frank? It was hard to say. They travelled to work and back on most days, he thought he would be able to keep an eye him, not that he ever thought Frank particularly needed looking over. He seemed to be like the other two boys, but more like Archie.

Albert took the first sip of his beer and suddenly felt exhausted. Not the physical kind; he had worked hard all his life and could count the amount of times he had been crook on one hand. This was different; he felt older. He hadn't acknowledged it before; he made sure his family—in particular his wife—were in good spirits. That had taken priority. But as he sat alone in a noisy pub, he felt the strain that came with seeing two sons off to war. By being preoccupied with concern for his eldest boys, he had possibly lost sight of the youngest, maybe most in need son. Albert reached into his breast pocket and pulled out the envelope Craig had given him. He promised himself to devote more time to Frank.

Albert tore open the bone-coloured envelope and noticed two separately folded letters. Intrigued, Albert looked at both, and then saw that one of them had Dad written on one side in bold letters.

Anzac
11 August 1915

Dear Dad,
I hope this letter finds you well. I took the liberty of mailing this to Cockatoo Island, hope I didn't get you into strife, as I wanted to let you know how we have done over here without alarming

Mother and little Alice. The other letter is for you to read at home.

I am not exactly sure what to write, but felt I had to write something as I could never have imagined the scenes that I witnessed over the previous few days could be brought to bear on any man. My mates and I have been involved in ferocious fighting, mostly hand-to-hand, at a place they call Lone Pine. We lost many good men, too many, but the ones that pulled through did our fallen mates proud, taking the Turkish trenches and holding them. My battalion, the 1st, was in reserve, but we were called forward less than an hour into it, to secure some trenches that had been taken. We really stuck it to the Turk and he, in turn, never gave up, launching counter attacks one after the other, hurling an endless supply of small bombs at us. I will never be able to explain the courage the Diggers showed. One bloke, Captain Sasse, led us time after time, attacking the enemy with bayonets, even though he was wounded more than once.

I don't know how I pulled through, but rest assured I'm fine, except for a case of the 'runs'. Having a rest from the front-line trenches at the moment, if you can call it that, still getting shelled and sniped at, so you have to have your wits about you. There has been a series of battles and charges resulting in heavy casualties, all part of a big push to get to our objective. Proud to have been able to do my duty for Australia and the Empire, but just as glad that Clarrie hasn't joined up and is sticking with the newspaper. When I think back to the day I set sail, I shake my head. I am not sure if I knew what to expect when I left, but I know now that I was innocent to the ways of the world, a boy really. Think of me when you go to watch Balmain.

Your son
Archie

And every other day son, every other day. Albert folded the letter like it would tear at the slightest breeze and placed it in his pocket—separate from the other letter. Two men who stood at the bar glanced at Albert. Both understood what he was going through; it was a ritual that had become commonplace in pubs from Manchester to Sydney.

SIX

The moon sat low over the western horizon, larger than one would normally view it. Surrounded by three elongated clouds, visible only by the light from the luminescent orb, they appeared strained to breaking point. A destructive force hidden by darkness attempted to tear them away from shining hope.

Clarence sat with his back against a bulwark of the HMAT *Warilda*. The ship's bow cut south through the calm sea. His senses were captivated by the lunar display and its portrayal of contrast. Somewhere over that distant horizon lay the east coast of Australia and thousands of souls at rest. His wife, unable to sleep, might gaze out through her window to accept the moon and its light, a transmitter between two points, a beacon for kindred spirits to find each other.

It was a boy. Without knowing how, he knew, and he felt love of a new but wonderful kind. With one knee tucked up to support a sketch-pad, he scratched away with a pencil. Clarrie tried to capture the mood of the men on this first night at sea. Along the starboard rail, he could hear the muttered voices, as men, congregated in small groups, told stories and made jokes. Each figure was a silhouette, indistinguishable from the other, until the reddish-orange tips of their cigarettes gave definition to their faces. Their banter comforted Clarence against a steely black sea.

'What ya got there, Miller?' blurted Private Jack Sullivan. He appeared suddenly out of the shadows and dropped to the deck to sit shoulder to shoulder with his mate. His back, like Clarence's, rested against the cold steel of the *Warilda*.

'Nothing really.'

'Doesn't look like nothin' to me, give us a look.'

'I would rather...' replied Clarence, but in one fluent movement, Jack or Sticks, as he was more commonly known, dug the knuckles of his left hand into Clarence's ribs and swiped the sketch pad from his grasp. His victim recoiled in pain.

'Thanks, Sticks,' said Clarence, as he rubbed his ribs.

'Not a problem, mate, now what do we have here? An artist!' Private Sullivan rubbed his chin with thumb and forefinger. He mocked his friend while he masqueraded as an art appraiser.

'Fair go, Sullivan.'

'Clarrie, you've got me all wrong mate, it's very good, very good. Is there anything you can't do? Journalist: artist, professor of general knowledge, what other talents do you have?'

'Righto, Sticks… give it back.'

'No chance, hey who wants to...'

Now it was Clarence's turn to give Sticks a dig in the ribs, and he delivered the blow where he wanted. Private Sullivan surrendered the sketch pad, doubled over in laughter, not pain.

'Sorry, Clarrie, just having some fun,' said Sticks. He chuckled while he rubbed his flank. It is very good though, fair dinkum mate.'

Clarence ignored Sticks's compliment. 'Where have you been anyway?'

'Oh… just played cards with some of the boys.'

Clarence looked at Sticks with a look a father might give a son when he had done something that lacked judgement, but with a wry smile of a mate.

'I know, I know. I said I would give the cards a rest but I thought I could get something off those bloody Queenslanders.'

'Skin you, did they?'

Sticks gave a nod. 'Bastards they are. Think they're running the joint,' he said through gritted teeth.

'Maybe cards isn't your go, Jack.'

'Not my go! You listen hear mate, I'll sort those bloody banana benders out, don't you worry about that. Just give me a day or two.'

Clarence smiled as he glanced back at his sketch pad. He admired his mate's dogged outlook on his dwindling finances. Clarrie shook his head and made a few minor adjustments to his sketch.

Jack Sullivan and Clarence Miller had become firm friends since their first day at training camp. Jack, a dock worker at Sydney's White Bay, stood about six feet two inches tall, and although thin, he had strength in his body's tight sinewy muscles. It could be felt in his firm handshake. He liked to drink, swear, play cards, and fight, usually in that order. They were things that had never really interested Clarrie, but it had not stopped him from enjoying the dock worker's company.

It was the same for Jack. He too had often wondered what had drawn him towards the well-dressed and fresh-faced cadet journalist. Jack had never understood how a man could prefer to read poetry over a game of cards, but he respected the fact that Clarrie wasn't afraid to be himself, especially when surrounded by men intent on showing the world how manly they were. Maybe that was real bravery, Jack would think to himself—but not for too long. Jack didn't like to complicate things. Clarrie and he were mates and that's all he needed to know, and that was all Wally Clarke knew after he called Clarrie a pansy after seeing his book on Keats. Poor Wally ended up flat on his back with his nose flatter and wider, courtesy of a left jab and right cross from Jack Sticks Sullivan.

Sticks tapped Clarrie on the shoulder; thoughts of avenged losses were put on the back burner for the moment. 'I will get us a good spot to put up our hammocks before the rest of these bludgers cotton on to it.'

Without a word, Clarrie nodded, gathered himself up, and followed Sticks below decks.

***

Balmain, 10 October, 1915
Frank Miller looked like any other boy in a Sydney suburb. He stood across the road from the Dry Dock Hotel, tossed his football in the air and caught it again. To a passer-by, he would look like a son who waited patiently to pass on a message from an exasperated mother to an inebriated father. Except that Albert Miller drank at the Exchange, not the Dry Dock.

It was close to dinner-time, and Frank felt he should probably head home. He had already received a tongue lashing from his father on the Saturday morning after his dust-up with Jimmy Taylor, and he didn't want another one or worse. But he didn't want to upset his new business partner either.

Frank had felt like a new person, a grown-up, since he met Mr Symonds. His father had told him to steer clear of people like him, and by the tone of his voice and the look in his eyes, Frank knew his father meant it. In the years or even months gone by, he would have heeded his dad's advice and not gone near the Dry Dock Hotel again. But for some reason, one he was not sure he could explain, he had ignored the Old Man.

In a chance meeting at Birchgrove Oval, Ron Symonds had given Frank and his mate Jim an opportunity to earn a few extra shillings, while, as Mr Symonds put it, providing a service for the community in tough times. Frank and Jim had taken the bait, hook, line, and sinker, and had started doing the rounds on Cockatoo Island during smoko over a fortnight ago.

At first, Frank had trod warily. He was well aware that he was only an apprentice on the island, well down the pecking order of importance, but as the days passed, he grew in confidence. He had noticed how men nodded g'day, and even the union representative, Ned Larson, would give him a greeting every now and then. Frank felt empowered in his new pastime. At home he was feeling unnoticed and alone. He missed his brother Archie more than he knew how to explain. He wanted to ask his mother and father questions about where Archie was fighting and when he would be back, but he felt a feeling of gloom come over his parents every time his brother's name came up and. He found it easier to get away and kick his football. When Clarrie had announced he was enlisting, he felt the strangest feeling of betrayal, which he knew didn't really make sense, except for that he felt it, wrong or right.

On the Friday when he had hit Jimmy Taylor, and Jimmy—knowing who Frank worked for—had not retaliated, it had changed Frank. It had turned his feeling of empowerment into sheer arrogance. While Frank and Jim may have swallowed Mr Symonds's line about providing a service for the ordinary man, who was unfairly rationed, while the rich still consumed the best of everything, he was well aware that Ronnie Symonds was a criminal, and a feared criminal at that. Nevertheless, as crooks do, and he was now one, he rationalised that he had provided goods for payment that otherwise would not be available. A business transaction between two willing parties, and as long as the second of those parties—the customer—kept up their end of the deal, incidents like the one that involved Taylor wouldn't have to happen.

Frank noticed a sturdy figure step out from a door on the College Street side of the pub. It was his boss, and he darted across Cameron Street to meet him.

'Frankie, my boy, sorry to keep you,' said Symonds, with a smile that suggested he actually cared.

'That's alright, Mr Symonds,' replied Frank, enthusiastically. Frank realised he didn't sound like the hardened crook.

'Frankie, it's Ronnie, please. Where's Jimmy?'

'He's not here.'

'Well I can see that, but is he coming?'

'I don't think so Mr, I mean Ronnie.'

'Cold feet, hey?' stated Symonds. He tapped his shiny leather shoes on the footpath as he lit himself a smoke and inhaled deeply. Ronnie blew a thick cloud of tobacco smoke over Frank's head, while his eyes narrowed, deep in thought. 'Not to worry,' he blurted. 'Had a feeling that might happen, but I have confidence in you, Frankie boy.'

'Thanks, Ronnie,' replied Frank. He glowed in the recognition.

'Got the list?'

Frank didn't answer, but promptly produced a folded piece of paper and handed it to his boss. Symonds studied the sheet and gave the occasional murmur, while Frank acted like he was suddenly distracted by the metal work on the awning above him.

'Very good, Frank. Any trouble? I know about Taylor.'

'Sorry about that, Mr Symonds, I lost my temper.'

'I would rather you leave that stuff to my boys, but it's fine lad, really,' said Symonds. He broke into a laugh, as he tussled Frank's hair. 'I would have liked to have seen it though; you've got balls, Frank. I will give you that, Taylor's no girl.'

Frank gave a slight grin but remained silent.

'I think you and me are going to get along just fine, Frank; I have big plans for you my boy. Just keep your head down and don't attract unnecessary attention.'

'Yes, Ronnie, it won't happen again,' replied Frank obediently.

'Same as last week, take the orders on Monday and bring the list to me after work. One of Ned Larson's boys will deliver the goods Wednesday, you distribute, Ned's man collects.'

'I can collect, Ronnie.'

'I'm sure you could, but how could you explain that sort of cash if questioned? Low profile son, low profile.'

'Yes, Mr Symonds.'

'Ned's man collects on Friday, you fill in who has and who hasn't, and pass it to me, easy as ABC. Got it?'

'Got it.'

'Good. Now remember Frank, loose lips sink ships. Don't give the game up by bragging, and if someone puts some heat on, what do you know?'

'Nothin'.'

'Good boy, now head home,' ordered Symonds. He put his hand out for Frank to shake; there was a ten-shilling note neatly folded in his palm.

***

'Boots!' Yelled Grace Miller. An automatic response when she heard Frank enter the house with the finesse of a Hereford bull. Frank slammed the heavy timber door behind him and took a few strides before the command registered. He paused and then back-tracked.

'Sorry!'

'You were last time too,' sighed Grace. She rolled her eyes as she continued to mix a cake batter. The bowl was cradled in one arm to allow her to use more force with her wooden spoon; the effort drew small beads of sweat to her forehead on a warm spring day.

'What are you making, Mum?' exclaimed Frank, as he entered the kitchen, boots clamped together in one hand, his football nursed in the other.

'Vanilla cake.'

'Can I have the bowl and spoon?'

'If you're good… Now, where have you been? Dad was looking for you to go to the football.'

'Oh, I forgot. I was just kicking the footy around,' he said. Frank felt slightly unsettled about lying to his mother. He was also truly sorry to have missed the game.

'Well he couldn't wait; he would have missed the tram.'

'I would've liked to have gone to Redfern Oval,' said Frank sincerely, like the threshold of the house reverted him to the boy they all knew, leaving the wannabe tough guy outside.

'That's what your father said. Here, sit down.' She passed the mixing bowl smeared with batter to her youngest son.

Grace sat down opposite Frank with her cup of tea. She watched her son as he scraped every inch of the bowl with the spoon, and then finger.

'Frank.' She stated calmly.

'Yes, Mum.'

'So, who were you kicking the football with?'

'Jimmy,' he replied, with a pause that hinted at guilt. It was barely perceptible, but rang like a fog-horn to a mother.

'Oh,' said Grace, as if the question had no significance other than kitchen table chit-chat. When your child starts to lie to you, it is a strange experience for a parent. Sometimes, as it was with Archie and Clarence, it is brushed off as one of those things that would inevitably happen, harmless and sometimes humorous, part of a kid trying to show that they can make their own choices. Other times, when you sense something amiss, it makes you feel sad. You realise that while you sit with a smile, a small piece of innocence has tumbled off into the abyss. Like a chunk of ice off an iceberg, it drifts perilously into warmer waters. Frank had begun to drift, she could feel it. And even though she could see that little boy she knew so well, as he attacked the mixing bowl with all the playfulness and enthusiasm of a pup, she couldn't ignore the subtle change that had overcome her son.

***

96 Beattie St
Balmain, NSW
Australia
24 October, 1915

Dearest Clarrie,
I think this will be my sixth letter since you left, none of them of course able to find you until you reach your destination. There

will be plenty for you to read when you do arrive, as I intend to keep writing. It makes me feel closer to you, and relieves some, but nowhere near enough of the anguish of not having you by my side.

I often lie awake wondering what life is like on an ocean-going vessel. I hope you are not seasick, I've heard it's terrible. I have been a little ill during the mornings with the pregnancy, but I am fine, and your mother, God bless her, says it's perfectly normal.

It is quiet sometimes in the house, with your father and Frank at work, but little Ally keeps us on our toes. Your father has been quiet of late, but he does have a lot on his mind, and we seem to see less of Frank each week. The bakery is quite busy, and I am doing as much work as I can, while I can. It also fills in the days. Can you believe that I have not seen one single person walk into the bakery with a volume of Keats in their hand since that infamous day? But come to think of it, I haven't seen another person like you before or since. When I think of how you were on that day, I smile and then miss you even more. Keep safe.

Your loving wife
Ruth

***

The awning that stood over the pavement outside the Dry Dock Hotel shielded Frank from the teeming rain that fell without a hint of respite. The downpipes choked and gutters overflowed, as the water fell in a sheet from the roof of the crowded pub. Inside, the public bar was clouded with tobacco smoke, and reeked of stale beer, but it was dry, and the only place to be for a working man on a Sunday afternoon such as this.

Frank stood patiently, but shivered. The cold damp air stiffened his joints, so he pulled his new flat cap down over his brow and began to pace on the spot. He was alerted by a rhythmic tap, and turned to see a well-dressed but frustrated man at the window of the busy pub. Eventually, the cold released Frank, and he recognised 'Hammer', Ronnie's right-hand man. Hammer was a bit annoyed at Frank's slow response, and looked set to lose his temper, when Frank suddenly deciphered his message and signalled the thumbs up.

Frank took a few paces to his right and entered through double glass doors framed in dark timber. He removed his cap and ran his fingers through his damp hair. Frank looked up to see a cheerful Ron Symonds and a not so happy Don Hammer Ryan.

'You sure about this kid, Ronnie?' snarled Hammer.

'Don't worry about Frank, he's a natural. Aren't you, Frankie?'

Frank didn't reply; he had determined that some of Ronnie's questions were in fact statements, and he had learnt that saying as little as possible was often a good bet. He had witnessed tough grown men converted into blabbering fools after they said something stupid to Ronnie.

'Well, he took long enough to get my message, he might be a bit dim-witted,' sneered Hammer.

Ronnie didn't answer Hammer; he winked at Frank instead. It was a hint that everything was okay, and that Hammer posed no threat to him. At least while Ronnie was happy. Ron placed his arm around Frank's shoulder and steered him towards a large timber door on the far side of the hallway, which Hammer opened for them both. They walked into the spacious dining room, where Frank was released from his boss's friendly but commanding grip. Frank turned and glanced around the room, more to give him time to consider what all this was about, rather than with any real interest in the furnishings. Two ladies, dressed in black with white aprons, were busy setting tables in preparation for meals, which began at six o'clock.

Hammer gained their attention, and without a word, the two ladies bowed their heads and exited through a side door.

Frank noticed the brief interaction, and although impressed, he didn't make a fuss. He turned towards the fireplace instead, and allowed the warmth of the flames to thaw his face.

'Have a seat, lad,' said Ronnie. He gestured to a chair that Hammer had pulled out for him alongside a neatly set table. Hammer then moved to the door to guard against intrusion. Ronnie paced steadily back and forth. He looked several times out the window and then back towards Hammer; he ignored Frank for the moment.

Don Hammer Ryan was Ron Symonds's most trusted associate. Wherever Ron was, Hammer wasn't far behind, and from what Frank could gather, it had always been that way. The two men had grown up together in Balmain. They had been brought up tough by going without, and had learnt that the only way uneducated sons of unemployed drunks got ahead was to use their instincts. They did whatever they could to survive. As young boys, the two mates had vowed to look out for each other, and had grown to form the classic pairing. Ron had shrewd street instincts and was the brains in the partnership, while Donald, who was solid in build and stood at six feet three inches, was the brawn.

Over time they had started to make a meagre living anyway they could. They would pounce on drunks who staggered home at night, but this proved limited, as most drunks, by nature, drank any money they had. Gradually they moved up the chain; they used their gifts to complement each other, and over time, built up a nice income on black market goods, along with a bit of loan-sharking.

With the outbreak of war, the need for black market goods escalated rapidly, and with the added income, Ronnie used his nous and Hammer's muscle to set up their own illegal gambling ring, run out of a small room in the Dry Dock pub. Their latest venture had proven very fruitful, and had allowed them to make inroads with union officials, which gave them access to the dock workers and Cockatoo Island, where Frank's story began. Now in their thirties, they had reaped the rewards of their efforts. Ron Symonds and Hammer Ryan dressed in the finest suits, and ate and drank the best of everything.

Ron took a deep breath and turned to look at Frank; his thoughts had drifted ahead to new ventures, and how his young apprentice would fit in. In some ways Frank reminded Ron of himself. He obviously hadn't grown up rough like he had; you could tell by the look of the lad. But there was something in his eyes, a quiet confidence that betrayed his shyness, a cold flicker in his gaze that hinted at ruthlessness, and it was this that interested Ron Symonds.

'This rain is enough to give you the shits,' said Ronnie with his customary smile; a nice opening to a casual business meeting.

'Too right, Ronnie,' replied Frank.

'I wanted to have a chat, lad… about your future.'

Frank raised his eyebrows slightly. He quickly glanced at the statue-like Hammer, who was still guarding the door. He was intrigued by what his boss had just said.

'Hammer and I have discussed the way in which you have handled things down at the Island. We've had good reports son, and I think it's time we had a talk about where you're headed.'

Frank shuffled in his seat a little; he felt he needed to respond to this endorsement, and with his chest puffed out slightly, he cleared his throat. 'I have tried hard to do a good job, keep my head down like you said, Mr Symonds,' said Frank. He nodded at Hammer to acknowledge his rank in the organisation.

When he felt a bit nervous, Frank would often revert to "Mr Symonds" instead of "Ronnie", a trait not lost on his boss. It actually made Frank appeal more to Symonds. It showed Ron that, even though he possessed inner strength and self-belief, he wasn't just some ratbag who lacked the necessary respect or common sense to know where he stood in the scheme of things.

'I know, Frankie, you have learnt fast. How would you like to get into something a bit bigger?'

'For sure, Ronnie, I'd be in it,' replied Frank quickly, before he adjusted his spirit to be more subdued. He had remembered Ronnie's advice about keeping your head down and not being a mug lair. 'What do you have in mind?'

'Nothing right now, we just want to know where you stand, if you know what I mean.'

'I have enjoyed the work, Ronnie.'

'And the extra money,' Symonds said with a smirk. 'That's not bad either, is it?'

Frank grinned and then looked at the carpeted floor. He admitted to himself that the extra money was indeed very appealing, a virtual fortune compared to his apprentice wage. While Ronnie turned to engage Hammer in conversation, young Miller glanced up at the smoke-stained walls, his attention grabbed—for no particular reason—by an old warship, complete with masts and sails and cannons blasting. He pondered, most unlike a fourteen-year-old, what Ronnie's enquiries would mean to the rest of his life. How it would change him? How would it affect his family?

Strangely for Frank, these thoughts or questions seemed almost irrelevant to the outcome of what lay before him. He somehow knew, without an explanation, that things had moved along with a life of their own. His destiny seemed pre-cast; the events of the preceding weeks and the responsibilities laid upon him felt like a natural extension of who he was. The confusion came from having feet planted in two paradoxical worlds. Home for Frank was safe, loving, and warm, but suddenly fractured. His other world, charged with energy, restrained by command and respect, was inherent with risk and its potential dangers. The exhilaration from this life was a fuel that overcame Frank's hidden inadequacies.

'I'm glad we had this little chat, Frankie,' said Symonds smoothly. The statement snapped Frank from his reflections.

'How's home life, no troubles?' While uneducated in the sense of not having attended school regularly, Ronnie Symonds was smart enough to know that he must keep tabs on all aspects of his business. Ronnie considered Frank as an asset, an asset that could be devalued by law-abiding parents, unhappy with their son's extracurricular activities. A happy home was important to Ronnie.

'Fine Ronnie… Dad had a little dig at me, but nothing to worry about.'

'A bit of advice Frank, and I want you to think about this,' said Ronnie sternly. 'Always keep the home front in order, whether it be Mum and Dad or when you're older… the missus.'

'Yes, Mr Symonds.'

'Your cap for instance, how would you explain that to the 'Old Man' or the foreman?'

'No one's asked,' replied Frank uneasily.

'No one's asked,' repeated Ronnie. He smiled, but with a hint of venom as he glanced over at Hammer, who still guarded the door. 'You see mate… these are the little things; the little things that matter. If you want to succeed, you have to be on top of it.'

Frank gazed back at Ronnie but didn't speak. A wiser choice he felt.

'Cover your tracks,' Ronnie continued, 'very important in this game son; can't emphasise it enough.' Ronnie wandered over to Hammer, said something inaudible, which resulted in Hammer producing a thick wad of five-pound notes. Ron returned to stand in front of Frank. He held the wad of cash inches from Frank's face; the apprentice crim did not flinch one inch.

'See this, lad?'

Frank nodded.

'Ask me where I got it,' said Ronnie insistently.

'Where did you get the 'deep sea divers' from Ronnie?'

Symonds turned to Hammer and grinned. 'See Don, that's what I like about this kid, cool under pressure, "deep sea divers", he says.

Ron paused and chuckled for a moment. 'The races, lad, that's where I got it… the races. End of story, have a nice day. Not oh, um, no-one's asked. Always be one step ahead, Frankie.

'Yes, Ronnie,' said Frank. The casual charm of his boss brought a smile to his face.

Ronnie Symonds glanced over at Hammer, then returned his gaze to Frank, with palms open and spread outwards, relaying to his understudy that what he had just explained could not be simpler.

'Same as usual this week, lad, Hammer will be in touch if I need you.'

Frank took this as his signal to leave and stood up. He placed his wool cap back on his head and shook hands with Ronnie and then Hammer, to cement their vague but binding agreement.

'That rain is a real a prick,' remarked Ronnie. He basked in his role as boss. He knew now that Frank had taken the step to commit, and was his.

SEVEN

Port of Alexandria, Egypt, 21 January 1916
Pressed amongst hundreds of their fellow soldiers, Privates Jack Sullivan and Clarence Miller stood shoulder to shoulder against *Warilda's* starboard rail. All of the men clambered for a view of the exotic city that spread out before them, as the tug-boats eased the troopship against the dock in the Port of Alexandria. The new recruits had become frustrated after two monotonous days and nights anchored in Alexandria Harbour while the ship's captain had waited for permission to dock. Tired of tedious drills and kit inspections, the Australians now bristled with excitement at the prospect of getting ashore.

The wharf was a hive of activity. Military personnel darted in and out of countless natives, as they made the last preparations before the soldiers disembarked. Almost every one of the local Egyptians appeared to be carrying produce or some other item, which they would offer for sale. The Australians on board had been warned about the hawkers and beggars, but they were impossible to avoid while in Egypt. The raw recruits had been left in no doubt as to what would happen, should there be any incidents that even faintly resembled the disgraceful and infamous 'Cairo riots'.

That day and night during Easter 1915 had left Australian soldiers with a tarnished name, and it was vice, according to their commanding officer, such as alcohol and immoral women, coupled with weak-willed individuals, that led to the distasteful events. The soldiers involved had seen their actions as justified reprisal for over-priced goods and watered-down liquor. They also targeted brothels and blamed the women, not themselves, for the spread of venereal disease. Headquarters said it was every man's duty to act as ambassadors, not only for Australia, but for the British Empire.

By this time, after a long and sometimes miserable journey, marked with sea sickness, bland food, mind-numbing drills, and more sea-sickness, the men could have been forgiven if they had unleashed their own colourful address to the officer in charge. But as those with no previous military experience, like Privates Miller and Sullivan had quickly learnt, army life was one endless play, and the only lines you needed to remember were, 'yes, sir!'

Clarence nudged Sticks in the ribs. He drew his attention to a particular group of local men, who had suddenly and violently clambered for a position on the wharf edge. They were only fifty yards away towards the stern of the ship, and some of their comrades had laughed with delight after they had tossed pennies towards the locals in exchange for oranges. The Australians were more interested in the melee that ensued than in the oranges themselves.

Too quickly, the fun was brought to a halt by a young and keen-to-please lieutenant. The jeers and moans from the infantrymen involved met with laughter and sarcastic applause from the rank and file.

With lines secured, a group of military police cleared a passage on the dock. This allowed for several motorcars to come forward, each with an important looking individual perched on the rear seat.

'Oh, look, Miller, our transport is here,' said Sticks sarcastically.

'Very good of HQ, I was prepared to march to wherever it is we are going,' replied Clarrie, continuing the banter.

As the gangway was fixed in position, the officers on board, or brass hats as they were known, filed past the enlisted men, deep in conversation. The officers appeared almost oblivious to their presence, and gave only the occasional glance at the team of porters that struggled with their personal luggage behind them. The regally dressed men paused in front of the vehicles and saluted each other, while the chauffeur of each car stood patiently with the door open. The crowd of natives surrounded them, but were restrained by the military police. The hawkers surged and subsided like the ocean surf, eager to have a chance to sell their goods to the khaki-clad soldiers that lined the ship rail.

Either not knowing the difference between an officer and an enlisted man, or too in need of money to care, a skinny man dressed in a dirty gallibaya—a traditional Egyptian garment—ducked under the outstretched arm of an MP and scurried for the party of officers. Another MP, positioned to the side of the vehicles, noticed the breach in security and stepped forward with his baton drawn. With one well-directed blow below the knees, he brought the half-starved peasant and all of his fruit to the ground. A tall thin officer in his late twenties, wearing a monocle and looking slightly more pompous than the rest, broke momentarily from his conversation to look at the native, writhing in agony. He looked at him in the way one may glance at a stray dog that lay in a public place. The officer gave a noticeable look of antipathy and then raised his eyebrows before he resumed his conversation. Two burly MPs dragged the would-be vendor away. The lesson on how to behave around officers was well and truly received by the hawkers and beggars who remained.

Eventually, Clarence and the rest of his rifle company were ordered to disembark, and the men gave a hearty three cheers to the captain and crew for landing them safely in this bizarre land. Happy to have his feet on dry land, Private Miller made his way along the pier, where orderly columns of soldiers had started to form. Clarence absorbed the sights and sounds as he strode along the ancient and exotic Port of Alexandria. He could feel himself been taken in by the allure of adventure and the comfort of comradeship that had developed on the voyage. He was beginning to understand the boy-like enthusiasm that most of the men around him showed for this enterprise.

At last the soldiers were ordered to pick up their kitbags and march for the train station. Weighed down by his kitbag, he breathed in the salty air of the harbour, laced with the smells of over-crowded humanity and their livestock. By chance, he had already answered one of life's most evasive mysteries, true love, only for it to be interrupted by fate. As he marched in formation, with his chin high and proud, Clarence had accepted where he was and how he had got there, and prayed silently that he could see it through.

The sergeant roared, and the men, shaded by their distinctive slouch hats, entrained efficiently, ready to depart for their training camp, its destination unknown.

***

Clarence sat on the floor of the rail car, which, before 1914, was no doubt used to transport stock of some description, but since hostilities, had become third class troop transport. As they did their best to get comfortable, some of the men joked that headquarters would have put them in fourth class, but it didn't exist, so third class it had to be. Clarence hadn't complained though; he was pleased to be off the *Warilda* and enjoyed the view of lush green crops through the gaps in the timber panels. As the scenery rushed past, a cool breeze enveloped the soldiers. It carried scents of ripened wheat on a mild but beautiful winter's day.

Back from one of his regular reconnaissance missions, Sticks plonked himself beside Clarrie, full of information. In his enthusiasm to relay his findings, he had inconvenienced a soldier or two.

'Watch it, mate,' snarled a burly looking man, who was trying to sleep against the hard timber panels.

'Sorry, cob,' replied Sticks.

'Bugger off, Sticks,' hissed the man, even more pissed-off after realising who had disturbed him.

Jack Sticks Sullivan had made himself quite well known during the voyage from Australia. The gamblers loved him; he had been a regular at any card or two-up game, and either through his lack of ability, or not knowing when to quit, he had contributed greatly to their wealth. Jack was also very interested in any information he could get his hands on. Knowing who knew whom, and what they might need, was vital to his other little pastime—trading, as he liked to call it. The card and two-up games were always a good source of gossip, but one of Private Sullivan's true talents was as a conversationalist. He could walk up to a group of men, and within seconds, they would be laughing and joking like old acquaintances. This talent didn't cross over to the fairer sex though. Sticks had been slapped in the face by more women than he cared to remember, and confided in Clarrie that he was genuinely confused as to why it was the case.

'Well, Clarrie, me boy, I don't think you're going to see that Cairo place you were so interested in, well not soon anyway.'

'Bugger,' spat Clarence. 'Where are we headed?'

'No one seems to know. All I could gather is that we're stopping at a place called Zagazig.'

'Did you make that up?'

'That's what I said to Ramsey; supposed to be a railway junction. Word is, brass hats don't want us near the temptations of Cairo, too much vice.'

'My brother Archie camped right near the pyramids when he came over.'

'No such luck for us, Professor. My bet is the Suez Canal.'

'Is it?' replied Clarrie dryly. 'Well we all know how you go at betting.'

'Bugger off, Miller,' said Sticks. He grabbed Clarrie's slouch hat and tossed it across the rail car before he rolled up his tunic to use as a pillow.

Clarrie resumed his spot after he had retrieved his hat. His soft nature got the better of him and he apologised to his mate, who grunted a reply.

'By the way, Miller, your brother's 1st Brigade is at Tel El Kebir.'

'What!' exclaimed Clarence, as he grabbed Jack's shoulder to pull him towards him.

'Easy, Easy.'

'Sorry, mate,' said Clarrie excitedly. 'What did you say about Archie?'

'Oh, that's how it is hey,' replied Sticks, still wounded by the gambling dig. 'Best mates when I can do something for ya. Isn't that lovely.'

'Knock it off, Jack, what did you hear?'

'Your brother's brigade is camped at Tel El Kebir,' said Sticks. He resumed his original position alongside Clarrie, with his back to the timber panelling. 'There are a few different camps in the Canal region and your brother is at the biggest. With any luck we will land at the same joint.'

'Archie, after all this time,' whispered Clarence. A glaze came over his eyes and his mind drifting over the ocean to Beattie Street, Balmain. He pictured the whole family around the table, happy in each other's company. Uninvited, a terrible notion crept in and shattered the glistening picture in his mind's eye. *Did he make it back? Pray God he has.* He tried desperately to suppress a vision of his older brother, alone and helpless in the dirt.

Sticks Sullivan casually turned away as a courtesy. He pretended not to notice his mate's emotions, allowing him time to take in the news. He was almost as keen as Clarrie to meet Archie, the big brother who he had heard so much about. Sticks gazed at three Egyptian men who tended their crops, and felt his own emotions. But he would be unlikely to acknowledge it as such, sentiment would be a better word, but not said aloud. *'Clarence Miller,'* Sticks thought, as he recalled the development of their unlikely mateship over the preceding months. *Gentle in nature, considerate, quick witted and intelligent, Clarrie is a softy, no doubt, but with a heart of gold, and tough in ways, definitely... unconventional, but tough all the same.* Jack realised Clarrie had opened his eyes to different ways of thought, an achievement in itself. *You're an odd one, my little mate,* he continued silently. *My little brother.*

Balmain, February 1916
Frank Miller placed the last of the tea chests, full of black-market cigarettes, on the floor of the shed. He moved quickly, but without panic. He closed the two large timber doors and secured them with a chain and lock before he turned and walked away. Frank withdrew a thick bundle of cash—wrapped in brown paper and tied with string—from inside his boiler-suit and handed it to the lorry driver without stopping. He made for home via the Dry Dock Hotel.

***

Albert folded the letter and placed it in his top pocket. He stood from the table, nodded to the barmen, and then exited the Exchange Hotel into the heat of a February afternoon.

Albert's visits to the Exchange had become more regular, and it wasn't just to read Archie's letters. While he had always enjoyed a cool beer, especially on a summer's afternoon, he had never been one to head straight for the pub after work, like so many of his co-workers. He enjoyed being at home with his family; he basked in the excited greetings of Alice and up until recently, Frank. The warm smile of his darling wife, the spirited debates with Archie on who was what in the world of sport, and oddly, now that he was overseas, Clarrie's sudden and enthusiastic assessments of current world events.

Albert found the quietness of his house slightly uncomfortable. It was a stark and vivid reminder that his boys had actually left to fight a war and it wasn't all just a bad dream. Ruth had definitely added some light to the house with the exuberance of youth and the glow of pregnancy. But she also carried her own concerns, which from time to time appeared in a vacant look through lonely eyes. Little Alice was always the same, and Albert was grateful for her antics, if only to keep Grace's mind engaged in something other than her boys' welfare.

The two eldest away on active service caused more than enough angst in the Miller household, without the added worry of Frank and his undoubted shift in behaviour. As crazy as it seemed, Albert sometimes felt more removed from his youngest son who lived under the same roof than from his two boys on the other side of the world. It wasn't as if Frank was being unruly or disrespectful, or rude to his mother. He didn't fight, except for that one time with Jimmy Taylor, which seemed to have been a one-off. Albert felt he could handle changes in young men such as that. It's what boys do at that age; but Frank had changed in a way that had caught Albert by surprise. He couldn't remember the last time they sat and spoke to each other as they had so often before. They had usually settled on football or cricket, and while he was happy and polite around the dinner table, he almost seemed more like a paying boarder than his youngest son.

Frank had developed an interest in horse racing. He had told his parents that he and his mate Jim had made a few bob walking horses for a trainer, which Grace wasn't too happy about. Albert had consoled her, and said, 'there are worse things a teenager could be attracted to.' Albert spoke to his wife with conviction, but he wasn't able to allay his own doubts about Frank's activities.

His mother had asked questions about a new cap, amongst other things he had purchased, but in his quiet and amiable way, he had described how an elderly gentleman connected to the stable had been nice enough to tip a few winners to him, and after he returned from Randwick one Saturday evening with a nice little parcel of groceries, courtesy of an alleged winning wager, the questioning became less frequent.

Albert often wondered if he allowed Frank to get away with more than the other boys; he couldn't tell. If he was honest, he couldn't remember what the others had tried. Not in detail anyway. It all seemed pretty straightforward then. Maybe that's where he had fallen down; he had forgotten.

The truth was, thought Albert, as he opened the front door of his home to the smell of sausages, was that he knew something was not right with Frank. He could now admit to himself that time after time he had chosen not to push the issue, for the simple reason that he didn't want the struggle that would come with the inevitable confrontation. That revelation alone made him feel slightly less of a man than the one he had always convinced himself he was.

'Daddy, Daddy,' screamed little Alice, her high-pitched voice sweet and innocent. A shower of relief washed over Albert Miller.

'Hello, Ally,' whispered Albert. He picked his daughter up and held the nine-year-old close to his chest. Albert savoured the moment and thought of simpler times. 'By crikey you have grown, Ally, I can hardly lift you.' His spirits had lifted and it pushed aside, consciously or not, the concern over Frank. Albert put Alice down, who immediately scampered off through the kitchen and out the back door to begin one of her imaginary adventures.

Following his daughter's path, Albert walked into the kitchen to find his wife at the stove, while Ruth moved cautiously around the table with a pregnant belly.

'Afternoon,' said Albert.

'Evening,' replied Grace dryly, but with no hint of anger. She gently reminded her husband what time it was.

'So it is. What's cooking?'

'Sausages, and they are almost ready,' stated Grace.

'I'll wash up and take a seat,' replied Albert. He smiled at Ruth as he made his way out the back.

Albert bent over to wash his hands and face from the tap connected to the water tank in the back yard, and then straightened. He reached for a small towel slung over his makeshift clothesline, and dried his face and hands. Hungry, he looked forward to his meal and was surprised when the back gate crashed against the fence that supported it.

'Son!'

'G'day, Dad,' replied Frank confidently.

'Go easy on the gate.'

'Sorry'.

'What have you been up to?' asked Albert, genuinely interested, but concerned it would be perceived as an interrogation.

'Went to a union meeting.'

'A union meeting?' stated Albert. He sounded perplexed.

'Well not really a union meeting, Dad,' replied Frank too quickly, 'just a few of the apprentices getting together for a chat. We have rights too, you know.' Frank tried his best to sound like a true Socialist, to cover his rather shadowy footsteps for that afternoon. Ronnie Symonds—the criminal tutor—would have been proud.

'Oh… well it's good for you younger blokes to stick together,' Albert replied vaguely. 'But be careful, you don't want to be seen to be a trouble maker as an apprentice.'

'She'll be right, Dad, we talked about boxing mostly. I can smell dinner.'

Frank excused himself and entered the house. He left his father more confused than ever.

***

The meal of sausages and mash passed with general chit-chat. Ruth relayed what the doctor had told her on her last visit; with a little over two months to the due date, all was reported to be going well. Alice was beside herself with excitement about the arrival of the baby, and asked questions relentlessly. The easy ones were answered, the more confronting gently deflected.

After Ruth and Frank had cleared the plates and Grace had brewed a pot of tea, Albert retrieved Archie's letter from his breast pocket and read it to the family.

It was dated October 10, and was general in its content, as were all the letters from Archie that Albert read at the dinner table. The tales of sacrifice and hardships—that were able to pass the censor—were read next to a glass of ale at The Exchange. Grace, Ruth, Frank, and Alice, listened intently as Archie sent his congratulations to his new sister-in-law, elated at the news of his younger brother's marriage, surprised but buoyant—having had time to digest the news via his mother's letter—on Clarrie's decision to enlist. Archie relayed news of his promotion to lance corporal, which brought a smile of pride to Frank's face. A story of a terrible storm that swept the peninsula two days before, with strong winds and torrential rain that cascaded down the numerous ravines and gullies, alarmed Grace. It caused substantial damage to dugouts and supplies. Archie finished off by sending everyone his love, and promising Ruth and his mother that he would watch his little brother like a hawk.

The moment after one of Archie's letters had been read was always one of quiet. Each member of the family went one way or the other. They occupied themselves with a chore or an old newspaper, as they pondered what Archie, and now Clarence—whom they hadn't heard from—were going through. The exception was Alice, who just went back to playing with her doll. But who was to know what went through the mind of a child.

EIGHT

Tel El Kebir Camp, February 1916
Lance Corporals Archibald Miller and Alf Conner rested in the shade of Archie's tent. Both men enjoyed a cigarette after they had toiled for most of the day, erecting lodgings for reinforcements, under a still mild but warming Egyptian sun.

After the evacuation from Gallipoli, Archie's brigade had spent some time recuperating on Lemnos Island before they embarked for Alexandria, and eventually for Tel El Kebir training camp. The camp was approximately seventy miles northeast of Cairo, and forty-five miles south of Port Said. It was about six miles in length, and home to thousands of soldiers, both veterans from the Gallipoli campaign, and reinforcements that had arrived from Australia.

'Do you reckon we will get leave to go to Cairo?' asked Conner, as he watched a plume of smoke he had exhaled rise steadily towards the roof of the tent.

'Not likely,' replied Archie, 'more likely...'

His reply was interrupted by the snap of canvas. Archie recoiled and raised a hand over his brow, as the glare of bright sunlight broke through the entrance of their little dwelling. Lance Corporal Miller was about to give the intruder what-for, but caught himself after he noticed the chevrons on the interloper's right sleeve.

'Attention!' yelled Sergeant Bourke. He announced his presence inside the tent with an arrogance that was usually reserved for commissioned officers. Bourke stood to one side and made way for the platoon commander, Lieutenant Davidson, a man who was respected by the whole battalion. In the glare, Davidson had not been seen by the two soldiers, who struggled to respond to Sergeant Bourke's command.

'On your feet!' barked the sergeant, his lack of self-confidence hidden by his loud, harsh, grating voice; a chance to use his authority never missed by a man with an insecure nature. The lack of regard for the sergeant was displayed in the way Archie and Alf rose slowly to their feet.

'Miller. Conner.' The lieutenant's calm voice registered with the two men instantly. It brought them to attention in one sudden and fluent move; the men's immediate display of respect for the lieutenant only fuelled the sergeant's feelings of inadequacy and animosity towards the men in his platoon.

'Lieutenant Davidson!' the men said in unison, while they executed a perfect salute.

Lieutenant Harold James Davidson stood at five feet eleven, with a muscular, athletic build. He was an officer with whom men liked to serve. Educated at the University of Sydney, he had excelled as a student of law as well as a sportsman, where he was more than accomplished at cricket, rugby, and to his family's displeasure, rugby league.

After graduating in 1910, he entered his father's legal practice in Neutral Bay, and gained experience in the militia, with the 1st Battalion, G Company, of the 1st Australian Infantry Regiment located in North Sydney. Enlisting within a week of the outbreak of war, he was given the rank of lieutenant and command of a platoon in A Company within the 1st Battalion, which was one of the four battalions—all raised in New South Wales—which made up the 1st Brigade in the Australian Imperial Forces, 1st Division.

A natural leader, Lieutenant Davidson had earned the respect of his men early. A perfectionist of sorts, he worked the men hard, being tough but fair in all matters, giving the average soldier the impression that he was in their corner, something that didn't sit too well with headquarters, and rumoured to have stalled further promotion. The respect and devotion afforded him by his platoon and battalion was taken to a new level while on the Gallipoli Peninsula, where the lieutenant was never found wanting in a fight, and it was widely remarked through the trenches and in cramped dugouts that there was nothing the men of 1st Battalion wouldn't do for Lieutenant Davo.

'At ease. I will get straight to the point. As you may be aware, the Australian Imperial Force has recently gone through a period of expansion. Two new brigades, the 14th and 15th, have been raised, and with the existing 8th, will form the new 5th division.'

Archie and Alf took a sideways glance at each other. They realised something was coming.

'Headquarters,' the lieutenant continued, 'has decided that the new brigades will consist of both experienced Gallipoli veterans such as yourselves and new recruits from Australia.'

'Here we go,' whispered Alf.

The lieutenant pretended not to hear Conner's remark. He allowed himself the faintest of smirks, knowing from experience what the lance corporal really wanted to say, after being shoulder to shoulder with him in the trenches of ANZAC Cove. The sergeant, lips pursed and limbs stiff, resented the comradeship that pulsated like an unseen force amongst the trio.

'Gentlemen, I have recommended both of you for promotion, and headquarters has acted on this recommendation, making you both corporals,' said the lieutenant. He saluted, and then relaxed his demeanour to step forward and warmly shake each man by the hand.

Both Archie and Alf returned his salute. The lieutenant, his moment of affection for his trusted soldiers expressed, resumed his previous stance and position as platoon commander.

'Corporal Miller and Corporal Conner, you have been reassigned to 14th Brigade of the 5th Division and will take charge of your own rifle section. You will report, along with Sergeant Bourke to 53rd Battalion headquarters, effective immediately. That is all.'

'Attention!' yelled Sergeant Bourke. The lieutenant saluted again as a prop to hide his eyes. He rolled them towards his eyebrows to mock the sergeant, and received a glint of acknowledgement in the eyes of the two newly promoted men.

Knowing it was time to leave, but wanting to say so much more, preferably over a beer rather than in a tent, and without the presence of a self-serving man such as Bourke, the respected officer and leader of men turned and then stopped. He pivoted on his heel and came to attention like he would at parade.

'It's been an honour and a privilege. You will always have a place as men of the First Battalion. Serve your new commander as you have me.'

***

Sergeant Kent approached the tent hot and bothered, with a thirst that had reduced his already short fuse. He had performed this task over forty times already this morning and silently cursed the AIF's restructure. The fact that it was Sunday and a day off made it all the worse. Kent wiped the sweat from his brow and adjusted his tunic; it allowed him a moment to compose himself before he entered. His current mood required a swift and proficient execution of his duty.

Sergeant Kent flicked the tent flap back as if his intention was surprise. He stepped into the dull light and spoke.

'Miller, Sullivan, Finch and Evans, pack your kit and report to 53rd Battalion headquarters, you've been transferred.'

'Sarge...' started Sticks.

'Shut your trap, Sullivan,' snapped the sergeant, '53rd headquarters, promptly.'

Jack Sullivan looked sideways at Clarrie; his mouth was still open from his unfinished sentence. He returned his blank gaze to the sergeant, who had already turned and exited for the next tent.

'I was only going to ask where 53rd Headquarters is,' said Sticks, stunned by the sergeant's response.

The question, along with his bewildered look, brought raucous laughter from the rest of the men in the tent.

***

They approached their new digs like kids who had swapped schools. Privates Miller, Sullivan, and Finch paused to gather their thoughts. Clarrie glanced at his new rectangular colour patch of black alongside dark green, stitched vertically on his sleeve, instead of horizontal like his 4th Battalion patch. The green represented the newly formed 14th Brigade, with the black—the colour of the 1st Battalion in a regiment—reported that he now belonged to 53rd Battalion.

Sticks pulled the tent flap back and motioned for Clarrie to enter. Clarrie gave his mate a dry smirk, which would have neatly translated into 'you bludger.'

As the men's eyes adjusted to the softer light of the tent, Clarrie surveyed the surrounds. He counted four men: two playing cards, one polishing his boots, and the fourth reading a letter. All of them were totally disinterested in their arrival. Clarrie made a quick summation, and gathered from their appearance, and more noticeably, from the way they held themselves, that they were all likely to be veterans of the Gallipoli campaign.

Uncertain as to what move he should make next, Clarence decided the best thing to do was to act like a soldier, and announce his presence.

'Privates Miller, Sullivan, and Finch,' shouted Clarence, a little too enthusiastically.

'Righto,' said the soldier with the letter, his eyes fixed to the page, 'give us a tick.'

Clarrie, Sticks, and Joseph stood patiently, and waited for the letter reader to finish. They had their attention diverted momentarily, when two more men entered the tent. Clarrie looked back towards the new arrivals and was amazed as to how out of place they looked. They moved nervously; their eyes bulged and darted like scared rabbits.

Geez, is that how we look to these men, said Clarrie to himself; *no wonder they treat us with indifference.*

Sticks moved to one side to make room, and then motioned for Clarrie to follow.

'Get that silly smile of your face, you look like a half-wit,' whispered Sticks. He had noted that their actions were doing little to disguise their status as untested reinforcements.

Clarrie nodded to his mate, and then to the man who read the letter. He had now made an effort to stand, but not too enthusiastically. The soldier yawned and then showed a lot of concern for a numb and itchy back-side.

He looked casually at each man. The reinforcements stood as best they could in the confines of the tent and waited.

'Welcome to number 5 rifle section of 2nd Platoon, A Company men. I am Corporal Alfred Conner, behind me are Lance Corporal Atkins, Privates Baker and Smith.' Each man raised his hand slightly in acknowledgment of their name being called. 'Unfortunately,' the sarcasm in the corporal's voice present for all to hear, 'Sergeant Bourke isn't present to meet you.' The two privates involved in a card game, Baker and Smith, smiled at the corporal's sense of humour, loaded with sarcasm.

'Sticks Sullivan,' said Sticks, as he offered his hand to shake.

'G'day, Sticks,' replied Corporal Conner, as he shook hands. 'I normally give out the nicknames.' He made a mental note of his new acquaintance's firm grip and overall physical build. *This one might be all right*, he thought to himself.

'Clarence Miller from Balmain,' said Clarrie, with a smile.

'Hello, Clarence.' *Officers' batman.* The corporal began to turn towards Joseph Finch and then spun back to Clarrie. 'Did you say Miller, mate?'

'Yes, Clarence Miller,' replied the happy-go-lucky private.

'Thought so,' said the corporal. He moved on, as if his question had meant nothing in the first place, but allowed the faintest of smiles to form on his lips. It gave away—to someone with a keen eye—the penny that had just dropped inside his head.

'Joseph Finch.'

'Now that's what I like to hear gentleman!' roared Corporal Conner, 'a name I can assign a nickname to.'

The two men that played cards and Arthur Atkins—the boot polisher—now stood and moved forward to great the new recruits, laughing in unison.

'From now on, Joseph,' said Connor, as if he waited for trumpets to blare and proclaim the announcement official, 'you will be known as Birdie.'

All four veterans cheered in unison, grateful to have a diversion from the monotony of labour that had been their life at camp this past month. The new recruits smiled, but felt like the kids who had just changed schools. They knew someone would be picked on, they just hoped it wasn't them. The exception of the group was Sticks. He had a grin from ear to ear.

Seem like a good mob of blokes, this lot, he said to himself, while he stared at Joseph. *He actually does look like a bird, now I think of it.* His own humour made him chuckle, which brought a sharp look from Corporal Conner for the breach in protocol during an unofficial, but very important "greeting ceremony".

The banter subsided and Alf Conner motioned for Clarence and Sticks to move apart, making a gap for a diminutive lad who had been content to stand in the shadows while the fun played out. The young man looked around nervously. He was no taller than five-foot-three inches and as slender as a bean-pole. Unknown to veteran and novice alike, he stepped into the spotlight with the eyes of each man fixed firmly on him.

'James Cook,' the young man said quietly, swallowing.

'Sorry cob, Cook is it? James?' asked Alf

'Yes, sir.'

'Please, James, don't call me sir. It makes me nervous.'

'Yes, sir,' replied Private Cook. He looked distraught.

Clarence stared at the poor boy. He knew what it felt like to be a duck out of water. He silently prayed that the private would hold himself together.

While he liked to have fun, Corporal Conner was by no means a heartless man. He put his arm around Private Cook's shoulders and brought him over to stand with the veterans. The corporal then held up his free hand for quiet.

'Men,' he started seriously, 'everyday you wake up, not knowing what to expect, what lies around the next bend… ANZAC taught us that.' The soldiers in the tent bowed their heads. They expected to hear something profound from Corporal Conner. 'Today, when they said we would get some fresh-faced recruits to bolster our new battalion,' continued the corporal, as he turned to the private to look him in the eye, 'never, I repeat never, did I expect to be out ranked by Captain James Cook himself!'

Alf Connor raised his arm in the air, undefeated champion of nickname bestowment. The men took a second to join the dots and then cheered enthusiastically. They tussled Private Cook's hair and then gave him three cheers. The young private looked so relieved that Clarrie thought he might faint.

***

The five untried recruits found their places in the tent and began to settle in. Clarrie wound up next to Sticks, with Private Atkins on his other side. They exchanged small talk and Clarrie learnt that Atkins was from a small town called Gilmurra, deep in southern New South Wales, a place Clarence wasn't familiar with. That surprised him a little, as he thought there weren't too many spots on the New South Wales map he couldn't place.

'Miller!' shouted Conner.

Clarence looked up to see Corporal Conner in conversation with Tom Baker. The corporal signalled for him to come and join them. Clarence rose and made his way across the tent, while Sticks followed.

'Yes, Corporal?'

'Are you his shadow or something?' Conner said to Sticks.

'We're mates,' said Sticks. He didn't want trouble, but he would be there for Clarrie should the earlier antics begin again.

'You don't say. All right, tag along then,' said Alf. He looked at Private Sullivan, still assessing the one newbie who hadn't seemed intimidated by their veteran status. He switched his gaze to Clarrie and smiled. 'Follow me, Miller.'

The bright Egyptian sun and its reflection off the yellow sand speared their eyes like a lance when they exited the tent. Their eyes closed to relieve the ache in their skulls.

'Surely someone could invent something to protect your eyes from that blasted sun,' hissed Alf to no one in particular.

Clarrie felt it would be better not to say too much, and decided not to ask where they were going. He followed obediently and then bumped into the back of the corporal when Conner stopped abruptly in front of a tent. It was identical to theirs and the thousand others that were lined neatly throughout the camp.

Sounds of laughter, much the same as had come from their tent, escaped through the canvas walls. It made Sticks wary as to what would unfold. Calmly, and with a warm smile on his face, Alf Conner leant over and grabbed an edge of the woven fabric; he pulled it back and invited Clarence to enter.

Clarence hesitated, but Corporal Conner urged him to proceed into the tent. Clarrie did not want to be seen as someone who wasn't game, regardless of whether he was or not, so he walked slowly towards the entrance. Sticks followed close behind.

Once again, the men's eyes adjusted to the change in light. The tent was crammed with men and various items of kit, and to Clarrie's eye, the soldiers were going through the same little ritual as they had only half an hour before.

'Go away, we have our full quota of "virgin soldiers"', shouted a larger than life voice; husky, but all too familiar to Clarence. The orator waved his arm towards the exit and didn't bother to turn his hunched body.

Clarrie suddenly realised the objective of the corporal's covert mission, and spoke louder than he normally would. 'Well, I wouldn't normally speak of such things in public. But I am a married man now... so your words are ill-chosen to say the least.'

Archie Miller straightened his back so quickly, it was like Clarence had pushed a red-hot branding iron against his rump. 'Clarrie,' Archie whispered. His eyes were wide, and his cheeks creased from a smile that threatened to split his bronzed skin. 'Clarrie, you little ripper,' he yelled, still with his back to his brother. Archie then turned so quickly, that he sent two of his mates to the ground.

It was something that Clarence was yet to understand, but for Archie, having clung to the unforgiving coastline of enemy territory, it was something that lingered within him. Having fought and survived the nauseating and hellish experience of Lone Pine, he had wondered what—if anything—awaited you once you felt the cold steel or hot lead from a foe, determined to end your life. To pass through those moments of fear and utter helplessness, whether to turn and flee in but the flicker of an eye, or to stand and fight—just a sequence of events that pushed you from one side or the other. To have an idea of something, then to have that idea twisted so far out of recognition, to be beyond explanation. To be surrounded by voices that were not of the living, but your tortured memories of what had lived—then suffered. To keep this inside, deep inside, hidden from view by whatever means necessary, only to be propelled forward by a single voice, a voice that defined all that was good, but stirred all that was suppressed.

To live, or to survive, with the objective not being a hill or a trench, but to live for the next day. A day which brought hope, hope that somehow things might return to how they were before young men felt the rush of patriotism and adventure. Before they knew the pain of loss, and their naivety had allowed them to live carefree.

As he hugged his younger brother, Archie soaked up all that he remembered and cherished. Clarence moved backwards a pace or two under the weight and exuberance of his brother's embrace. He felt all the emotion, but could only interpret it as joy in the re-uniting of siblings, for he was still in that world that Archie longed for but could not reclaim, as it was as dead as any soldier on the battlefield.

***

Archie and Clarence walked up and down the criss-crossed streets or sandy paths that were created when thousands of peaked tents were erected at the Tel El Kebir military camp.

For Clarrie, it almost seemed surreal to be alongside his brother again, both in army issue, and both in the desert, thousands of miles away from Beattie Street. Luck had put them in the same battalion, and Archie couldn't get enough of any news from home. He listened intently to the smallest event or happening amongst his family and friends. He would ask Clarence several times to repeat things and then pause to smile, savouring the moment like a cool beer in summer.

'Did you know there was a battle right near here,' declared Clarence. He scanned the horizon, as if he expected to see some evidence to support his statement.

'No, I didn't, mate,' replied Archie. He smiled at his brother and his love of—in Archie's opinion—useless bits of information.

'1882, between the British and some Egyptians...'

'Tell me about this wife of yours, little brother,' interjected Archie. He feared a full-blown history lesson. 'Mum adores her, judging from her letter.'

'Ruth is... how can I describe her?'

'Here we go, out of the frying pan and into the fire,' exclaimed Archie, jokingly. 'Reveille's at 05:00, so keep it as brief as possible.'

'Impossible,' replied Clarence, Ruth's face, the sound of her voice, the smell of her hair, invaded Clarrie's senses all at once.

Archie noticed the look on his brother's face and could tell what she meant to him, but he wanted to hear it anyway.

'Just try for me, little brother,' replied Archie, 'I'm out of the loop, my brother gets married and I miss it.'

'I knew from the moment I saw her.'

'Knew what?'

'That I loved her.'

'Bullshit!' scoffed Archie. 'I mean fair dinkum. Sorry, mate, I didn't mean that.'

'That's okay, you'd know if you saw her,' Clarence replied. 'Couldn't speak the first time I saw her, made a right fool of myself. I ordered a loaf of bread and I was...' Clarence chuckled to himself, as he took off his slouch hat and twirled it from one hand to the other. He replayed the scene from the bakery in his mind. He could smell the bread and feel the sensation of suspension, as he stared at his future wife.

'I wish I could find a girl like that,' said Archie. He meant every word of it.

'What do you mean,' laughed Clarrie, 'you've had plenty of girlfriends.'

'I know that, ya dim wit, poked a few of 'em too, but none of them special.'

'Oh,' replied Clarrie, a little embarrassed by his brother's frankness. 'What's the family like?'

'Fairly normal, her mum's a bit high strung, her father's a good bloke though, a baker, Reynolds's bakery.'

'I know the one, Darling Street, near the butchers.'

'That's right. Ruth still works there or maybe she isn't now,' said Clarence with a puzzled look on his face. 'The baby is due in April. This mail situation really gets under my skin, haven't seen one letter yet.'

'It stinks,' replied Archie, 'you get none and then suddenly you'll get eight, typical… what did you just say?'

'The mail's getting me annoyed.'

'Before that.'

Clarence scratched his head. He ran the conversation through his mind, and then, casually, like he had recalled a lost melody, he blurted, 'The baby's due in April.'

'The baby's due in April?' replied a stunned Archie. He stopped in his tracks alongside a water cart. He forced Clarrie to stop and turn to face him. 'Baby, what baby?'

'Ours… mine and Ruth's.'

Archie was gobsmacked and stood motionless on the sandy road. His face was fixed in an expressionless stare, while other soldiers passed. They paused, as if he might need assistance; touched by the sun, they probably thought.

'You all right, Arch?' enquired Clarrie.

'Yeh mate… just shocked. A baby, Clarrie, you're going to be a dad!' The news of new life added weight to what Archie had felt inside the tent.

'Yes, Arch, you could have knocked me down with a feather when Ruth told me.'

'My little brother,' whispered Archie. He moved sideways to lean against the water cart, a glint of joy in his eye. The news touched a part of Archie's being that he hadn't been aware of; the part of an individual that, without them knowing, makes them paternal. When

Archie had leapt aboard the troopship, arm-in-arm with his mates, the only other thing that he thought could occupy his mind and life in this world was football. In one short sentence, he had just found out what his real vocation was.

'You sure you're all right, Archie?' asked Clarrie, surprised at his normally boisterous brother.

'Over the moon,' exclaimed Archie. He sprang to attention and held out his hand to offer his congratulations. 'Sorry, Clarrie, I couldn't be happier for you. So much has happened… I've only been gone a bit.'

'You're right, Archie, sometimes I can't believe how my life has changed and so quickly, but when I think of Ruth, I feel like I have known her my whole life and everything that has happened was meant to happen.'

'Well, that may be true shagger,' said Archie with a return to his masculine self. He grabbed his brother in a headlock and ruffled his hair, 'but I do know something that is definitely meant to happen.'

'And what's that?' asked Clarence, pleased to see his brother like he knew him.

'We are meant to get a leave pass and celebrate.'

'But I don't drink.'

'I'll teach you.'

NINE

Balmain, February 1916
'G'day, Hammer,' said Frank, as he took a seat alongside the strongly built man, on a bench between the waters of Snails Bay and Birchgrove Oval.

'Ronnie wants you to go "cockatoo" tomorrow afternoon,' said Hammer. He stared out over the water and made no acknowledgment or reply to Frank's greeting.

'No worries. Where?'

Hammer stood and removed a folded piece of paper from his coat pocket. 'Hat on if all clear, hat off if you see anyone that shouldn't be there. Three o'clock, don't be late, address is here,' said Hammer. He passed the piece of paper to Frank. 'Sweet?'

'Got it,' replied Frank

'Don't stuff it up,' warned Hammer, before he turned and walked west towards Louisa Road.

***

Tel El Kebir Camp, March 1916
Sticks Sullivan burst into the tent with his head bowed and shoulders slumped. He stomped his feet like a two-year-old throwing a tantrum; his toxic mood had not considered Clarence, who was in the middle of a whole bundle of letters he had received from home. Most of them

were from Ruth, but there were a couple from his mother and even one from his former editor, John Blake.

Clarrie realised that his mate had made a ruckus to prompt him to ask what troubled him, so he obliged. The list of baby names Ruth had picked out would have to wait.

'What's up, Sticks?'

'Flamin' 15th Brigade bastards!'

'Who?' Clarrie stifled a laugh and changed to a sitting position. He was now more intrigued than usual by one of Jack's predicaments.

'Bloody Victorians, that's who. Bloody 15th. You can bet all the tea in China it's rigged.'

Clarence suddenly caught on. *Again*, he said to himself as he placed a photo of Ruth— included in one of the letters—in his breast pocket. 'Lost the lot, mate?'

Sticks shrugged to confirm what Clarence really didn't need to ask.

'You have to lay off the cards, Jack, it doesn't seem like much fun to be losing your money all the time.'

'Thanks for the advice, Mr "I don't do a thing wrong," but it's a bit late now. Anyway, it wasn't cards.'

'Well two-up then,' snapped Clarrie, 'what's the difference?'

'Wasn't flaming two-up either, ya big sheila,' moaned Sticks. He looked despondent, as he half-heartedly kicked his kit that lay on the floor.

'Well what was it then mate?' Clarrie softened his tone.

Jack lit a smoke and drew back deeply. He held his breath for a few seconds, as if in thought. Suddenly he blew a cloud of smoke towards the roof of the tent and said, 'beetles.'

Clarrie sat silently, not sure if he had heard correctly. 'Sorry, mate, did you say beetles?'

'Yeh, beetles. That's right.'

'I know I'm not up to speed on these things,' replied Clarrie, a broad smile on his face. 'But how on God's earth do you bet on beetles.'

'It's really quite simple,' said Sticks calmly. 'You catch a Scarab beetle.'

'Scarab beetle?' asked Clarrie, amazed.

Sticks nodded, a little annoyed at the interruption. 'You get the beetle, make a circle in the sand and build up the edges so it can't escape.' Sticks looked intently at Clarrie while he illustrated the process with his hands, as if he was the expert instructor and his mate had paid good money to be at his tutorial. 'Then you make three gaps in the wall and bet on which one he leaves through.'

A brief silence was shattered by a laugh from Clarrie that even surprised himself. Clarence Miller rolled on the tent floor with tears in his eyes. The laugh came from deep in his belly, but it changed to a kind of squeal when he had to catch his breath.

'Righto, Miller, get a hold of yourself,' cried Sticks.

Clarrie took a few giant breaths in an effort to control himself. He raised himself to a sitting position once again and rested his forearms on his knees. He looked up at his tragic but lovable mate and couldn't resist the temptation. 'Beetles,' squealed Clarrie, as he broke into another fit of laughter.

'Get nicked, Miller,' barked Sticks as he playfully kicked him in the guts. 'This is serious, I'm broke.'

Clarrie pulled himself onto his knees. He still laughed quietly, but he held his right palm outstretched in a sign of truce. Clarrie looked straight at his friend and then towards his pack. A quiet voice in his head warned him of the dangers of what he contemplated, but a louder voice knocked the quiet one off its perch.

Private Miller thrust his arm into his kit and rummaged around. He withdrew his hand and revealed a thick, leather-bound notebook with large pieces of paper of various sizes and colours protruding from top and bottom. Clarrie undid the buckle that secured it and opened the book. He flicked through the pages and pulled out several ten-bob and five-pound notes that were a part of a thicker stash.

'You never saw that,' said Clarence as he rose to his feet.

'Not a thing, mate.'

'Come with me, Sullivan,' said Clarence, as he looked straight into his mate's eyes. 'Let's go and sort these Victorians out, the 14th can't be pushed around. What do you say?'

Sticks, in a state of mild shock, was almost lost for words. He spoke through gritted teeth. 'You bloody beauty.'

Both men strode through the tent opening and turned right towards the 15th Brigade area in the Tel El Kebir camp. They walked side by side, linked by that fundamental ingredient of mateship; when the time comes, you help your mate, no matter what. Clarrie didn't understand what drove men to waste good money on gambling, but he could sense his friend was despondent, and apart from his desire to pull Sticks out of a hole, he was also exhilarated by the prospect of doing something, although not out-and-out criminal, against army regulations.

***

'Back for a bit more punishment, Sticks?' sniggered a well-built private, who pretended to read an old newspaper. He sat on an upturned crate outside one of the many tents erected in neat rows at Tel El Kebir. His barb delivered, the private returned his attention to his paper; he did his best to disguise his real role of being point for the gambling school inside. Casually he looked up again, as if in general and meaningless conversation. He looked left and then right to pass his trained eye over the other tents. 'Who's your mate?'

'Miller.'

'Wants in does he?'

'Yes, thanks,' replied Clarrie, a little too eagerly.

'Who asked you?' hissed the sentry, as he stood to reveal his impressive height.

'He's keen to give it a go,' intervened Sticks, 'never gambled before,' he added from the corner of his mouth. 'Wants to see what all the fuss is about.'

'Does he now?' replied the Digger, his interest in Clarrie suddenly enhanced. 'Wait here.'

The tall, well-built soldier with bronzed skin gave a short sharp whistle before he pulled back the tent flap to disappear into its void. Sticks turned to Clarrie and gave him a few tips on how to handle himself, once inside.

'Don't bet too big too early, ok.'

'You told me that.'

'We don't want to scare them off. If you go in hard they might think something is up and pull up stumps,' instructed Sticks.

'How much to start with?' asked Clarrie.

'Wait till we get inside, but probably a quid or ten bob. By Christ, I want to nail these bastards.'

Clarrie laughed, and then turned it into a cough as he saw the point-man emerge from the tent.

'Five bob each to get in, ten bob minimum bet,' stated the private, with a smart-ass smirk on his face.

'What!' exclaimed Sticks. 'Ya thieving sod, I was just in here twenty minutes ago.'

'Take it or leave it Sticksy, and watch your mouth,' said the private. He loosely shadow-boxed to continue the charade of banter amongst friends, while letting Sticks and Clarrie know that they could be knocked out with either one of his impressive fists.

'No problem,' said Clarrie. He stepped forward confidently with his hand outstretched for the smug sentry to shake. Disarmed by Clarrie's unexpected move, the impressively built private switched his focus to the novice gambler and tentatively grasped the turned palm. He instantly felt the touch of folded paper, and while he welcomed the discreet move, the calmness of the act sent up a small flare of alarm in the racketeer's mind. The look-out glanced left and right again, and then stood to one side, while he pocketed the ten-bob note.

The two mates passed into the gloomy light of the tent; a brume of stale acrid air hit them as they inhaled the by-product of twenty or so perspiring soldiers whose skin hadn't seen water in days. Sticks surveyed the room and spotted 'Bomber' Kendall. The nickname was said to have originated from his penchant for blowing things up in his life as a civilian on the streets of St Kilda.

Private Christopher Bomber Kendall chose to enlist in the army, but he wasn't your regular citizen who had reacted to a call of patriotism, nor did he possess an idealistic grudge that fed a desire to fight the Hun. Christopher Kendall was a small-time, but nasty, Melbourne crook. He had crossed paths with the law on one too many occasions, and had been given the choice by the local magistrate to either join the AIF or go to the clink. Bomber had surprised and aggravated the magistrate at the time, when he had taken a few moments to make his decision. But after he had remembered a few members of the Melbourne underworld that were behind bars and would eagerly await his arrival, he elected for the Infantry.

Bomber Kendall made eye contact with Sticks, and welcomed the hapless gambler with the warmest of smiles. He was more than happy to take his money, and if his mate was only half as hopeless as Sticks, he could make plenty off him too.

'Sticks, good to see you again mate,' Bomber said softly. He observed his own rule of muffled speech. Two men, almost identical to the bronzed sentry outside, stood at each shoulder to keep an eye on everything and everyone.

While Clarrie and Sticks had just entered into a thriving little gambling school, it wasn't your regular venue. The military police or 'Jacks', as some called them, would love nothing more than to discover this unusual, yet profitable little enterprise, bust the game up, and crack a few skulls in the process. The bronzed Aussie who guarded the front door was on constant lookout not only for MPs, but also for officers and banned clients, and had developed a series of whistles that could be used to warn Bomber. Any patrons who shouted, or made a nuisance of themselves in general, would be expelled from the tent.

Bomber returned his attention to the game in progress, while Clarrie glanced around at the rest of the faces that circled the small sand arena—a miniature Coliseum. The frenzied crowd hissed through gritted teeth as they willed the sacred symbol of Egypt towards the gate they had bet on. Clarence found the incessant noise unnerving, and although it was subdued and most likely inaudible outside, the repetitiveness of the sound made the tent feel smaller than it actually was.

Clarrie watched on intently. He realised that what had initially seemed like a ludicrous and moronic concept had captivated him to the point where, after only a few minutes, he found himself silently egging the tiny beetle towards any one of the three gates. After a few minutes of indecision, the beetle finally settled on a course and passed through Gate Two. Men pumped their fists or mockingly pushed a mate in the back of the head, as a flurry of monetary exchanges took place in an orderly and precise manner.

All debts settled, Bomber, with the beetle gently held between his thumb and forefinger, called for new bets. He handed the struggling insect to the starter—another Digger in his employ—before he held up his hand up for bets to be finalised. Clarrie and Sticks held a brief conference, nodded to each other, and then placed a bet of ten bob on Gate Two.

All gates had odds set at even money, put ten bob on, get ten bob back. Everyone had to bet with the house; side bets were not allowed—nothing in it for Bomber—and the beetle had three minutes to make his exit. If he failed to pass through a gate—unless you bet that way—it was a win for the house, as it was if you bet on a losing gate. Not the best odds for the punter, but beggars can't be choosers, and in the case of most Australian soldiers, who would be likely to bet on two flies that crawled up a wall, Bomber's tent was as good as it got in the Egyptian desert.

Call it beginner's luck, but Clarrie won on his first three bets, all on Gate Two. He took a loss on Gate Three and then won another two on the faithful Gate Two. With punters being superstitious by nature, he was beginning to draw attention from men either side of him. Some delayed on their bets until they could ascertain which way the newcomer had gone. Sticks looked up to see Bomber whispering to his starter. The starter then casually reached into his pocket, and under the cover of bets being exchanged, placed an unknown substance on the beetle's legs.

Being witness to the act, Sticks casually feigned interest in bets being placed with the bagman, while he discreetly tugged on Clarrie's arm.

'Hold off, mate,' whispered Sticks.

'Why, I've got the hang of this.'

'Up your bet and go no-gate,' hissed Sticks. He tried to appear calm but there was stress in his voice. He could see an opportunity vaporise in the dingy air of the makeshift gambling den.

'You're mad, Sticks, the beetle loves the Two Gate.'

With time running out before bets were closed, Sticks was about ready to throttle Clarrie. He took a deep breath and lent towards his mate's ear. He spoke slowly, and in accordance with house rules—softly.

'Clarence. Just fucking do it!'

Clarrie was slightly shocked, but realised the tone in Jack's voice left no room for debate. He nodded in the affirmative, and in an attempt not to announce their bet to the rest of the mob, folded two five-pound notes into the palm of his hand, before he approached the bagman.

'Ten quid on no-gate,' whispered Clarrie. Private Miller slipped the equivalent of a month's wages into the money-man's hands.

A concerned look came over the bagman's face. He wiped his

sweaty forehead with his upper arm and then turned to speak to his boss. Sticks pretended to be interested in goings-on elsewhere and tried desperately not to smile, as he lip-read each swear word that came from Bomber's mouth. Kendall realised he was cornered and reluctantly approved the bet. He knew that a rejection could spread doubt throughout his clientele, which would cause bigger losses than the one he was about to receive.

Anyway, Bomber thought, *all the other stupid pricks will bet on a gate, I will still win, but not as much as I would've.*

When the three minutes lapsed and the beetle had barely moved, let alone pass through a gate, all the punters, except Clarence and Sticks, cursed. Bomber's gaze could have burnt a hole through the pair of mates from 14th Brigade, and if he was back in St Kilda, he may have attempted something just as painful. Bomber stood still and tapped his foot repeatedly on the soft floor. His glare was fixed across the tent, while he whispered something to one of his henchmen, who nodded and then circled the crowd.

Sticks rubbed the top of Clarrie's head in jubilation and then punched him in the arm. 'You little ripper, Miller, I told ya! Didn't I?' said Sticks, in a hushed but excited voice.

'You did, Jack, and I wasn't about to argue the point.'

'Yeh, sorry about that, felt I had to get the message across.'

'It worked.'

'You two, follow me.' Their joyous exchange interrupted by a third, and distinctly abrupt voice.

'Huh?' moaned Sticks He did not appreciate being ordered about, especially now that he had won. 'Go follow ya fuckin' self,' blurted Sticks, his blood still up from the big win.

The voice, who had continued on as soon as he delivered his orders, expected them to be obeyed—as they always were. He stopped in his tracks after Jack Sullivan's suggestion and turned slowly enough for his eyes to change from white to blood-shot red. Clarrie saw that the body that carried the voice was as big as any man he had seen, and leapt to his feet in an attempt to calm the situation. He intercepted Bomber's bouncer, just before he reached Sticks, who, being a dock worker and a proud man, was on his feet as well and ready for anything.

'Did you say something, old mate,' asked the bouncer over Clarrie's shoulder. His eyes were an inferno but he remained calm outwardly. He knew that any ruckus could bring unwanted attention and a reduction in his slice of the takings by an unhappy boss.

'Listen, mate, we're not here to cause trouble,' said Clarrie nervously. The bouncer's body pressing against Clarrie's; the rock-hard muscles and weight of his stance, elevated Clarrie's already heightened sense of alarm. 'We were just about to leave.'

The bouncer completely ignored Clarrie's attempt to keep the peace; instead he continued his death stare towards Private Sullivan and waited for the slightest provocation.

'I think you know exactly what I said, Princess,' taunted Sticks. The final words were delivered with the added insult of a smirk.

The left hook came quickly, but Sticks had more or less asked the bouncer to hit him, so he was ready for it. He ducked down and slightly to his left, while he protected his face with his right forearm. His left fist was tucked under his chin, cocked and ready to fire. The bouncer's blow glanced of the top of Stick's head and crashed into the jaw of an unsuspecting soldier, sending him to the sandy floor. The bouncer's balance had been tipped after he had overshot his mark. It caused him to lurch forward and force his substantial weight onto Clarrie, who buckled under the strain, landing beside the punched soldier.

Sticks seized the moment and sprang from his slightly crouched position. His right arm still protected his face; he used the drive of his legs and his hips to deliver a left hook that crushed the bouncer's ribs. A split second later, the right hand that had protected his face was unleased in a lethal overhand punch that landed squarely on the bouncer's jaw.

The sound from bone on bone when Jack Sullivan landed his own 'Howitzer' on the huge man was like the crack of a stock whip. It brought a stunned silence to the tent. Clarrie, still sprawled on the ground, looked across to the bouncer, spread-eagled on his back. He slept like a baby under the triumphant shadow of Sticks Sullivan. A quick glance around the gambling den by Sticks revealed a dozen or more shocked Diggers and one incensed Bomber Kendall. His teeth were clenched so tightly that it changed his appearance; Sticks realised then and there that he had made an enemy for life.

Sticks hoisted Clarrie to his feet, pocketed the winnings and made for the tent flap. The sentry outside had not been alerted to the commotion, so swift was the encounter. As they approached the exit, a self-assured Private Sullivan couldn't resist the temptation. He paused and turned to face Kendall.

'I kept it quiet, Bomber,' whispered Sticks. 'I didn't want to bring the MPs down on a decent honest bloke like yourself.'

Whether through the threat of visiting MPs or Jack Sullivan's fists, Clarrie wasn't sure, but he was surprised when Bomber Kendall didn't utter a reply. Being a naive romantic, Clarrie was unaware that people like Christopher Kendall preferred to work in the shadows. Sticks Sullivan, a man with more of life's experiences under his belt, was all too aware that while ever Bomber Kendall was around, he would need eyes in the back of his head.

TEN

Balmain, March 1916

'It's here; it's here,' screamed Grace, as she entered the house. Her apron was tucked up with one hand, as she tried to move as quickly as possible, while the other hand held the letter aloft like a trophy. 'Ruth, it's here!'

Ruth raised herself slowly from her seat at the kitchen table. She could feel the weight of her unborn child bear down as she did.

'Here luv, let me help you,' said Grace. She reached her daughter-in-law, and her voice reverted to its normal calm tones when she witnessed Ruth's discomfort.

'This baby must be a giant,' said Ruth, her face suddenly flushed.

'It's a letter from Clarrie, luv, finally.'

'Clarence?' asked Ruth quietly. She inhaled and caught her emotions before they escaped.

'Yes, dear,' replied Grace, excitedly. 'Would you like some privacy?'

Ruth took a few seconds to answer, anxious at finally having received what she had waited so long for.

'No, of course not Grace,' Ruth replied with love and sincerity in her voice. 'This is yours and Mr Miller's letter, as much as it is mine.'

'That is very kind of you, I have thought of him every day. Shall we have a seat, maybe you could read it aloud for us both?'

They sat at the kitchen table, like they had so many times over these last months. Ruth opened the envelope, inscribed with her husband's hand, and, after a deep breath, she began to read.

HMAT Warilda
Port of Alexandria
21st January, 1916

Dearest Ruth & Family,
Well, here I am, safe and sound in Egypt, the land of the Pharaohs. Not quite actually. We are still on board and anchored in the harbour itself, waiting for permission to dock, which could be days.

Ruth paused to giggle at her husband's familiar bumbling.

Still, it is exciting to be in a foreign land, and judging by the interesting architecture and intriguing smells that waft over the bay, along with the tiny vessels laden with goods that hover around our ship trying to make contact, who knows what we will find once we finally dock.
The departure from the Quay and the days after were difficult, and I spent many evenings on deck staring towards the horizon, wondering what you were doing, picturing you in all your beauty.

A small tear hit the page, blotting the ink on the previous line.

Being on a ship at sea, I didn't think we would get a chance to get mail away, so I sketched instead (two enclosed). Hoping to see mail from home, maybe on the next ship. I hope you are well. I still have to pinch myself about becoming a dad.
We were kept fairly busy on the voyage over, with exercise and basic drills, but a great many could take no part due to

sea-sickness, which is no laughing matter when you see what some of the poor chaps went through. Thankfully I was all right.

Have become good friends with a fellow from Glebe named Jack Sullivan; everyone calls him Sticks. A larrikin to say the least, but a very decent chap, can't wait for you to meet him one day.

Give everyone my love and I will write again promptly. I will be making enquiries about Archie's battalion at first chance. Tell Frank there are a couple of boys from Balmain Rugby League Club on board. Tell him to keep up his training and he will make the grade one day. The boys had a good laugh at my expense when we were passing the ball on deck one evening. I am sure Frank could appreciate that after my efforts at home.

Thinking of you always.

With love from your Husband
Clarence.

***

Frank found the address in Phillip Street that Hammer had written on a scrap of paper. It was a dilapidated terrace house, typical of the area. He glanced at the piece of paper once more and confirmed he had the right location, and then looked across the street at the small park. Frank immediately crossed the road; he felt it would be a more innocuous place to wait.

With his back against the sandstone wall that bordered the park, Frank watched two men—both in well-worn, dark brown suits—walk up to the door of the same terrace house where he was to meet Hammer. He knelt on the pavement and pulled his wool cap lower over his brow. Frank then picked up a few stones and pretended to amuse himself with a game of Jacks, like a normal kid would. With his back at forty-five degrees to the terrace, he turned his head slightly; it allowed him to view the two men without drawing attention.

Both men stood at the door in conversation, before one of them dropped to his knees. The other man looked left and right, and occasionally upwards towards the upstairs room of the terrace.

What are these blokes up to? Frank whispered.

Hammer had said to meet him here at three o'clock, but he couldn't remember if he had mentioned anyone else. He assumed Ronnie had arranged some sort of meeting, and he would be standing cockatoo; maybe he would run errands; Ronnie had many places he owned and used in Balmain, low-key and out of the way, but this was Frank's first time at this particular address. The Dry Dock Hotel had too many ears for certain dealings.

He continued to survey the scene, but not for longer than would be suspicious. Frank's concerns were raised when he noticed that the man who acted as lookout held a parcel covered in brown paper. It was roughly the same size as a football; the other bloke, he now realised, had worked the lock.

The hairs on the back of Frank's neck bristled and his instincts told him that this wasn't a common burglary job. His mind raced. *What should I do, investigate?... no.* They were two grown men, and while he was a strongly built fifteen-year-old, he was still only fifteen.

Think, Frank said to himself. *Think.*

Frank looked left up Phillip Street and right towards Bay Street. His heart pounded as he heard the faintest of sounds from across the street. He peered from under the cover of his peaked wool cap and saw the hunched man win his battle with the lock. Frank turned completely away from the terrace house and resumed his act as the playing child. He realised he had seen all he was going to see.

After he heard the dull thud of timber meeting timber and the metallic click of the lock finding its original, secure position, Frank rose to his feet and began striding towards an elbow in the road. It was a position from which he could view the terrace house but remain out of sight.

Minutes that seemed like hours dragged on, with no further sightings or even sounds from inside the terrace. The sun was unusually hot for March, and it felt like a blacksmith's iron on the back of Frank's neck. It made rational thoughts more difficult than they would normally be in a situation like this. Squinting towards the terrace for the slightest sign of activity, Frank's heart skipped a beat when he saw the pair exit the run-down dwelling and turn in his direction. He didn't waste a second and leapt the fence that bordered the street from the park on the edge of Mort Bay.

Frank held his breath and then slowly lifted his head to look over the sandstone wall. He listened to the muffled voices of the two men. They were no longer concerned with being seen or heard now that they were well clear of the terrace house. Strangely, after things had happened so quickly, Frank felt a level of calm and awareness about his situation. As they passed his line of sight, he was able to get a good look at the man closest to him; he was the one that held the package at the front door; the other man's face was obscured by his companion. Frank searched earnestly for anything that could help identify them. He was sure his boss would want to know who they were.

'No package,' he said in a hushed voice. He swivelled around to sit with his back to the wall. 'The package is gone.'

Frank wasn't sure what it meant exactly, but every nerve in his body told him it meant something. He took a couple of deep breaths and then stood. After a quick glance around, Frank jumped back over the fence and headed in the opposite direction to the brown-suited men.

As he strode along Phillip Street, Frank looked at his watch, and noted that it was still a couple of minutes to three o'clock. 'Good, Hammer should be here.'

Frank approached the terrace for a second time, but once again, he stood on the opposite side of the street. He felt inexplicably nervous, and when he spied Ronnie and Hammer only thirty yards away and on the same side of the street as the terrace, he acted intuitively and made a bee-line for them.

'Frankie, my boy,' said Ron with enthusiasm, while he noted the look in his young apprentice's eyes.

'Turn around!'

'Huh?' exclaimed Hammer, taken aback by the boy's directness.

'Turn, and follow me to the park,' hissed Frank, as he passed his two bosses. Deliberately, Frank didn't stop. He wanted to let them know he wasn't making idle chit-chat.

Ronnie acknowledged Frank's mood, and turned without hesitation. Hammer followed because Ronnie did, but he wasn't happy that he had just been barked at by a kid.

They reached the sanctuary of the park and the shade of its trees, but with the terrace house still in view. Hammer couldn't contain himself and grabbed Frank by the shoulder and spun the boy around to face Ronnie and himself.

'What the fuck was all that about, ya little prick,' yelled Hammer.

'Easy, Hammer,' said Ronnie quietly.

'Easy! I'll smack the little bludger in the mouth.'

Not perturbed by Hammer's outburst, Frank waited a few seconds before he spoke.

'Ronnie, who were you meeting today?'

'Why you little....' started Hammer, but was silenced by a raised palm from Ronnie.

'What do you mean Frank?' asked Ron calmly. Frank's seriousness registered with every criminal aspect of his being.

'I mean, I came to the address Hammer gave me. Got here a little early, to be sure, and two blokes turn up.'

'Did you know them?' queried Ronnie.

'Nah. At first I thought, Ron is having a meeting, but it still seemed strange they were here before Hammer,' said Frank. His voice was clear, calm, and precise.

Ron Symonds glanced at Don Hammer Ryan, who replied by raising one eyebrow.

'I thought something wasn't right, so I took a bit of cover and pegged them out. I couldn't believe it when the codger started working the lock.'

'What the...' Ronnie held up his hand again, and Hammer fell silent. Ronnie inhaled deeply through his nose, as if he quenched his anger with the extra air, and began again. 'Thieves maybe?'

'I thought the same, Hammer,' replied Frank. There was no animosity in his voice, all business. 'But they were in suits, a bit old and worn but still suits. And a package, one of them carried a package.'

'What sort of package?' said Ronnie sharply. He showed his first hint of unrest, but recovered quickly.

'About the size of a football and wrapped in brown paper.'

'Are they still in there?'

'In and out in under three minutes.'

'Shit, Ron, do you reckon Farnsworth sent them?' exclaimed Hammer.

'Nothing would surprise me,' he replied, 'but why?' The question hung in the air like a dark cloud; its malice grew larger the longer it remained unanswered. Ronnie's head was abuzz with hypotheticals; he took a few steps away from his two colleagues and attempted to piece together recent events. He probed every recess of his memory for the clue that could bring some clarity. *Could it be Ned Farnsworth, looking to expand his territory?* he thought. *I wouldn't put it past the prick.*

Frank stood back and resumed his proper position in the organisation. The alarm raised, his job done, he would only speak now if asked. Ron Symonds gestured to his mate, and Don Ryan went to his side immediately, where a short sharp discussion ensued.

Both Ron and Hammer made their way over to Frank, but Hammer continued on to the gate in the sandstone wall to examine the quiet street; in particular the area that surrounded Ronnie's little slum.

'Frank… mate,' said Ron sincerely, 'good work. 'That's why I have faith in you, always on the ball; would you recognise the bastards if you saw them?'

'I got a good look at one of them; the other had his face hidden.'

'Good, find one, find the other I reckon.'

'Can't see him,' shouted Hammer, shouting from the gate, I'm going for a look-see.'

'Ten past three, I have a feeling the arse-hole isn't going to show.'

Ron motioned for Frank to follow him and the pair walked casually through the gate. They turned right towards the terrace house and into the heat.

Frank saw the cloud of smoke and debris before he actually heard anything. Hammer's body, all six feet and three inches, was engulfed and thrown against the sandstone wall like a rag doll. Almost instantly, Frank and Ronnie were hit by the shockwave of the thunderous blast. It carried choking smoke and splinters of timber and glass, and dropped them both to the ground. The pair cowered, as shrapnel-like pieces ripped at their clothing. The concussion of the blast burst their eardrums, with a pain that drew Frank's hands to the side of his head.

Frank's arms and legs were heavy and unresponsive; he felt himself being hoisted onto his feet. He could hear a voice, but it was distant and faint, drowned by a continuous ringing in his ears. He struggled to open his eyes, but he recognised Ronnie. His face was only inches from his own and he yelled like a madman. The scene confused Frank, as there was little or no sound. Ron's eyes were crazed like a warrior in battle.

Frank's head rolled around on his shoulders like a newborn. He staggered, but was caught again by Ronnie, who propped him against the sandstone wall. The crime boss waited a moment—dazed and staggered himself—before he headed down the street towards his mate Hammer. Frank's head cleared slightly, and he could see smoke that spilled into the air from Ron's terrace house. Pieces of timber, brick and tin were scattered all around the derelict building. Frank looked down at his hands and noticed streaks of blood, and he began to search for the source. His hands moved clumsily—as if controlled by an inexperienced puppeteer—but he eventually located the injury at his ears.

He peeled himself off the wall and began to shuffle towards Ronnie. An image of a woman in the middle of the road entered his peripheral vision; her face was tortured with anguish, and her lower limbs were sprawled in hopeless resignation as she cradled the limp body of a child. Her screams were barely audible through Frank's shattered eardrums, only the sight conveying her loss.

The bomb, which the brown suited men had planted, was a crude but effective combination of dynamite and long fuse. It had nearly demolished Ron's place, as well as the neighbouring dwelling.

With the bell of the fire brigade ringing in the distance, Frank slumped to his knees, just short of a motionless Don Ryan. Hammer was flat on his back. His white shirt was soaked in blood, and his chest was impaled by a splintered window frame. Frank watched on, his numbed brain unable to comprehend what he saw. His gaze switched from the lifeless body to his boss. Ronnie knelt with his fists clenched tight against his temples and his chin tucked into his chest.

***

Frank woke, but struggled to open his eyes. They closed and then slowly re-opened, while he fought the heaviness of concussion and his desire to sleep. He tried to focus on the two figures directly at his side. Their image became clearer with each attempt to stay awake.

A soft murmur of voices crept into his consciousness at the same time as a skull-splitting pain, reminded him of the explosion. He recognised his father and his familiar but muffled voice that urged him to rest.

'Mum, Dad, where am I?' shouted Frank. His injured eardrums prevented him from gauging the volume of his own voice.

'Hospital, dear,' replied Grace. She put her mouth close to his ear and then kissed his forehead gently. 'What happened Frank? They tell us you were near an explosion.'

Barely able to hear and with a headache that throbbed at the base of his skull, Frank stared back at his mother, confused, while scenes of what had taken place gradually came to his mind's eye. The sterile environment of the hospital unsettled him further.

'Grace,' said Albert, 'he can't hear, let him rest. We will come back tomorrow.'

'Can't we stay?' she replied.

'It's pointless, luv. Sleep is the best thing for him, the doctor said so himself.'

Torn between a mother's instinct to nurse her child, and the practicality of her husband's words, Grace reluctantly got up to leave. A pang of sadness made her turn suddenly for one last word, only to see Frank already fast asleep. As a tear rolled down her cheek, Grace leaned over and kissed her youngest son on the forehead—like she had before adolescence had brought on all of its awkwardness. She brushed his hair with her fingers as she pulled away, and felt a heaviness develop around her.

Albert and Grace left the ward and stepped into a large hallway, typical of many hospitals. The light was dull and the air cold; it felt like it conflicted with the purpose of healing. They turned right for the main entrance and passed a man who was dressed neatly, of medium build, and in his mid to late thirties. He spoke with the doctor who had looked over Frank's chart only moments before.

The Millers continued on towards the main doors of the hospital, but Albert stopped after he had felt a hand on his bicep.

'Excuse me, sir,' said a soft male voice.

Albert turned and noticed it was the man who had been conversing with the doctor. 'Yes?' replied Albert quietly, mindful of the hospital patients.

'Mr Miller, isn't it?'

'Yes, that's right.'

'Detective William Tyrell, Mr Miller,' said the policeman. He displayed his credentials and then nodded to Grace politely.

'How may I help you, Detective Tyrell?' asked Albert calmly. Little alarm bells gave off a quiet but distinctive ring in the depths of his awareness. Grace was nonplussed, and stared at the detective. She smiled politely, but was at a total loss as to why he had introduced himself.

'Just a routine follow-up in regards to the explosion your son was caught up in,' said Detective Tyrell. He reached into his coat pocket and produced a pencil and notebook. 'Could I ask a couple of quick questions?'

'Certainly, but I'm not sure how much help I will be,' replied Albert. He anticipated the need for comfort and took his wife's hand in his. 'From what I have been told Frank was in the wrong place at the wrong time.'

'Yes, like I said, just routine. How is your son?'

'Knocked about... but all right thank you Detective,' replied Albert, a little more defensive than before. 'He is heavily concussed and his hearing isn't good... burst eardrums from the explosion, the doctor told us.'

'How old is Frank?'

'Just turned fifteen.'

'Donald Ryan, Mr Miller. Does that name mean anything to you?'

'No, can't say I have heard that name,' replied Albert. 'Who is he?'

'Unfortunately, Mr Ryan was killed in the blast.'

'Oh, that's terrible,' gasped Grace. 'His poor family.'

'Tragically, a young boy was killed as well,' added Detective Tyrell.

Grace Miller let out a high-pitched shriek. She caught it by placing her hand to her mouth. Albert pulled her in closer.

Detective Tyrell made a couple of quick notes in the small book he carried. He surmised, as he wrote, that Mr and Mrs Miller were your average, law-abiding couple. Mr Miller's answers were honest and forthright, the trace of defensiveness understandable considering the circumstances. Their son, however, puzzled him. At first glance, he appeared like any other teenage kid, but what was a kid from a nice family doing anywhere near Donald Hammer Ryan, let alone the other injured man who had left the scene? Witnesses described him as someone who looked a lot like Ronnie Symonds, and after a bit of digging, the detective discovered that the terrace house gutted in the explosion belonged to him.

Albert watched Detective Tyrell make notes. He had the distinct impression that these enquiries were anything but routine, and decided that the less he said from now on, the better. At least until he had a chance to talk to Frank.

'Detective Tyrell.'

'Yes, Mr Miller,' replied the detective, looking up from his notebook. 'Sorry about that, I need to keep notes, not as sharp as I used to be.'

'Could we continue this at another time?' asked Albert. 'It has been a tiring day for my wife, and I think it would be best if I get her home.'

'Certainly, Mr Miller, you have been most helpful. You can come down to the station; I will need to speak to Frank when he is discharged any way.'

'Excuse me?' replied Albert sharply.

'I will need to speak to Frank, after the doctors give the all-clear, of course.'

'You're not suggesting Frank had anything to do with this, Detective?' Albert Miller's voice was restrained, but had a bite in its delivery.

'Not at all, Mr Miller,' replied Tyrell, calmly. He absorbed Albert's aggression. 'I will be interviewing everyone who was at the scene at the time of the explosion.'

'Of course,' said Albert. 'You're just doing your job. I apologise for my tone, like I said, it has been a long day.'

'I understand completely,' replied the detective. He offered his hand for Albert to shake, before he excused himself and walked away to intercept the doctor he had spoken with before.

***

Apart from feeling upset after her son was injured in the explosion, Grace Miller was tense. Her nerves were stretched tight after the unexpected encounter with the detective. Her mood was jittery. Each sound, in an otherwise quiet hospital, was louder and more intrusive than it actually was.

With her arm linked in her husband's and her face angled towards the floor, Grace made for the hospital's main entrance with quickened steps and shortened breath. She had tried at first to avoid, and then out-run, a wave of emotion that began with Archie's departure. Slowly but surely, it had gathered itself to gain strength, and reached a point where containment was no longer an option, only escape.

Grace broke away from her husband and let out a small and muffled cry as she began to run down the cold and sterile hallway. One hand was clasped to her mouth, the other over her stomach. Desperate and ungainly, she struggled feverishly with the heavy door that barred her escape. Her only thought was for the wall of emotion that cascaded from behind; it threatened to her engulf her in a flood of her own fear.

Albert reacted immediately, and was able to catch up with his wife. He covered the ground between them quickly and placed his arm around her shoulders. He did his best to comfort Grace as she sobbed uncontrollably in his arms, his heart ripped apart by his wife's agony. He knew, through his own darkened moments, exactly where this outpouring of feeling was coming from.

For Albert, the head of the family, his role was clear. He must be the one immovable figure in a howling gale; the person that could be clung to when the hurricane of change threatened to move and displace his family, like it would trees in a wild storm.

'It's alright, luv,' whispered Albert, as he calmly opened the door. He noticed a bench to his right on the hospital verandah, and gently steered his wife towards the small stone slab. He spoke gently to her as he did.

'Frank will be fine, Grace, everything will be fine,' said Albert. He knew that Frank's condition, although very upsetting, was only part of the reason for his wife's loss of composure.

'What is happening, Albert; Frank hurt, the police?' cried Grace. Her tortured sobs were replaced by sniffles; her nerves, which had been wound tight, were released by the outpouring of emotion.

As Grace calmed, a soft glow of embarrassment crept across her face. She realised the scene she had created. 'I am sorry for how I behaved, Albert, I lost control,' said Grace with more composure. She was raised not to put family or personal issues on display, where they could be viewed by a conservative and disapproving public.

'Think nothing of it, Grace,' said Albert. He passed her his handkerchief. 'No one noticed. Are you all right?'

'Much better,' replied Grace. 'But I still feel foolish, carrying on like that, when poor Frank is injured and in pain. I'll be back first thing in the morning with something nice,' she continued cheerfully. 'Maybe I could bake some scones for him; that will lift his spirits.'

'Frank would love that Grace,' replied Albert, which brought comfort to his wife. Albert pondered the likelihood of Frank's accident being a case of simple misfortune. Saddened by what he had witnessed, he did not want to dwell on the matter. He knew his wife would want to deal with what had happened in her own way, so Albert changed the subject by suggesting they walk home; Grace agreed at once.

An image appeared in Grace's mind of a wounded Frank that unexpectedly morphed into Clarence, alone and afraid. It made her gut taut like a weighted rope.

***

The night was balmy, which made access to the ward easy, by way of a window left open in hope of a cooling southerly change. Aware of the need for stealth, but desperate to get his message across, the lone figure moved slowly past several beds in the hospital ward. Assisted by moonlight, he limped forward, slowed by a slight but consistent pain in his hip. It was the result of a deep laceration sutured by a backyard doctor in the cellar of the Dry Dock Hotel.

Ronnie Symonds paused and scanned the row of beds in search of Frank; his attention was diverted momentarily by the silhouette of a nurse who walked on the other side of a glass-panelled door. Confident the threat of detection had passed, Ron Symonds began to move in Frank's direction. As he did, he retrieved something from his pocket, fully aware that he must act swiftly. Crouched at the side of Frank's bed, Symonds placed his hand firmly over Frank's mouth. It snapped the patient out of a deep and peaceful sleep.

Frank was startled, and fought as hard as his weakened body could under his attacker's grip. He succumbed quickly when he recognised his boss's face, illuminated partly by the lunar glow.

The patient in the next bed stirred but didn't wake, reminding Symonds that he could not afford to be discovered. He placed a finger to his lips for silence and then grasped Frank by the wrist. Roughly, Ron placed a piece of paper he held in the palm of Frank's hand and then leaned over to position his mouth within an inch of his apprentice's ear. He began to speak slowly, but with enough volume to overcome any misunderstanding.

'Read this, then destroy it, destroy it—understand?'

Ronnie stood up and held his thumb up as a signal for comprehension. After he received a nod from Frank, he made a quick exit just as the nurse on duty entered at far end of the ward.

ELEVEN

The walls of the small interrogation room were a pale green, like moss that had dried hard on a sun-baked rock. The ceiling—once white—had turned a yellowy-grey from years of tobacco smoke, blown in the air by handcuffed citizens.

While Frank was not handcuffed, he was certainly being questioned, and as he sat on a timber chair, alone, except for a bare table, his mind spun like a top. He tried to take in all that had happened in the last three days.

The shock of seeing Don Ryan lying dead on the street, impaled by a piece of timber, had shaken Frank Miller. The excitement and exhilarating rush that had come with his new-found profession suddenly took a cold and sobering twist. Frank's steady rise under Ronnie's tutelage, the responsibility of dealing with large sums of cash, and the overall trust his boss had placed in him, had established him as a mostly unseen, but important part of the business. It had sent his self-belief sky-rocketing, and infused him with a euphoric sense that he couldn't be touched.

The euphoria was now checked, but not extinguished; a thin but permanent crust—imperceptible but life altering—had formed over his resolve after a heated exchange with his father. That had been the case for Frank after each obstacle or challenge he faced in his new trade; absorb it, then deal with it, just like he was on his first trip to the police station.

His hearing was still affected, so he had been forced to write some things down for the detective, such as name, address, and occupation. But as disoriented as he was, he still remembered Ronnie's advice. He told the constable at the scene of the explosion that he knew nothing. After Ronnie's visit during that night at hospital, his line of reply had remained constant, and he admitted to police that he knew Ron Symonds, but only through doing the odd job for extra money. A bit of house maintenance here and there, as he had intended to attempt on the day of the explosion. Frank had frustrated the constable, then the sergeant, and now, the detective. His unwillingness to talk had stalled proceedings and brought him to his current impasse.

Frank heard the metallic sound of the heavy bolt being unlatched on the other side of the door, and he prepared himself for further questions from the detective. He recited what had been on the note that Ron had delivered to him. 'I pay you a bit of cash to do odd jobs on my properties. Nothing more. Keep it simple. Never explain yourself. You knew Hammer to say hello, that's it.'

The door opened and Frank took a deep breath. He exhaled slowly and steadied himself for the detective's next round of questions. The constable opened the door and stepped to the side to allow the person behind to enter the room. Frank felt his confidence return, and was ready for what was to come, but was completely shocked to see who had entered the small dull room in the policeman's place.

***

'Are you sure this is the right thing to do, Detective?' queried Albert Miller. He fidgeted in his seat across from Detective Tyrell, who was seated behind his cramped, but organised desk.

'I admit it is unorthodox, but I, and forgive me for saying, you have gotten nowhere with young Frank so far,' replied Detective Tyrell.

Albert Miller, sat upright in his chair, offended at the detective's intrusion into his personal life; the 'gotten nowhere' remark stung. The father of four took the comment as a summation of his fifteen years as Frank's father, not, as the detective intended, a note on what had transpired these last days.

'Mr Miller,' said Sergeant Hobbs, from the side of Detective Tyrell's desk. The sergeant spoke firmly, but without aggression, and looked Albert straight in the eye. 'We firmly believe that Ronald Symonds and his former associate Don Hammer Ryan ran everything in Balmain from illegal gambling to protection rackets and black-market trading.'

'Now, Mr Miller,' began Detective Tyrell. He leaned forward in his seat to engage Frank's father, and regained his ascendency in the process. 'We do not believe that your son had anything to do with, or was a target, for that matter, of the bombing.'

'I should hope not,' retorted Albert, shocked by the gravity of the statement, not the statement itself. 'Should I be getting Frank a lawyer?'

'Mr Miller, if I may,' said the detective. He raised his hands like a preacher would in an attempt to subdue Mr Miller, but in doing so, showed his first signs of impatience through his voice. 'While we don't believe he is involved, it is my gut instinct, my police officer's voice, if you will, that tells me that Frank knows a hell of a lot more than he is letting on about Ryan and in particular Symonds, and… what they may get up to on a daily basis.' Tyrell calmed his voice and continued. 'We want to help Frank, Mr Miller, and no, he doesn't need a lawyer, but we want to know he is on our side.'

Albert Miller's shoulders slumped. He resigned himself at that moment to all the doubts and questions that had plagued his mind these past months. All the issues he had promised to engage, but failed to pursue. He reassured himself that his status as Frank's father would be enough to ensure honest and reliable answers, even when those answers were unnervingly calm and confident.

'I've been a father for twenty-odd years, Detective,' remarked

Albert, quietly and somewhat despondently. 'I've worked hard, saved what I could and looked after my family. My two eldest are serving...'

'You're a good man, Albert,' interjected the detective. He motioned to the sergeant to leave the room. The detective sensed a pivotal moment, of sorts. 'I could tell the first time I met you and your lovely wife.'

Albert shrugged in response to the detective's comment and stared at the ground near his feet. He wanted to relieve himself of what he held inside. 'I think I knew all along. I think I knew but didn't want to. I'd ask a question, he would answer it—calm as you like. "Where did you get that son?" "Did some labouring," he would say. "That's a nice cap." "Got a job walking horses at the race track."

'Mr Miller, I have been a police officer for sixteen years, worked my way up to detective, heard and seen most things. Time and patience, Mr...'

A knock on the door interrupted the detective; a young constable entered the office.

'Sorry sir, but Mrs Miller has entered the room—thought you would like to know.'

***

'Ruth?' said Frank. He was confused, and had a guarded look on his face. 'Why are you here?'

'How are you, Frank?' replied Ruth in a raised voice to allow for his injury. She deliberately avoided his question. 'Can you hear me alright?'

Frank made a sign with his hand to inform Ruth that his hearing, while not the best, was not hopeless either. Ruth took it as, 'I will hear you if it suits me.'

'I made you a sandwich,' continued Ruth, as she produced a brown paper bag from a small basket. Her cheerfulness was not dented by Frank's lack of enthusiasm for conversation.

Frank reached over the table that separated them. He accepted the sandwich with a nod, still sceptical, while he gazed at Ruth's protruding belly.

'It's due next month,' said Ruth in response to Frank's unspoken question. 'I can't believe it myself.' Ruth paused to rub her stomach. 'It all seems so surreal in a way. Just think Frank, you're going to be an uncle.'

Frank sat silently. He tried to recalibrate his thoughts, after been caught off-guard when Ruth had entered the room. He chewed on the sandwich his sister-in-law had prepared for him, and shifted his gaze to the surrounding walls. He never looked at Ruth for more than a second or two, while she chatted merrily.

Frank wasn't sure what it was, but Ruth made him feel a little nervous. Not nervous as in being afraid of what might happen. He had executed dealings with tough, burly men, confidently and professionally. It was more like being conscious of not having the right thing to say, or being made to feel silly. In fact, he found making eye contact with Ruth almost impossible. To him, she was as mysterious as anyone he had come across. Part of him wanted her to reach over the table and hug him, wrapping him in that faint and intoxicating floral scent that would catch him unawares at the dinner table. The other side of him wished she would get up and leave, so he could resume what he was most comfortable with.

Ruth looked around the room. She stared at the pale green walls and allowed the silence to linger for a moment. She contemplated her next move. *Frank is an enigma*, she thought; *tough on the outside, but still a kid in many ways*. His eyes, from what she had seen, never gave much away. They were dark like the ocean. His wariness made her cautious, fearful that the wrong enquiry could see him withdraw further. She also could sense something else in those deep eyes, something that flowed slowly, like molten rock in the depths of a volcano, ever present, the essence of the being, but rarely shown in its fullness. It was kept in check for the most part, only allowed the occasional vent for someone with a watchful eye—like Ronnie and now Ruth—to identify it's presence. *Is it good?* Ruth pondered. *That depends. After all, how did he come to be here? Was it bad luck, or just fate catching up with him?* Her husband was also a mysterious person, but not in the same way Frank was. Clarence was a thousand thoughts being processed at once, open and spontaneous. His eyes, though also dark, glistened, and radiated what was at his core. If Frank's inner being flowed like lava, then Clarence's danced like a butterfly atop the tips of spring grass.

'Did you read the letter from Clarrie?' asked Ruth suddenly. She had decided on her approach.

Frank squinted and turned his head towards Ruth.

'Clarrie's letter, did you read it?' she repeated, louder and slower.'

'No!' barked Frank.

Ruth looked quickly through a small bag that was in her basket and produced a well-worn envelope. She held it up triumphantly, before she reached across the table to hand it to Frank. Her face beamed with a smile, brought on by the thought of her husband.

Trapped between his two worlds, Frank was confused as to how he should act. The mention of his brother Clarence brought an instant spark of interest, but the pale green walls he was surrounded by reminded him where he was and what had got him here. He stood to accept the envelope from Ruth and eased himself back into his wooden chair. With little emotion, which he realised would seem strange, but necessary in the current climate, he unfolded the letter and began to read.

Ruth sat and watched Frank with interest while she placed the basket on the table. She tried to make herself more comfortable on the hard chair, but it was not an easy task at this stage of her pregnancy. Ruth knew the letter by heart, so she studied Frank's face to note the small changes in his expression: the raised eyebrow, the upturned corner of his mouth that hinted a smile, or the reflective pause. All of them suggested to Ruth that the letter might prove to be quite the interrogator.

Frank's face split like a peach. It formed a smile that warmed Ruth's heart, and she knew he must have read about his brother's lack of coordination. The release of happiness in Frank, while pleasant for Ruth, also gave her a small insight as to what it was to be a parent. To see the innocence in a person you have nurtured and loved while you guide him through childhood. To teach him—as far as you know—how to function in society, before being silently grasped and overcome by influences outside of your control. Those influences taking its victim in a direction you can't—or don't want to—see.

'It's good to finally hear from Clarence, isn't it?' said Ruth. She remained cheerful, determined to have an impact on Frank.

'Yes,' replied Frank. 'Where's Egypt?'

Ruth's skin tingled, as she witnessed the boy as he attempted to emerge through the recently formed crust of his adopted persona. 'At the top of the African continent, although a little to the right,' replied Ruth enthusiastically. 'Could you imagine Clarrie; all of his army mates bored to death from his stories about the pyramids and pharaohs?'

Frank laughed at the thought; the laughter caused his ear to ache, and he instinctively put a hand to it.

'Sorry Frank, I forgot about your ear.'

Frank shook his head and waved his hand to indicate that it wasn't a problem, and sat for a second before he spoke.

'Have you got one from Arch?'

Ruth could have cried as she watched the expression on the young man's face. The preceding nine months had seen great turmoil and upheaval in everyone's lives, all of it taking its toll. The adults had done their best, Ruth and Grace in particular; they had been there for each other. Albert, as you would expect, was strong and stoic, but a little quieter than normal. In all the hustle of daily life,

Ruth now realised that while Frank sat around the table and listened to letters from Archie, she, and as far as she knew, Albert or Grace, never talked to him about his brothers. She knew Albert and Grace had concerns for Frank in general; she had seen Albert doing his best to strike up conversations. And it would have been difficult for Albert to agree to the detective's suggestion about a female family member meeting with Frank. But there it was. It glared at her. His inner torment, barefaced and exposed, as obvious as anything she could choose to look at.

Frank, the youngest of three boys, had lived life secure in his siblings' shadows. He emulated Archie in any way he could. His dream was to be like his eldest, football-playing brother; the sight of Archie in his military uniform was amongst his most memorable days. When Clarence had enlisted, Frank had been surprised by his own reaction. Although not really interested in the same things as Clarence, he had always felt reassured—without really knowing it—by his calm and confident manner. Shocked like everyone, when Clarence had announced his intentions, Frank had felt let down, and while he didn't intentionally rebel, circumstances, such as his fractured family unit and new acquaintances, drew him gradually and unknowingly towards different mentors.

'I'm sorry, Frank, I...'

'Doesn't matter!'

'You must be very proud of Archie,' said Ruth.

Frank shrugged. He was aware he had let his guard down, but was enticed to go further by Ruth's disarming ways. 'None of my mates had a brother at Lone Pine.'

Ruth forced a smile, and nodded, and allowed Frank to bask while she pondered. The thought of Archie being in battle immediately drew her to think of the perils Clarence would encounter.

She felt things were going well, so Ruth decided to widen the discussion. 'The explosion must have been frightening; did you know the man that passed away very well?'

Frank froze; an odd look came to his face. Ruth interpreted his expression as confusion after not having heard the question. But in fact, it was his brain, which had kicked into gear. The dark voice from inside him said, *Where it should have been in the first place. She's like the rest.* Frank was angry at himself. The warm and comforting thoughts of his brothers were flung violently from his mind. *Stick to your plan, or she'll do you in just as good as a copper would.*

She repeated her question. 'Did you know the poor man very well, Frank?' Her voice trailed off as she witnessed a look of smug self-confidence transform Frank's appearance.

'No, not very well,' replied Frank. 'I mean, I had seen him around, said g'day, but that was about it,' continued the young crook, so calmly that Ruth felt she was in the presence of another person.

Ruth sat quietly, unnerved by the young man she now faced. The Frank Miller she had known had disappeared without a trace, as if he had sifted like sand through a crack in the floor. The wrong line of discussion, the one she had feared to mistakenly take, had been taken, and she cursed herself for diving in too quickly. Had she and the detective hoped against hope? Was the boy's path already chosen, the policeman's unorthodox plan doomed to fail before it was enacted?

Frank could see the look of defeat in Ruth's eyes, and it gave him a sense of satisfaction. The burgeoning part of his character, the one that relished the thrill of shady backroom deals, grabbed his softer emotions like a bouncer would grab a drunk, and beat them to a pulp. It eliminated them as a risk, and prevented the unreliable feelings from ever surfacing again to cloud his judgement and put him in harm's way.

'Thank you for the sandwich, Ruth,' said Frank, as he rose from his seat, 'it was very nice of you. If you see Dad on the way out, could you ask him to tell the detective that I would like to go home… if he has no further questions?'

TWELVE

A week and one day after the explosion, Frank Miller was back at work on Cockatoo Island. His hearing, while not perfect, had steadily improved. The doctor had completed a thorough examination on the Friday before, and stated he was confident of a full recovery.

Frank's return to home life had not been easy, but he had expected that. His father had barely spoken to him, and only broke his silence to warn him of the consequences if he was seen associating with Ron Symonds. Consequences Frank couldn't give a rat's arse for. He had heard his mother and father arguing late at night in the kitchen, with his name coming up several times. It prompted the quietening of voices on occasion, no doubt at the behest of his mum. Ruth had been polite but distant, and Frank had found himself having thoughts about her that had never previously entered his mind. Alice's affections remained the same. She too had heard the arguments and noticed the silence, but a couple of small gifts from her youngest brother had soon allayed any concerns.

Halfway through his first day back, Frank received a tap on the shoulder from the foreman, Bob Timmins. He asked him to clean the storeroom before lunch. Frank looked at the foreman, confused and slightly annoyed, but was persuaded to do as he had asked when Timmins gave him a sly wink.

Frank reached the storeroom and entered cautiously through the swinging timber door. He knew he had been sent there for a specific reason, but was not sure if it would be good or bad. Slowly, he poked his head over the counter that barricaded the rows of shelving from the entrance, and looked left and right before he reached over to unlatch the hip-height door to his left.

'Took your time,' said a voice directly behind Frank. It made him spring to an upright position before he could complete the task of opening the counter door. 'A bit jumpy, Frankie, haven't lost your nerve?' continued Ronnie Symonds.

'Ron, you scared the shit out of me,' replied Frank, startled but pleased to see his boss.

'I know.'

'What are you doing here?'

'Oh, just come to say hello, catch up,' said Ron, as he turned to shut and lock the entrance door before he moved around Frank to release the counter door from its latch. 'Step inside Frankie.'

'I didn't let on to the police.'

'I know,' replied Symonds.

'How?'

'I just do,' said Ronnie, calmly, before he lit a smoke. 'You did well... but enough chit-chat. I found out the names of the bastards who killed Hammer.'

'Who are they?' Exclaimed Frank.

'You'll find out soon enough, but I need to know if I can rely on you to be there when the time comes to sort them out.'

'Count me in, Ron, those pricks could of killed us all,' said Frank through gritted teeth. 'Just tell me when.'

Ronnie Symonds moved towards Frank and placed his right palm on the nape of Frank's neck. He gripped Frank firmly, while he rested his forearm on Frank's collarbone. Symonds looked him dead in the eye and spoke in a low growl that made the hair on Frank's arms stand on end.

'The slimy scum that killed Don Ryan, my mate, will get what is coming to them. What you have to do is not get excited and fuck this up.'

'But… '

'No fucking buts. In case you have forgotten, you were in a police station last week. They will be watching. People here on the island… will be watching. Lay low and I mean low, and when the time's right I will find you.'

'Yeah, no worries Ronnie,' said Frank. He nodded his head once and then took a step back as Symonds released his grip.

'No coming to see me at the pub, nothing. Your rounds here will be taken on by someone else, got it. We don't know each other.'

'Whatever you say, Ron.'

Ron Symonds took a deep breath to calm down. With hands on hips, he looked towards the ceiling, and then back down at the floor. He stood motionless, except for a gentle tap of his right foot on the painted concrete.

'This has to be done right, Frank,' said Ronnie. Slowly he lifted his chin to look at his new right-hand man. 'Patience… patience and silence, and the will to get it done, that's all.' Ron stepped forward and shook Frank firmly by the hand. It bound the contract as the siren for lunch sounded. 'Get back to work, Frank.'

Thiennes, France, 30 June, 1916
The barn had a pungent but earthy odour, and bristled with activity as the last of A Company from the 53rd Battalion of the Australian Imperial Force settled into their new billet. They were in the rural community of Thiennes, part of the Armentières sector of the Western Front, also known as The Nursery. It was a place where inexperienced troops could get a gentle introduction to trench warfare.

The soldiers had marched from Blaringhem and the railway junction of Hazebrouck, where they had endured light but constant rain. They were grateful for the chance to take shelter; the fact that their digs were normally inhabited by cattle, horses, and pigs, didn't seem to bother them. They were one step closer to the front, and after four months of training as a battalion—longer for the new recruits—

they were bored senseless with monotonous drills and instruction.

Clarence took up a spot against the barn wall, which was completely made of stone except for the timber fittings such as doors and shutters, and the gabled roof above; its thick beams and trusses were fashioned from ancient French oak. As always, he was alongside Sticks, and the Gallipoli veteran, Tom Baker, whom Clarence had become mates with while in Egypt.

A large and open space, the barn was a rare opportunity for the whole company to be quartered together. Tents and smaller billets usually required the men to be divided into their rifle sections, or at best, platoons. Clarence allowed his eyes to wander around the large expanse. He admired the massive dark timbers that supported the impressive roof, and allowed his eyes to linger on the soft, cloud-filtered light, which passed through the open timber doors and glassless but hatched windows. Their frames were painted blue, and they blended comfortably with the light ash colour of the stone. It gave the place a homely feel. The darkened oak provided a nice contrast.

How pleasant, Clarence thought, *to be in such a beautiful country, after the harsh and unforgiving conditions of Egypt.* It appealed to his nature; the rich but soft colours that seemed to blend and become one with the countryside. The vibrant and charismatic people, whose approach to life centred on family and enjoying the gifts that God had provided. He could see himself in such a place with his beautiful wife.

Clarence caught sight of his brother on the opposite wall. Archie barked orders at a private who dallied. Clarrie smiled as he watched the private jump like a cat on a hot tin roof, fearful of not living up to Corporal Archie Miller's standards. Archie had the respect of all the men around him, which included those of higher rank. The rank of corporal meant he would lead a rifle section, which usually contained a lance corporal and eight privates. Some corporals liked to remain chummy with the rest of the section. They had been privates once themselves. They didn't like to be seen as being hard on their mates.

Archie was a mate in many ways to his men, and his ability to lighten a tense mood endeared him to those who knew him. But overall, he saw his role a little differently, as a protector of sorts, who looked after his men through hard work and discipline. Influenced by his experience at Gallipoli with Lieutenant Davidson, he knew this would give them their best chance of pulling through.

As he opened a novel he had borrowed from a Digger in Marseille, Clarence watched his brother share a joke with the man he had just chastised. The camaraderie he witnessed, each soldier connected to the other by a common cause, took his mind away from his book and back to Egypt on a damp foggy morning in March. It was the beginning of the three toughest days to date in Clarence Miller's young life, and a moment when he learnt the meaning of mateship.

Clarence sank deeper into reflection; he remembered the heaviness of the damp air on his tunic and the squelch around his woollen socks, as the moisture from the wet sand penetrated his boots. The difficult memories brought on a nervy chill amid the exuberance and warmth of his fellow Diggers in the French barn.

***

They stood in formation, in full marching order, outside of Tel El Kebir Camp. Clarence felt nauseous as he anticipated the march across the desert sands to the part of the Suez Canal defences called Ferry Post. The consensus amongst the men was that it would be a very trying exercise for the most seasoned soldier, let alone inexperienced recruits. In battle dress, the soldiers would be asked to carry full packs while they endured the intense Egyptian heat.

Newly appointed Commander of the 5th Division, Lieutenant General James Whiteside McCay, had ordered the march. Although a courageous soldier, McCay was not well liked. Many believed he had gained his position through powerful political connections; his lack of regard for the troops had brought his ability to command into question.

Clarence, along with many other men, had struggled from the outset in the horrendous conditions. With uniforms wet from the fog, the skin on various parts of the body began to chafe. Many men fell out and sought medical attention before the first halt. As the temperature rose and the fog burnt off, the soldiers were subjected to the harsh sun and the incessant glare off the sand; the number of men in need of assistance climbed to an alarming rate. The soldiers were dehydrated and exhausted; all discipline among the untried troops went out the window. Men began to wander off in search of water, and piquets had to be placed on the Sweet Water canal to prevent soldiers drinking the tainted liquid.

At this point, Clarence was ready to quit. His body was dehydrated and weakened, his feet blistered, and his groin chaffed red raw. He lay against his pack on the hot sand, a pitiful sight for anyone to see. He was lifted to a sitting position by a strong arm that cradled his head. Clarrie squinted to see his brother, who held a canteen to wet his lips; his own bottle had been emptied miles before. While Clarence drank, Archie bandaged his feet. He winced in pain as the skin came away with his socks. Archie spoke to his younger brother constantly, and did his best to motivate his demoralised sibling. He realised Clarence had a lot to overcome before he made it to Ferry Post.

Startled back to the present by a clip over the ear from Sticks, Clarence heard the words that Archie spoke on that day, as clear now as they were on that hot desert sand. 'What are you going to tell that son of yours when you get home? Get up!'

Clarence had thought about what his brother had said to him, over and over, and he still couldn't say why he responded as he did. Archie hadn't spoken with any real aggression or disdain. The words were unlikely to have his fellow soldiers jumping to attention, but they had pulled Clarence from the mire. He made the bivouac at Mahsama that evening, and then rested. Eventually he reached the pontoon bridge for the crossing to Ferry Post.

Archie had never brought it up, and strangely Clarence had never thanked his brother. They had just continued on, the only difference being that Clarrie had emerged a man. No more a man than he was when he married his true love; just the man that he needed to be for now and what lay ahead.

'Wake up, Miller,' shouted Sticks, as he positioned his hand for a clip to his mate's ear, while Tom Baker stood to one side with a smirk. 'You look like a stunned mullet. Thought there might have been a Hun sniper in the loft, got you while we weren't looking.'

'Just thinking,' replied Clarrie wearily.

'Well, you're always doing that, just try not to do it too much when we finally see some action.'

'I'll do my best,' replied a detached Clarence, his mind still partly in Egypt.

'C'mon, tucker's ready,' said Sticks enthusiastically. He held his mess tin, or dixie, as it was known, and began to look impatient. 'We better make the most of this while the other Divs aren't here.'

'Be right there… you two go ahead and I'll catch you.'

'Have it your way,' said Sticks, as he turned with Tom and headed for the large double doors of the barn that opened into a stockyard, which now served as a kitchen.

Clarence forced his book down one side of his heavily laden pack for retrieval at another time. As he did he disturbed some letters bound in twine. Ruth, he said silently, his thoughts turned to their child. *He… or she… would be born now, everything going well.* He had prayed for them on so many nights. *More than two months old, how would Ruth be coping?* He wondered. *Fine with Mother about. What does he look like?* He said 'boy,' but he really didn't care, it just came to his lips, just as it had for Archie on the desert sands in Egypt. 'Blasted mail,' Clarence cursed out loud. 'I should get word soon.'

The heavy workload before the brigade embarked at the port of Alexandria, and then disembarked and entrained at Marseille, had not allowed Clarence to even enquire about the possibility of a telegram. If he was completely honest with himself, there were times when he had almost forgotten he was in fact, a father-to-be. The thought, as he walked out into a cleared French sky, made him feel a little ashamed; but how do you miss something you have never experienced? Alf Conner had said, 'To find out that you will be a father is the best news you will ever receive. To hold that baby in your arms is something else altogether.'

Clarence felt he understood what Alf meant. He had felt the pure elation on the dock in Sydney when Ruth had delivered her news, but he could tell, as he recalled the tone of Alf's voice, that it was something you had to experience to truly understand. Clarence joined the line of soldiers with dixies in hand and felt a pain of longing in his stomach that surpassed any desire for food.

THIRTEEN

Thiennes, 8 July, 1916

The whistle sounded in the morning's mild and breathless air. It signalled the all-clear, and allowed the men of 14th Brigade to remove their gas masks. Although they had drilled the donning of their protective apparatus many times, this was the first time they had been subjected to an actual cloud of poisonous gas.

The brigade as a whole was marched into a field where numerous bombs were exploded that contained the poisonous substance. The men were assembled in mass formation and stood with discipline and calm while they were subjected to the nerve-wracking experience. Many men silently prayed that they had paid the necessary attention to their equipment, as the ghastly looking hood was all that stood between them and a terrible experience.

'General,' said a middle-aged colonel, who stood to attention and saluted at a safe distance from the vapour. 'The commanders of each battalion report no ill-effects suffered by the men during the drill.'

'Excellent Colonel, General McCay will be pleased. Carry on,' ordered the general while he executed a perfect salute. He wasted no time as he turned sharply towards his staff car.

The brigade split into battalions and marched back to their various billets. The Diggers were given the afternoon off after a tense morning, and were encouraged to use the time in kit and weapons inspection; advice taken by the men, as a move to the front at any time was anticipated.

Clarence, Sticks, and Tom, entered the cool stone barn and tossed their packs against the wall. They chatted freely, relieved to have the mandatory gas test out of the way. To a man, the battalion was enthusiastic to be thrown in against the Hun. As a unit, they had come together to form an efficient and physically fit infantry brigade, now praised by headquarters. It was a far cry from the dishevelled band that limped across the Egyptian desert, unfairly criticised by General McCay.

A commotion, which had begun outside and then filtered into the barn, caught the attention of the three men from Number 4 Section of 2 Platoon, A Company.

'Mail!' yelled Private James Cook. 'The mail's come,' he repeated, with the enthusiasm of a child on Christmas morning.

'Well I'll be buggered,' remarked Thomas Baker, direct and to the point.

The three mates, along with the rest of the company, ran for the double doors of the barn; every man was desperate for news from home and loved ones. The imminent departure for the front gave this particular delivery more emphasis.

A tightly packed crowd formed quickly around a large wagon pulled by two aged geldings. The two bays stood quiet and unmoved by the crowd that now pushed and shoved; the horses no doubt appreciated their assignment, and had quickly evaluated the difference between this mob and an exploding shell. Two MPs did their best to keep the soldiers at bay, while three startled privates and one furious sergeant attempted to distribute envelopes and packages.

'Private William Cooper!' yelled one of the privates, a bundle of letters held above his head.

'Yes,' came the loud reply, the package was immediately thrown into the crowd to be passed back to its intended recipient.

'George Smith, Joseph Finch,' continued the calls.

'Good on ya, Birdie,' remarked a voice from the crowd, pleased that his mate Joseph Finch had received something.

'Clarence Miller!'

'You lucky bastard,' said Sticks while he poked his mate in the ribs. Clarence stood on his toes to catch sight of what may come his way.

His eyes bulged and calf muscles strained as Clarence watched the single envelope dance across the fingertips of his countrymen until it landed in his grasp. He turned to escape the mass of men and bumped straight into his brother and Alf Conner.

'Archie… Alf,' said Clarence. He stared at them like a husband stares at his wife when he's had one too many ales.

'Don't just stand there! Open it, you useless prick,' grinned his brother affectionately, in a vernacular that was unique to Australian men.

Clarence wondered over to the post and rail fence that bordered the yard and eased himself down to rest against it. He never once took his eye from the off-white envelope, covered in the elegant handwriting of his wife.

Sticks Sullivan, almost as excited as Clarrie to hear the long-awaited news, began to walk towards his mate, but a strong forearm barred his way.

'Let him have a minute Sticksy,' said Alf Conner.

'Too right,' replied Sticks, embarrassed at his thoughtlessness.

Excited and nervous, Clarence tingled with anticipation. He opened the envelope while the voices of the mail-men continued in the background, subdued and softened by Clarrie's heart that pounded against his chest. He stared at the script and took a moment to focus. The page—in his delirium—appeared as a scattering of unintelligible lines and curves. He took a breath, composed himself and began to read.

Beneath the Willow

96 Beattie Street
Balmain, NSW
Australia
26th April 1916

Dearest Clarence,
Over the months, I have wondered many times how I would write this letter. Now that the time has arrived, I am filled with a sense of joy, so overwhelming and uplifting. It has opened my heart and mind to something so wonderful in its purity. My darling, you are the father of a beautiful baby Boy, Reginald Clarence Miller, eight pounds and two ounces.

With his eyes closed, Clarence paused to look skyward. The warm sun bathed his skin tenderly and anointed him with the sacred rights of fatherhood. His breaths became deeper, and he caught every scent delivered by the soft breeze; it filled his soul with the answers to his existence.

Both I and your healthy son are doing well. He was born exactly at eight o'clock on the 25th. He is perfect in every way and looks just like his father. I will get a photograph taken as soon as I can, so you can see how adorable he is. I feel so happy to have given you a son; my only sadness has come from not having you here. I take comfort knowing you will return to me safely, to continue the life we began together, only now with a child.

Every thought is with you, my love. I cherish each letter you write and read them over and over. I write to you constantly, not knowing how many get through. Keep safe.

Your loving wife and son.

P.S. Reginald was my father's father's name, he was very dear to me, I hope you don't mind. My father was very proud. Both he and Mother send their love. Your parents have been wonderful.

***

Clarence stood upright and held his arms in the air like a prize-fighter, the emotions conveyed through his wife's letter absorbed to become part of himself.

'I have a son!' he yelled.

His platoon responded as one and cheered his good fortune. Archie, Alf, Sticks and Tom rushed over to shake his hand, elated at the news. His brother suddenly broke from the group and sprinted towards the barn. He returned moments later with a bottle of French champagne, which he had stashed away for this very occasion.

Archie popped the cork and showered his brother with a little of the foaming liquid, before he passed him the bottle to take a large swig in honour of his new son. Clarence grabbed the bottle enthusiastically, and took a long draught. But as a non-drinker he soon found himself coughing and spluttering, which brought cheers and back slaps from his mates. Each man around the circle, which now included Arthur Atkins, George Bluey Smith, and Francis Tench, took a small mouthful from the bottle to toast their mate, who had become a father.

***

Balmain, 10 July 1916
The rain fell as drizzle. The small droplets, which were driven sideways by a cold southeast breeze, hit Frank Miller in the face as he stepped off the ferry and onto the wharf. It made him begin to dread his walk home. The past months had been mundane for a young teenager who had become accustomed to excitement and responsibility. His

thirst for his old job had left him, at times, crazed and maddened, like a parched explorer who stared at an ocean of water he cannot drink. He had followed Ronnie's orders to the letter and kept his head down. He had even mended his relationship with his father to a degree, attending several Balmain Rugby League games with him, and helping out around the home. But it was the fast-life he yearned for, so he waited patiently for the call from Ronnie.

Frank walked with his head down and coat collar up. He turned into Darling Street and hoped to get some relief from the rain beneath the shopfront awnings. Frank stopped to look in a store window and caught the reflection in the glass of a tall man directly behind him. He had seemed to appear from nowhere.

'Look forward, son,' said the voice harsh and gravely. 'Listen, 'cause I will only say this once. This Saturday morning at nine o'clock, be at Central Station. There is a bench opposite the ticket windows; take a seat and wait. Got it?'

Frank nodded. A flat cap and the gloom of the rainy day hid the man's identity among shadows and reflective distortions. The stranger touched the peak of his cap, turned and was gone. Frank continued his interest in the shop-front for a minute before he turned and crossed Darling Street, into the miserable rain. He was cold, but he glowed inside. He had received his long-awaited recall.

FOURTEEN

Fleurbaix, 14 July, 1916

The half-moon gradually appeared from behind a solitary cloud that drifted steadily across the night sky. It threw enough light on the timber barn so Clarrie could make out the bodies that slept in 2 Platoon. The 14th Brigade had marched out of Thiennes three days earlier for the Fleubaix-Fromelles sector on the front, while Clarence's 53rd Battalion, along with the 54th, had been held in reserve. They took up billets in Fleubaix, while the 55th and 56th Battalions had gone forward to man the front line.

The news that their brigade was being moved to the forward lines was greeted with great enthusiasm, and although Clarence's mind had been pre-occupied with the birth of his son, he too had been caught up in the wave of excitement that swept through each company.

A tough twenty-mile march had awaited the men after they left Thiennes. The hard cobble stoned roads had taken their toll on some men, with stragglers noted before the first rest point. Sergeant Kent, a hard but respected man, tore strips off the soldiers in question and told them in no uncertain terms that they were now at the 'pointy end of the stick'. Slackness of any kind would not be tolerated.

The sergeant's blast had the desired effect, with not one dropout for the rest of the march. The men now realised that their training was exactly that—training. What lay ahead was real, and ill-discipline could result in the man next to you getting killed.

Clarence lay awake in the musty timber barn. It was not as spacious or clean as their last billet, but with their minds on other things, there had been no complaints. In the distance, artillery thundered like storm clouds and then faded, to be replaced by the faint knock, knock, knock of a machine gun—from which side, Clarrie wasn't able to tell yet. He listened to the activity, miles away, and felt a bizarre sense of detachment. After all the training that seemed never ending and monotonous, the route marches, the drills and parades, musketry practice and bayonet instruction, he was at odds with himself. He felt some excitement at the anticipation of what lay ahead, while being secure where he lay. So close to where men battled, yet far enough away to sleep in comfort.

Each man in the Australian Imperial Force had volunteered for active service and knew what that entailed. But Clarence received the distinct impression, as the different platoons went about their respective duties in preparation for battle, that the prospect of death in combat was far removed from anyone's mind. The rumble of distant guns began again, and Clarence closed his eyes in an attempt to sleep. His thoughts immediately drifted back to his young family.

***

Sydney, Central Station, 15 July
He arrived half an hour early and purchased a newspaper before he casually proceeded to the bench across from the ticket window, as instructed by the stranger in the cap. Frank looked towards the high ceiling of the main concourse, and pretended to be like any other commuter with time on his hands. He admired the expanse of the impressive structure, and slowly glanced towards the numbered platforms to look for anything out of place or unusual. Frank turned his gaze towards the brick arches that led to offices and dining rooms and, satisfied he was not in any immediate danger, he eased down onto the timber bench to wait.

Frank stretched one leg outward to fight against feelings of irritability and the loss of pay after taking the morning off work, when his eye was caught by a dark-suited man with a familiar swagger.

'Hello, son,' said Ron Symonds. 'Haven't kept you, have I?'

'No, Ronnie.'

'Good, sorry to drag you all the way over here, but there's a reason for it. You hungry? I'm starved! Let's get some breakfast.'

Ronnie didn't wait for a reply and started to walk towards the dining room. Frank left his paper on the bench, stood up and followed.

The pair entered the busy hall filled with tables occupied by hungry overnight travellers; Ron paused, and then made a bee-line for a table already occupied by a tall man with broad shoulders and thinning dark grey hair. Frank followed.

'Cliffy,' exclaimed Ronnie, 'sorry to keep you.' He touched Cliff on the shoulder as he passed him and took a seat at the table. He pulled the third of four chairs out for Frank to sit in. 'Frank, meet Cliff Ryan; Cliff, Frank Miller.'

'We've met,' mumbled Cliff.

Frank instantly recognised the voice as the man in Darling Street. He also caught the surname; *no coincidence*, he thought.

'You have too,' said Ronnie, while he casually turned to a waitress. 'Three bacon and eggs please and a pot of tea… thanks, luv.'

Frank sat silently and looked around the room; he focused on nothing in particular and avoided eye contact with the surly Cliff.

'Let's get down to it then,' said Ronnie, as the waitress placed a pot of tea and three cups and saucers on the table. Ronnie waited for her to leave before he continued. 'Frank, I have a plan that, if executed with patience and discipline, will bring satisfaction to all of us.'

Cliff poured himself a cup of tea and then placed the pot down without offering it to Ronnie or Frank. He stirred his cup and then tilted his head to look directly at Frank. The family resemblance between Hammer and Cliff was unmistakable.

'Ever worked in a pub, son?' asked Cliff.

'No, Mr Ryan… never.'

'That doesn't matter,' he replied. Cliff leant back as the same waitress placed a plate of bacon and eggs with toast in front of each man. 'In about twenty minutes,' Cliff continued, 'I will take you across to Pitt Street and the Lions Gate Hotel. They're looking for a lad to do some grooming and odd jobs of a Sunday morning while they are closed.'

Frank shot a quick glance at Ronnie, who saw that Frank was a little lost, and while Cliff was preoccupied with his meal, he continued in his place.

'What I want from you, Frankie, is to take the job on and get familiar with the joint. Keep your ears and eyes open, while not attracting attention—you know how it's done.' Ron cut his egg into several pieces and then paused. 'The travel will be a pain in the arse, but what else would you be doing, and besides, it will be worth it. Cliffy here will keep in contact and relay it to me.' Ronnie pointed his fork now wrapped in bacon, and then dangled the necessary bait. 'We get this sorted, Frankie, and we can concentrate on more profitable things,' he said. Ronnie smiled at his protégé and gave him a harmless jab to the arm.

***

Fleurbaix, 15 July
Attached to a work detail of two platoons from his battalion, Clarence held a sandbag while Sticks filled it. Clarence lifted the bag onto a trolley which, when full, would be pushed to a lorry by a soldier, who would curse his luck at having landed the heavy work. This small operation, along with many others, extended from the front line all the way back to the reserve units.

The increase in activity had begun rumours of an imminent assault, and the men asked each other if and when they would be involved. Clarence wondered if the Germans had noted all the activity from their elevated position upon Auber's Ridge.

One thing that had struck each soldier within the 5th Division upon coming into the sector was its flatness. There was barely a notable landmark around, with the exception of a couple of church steeples and Auber's Ridge, which would barely rate a mention as a ridge if not for the surrounding countryside, and the fact that the Germans occupied it.

Sergeant Kent looked at his watch, noted 0900 hours and called for a smoko. The men dropped at the first available shaded spot and eagerly waited for the water that was supplied in old petrol tins.

Sticks returned from a conversation with some men from 1 Platoon, which included Clarrie's brother Archie. He dropped beside his mates Clarrie and Tom under the shade of an elm tree.

'Anywhere will do, Sticksy, ya clumsy sod,' cried Tom.

'Righto, Tommy, settle down,' replied Sticks. 'I'll get you a handkerchief to wipe away the tears in a minute.'

'C'mon, boys,' said Clarence, the peacemaker.

'What's the latest?' enquired Tom, the abrasive exchange forgotten.

'Well,' said Sticks, at home in his favourite role. 'The boys from 1 Platoon say there is a very big chance we will head to the front tomorrow to relieve the 55th.'

'About bloody time,' interjected Tom.

'Word is,' continued Sticks, 'HQ is being moved further up the road towards the front, to a place they're calling Croix les Cornex.'

'Sounds like brass might be planning something big.'

'That's what I said, Tommy,' replied Sticks.

Clarence sat with his back to the elm tree. He listened but did not respond to the news Sticks gave; a picture of the girl in a white dress with a tobacco tin flashed into his mind.

***

The afternoon had been used to check and re-check equipment, as well as clean and inspect rifles and scrutinise gas masks. Some of the veterans spent hours going over the one hundred and fifty rounds of ammunition they had been allocated. They would remove each one to wipe away dust or any other matter that might cause the rifle to malfunction.

The men of the 53rd had received their orders to move to the front lines along with the 54th Battalion under the cover of the pre-dawn darkness, on the morning of 16 July. They would relieve the 55th and 56th Battalions, who would move to billets at Bac St Maur. The mood was electric but quiet as men went about their business. Some would reflect; others like Clarence would get a word of advice from a veteran; the battle-scarred soldier would do his best to prepare the novice for action.

'Just remember, Clarrie,' said Arthur Atkins, 'keep calm but stay alert. When we're asked to jump the bags—which we will be—keep moving, never stop, never! Right, mate. You'll be fine—just fine.' Arthur slapped him on the shoulder and then moved in the direction of Private Birdie Finch; another member of their section who looked like he could use an encouraging word.

'Clarrie,' said Archie quietly, as he crouched down to be at his brother's side. 'All set, mate?'

'Good as gold,' replied Clarence, not too convincingly. A look of apprehension was noted by Archie, but not commented on.

'Good mate, good; I saw you chat with Arthur, he's a good man. Follow his lead and you'll be right.' Archie looked at the ground for a minute and picked up a pebble. He rolled it between his fingers. 'Who would have thought hey… you and me… in France together.' Archie went silent and focused on the pebble.

Clarrie didn't reply. He allowed his brother to convey through silence what he couldn't say in words.

'Remember that time, Clarrie, when we got in that fight with those Thompson kids.'

'You fought, I watched,' said Clarence with a smile.

'Didn't have much choice, they were going to pinch that bloody poetry book of yours,' blurted Archie. He stopped suddenly and looked up from his pebble, eyes filled with brotherly love.

'They got a bit more than they bargained for, didn't they,' added Clarence.

Archie placed the pebble down gently on the dark soil and shook his brother's hand firmly, while he brought his left hand across to grip his brother's forearm. 'Best be off,' said Archie before he released Clarrie's hand. 'I have to go and see Lieutenant Davidson for a briefing; he's been transferred from the 1st over to us—given the boys a bit of a lift it has.'

***

Tom Baker sat next to Clarence; a smoke dangled from his mouth, which left both of his hands free to relieve Clarrie of his Lee-Enfield rifle. Tom immediately began to inspect the weapon, and with dextrous fingers, he removed and replaced the magazine and worked the bolt action several times, before giving his approval.

'Trying to make Lance Corporal, Tom?' joked Clarrie.

'Piss off, Miller,' snapped the Gallipoli veteran. He used an open hand to clip Clarrie over the back of the head as he spoke. 'Just want to make sure Fritz doesn't get me because your bloody rifle jams.'

Clarrie copped the tip and continued to work on his weapon. The light-hearted banter relieved some of the butterflies that tormented his stomach.

'Hey, Tom,' said Clarrie. 'Where's...'

'Righto boys,' shouted Corporal Connor, 'gather round.'

The ten men of 2 Section moved swiftly to form a semi-circle around Alf Conner, who had knelt alongside a water cart.

'Men, I have just been briefed, along with the other three section leaders, by Lieutenant Sharp. We will assemble at 03:00 hours tomorrow and step off at 04:00 hours. We will march in company formation initially, and then after the first stop we will split into platoons, and then finally sections, when we near the front itself.'

Corporal Conner drew back on his cigarette and exhaled slowly before he proceeded. 'There is an attack planned for the 17th and it involves our 5th Division and the British 61st Division. The battle further south at the Somme has recommenced in earnest. We will engage the enemy here and do as much damage as possible, so Fritz cannot send reinforcements south.'

'Corporal?'

'Yes, Birdie.'

'Will we be put into battle straight away?'

The rest of the section cringed at the question asked by Private Finch. No one wanted to seem unwilling at this point, but none of the men would deny, if asked in seclusion, that they would like it answered.

'I can't say at this point, Private Finch,' replied the corporal, very aware of what effect anxious questions could do to the men's confidence or trust in each other, elements that are essential in the heat of battle. 'All I can tell you is that we are headed to the front line in the morning, and I have the utmost confidence that each of you will do your duty with honour.'

The five Gallipoli veterans looked serious but calm, while the men who hadn't seen action made small movements that betrayed their nervousness. They shuffled from one knee to the other, wiped a brow, or peered off into the distance.

'The way those clouds have built up,' said Private Dave Smith, another of the section's veterans, 'who knows what the Brass will do.'

Alf Conner tilted his head to the side and sort of tweaked the corner of his mouth, a non-committal gesture that neither refuted nor accepted Private Smith's statement. He was just glad for the diversion from Birdie's question.

'Now, boys,' continued Corporal Conner, 'there is no need to tell you again, but we will move quietly at all times, all kit stowed and secured properly, no sly smokes, nothing that can draw attention on us. Get some tucker into you, rest up, and I will see you at 03:00 hours.'

FIFTEEN

Fleurbaix, Front-line, 53rd Battalion Sector, 18 July
A shell whistled through the cloudy air and drowned out the machine gun fire that raked the parapet only a hundred yards away. Clarence threw himself against the damp sandbags that made up the breast works of the front line. The contact smeared his already dirty undershirt with mud.

'That one wasn't even close, Clarrie,' said Sticks, who stood motionless. He stared at his mate, as the uplifted earth—sent skyward by the projectile—settled to the ground more than fifty yards away in no-man's-land. Sticks, who had taken less than twenty-four hours to gauge the trajectory of a shell, continued on with his load of water tins, and distributed them to soldiers who manned the fire step below the parapet. As he moved, Sticks collected empties, which he took to the rear to be refilled. Clarence wiped a forearm across his face and resumed his position behind a wheelbarrow load of empty sandbags, destined for points along the front line. The bags would be distributed to soldiers involved in the first waves of the assault. He was suddenly reminded that one of those soldiers would be him.

The attack on the German positions in the region of Fromelles and Fleurbaix had been scheduled for the 17th of July, but poor weather, which started on the 16th, had seen those plans abandoned. As a result, the 54th Battalion had been taken out and put in billets at Bac St Maur, while the 53rd remained and held the whole 14th Brigade sector overnight. With more bad weather presenting itself on the 18th, the brigade was put on standby, while the 54th resumed its position alongside the 53rd. Orders were received that the attack would take place on the 19th. Zero hour was yet to be confirmed.

Exhausted by the mental tension of the postponement, the men of the 5th Division were also physically drained. They had to complete a whole range of demanding jobs in a very limited amount of time. The 14th Brigade under Colonel Harold Pope still had ammunition dumps to complete. Brompton Avenue, the main thoroughfare for the brigade, needed to be cleared, a job that was best done at night to avoid enemy artillery fire; while a tramway, designed to move a range of equipment to the front lines, was still under construction.

The 15th Brigade, situated on the right flank of the 14th, and the closest to the Sugarloaf salient—the main objective of the operation— had experienced similar problems to the 14th, as had the Australian 8th Brigade, who were on 14th's left flank. The British on the right half of the salient manned a line that ran roughly south-west. They had the unenviable task of silencing the menacing protrusion known as the Sugarloaf; the responsibility of that enormous undertaking fell to the 184th Brigade. The 183rd Brigade was to their right, and the 182nd took up a position further along the line in front of the smaller, but still formidable, Wick salient.

As Clarence continued with his job, he wondered what would become of him. How would he perform under fire, what would he do? He knew it wasn't wise to encourage these kinds of thoughts, but his mind asked a lot of questions of itself. It's just the way he was.

They had been informed by their platoon commander, Lieutenant Sharp, that the assault would be an operation comprised of two divisions, the British 61st and the Australian 5th. The three brigades of each division would line up in a two-battalion front. Clarence's 53rd, along with the 54th, were appointed the 14th Brigade's attack battalions, with the 55th designated to carry and re-supply duties. The 56th would be held in reserve.

From the 53rd Battalion, A and B companies would take part in the initial assault. Clarence felt a cold shiver run down his spine after he heard the news. *At least I'll be with Archie*, he thought. The plan was for the assault companies involved in the first wave to assemble at the parapet during the prolonged artillery bombardment, which began at zero hour. Companies C and D would advance behind them, followed by the 55th Battalion, who would be close behind with much needed supplies. During the bombardment, there would be several 'lifts'—pauses in fire—which would see the men closest to the parapet lift their bayonets skyward, as if ready to attack. This would draw the enemy to man their positions upon their own parapet, only to have the bombardment commence again, hopefully killing German soldiers and further weakening their defences.

At an allotted time, depending on the depth of ground to be covered and relative to the different brigade positions along the line, the barrage would recommence. A and B Companies from the 53rd and 54th would move into no-man's land and position themselves as close to the enemy positions as possible, while being behind the protective blanket of their own artillery fire.

Once the final barrage had lifted, it was the job of the forward assault units to dash across the ground that remained to take the enemy front line trench before the enemy could regain their positions. Once the enemy was removed from their own front line trench, the initial assault companies were to fortify that position and create a secure line of fire. The subsequent waves would then leapfrog them and move into the German support trenches. It was at this point that Lieutenant Sharp had stressed some points.

'Men,' said the lieutenant, 'from the information we have received from our own reconnaissance, our objectives beyond the German front line should be no more than 150 yards. Under no circumstances should you look to go beyond that. Our job,' he continued, as he raised his voice slightly to emphasise his point, 'is to take their front line and turn it into a secure defensive position. Pay special attention to your flanks, as we will rely on the success of the 15th Brigade; they too will be dependent on the success of the British 184th. God speed and good luck; your section leaders will go into more detail, dismissed.'

'You heard the lieutenant, back to it,' barked the infamous Sergeant Bourke.

'I'll give him back to it,' hissed Tom,' while he loitered with the other men. Sticks lit a smoke for Tom and Dave, as well as one for himself.

'I'll be stuffed how they got that recon on the German trenches,' said Dave in a low voice. 'You couldn't see two feet in front of you yesterday with that mist; how could an airman see what was what?'

'They know what they're doing,' replied Sticks, optimistically.

'Sullivan, if I've learnt one thing from this blasted war, it's this. The Brass couldn't find their own arse if they shit 'emselves.' Stated Dave.

'That's a fact,' said Tom.

'Move on you lot,' hissed Sergeant Bourke, 'work to be done.'

***

Fleurbaix, Front line, 19 July
A thick mist lay over the men like a heavy quilt, but unlike the comfort of being tucked in bed on a Sunday morning, this blanket sat cold and menacing. It forewarned the men of what lay ahead.

Alf Conner made his way through a group of soldiers from 2 Platoon and stopped to exchange a few words with old acquaintances before he sat on the bare earth among his men. He looked at the group of silent infantrymen and studied their faces. He knew, for many, it would be their last hours on this Earth. Having been baptised into war on the Gallipoli Peninsula, Alf Conner knew that all men handled battle, and in particular the hours that led up to it, in different ways. Some like Arthur Atkins and David Smith were relaxed; they ate and talked quietly amongst themselves. Jack Sticks Sullivan had the same easy way about him, which surprised Alf, because novices weren't usually like that. Others, like Francis Tench and Birdie Finch, expressed their anxiety through movement; the confined spaces of the support trenches were like a cage for them. The virgin warriors released their pent-up tension by a tap of the foot while they wrote a letter, or the frantic movement of a thumb and forefinger, as they cleaned the barrel of their rifle.

The person that caught Alf's eye more than anyone in his section was Private Clarence Miller. Corporal Conner watched as Clarrie sat with his back against the sap wall. His expression was a mixture of detachment and serenity. Alf would say he was scared, but his eyes told a different story. It was like—in a strange way—he wasn't with them. He would respond to a request, if asked, but then resume his pose as before. His eyes saw something other than the damp smelly earth, covered in opaque moist air.

'Boys, listen up,' said Corporal Conner. The men responded instantly to his call; James Cook and 'Smelly' Tench lifted their pencils and looked up at their section commander with bulging eyes. 'Zero hour has been set for 11:00 hours.' The men stared back at Alf. All of them had accepted that this moment would arrive, but the words that the corporal spoke brought a reality to the situation that affected them all. James Cook, scared, allowed a small trace of urine to escape his bladder; the young private arrested it with tensed stomach muscles, and twitched as a result.

'The barrage will last for seven hours,' continued Alf. 'Our A Company will deploy into no-man's-land, along with B Company, at exactly 17.43 hours, under the cover of artillery. We will move up as close as we can to the enemy position and take cover to wait for the final lift in the barrage. That will be the signal for us to attack.' Corporal Conner paused for a moment and allowed what he had just said to register with his men.

'Bugger,' said Sticks Sullivan.

'What's up Sticks?' enquired Alf.

'Just cut me bloomin' finger on this bully-beef tin.'

'Stretcher bearer,' said Tom Baker, in a muffled roar.

The rest of the men, as well as James Captain Cook, laughed, not only at Sticks and his reaction, but his apparent lack of concern for what lay ahead.

'Righto, settle down boys,' said Corporal Conner. 'Thanks Sticksy.'

'It bloody hurt.'

'I bet it did,' said Conner, as a lone German shell sailed harmlessly overhead. 'If I may, Private Sullivan?'

Sticks nodded his head towards Alf, while he placed his cut finger in his mouth.

'One thing I can't emphasise enough is to keep moving once you're in no-man's. Brass has told us that our guns will have Fritz tucked away in his shelter, but nothing ever goes to plan, so be ready for anything.'

'Corporal Conner's right, men,' said Lance Corporal Atkins. 'Get to cover as quickly as possible and when that barrage lifts, run like scalded cats into those enemy trenches and kill every fucking German you see.'

'Rest up for now, boys,' said Corporal Conner, 'we will move into position soon.'

***

19 July, 1916 Fleurbaix

Dearest Ruth and baby Reginald,
Last hours before battle and my thoughts are with you. Send my love to all. Archie is well and will do his section proud. The men are in good spirits, my mate Sticks making everyone laugh. All my love, Clarence.

    If my fate should be, that I stay in these fields,
    Know that I loved my life's love,
    the life of our love living on.

Beneath the Willow

***

Chunks of earth fell on steel helmets and hunched-over bodies. The German shelling, which had increased significantly since 14:30 hours, coincided with the bringing up of troops. It had a deadly and debilitating effect on the stationary soldiers. Already, three of the four company commanders from 53rd Battalion had been killed. It increased the confusion within the ranks, and the likelihood of failure, before they began.

Screams of agony from men shredded with shrapnel pierced the senses of those untouched, as soldiers, limbs torn from bodies, lay strewn amongst their comrades. Dead or wounded, the essence of their youth leached into the Flanders clay.

Huddled against the breast works and each other, the soldiers gritted their teeth and prayed. The enemy barrage approached like a storm of death and hit targets indiscriminately.

'Our Father who art in heaven… ahh!' screamed Clarence in anguish, both arms wrapped around his head. The blast from a German shell toppled sandbags from the parapet onto him and the men close by. In an attempt to break out of the tomb, Clarence frantically twisted and contorted his body under the weight of the bags. He tried to move, but both arms and legs were pinned around his neck on the duck-boarded floor. After a short and futile struggle, Clarence was suddenly imbued with a bizarre feeling of security. His survival instinct, sharp and non-consultative, had reacted to the danger of being buried alive. It suddenly remembered the scene he had just left.

Could I lie here in peace? Clarence thought. Mud from the trench floor oozed through the duckboards and pressed into his eyes and mouth. *I'm wounded, aren't I? The battle is over for me.* A feeling of relief mixed with guilt washed through Private Miller, as a quick release of weight from his back caused a rush of air to enter his lungs; the light from a dust-filled sky hit his face as he was rolled onto his back by the rescuer's arms.

'Thought we lost you there for a second,' yelled Dave Smith. The private picked up Clarence's steel helmet and slapped it back on his mud-covered head. 'Don't go anywhere without this,' said Smith, as he passed Clarrie his rifle.

Clarrie nodded a thank you at Dave for saving him—not entirely convinced if he truly was. Dave slapped him on the shoulder and then continued to lift the fallen sandbags into a pile. Private Baker attempted to throw them back on the parapet, but was met with machine-gun fire, which saw him dive for cover. Mortar fire from a *Minenwerfer*—German for mine launcher or light mortar—followed directly after the bullets; they struck the parapet wall where Clarrie's unit was bunched. Private Miller pressed himself against the breast works once again, while he placed one hand on top of his helmet. With his eyes shut, he held his breath and prayed. He prayed that the smaller shell of the Minenwerfer would fall short of their target, and several of the feared projectiles did just that. Until a single shell—its trajectory affected by a sudden change in wind—cleared the parapet wall and detonated amongst the duckboards only thirty yards from Clarence.

Splinters from the temporary flooring, pieces of mud and human flesh, showered men either side of the blast. A cloud of dust receded to reveal an armless Francis Tench, who staggered towards where Clarence and David Smith sat, dazed and disorientated. Blood pulsed from the cavity that was once his shoulder. He stopped and stared blankly and gasped hoarsely for breath. His hair was saturated with blood and his face—on one side–was grotesquely scarred from heat and debris. He collapsed and died. A hole in the dead soldier's back, the size of a man's fist, held Clarence's gaze.

Propelled by fear-induced adrenalin, Clarence rushed to Tench's side, then practically, but shamefully, he moved on. Clarence noticed more casualties, and knew nothing could resurrect the quiet and meek Tench. He crawled on hands and knees to a uniformed body, slumped in the foetal position; Clarrie reached out with his left hand

and grabbed the soldier's tunic. Clarence talked to the man as he pulled.

'It's alright, mate, it's alright,' said Clarrie. He felt the dead weight of lifelessness in the body. He suddenly realised it wasn't all right as he had promised. 'It's al... No!' Clarence reacted sharply. 'No, get up, no! Somebody help me!' screamed Clarence, demented and horrified. Clarrie turned the corpse over to reveal a calm but barren face. Enraged, the veins in Clarence's temples were dark, and they protruded like they threatened to burst under the strain. He lifted his face skywards while he clutched Jack Sullivan's bloody tunic with both fists. The rage subsided to hopeless grief. His chin fell to his chest and acid tears rolled down his face.

Clarence slumped to sit alongside his dead mate. He remained unmoved as another shell exploded dangerously close to their position. Distraught, he held his head in his hands and then inhaled deeply. He moved mechanically, and gently opened Jack's pockets to remove some personal items to place in his own tunic. Clarence received a tap on the shoulder followed by a calm word. He then picked up his rifle and moved like a zombie back to his position next to Dave Smith. He gripped the rifle firmly as he squatted, the weapon helping to hold his nerve as much as his balance.

In a cruel twist that demonstrated the uncertainty and arbitrary nature of war, the guns that had pounded ceased their carnage on the forward line moments after Jack was killed. The silence was shattered as another German barrage opened up, this time on the support trenches.

***

Front line, 17:40 hours
'Three minutes, Arthur,' said Corporal Conner from the fire-step, ready to lead his section into no-man's land.

'Three minutes,' relayed Arthur Atkins. The message was passed down the line, as shell after shell from their own guns whizzed high overhead before they crashed into the fortified German front-line.

'How are the men in your section, Corporal?' enquired Lieutenant Sharp.

'Good, Lieutenant,' replied Corporal Conner, 'two casualties from the bombardment.'

'See you in the German lines, Corporal.'

Lieutenant Sharp knew how crucial events to their right would be in determining their own fate. He turned to Lieutenant Colonel Norris, 53rd Battalion commander, and had a brief and intense discussion before the lieutenant colonel moved towards 1 Platoon. Lieutenant Sharp knew it would be critical that the 15th Brigade on their right, in particular the 60th Battalion, which were the 53rd's right flank, reached their objective. They in turn were reliant on the success of the British 184th Brigade, who had the toughest assignment of all, a frontal attack on the Sugar Loaf salient.

Clarence stood on the fire-step between Tom Baker and David Smith and wondered if Archie had made it through the barrage. *Maybe he had got a minor wound and is already back at a dressing station*, Clarence thought, and hoped. The ground rumbled from the relentless bombardment, and sent vibrations up through his feet, that were close to being numb with fear. Clarrie glanced along the line and spotted Sergeant Bourke with Alf Conner. The sergeant consulted his timepiece, and then waved his arm in a signal for his men to move over the parapet.

His mouth dry, Clarence took short sharp breaths to ready himself for what lay over the sandbags. He cleared the parapet, rolled and then sprung to his feet to see the sparse, featureless ground spread out before him. Clouds of smoke and debris formed ahead as the artillery punched away at the German lines. With roughly two hundred and fifty yards to cover, Clarence ran. The sound of his heart registered above the clamour of battle. The crack of sporadic rifle fire

Beneath the Willow

drew his attention, while the dreaded knock, knock, knock of the German machine gun was faint and far to his right.

He passed some brush, knee high and spread out to his left. He saw, one, two, and then three men fall from 5 Section. He felt a rush of adrenaline as he sprinted to make the relative cover of the enemy parapet. The British barrage continued. Clarence was knocked off his feet, but uninjured, when a shell, commonly known as a drop-short, exploded ahead of him.

'Useless pricks,' yelled Tom, as he pulled a stunned Clarrie to his feet.

'Keep moving, Miller,' shouted Sergeant Bourke. He waved his arm to encourage Clarence. Bourke's movement ceased when a bullet from a German Mauser rifle pierced his eyeball. It exited in a gush of blood and brains through the back of his skull. Fragments splattered Clarence's face, but a push in the back from David Smith urged Private Miller forward, and Sergeant Norman Bourke into memory.

The Diggers had to pause as they approached the German wire entanglements, which put them in great danger of being picked off. The gaps, narrow where they should have been wide, caused a bottleneck. The soldiers were forced to scamper through as best they could. The only saving grace was the lack of enemy fire. To their right, the sound of relentless machine-gun and rifle fire filled the air. It had devastated the men of the 15th Brigade.

With his eyes strained to catch sight of danger, Clarence cleared the wire and sprinted for a crater close to the enemy defences. He hit the dirt hard, and was jolted from behind by Smith, and then Baker, who rolled over the top of him as he gasped for breath.

'Jesus fucking Christ,' mumbled Private Baker, 'that wire was supposed to be gone.'

'Keep it down,' hissed Smith. 'Looks like most of the Germans have pissed off… a few brave bastards have hung around though.'

'Salient hasn't been knocked out,' whispered Clarrie. '15th have copped it.'

'Poor bastards,' sighed Baker, as artillery fire struck all around them in clouds of dust and grey-brown smoke.

The three men spun around violently, startled by two more men who had leapt into the improvised shelter.

'Christ, Arthur,' hissed Private Smith, 'where did you come from?'

Lance Corporal Atkins jerked his head to the right to answer the question. He pushed Joseph Finch's head down into the dirt, just as Finch lifted it perilously high. The young private was dazed and confused; his eyes darted every which way. Atkins moved close to Baker and Smith and reminded them of their objectives. He told them that Corporal Conner and Private Cook were to their right, and that 1 Platoon would probably need assistance to secure the flank, as the 15th had been hit hard on the right.

'Soon as that barrage stops,' said Atkins, 'you boys go like hell.'

Smith and Baker nodded in acknowledgment and then focused on the defensive position in front of them.

'Keep Birdie with you,' added Atkins before he crawled out of the crater to link up with Alf Conner.

***

Like most things unwanted, the end of the artillery barrage came without consideration or introduction; the seconds after its cessation were like hours. The silence was debilitating for the men, as it signalled the beginning of the real battle—the fight with enemy soldiers. Tom Baker and David Smith screamed as though they would breathe fire and charged for the enemy front line. Joseph Finch stood hesitantly and moved forward. He cart-wheeled backwards to lie at the bottom of the crater—shot by a German sniper. The bullet removed half of his face. Clarence stared, frozen to the spot. His body and mind wanted to rebel at the unrelenting violence.

'Move forward man, or I will shoot you where you lie,' screamed Lieutenant Sharp. The officer moved up from behind. His tirade was aimed at Clarence as he sat motionless, mesmerised by what was once Birdie Finch.

'Move, Private, or so help me!' roared the lieutenant. Clarence turned his head towards the lieutenant; his mouth gaped like he was ready to receive Communion. Clarrie watched, detached, as the lieutenant drew his revolver.'

The hand-gun fired, and Clarence was snapped from his trance. He scrambled from the crater and ran with his rifle out in front. The lieutenant's tirade still rung in his ears.

For the 14th Brigade, and the 8th to their left, the artillery barrage had taken some effect. The German soldiers, bar a few resolute and courageous men, had left their posts for the safety of the underground shelters. As they attempted to return to their guns, the Germans were surprised by the Australians, and were unable to fire weapons from their designated positions. Hellish hand-to-hand fighting ensued.

Clarence flung himself over the parapet and into the German front line trench. His blood raced after he was driven forward by Lieutenant Sharp. Men fought, locked chest-to-chest, hands on throats, or clenched onto wrists. They struggled to hold off the hand that held a sharpened knife, which threatened to end their life. The scene that greeted Private Miller was war in all its frenzied madness. Military objectives forgotten, it was brutal in its simplicity; kill the enemy before he kills you.

Clarence looked to his right and saw his mate Tom engaged with an enemy soldier. The German held Baker's own rifle sideways against his chest. He overpowered the Australian in an instant and forced him to the ground. The German drove his knee into Private Baker's gut and it knocked his wind out, along with his remaining strength. Seeing 'Fritz' reach for a knife, Clarence lunged forward with his rifle in the confined space and drove the tip of the bayonet into the German's throat. The air from the man's lungs escaped with the blood from his artery and gurgled. Clarence removed the blade quickly and watched the soldier collapse, lifeless. Private Baker recovered quickly and thrust outwards with his arms to move the limp body off him. Without thought, Baker rolled to his knees, steadied, and fired a shot at a range of eight feet straight into the abdomen of a German, whose arm was raised high, ready to thrust a dagger into Clarence's back. Baker worked the bolt action and directed his aim to two-o'clock, above the trench. He squeezed off another round to drop a German officer with a Luger pistol pointed towards the pair of Diggers.

'Thanks, Miller,' said Baker. He stood and looked up and down the trench. The scene somewhat calmer than it was only minutes before.

Clarence nodded, and then glanced towards the German he had speared through the throat. The man lay motionless on the trench floor. Maybe a father—definitely a son, but now, because of Private Clarence Miller, a lover of poetry—a corpse. Clarence relived the look of the man, eyes bulged and features contorted, allowed cruelly to contemplate the shock of being killed before death finally arrived. The image was seared into Clarence's conscience, never to leave.

Baker noticed Smith and Cook to their left. He slapped Clarrie in the chest and signalled him to follow.

'Come with me, Miller, and secure this section of the line.'

Clarence followed Tom but chose not to speak. *I have just killed a man*, Clarence said to himself, *and Tom killed also, twice, in a matter of seconds. Both times he saved my life. All in battle, I know, and in defence of each other, but killing none the less. So what am I now?* he asked, as his eyes darted left and right, up and down, alert and prepared for the enemy. *Now that I have taken something only God can give.*

Tom and Clarence linked up with what remained of the sections that made up their platoon. They secured a stretch of front-line, as soldiers from C and D Companies in the second wave leap-frogged them to continue the assault and secure the German support trench.

SIXTEEN

A curtain of darkness, almost drawn, allowed dim light to reveal darkened, beastly shapes dart in and out of view. The stress took the men of 53rd Battalion to the point of madness. Clarence held his rifle close to his prone body, and listened, as much as he looked, for any movement in the fading light. The position he held along with Conner, Baker, Smith, and Atkins, was tenuous at best.

After they secured the line that was once the German front, the men from A Company had moved forward to help defend the capture of what was thought to be the enemy support line. Word had passed from soldier to soldier that Lieutenant Colonel Norris, in an act of great valour, and with a small party of men, had been cut down by heavy machine-gun fire while he tried to advance. The death of Norris added to the high number of officers either dead or wounded within the 53rd Battalion. Command now passed to Captain Charles Arblaster from D Company.

With officer numbers depleted before they left their own lines, the troops rallied, and had initial success, but were hamstrung by a lack of instruction and quality reconnaissance. Soldiers broke into the German support lines and found nothing that resembled the information they had been given. They wasted valuable time in a series of old ditches. The supposed support trench was a water-filled drain, which may or may not have once served as a defensive position.

The 53rd put up a strong fight, but were now scattered across a series of small detached positions forward of the old German front line. They were in danger of being isolated further as the Germans gathered themselves for the expected counter-attack. Communication among the battalion was poor, owing to gaps in between positions, and contact with the 54th, on the left, was under extreme pressure. The position of 1 Platoon within the 53rd was critical, as they were on the extreme right and closest to the hard-hit 60th Battalion. 1 Platoon was forced to wheel right in order to protect the battalion flank.

'Atkins, Miller,' hissed Corporal Conner from inside their hastily built defences, a shallow ditch crested with the few sandbags they possessed—all they could manage under never-ending fire.

Lance Corporal Atkins and Private Miller crawled on their stomachs to lie alongside Corporal Conner. The artillery barrage that continued around them and towards the rear, where the 14th Field Company attempted to construct a communication sap with explosives, created a cloud filled with dust and smoke. It made visibility all the more difficult.

'Yes, sir.'

'See if you can get to our right flank and make contact with 1 Platoon. We have to get this line sorted or we will be cut off.'

Atkins nodded. He realised the urgency of the matter. Clarence looked towards Atkins for reassurance. The phrase 'cut off' struck him like the report of a Mauser rifle.

Atkins tapped Clarence on the shoulder and then made hand gestures to relay his instructions before he crawled out of their makeshift trench. The two soldiers had gone no further than ten yards when a German flare fizzed into the air, Atkins and Miller became statues, frozen to the spot. A fearful twitch came over Clarrie, as he fought the urge to run for the nearest crater; a reaction that would bring a concentration of machine-gun fire and certain death. With their eyes closed to retain optimal night vision, the men waited while the flare, with its deathly crimson glow, fell to earth.

Clarence opened his eyes and followed the lead of Arthur Atkins; his experience from the Gallipoli Peninsula was invaluable to the combat novice. After a few paces, Atkins saw an odd shape in the distance, and crouched low. Clarence mimicked him. After a minute, which seemed like an hour to Clarence, the lance corporal decided to throw caution to the wind.

'Wallaby,' said Atkins, in a hushed voice. The division as a whole had decided on Australian native fauna or flora as calls when they approached positions. The return call had to be different to the call made to give the all-clear.

'Emu.'

Atkins and Miller made a quick but controlled dash to the position ahead; a machine gun fired at random with no visible target. It caused Clarence to stumble and fall on the edge of the ditch that made up part of the 53rd's right flank. Two sets of strong hands reefed Clarence's body into the safety of the small trench, as a machine gun, this time with intent, sprayed the ground thirty yards either side of them.

'Easy, mate,' whispered the soldier, 'you'll get us all shot.'

'Archie,' said Clarence quietly, while he lay helpless on his back.

Archie Miller didn't respond; minimising talk was crucial in their position. Exhilarated, with the need to be contained, he pulled Clarence towards him and embraced his brother firmly, before he turned his attention to Lance Corporal Atkins.

'Things aren't much chop, Arthur,' said Archie.

Arthur gasped for breath and then spoke. 'The line's all over the place, Archie, gaps everywhere. We are on your left, but we've lost contact with our left flank.'

'Shit,' hissed Archie. 'I don't know where the 60th are, but we've had fire from our right flank, and there are three saps that run from the German positions straight for us. They shield Fritz from our fire. Got any Mills Bombs?'

'Here comes Fritz,' said Bluey Smith, before Atkins had a chance to answer.

Archie spun around and positioned his Lee-Enfield to fire as he turned. He reeled off three shots in quick succession from on top of the sand-bags. The brave act exposed him to enemy fire while he masterfully worked the bolt of the rifle. His salvo delivered, Archie ducked behind cover while George Smith and Arthur Atkins lobbed a Mills Bomb each into the darkness. They waited behind the bags while the hand-grenades did their work. Two explosions, one after the other, and then muffled screams told Archie and two other privates to react. They quickly leapt into the cloud of dust and bayoneted two Germans. A third enemy soldier, who had positioned himself to the right of his comrades, fired at the Australians and killed the private who stood next to Archie; the German collapsed a split second later from a bullet wound to the chest, fired by Arthur.

Clarence squinted as his eyes attempted to penetrate the darkness. He fired at a German helmet silhouetted by the glow of a distant flare; the faint thud of a body as it hit the earth could be heard. The target Clarence had in his sights had not reached the safety of the communication sap.

'Good shot, Clarrie,' whispered Archie. 'Keep watch on the area directly in front, and to three o'clock on your right.'

Archie rolled away from his brother towards the private who had made the bayonet charge with him. Whether through flinty toughness or the pain killing abilities of adrenalin, the young private had not let on that he had been wounded in the thigh. Corporal Miller noticed his trousers, wet and darkened with blood.

'You alright, Private Louth?'

'Good as gold, Corporal,' lied Louth.

'Private Cooper, see to Louth's leg,' whispered Archie.

In Archie's peripheral line of sight, a ghostly figure danced and then disappeared. He jerked his head towards the apparition and his heart skipped a beat. His instincts told him what it was; his sense of hope prayed it wasn't. He crawled to the rear of their position, closed his eyes and pulled the helmet he wore over his face to make his surrounds as dark as possible. Archie waited a few seconds, lifted the helmet and then opened his eyes to allow whatever light there was in the atmosphere to flood into his pupils. There it was again.

'Christ, they're behind us,' he barked, while he fired two rounds.

Smith and Atkins sprang to Archie's aid and fired rapidly; Cooper, having dressed Louth's leg, joined the fray. He tossed his last Mills bomb in the direction of his mate's fire. In the distance, rifles and machine gun fire opened up from the Australians in the old German front-line—a knee-jerk reaction to the shots fired from Corporal Miller. The sound of the Vickers machine gun was welcomed by Archie and his men. It had tied down and possibly killed the Germans that lurked, but it would do little to help their overall situation. With enemy troops in behind their position, it could only mean that the 15th Brigade had failed in their objective, and the flanking force that curved away to their right had been overrun or was like them—isolated.

'Bluey, we can't stay here much longer,' said Archie.

To their right a series of flashes could be seen. A short and sharp bomb battle ensued with small arms fire towards the old German line. It confirmed Archie's worst fears.

'Louth and Clarrie, keep your eyes on those comm-saps,' said Archie, in a low voice.

Archie Miller looked into the darkness and ran through his options silently. In the distance, hundreds of yards past their right flank, a sickening discharge of machine guns filled the night sky with an apocalyptic howl. A chorus of tortured voices met the evil clatter, but did not outlast it. Archie cursed this madness and decided the only course of action was to deliver his men from certain death.

He moved to the front of the trench to be near Louth and Clarence, but with his back against the sandbags so he could watch the rear.

'Men, our situation is critical. Fritz has moved in between us and the old front. We have no contact with the rest of our line, if it still exists, and we've run dangerously low on ammunition.' Archie paused for a second and gauged the mood of the men. 'We have no alternative but to make a dash past these Germans and break out to the position our brigade holds in the old German front line.'

'Corporal,' said Private Cooper, 'what about Louth?'

'We'll carry him.'

'I'll only hold you up,' whispered Private Cyril Louth. 'Leave me some ammo, and I'll keep the bastard Hun busy.'

Archie looked at the lad, a face plastered with grim defiance, a young man with a whole life to live, unwilling to put his mates at risk. Instead, he would choose to pay the ultimate sacrifice for the greater good.

'Don't be stupid,' replied Archie, 'we'll get you out.'

'I'll stay with him, Corporal,' said Private Cooper. 'Sort those Fritz out behind us and send stretcher bearers for Louth.'

Corporal Miller knew there would be no stretcher-bearers for Louth, or anyone else in this most dire of predicaments; Private Cooper's bravery was remarkable and tragic, like that of so many soldiers strewn across France and Belgium. Archie also knew that the men faced an arduous task in their attempt to break through the Germans. Impossible if they were being shot at from behind.

Archie closed his eyes to see a vision of his mother and father in front of their Beattie Street home. He opened them to see the fear-stricken faces of his fellow infantrymen and knew the decision he would take gave them their best chance of survival.

'You're going with the other men, Cooper.'

'Louth needs...'

'I will stay,' said Archie calmly, placating Private Cooper. An image of his mate, Bert Glanville, entered his mind. Archie never saw him after he died on Lemnos and it hit home as he talked to his men.

'Arch,' pleaded Clarence.

Archie ignored his brother's plea, fully aware of his fate. 'Lance Corporal Smith, you are in charge, organise your men.'

George Bluey Smith stared at his mate. He wanted to argue, but he knew it would be both pointless and dangerously counter-productive. His sole responsibility now was the safe transfer of souls across the dark cratered stretch. Bluey searched for words that could encompass what they had been through, both as soldiers and men. He swallowed hard and realised there weren't any. George Smith gripped Archie's hand firmly to wish him luck, for as men there could be no thought of farewells. He then turned and briefed the small party of men under his command. Clarence made an attempt to move towards his brother, but Archie bluntly rebuked him, with a jerk of his head towards Smith.

***

Clarence stood three feet to the left side and slightly behind George Smith. Another Digger, Private Barry was to his left, with Atkins and Cooper on Smith's right. They crept blindly through the night in an arrowhead formation. The air was heavy and lacquered the senses with the pungent odour of smoke mingled with the ripe scent of death. All around them, the mutilation of body, mind and spirit was sown into the earth, to be harvested when the guns had fallen silent.

Lance Corporal Smith halted and held his palm up; he was barely visible to his comrades. He made sweeping gestures and ordered Private Barry, on Clarence's left, and Cooper, on Atkins's right, to make a flanking movement on the German position. A shell crater full of Germans lay twenty to twenty-five yards in front. Smith thrust an open palm to instruct Clarence and Atkins to make the frontal assault.

Three of the German soldiers who occupied the shell-crater were busy setting up a machine gun. Once operational, it would traverse the ground with enfilading fire, and make the approach that the band of five Australians now attempted impossible. In order to protect themselves and their precious weapon, three of the remaining four Germans busied themselves filling sand-bags to make a parapet of sorts. The last soldier, a lookout, scanned the darkness that protected the Australians.

Clarence and Arthur surprised their German foes. They drove the cold steel that protruded from their rifles deep into the machine gunners' stomachs and withdrew them amidst horrid screams. Arthur then transformed his weapon into a club and swung it in an arc. The stock of the Lee-Enfield smashed into the temple of the third man in the detachment and cracked his skull, as he desperately gripped the handle-block of a weapon, unable to fire.

Lance Corporal Smith emerged from the darkness to shoot a soldier at point blank range. The German, his face locked in an expression of horror, clutched at his chest as he fell. Private Barry and Private Cooper roared like men possessed and entered the crater from the flanks. They bayoneted and shot almost simultaneously two men that held sandbags. A solidly built Fritz, left unharmed by the exchange, reacted quickly and cut into Private Barry's neck with a spade. Still connected to his enemy via timber and steel, Richard Barry fell to the damp earth and twitched spasmodically. Pulses of blood at first spurted, and then oozed from his dying body. Private Barry's killer, his eyes still engaged with his victim, received a bullet to the brain by a blood-splattered Private Miller; the German's efforts to defend his countrymen heroic but in vain. The final member of the Bavarian unit held his hands high in surrender. His eyes darted from one Australian soldier to the other as he considered his fate. Arthur Atkins, conscious of their position, stepped forward to mute the prisoner. He applied a gag and bound his hands as a precaution against any further heroics, while Private William Cooper held the incapacitated German in his menacing gaze.

***

Intermittent fire, random and hasty, landed around the captured crater that sheltered the Australian men. The bullets faded away amongst muffled and indistinguishable chatter. The darkness and emptiness of night made it difficult to fix their locations and get a bearing that would be vital in determining their next move.

'I guess it's about eighty to a hundred yards to the old German line,' whispered Smith.

'No telling how many Hun are out there,' replied Atkins.

'We'll have more chance by splitting up,' Smith said, unconvinced, but required as a leader to make a decision. Indecision was the beginning of calamity.

'I agree. What do we do with old Kaiser and the machine gun?'

'Slit his throat,' hissed Private Cooper.

'Shut your fucking trap, Cooper. I'll take the prisoner. Arthur, you take the MG. Start moving the men.'

George 'Bluey' Smith slid towards the prisoner. The gagged man recoiled in the confined space, his eyes distorted with the fear of his own demise. Smith made several hand gestures towards the captive to let him know what was required and what would be the consequence of non-cooperation. George Smith then rested on one knee and nodded towards Arthur Atkins, while he held his prisoner at gunpoint. As they waited, Private Cooper slithered out of the hole and into a darkness that was alive with the enemy.

Clarence peered towards the safety of the old German line and readied his nerve to face the unknown. He fell into a state of panic when he remembered his brother lying like a tethered lamb in among a pack of wolves. Although compelled by orders, the shame of leaving his brother gripped his chest and constricted his breathing, shredding the possibility of logical thought.

Clarence turned and scurried on hands and knees. He moved frantically to the other side of the shell crater, in the direction of his marooned brother. His movement was suddenly arrested by an oppressive weight; a firm and unyielding force that pressed into the base of his skull and sank his face into the dank mud. His heart yearned for his brother, but the strength in his body gave way to self-preservation. Clarence sobbed in coughs while he moaned his brother's name. Clarence implored God and all his saints to protect Archie and free him from the guilt of desertion. As he began to abandon hope, Clarence felt his sanity about to shatter.

'Miller… Miller, get a hold of yourself,' barked Arthur Atkins. The lance corporal had dropped the German machine gun to prevent Clarrie's mad dash. His mouth was an inch away from Clarence's ear.

'Archie,' moaned Clarence.

'Listen,' said Atkins through gritted teeth, as he released some pressure on Clarrie. 'Corporal Miller gave an order and you are to follow it, He wants you to live, not commit suicide. Think of your son and pull yourself together.' Arthur turned Private Clarence Miller and pulled him to a sitting position before he handed him his rifle.

Clarence, light-headed and full of self-loathing, pictured his beautiful wife and the son he had not met, and crept his way to the crest of the crater. Behind him, in the distance, he heard the sound of a Mills bomb explode, and then another, followed by several rifle shots, and then silence. *Was that Archie fighting for his life and that of Louth, or was it his mate Alf Conner and the remnants of his section?* Men whom he had, over the last hour or so, forgot existed.

Why am I here? he asked, while crouched over; the sound did not escape his lips, but burned like acid through the lining of his gut. *Get to that trench.* Images of his wife danced through his field of vision as he crept out of the crater. His heart jumped at the sight of a figure to his right, gone before he could determine if it was friend or foe. Intense gunfire, which made him twitch, came from far to his right. *Was that the 8th Brigade?* Clarence turned to the sound of a German machine gun, as it opened a withering burst of fire to his left. It aimed for targets in the direction he had come from. The glow from a flare revealed the abhorrent scene of a helmeted soldier that grasped a Maxim. His arms and torso shuddered to become one with the machine as it breathed its rain of death on two soldiers; one was bound at the wrist and gagged, the other was a lance corporal.

Doggedly still, Clarrie closed his eyes to avoid staring at the terrible scene, but the illumination of the flare that unveiled the deathly picture caused it to play and replay in his mind, until it faded into black as the flare hit the ground. He opened his eyes and could faintly make out the parapet of the old German line forty yards ahead. The position was securely held for the moment by his brigade but was under increased fire from German machine guns.

Clarence crept forward and was forced to leap to his right as particles of earth erupted near his feet from machine gun fire. He rolled into one of the many craters that dotted the landscape and covered his head with his arms, as a concerted barrage of fire from his fellow Diggers homed in on his position.

Clarence composed himself and then slowly rolled to his right. He gasped in horror at the sight and feel of a dead soldier. Its face was set in a cast of shock; a single bullet wound through his head had given the man no warning of his demise. Confronted by the possibility of being shot by his own countrymen, and pressed from the rear by the enemy, Clarrie had no option but to act.

'Waratah!'

Rifle fire, nervous and without aim, whizzed past, high and to the left of where he lay. Faint mumbles could be heard, carried on the still night air, but buried by the *knock-knock-knock* of an out-of-range machine gun.

From directly behind, and at a distance disguised by mingling sounds and the debilitating effect of fear, a voice whispered.

'Miller.' The sound reached Clarence as a garbled hiss.

A pause followed; sweat trickled from every inch of Private Miller's skin, so close to refuge, but stalked by death. As every sinew tightened, and each nerve stretched under unimaginable mental strain and physical punishment, Clarence was unable to trust his own judgement. Quietly he rolled back to his left and dug the heels of his boots into the soft earth—a sub-conscious act of flight. His back was pressed firm against the crater wall that faced the old German line, and the muddied slope barred his escape from the sound that now tormented him. Gently, he extended his rifle in front and prepared for the unwanted confrontation; breathing quickly in shallow sniffs, his teeth were clenched tight and his hands shook.

'Miller, hold your fire.' The voice wasn't German, or was it?

Clarence held his rifle a few inches higher and felt his feet involuntarily dig into the pliable clay further.

'Clarrie, it's Atkins, don't fire, I'm coming to you.' Another misguided bullet flew high over-head.

Clarence froze. The words reached his ears but were held in suspension—unable to enter his reason. A figure appeared low to the ground but above Clarrie's eye-line; a soft drab shape covered in a blanket of darkness. When the form that approached passed the point of no return, Clarence realised that the intention of the oncoming being would have no bearing on his response. For, as he lay there, petrified, and as urine flowed through his trousers and faeces soiled his under-shorts, he knew he was incapable of any action.

'Miller, it's me Atkins—Christ!' muttered the lance corporal. He had noticed the body to the side of Clarence and dragged himself closer to investigate. Positive identification was important in the aftermath of a battle.

'It's Rawlings,' announced Atkins. 'Bugger!' He added, as he pocketed a letter and notebook from his tunic for repatriation.

Clarence turned and looked at Atkins with blankness. His mind had shut out the horrors that lay across every inch of this poisoned earth.

'I'm going home,' said Clarence. He pushed the stock of his rifle into the mud and used the weapon as a rod to lever himself onto his feet.

'What?' Atkins did not understand at first, but then reached out in desperation to grab Clarrie as he realised the private's intentions. 'Miller, no!'

The mud that lay everywhere, and on Private Miller's trousers, slipped through Arthur Atkins's outstretched fingers. The mechanical and trance-like figure topped the crest of the shell hole and stepped into the open. Unable to cope, he bared himself to the gods of war and all their violent ways.

Atkins scampered up the slope and threw himself down to taste the filthy mud as a bullet gouged the earth to his left. A second flew high and whizzed within ear-shot, the lance corporal's helmeted head unseen, and not the intended target.

'Don't shoot,' yelled Arthur hopelessly. He raised his head to place his own life in grave danger, but his voice was lost in the report of the Lee-Enfield that fired on its own. 'Hold your fire,' he screamed, 'we're from the 14th, for Christ's sake.'

The fire from the Australian line ceased. It brought an eerie silence and stillness to the war-torn plain, as the uncertainty of the defenders hung in the air. During the quiet, Clarence seemed to break from the daze that had encompassed him. He stopped and turned to look towards the crater he had vacated and became aware of his complete vulnerability.

'Get down, Miller!' shouted Atkins, likely to draw attention, but desperate to save the frayed and battle-scarred private.

Atkins stared at the man. It tore at his heart to watch a helpless and defeated soldier resigned to death. The terrible sight caused the Gallipoli veteran to claw his fingers into the ground and grind his teeth. The isolated man, shrouded in darkness and a developing mist, swayed like a drunk. He appeared as an apparition to Arthur.

The body spun before Arthur or the men who held the old German line heard the shot. The Mauser's report pierced the dark night and reached them as Clarence hit the ground. Arthur reacted instinctively and sprinted towards Clarence from the cover of the crater, without thought for his own life. He shouted 'ANZAC!'—in hope of being recognised—and kept as low as possible. Arthur reached the limp body under intense enemy fire. The men of the 14th Brigade reacted to the lance corporal's shout and incredible act of bravery and opened a barrage of covering fire, as Lance Corporal Atkins hoisted Private Miller over his shoulder.

Arthur ran for his life. The sound of rifle fire and a Lewis light machine gun, which cackled like a typewriter, mixed with the sounds of his own breath. The adrenaline that pulsed through his body fuelled his muscles, burdened under the limp weight of a man.

'C'mon, Cobber,' yelled a Digger from behind a mound of sandbags; his mud-encrusted arms swung his weapon above the makeshift parapet to shoot a series of rounds towards the incoming fire. 'Get that into you bastards,' continued the rifleman. He fired his weapon like a man possessed.

Atkins reached the line and allowed Miller to roll off his shoulder into outstretched arms. Exhausted, he flung himself against the rear wall of the ditch, which only hours earlier had served as a firing step for the Germans. Arthur lay on the trench floor and gasped for breath. He lifted himself to his knees to see a wiry man with bulging white eyes on an unshaven and dirty face. Two other soldiers hurriedly stepped over Arthur to attend to Clarence.

'Haven't seen too many braver things than that mate,' said the rifleman, 'Atkins isn't it?'

Arthur nodded, still unable able to breathe, let alone speak.

'Thought so, bumped into you at ANZAC. Jacko's the name,' continued the rifleman. 'We're under the pump here mate, but we'll get you out through the sap they've almost finished across no-mans. Sooner the better for your mate, he's not good.

Atkins looked over at Clarence. Two men worked desperately on him but were hamstrung in the conditions.

'Can you walk, Atkins?' asked Jacko.

Arthur nodded at Jacko, not quite sure why he asked. He attempted to stand, but his left leg buckled underneath him. A bullet had passed clean through his calf muscle. It left his lower leg minced, with muscle and tendons torn apart.

SEVENTEEN

Balmain, August, 1916
Ruth weeded the ground beneath the small bed of roses that lined the Miller's front fence. The sound of footsteps, light and slow, persuaded her to cease work and lift her head. The transfer from one state of mind to another can sometimes come as a complete shock, as it does after a plunge into cold water. Or, it can be met with the complete confusion of being woken from a deep slumber.

As Ruth knelt on the small patch of grass next to the rose bushes, she felt a combination of both. The image of a teenage boy dressed in a black uniform, his babyish face partly obscured by an official looking cap, paralysed every muscle and nerve in her body. The pink telegram loomed large in her line of sight, and it singed her eyes like hot coals; its presence was the realisation of countless nightmares.

'Mrs,' said the boy sheepishly, scarred from so many similar deliveries. He was too young and impressionable to deal with anguished faces that met his every stop. He was not yet resilient enough to deal with the frenzied shouts that would, on occasion, prevent him from completing his job. 'Telegram for Mr Albert Miller,' he continued. The boy stood rigid and acted in the most respectful way he knew. He did his best to follow his boss's advice on the etiquette of delivering bad news.

Ruth extended her arm to receive the pink notice; the sound

of Albert's name released the young mother from her paralysis. A faint voice suggested to her that the telegram, addressed to her father-in-law, was likely to be news of Archie and not her beloved Clarence. A wave of shameful guilt washed over her. Tears welled in her eyes at the misery of having to hold onto such hope. As Mrs Clarence Miller, Ruth had imagined her name on the telegram, but when enrolling to enlist, Clarence had filled out the attestation form naming his father as next of kin, in part to protect Ruth, but also because he wasn't yet married.

Unmoved, Ruth stared at a black ant that moved from one blade of grass to another. She possibly held her life's worth in her hand, but Ruth was strangely motivated by the tiny insect and its continual struggle. Ruth nodded at the boy and rose to her feet. She straightened her dress and walked inside to see Grace.

Grace greeted Ruth with a smile like always, but her eyes widened and her complexion turned ghostly white when she noticed the telegram in her hand. The mixing bowl that she cradled dropped to the floor and she groped for the bench. Ruth rushed to her side. She realised that there was no lesser evil in what was contained in the message, for the woman who had been her guiding light in Clarence's absence.

'Who is it?' asked Grace. Suddenly, she was left breathless and hunched over; the effort of the question was too much.

Ruth did not answer. She chose to embrace her friend instead, for comfort's sake—her own as much as Grace's. The news would be dealt with in time. Ruth escorted Grace to the kitchen table. Both women sat, while the telegram lay flat on the table, her husband's name scrawled across the envelope.

'I cannot sit and look at this thing until Albert arrives home,' stated Grace and she picked up the pink paper and opened it.

COMMONWEALTH OF AUSTRLIA
POSTMASTER-GENERALS DEPARTMENT,
NEW SOUTH WALES
URGENT TELEGRAM

Dear Sir,
It is my duty to inform you that number 3281 Pte C A Miller 53rd Battalion was wounded in action 19 July 1916.

Lt Col Bradstreet
14th Bde

Ruth gasped while she breathed deeply; the sound of the cry that escaped contained both anguish and relief. Thankful that the telegram had not reported the death of her husband, she was distressed at the thought of Clarence stricken with pain in some foreign land.

'What does that mean, Grace?' she asked, desperate for comfort. 'Where is he?'

Grace didn't have the answers for Ruth; the telegram lacked any information other than the fact Clarence was wounded. How badly was he hurt? Was he in a hospital or on his way home? These questions had immediately sprung to mind but were left for the mind to ponder.

Grace cradled Ruth's head against her chest like she would hold Alice. The young mother, without a husband to lean on, cried tears of loneliness and despair. Grace's thoughts drifted to her eldest boy. Foreboding, heavy like oil, lay at the base of her stomach.

A week later the same boy dressed in black arrived at 96 Beattie Street and knocked on the door. He kept his head down and shifted his feet with nerves. The boy had simply held out his hand and waited for the telegram to be taken. To be the bearer of such news was too much for a child, too much for anyone.

Ruth placed her baby in its cot and suggested Grace sit at the kitchen table. She attempted to reciprocate the role of consoler as she walked calmly—while feeling weak. Ruth turned the handle and opened the door to meet the outstretched hand; the boy was an image in penitence. In an act of compassion, Ruth knelt and placed a hand on his rounded shoulder. She gently kissed him on the cheek and then whispered a soothing word.

The words, 'missing-in-action', fell over the room with that heavy fog, a chilling presence that had visited the house before. The mist carried the message to Grace in a way the telegram could not. Her son was dead. By the same feeling that told her she was to be a mother twenty-one years ago, she acknowledged its loss. She rose from the table in one uninterrupted movement and walked out the back door. Ruth felt helpless and let her go. She waited a moment and then walked to her bedroom to cradle her own son. She held him close and wet his face with tears.

***

England, Harefield Manor, August 1916
The English summer sun bathed Clarence with warmth in the picturesque village of Harefield Middlesex. Try as it may, the sun could not penetrate the chill that had settled within the wounded soldier since his experience in France. With a royal blue and beautifully decorated hard cover edition of *The Pageant of English Poetry* on his lap, closed, but held like one may hold a bible, Clarence held a fixed stare towards the tree-lined horizon.

He shifted uncomfortably in the rigid wheelchair that had been pushed to the lawn outside the manor-come-hospital and winced in pain as the partially healed wounds grabbed. His mobility was reduced to practically nothing, which had deepened his morose outlook. The discomfort from the bullet that struck and shattered the left side of his pelvis was insignificant compared to the desolation that had overtaken his soul. Surgery was performed in less than perfect circumstances in France, and the wound had become infected while en route to England. The follow-up surgery, a close-run-thing, had saved Clarence's life. The slow and agonising awakening that is the preface to the comprehension of lost mates, close mates, the experience of killing—regardless of the cause—was for Clarence a scorching of emotions: an entombing of treasures that had naturally blessed his person.

During his stay at Harefield Park, Clarence had learned the fate of the men in his section on that most horrific and senseless of nights. After being ordered to link up with their right flank, only David Smith had made it back from the men Atkins and he had left. Tom Baker had been taken prisoner, and Corporal Alfred Conner had scouted to the left of that precarious position and disappeared into the night, never to be seen again.

Tench and Cook, Birdie; Clarence had pictured their faces—so young, so ill-equipped for war. Tortured by feelings he could not interpret, Clarence sat in his chair while a gentle breeze brushed by. It carried cheerful and melodic songs from varying birds and was so at odds with the sounds that replayed inside his head. He slumped and thought about war, the war that for him barely lasted twenty-four hours. A day, which in his civilian life, could be the product of practically nothing. Yet it was enough, in a foreign land, to unleash man's most brutal and heinous traits upon inexperienced but brave men.

At night, Clarence would turn his head to see Sticks by his bedside. He would smile, pleased no doubt, that he had obtained some vitally important news pertaining to the brigade. Clarence would feel warm and comforted; he could sense his body move towards his mate, and then suddenly and violently he would gasp for air, as Jack's face melted into clay. The distortion of his face would bring Clarence to consciousness; covered in sweat, he would begin to cry. Confused and disorientated, Clarence would be tended to by a nurse, her bedside manner calm and reassuring.

The nurses were the same with all the wounded soldiers who

woke from a nightmare or instinctively took cover after a loud noise. The nurse's concerns, when raised with Doctors were often brushed to one side. One doctor, a major who had never seen active service, was overheard remarking to a nurse: 'that it was often the ones with less intestinal fortitude that reacted that way.'

Clarence had done his best to relieve any anguish Ruth or his parents may have felt on the other side of the world. They had no doubt received a telegram that he had been wounded in action, and he had heard they were blunt and without detail. By the kind-heartedness of a young Australian nurse from St Kilda—who had casually enquired if he had been on Lemnos Island—he was able to let his family know he was alive and well in England; they seemed the appropriate words. The telegram sent and a letter penned, Clarence was confronted with further doubts about his manhood; things that he had never had cause to examine. They unlocked apprehensions about returning home to the one he cherished.

During all of Clarence's days in recuperation, bearing the pain of his wound and the endeavours of the medical staff to get him mobile again, Clarence had not addressed what had happened to his brother. Conveniently for his state of mind, whether through hope or a sub-conscious act to relieve him of responsibility and therefore guilt, he had not been asked, nor had he spoken of his brave and dutiful sibling. Archie's decision to stay behind with the wounded Louth and provide cover while the remainder of men withdrew was, in Clarence's eyes, typical of his brother's protective qualities. The outcome for a man who tried to fight his way to safety in such a predicament could only result in death, but Clarrie would only allow the consideration of the more improbable. The likely scenario was destined to unhinge the man seated in a wheelchair. Clarence was aware that he was alive, not by his own gallantry, but by the selflessness of someone much like his brother.

EIGHTEEN

Sydney, Central Station, September 1916
Without acknowledging him, Frank took a seat next to Cliff on the timber bench in the covered concourse of Central train station. He stared straight ahead and waited. Without greeting or preamble Cliff spoke from behind a newspaper.

'At ten o'clock, take your empty crates to the side alley, as normal.' Cliff paused to cough; he rustled his paper before he continued. 'You will see another crate covered with blue canvas. Carefully, and I mean carefully, take the crate back into the pub. Inside is a leather satchel. Take the crate with satchel in it and place it on the trolley you use when doing the rounds.' Cliff ceased talking as a mother stopped in front of them to tie her young boy's shoelace. Finished with the task, the mother clasped the child's hand and hurried away for her train.

'Like usual, you will clean the dining room, as you do before each of their meetings, but this time you will leave the satchel under the table that sits against the far wall.'

Frank nodded to acknowledge his understanding of the instructions so far. He inclined his head a little as he did, indicating that he was impressed by Cliff's detailed knowledge of the dining room.

Like a good card player, Cliff picked up on Frank's body language, and smiled before he spoke.

'Don't worry, the long tablecloth will hide the satchel from view, and yes, you're not the only person that provides me with information. The meeting is at eleven o'clock. Finish the room as close to eleven as possible, but no later.'

Frank nodded.

'And Farnsworth is definitely going to be there?'

Frank nodded again. 'Charlie Watt will be on the door,' whispered Frank from the side of his mouth, 'and Tiger Black will be inside the room, just to the left of the door, so he can relay any messages to Farnsworth.'

'What else?'

'They will have a man out front,' replied Frank.

'Won't be a problem.'

'The rest of his crew will be around the table,' added Frank.

'A bonus, but it's Farnsworth, Watt, and Black we want,' said Cliff bluntly. 'As soon as you finish that room, make an excuse and go.'

'Done; meeting the grandmother off the train.'

'All right. Keep your nerve and go about your business as usual. Red bar towel on the empty kegs in the lane if anything is wrong.'

Frank nodded once more, stood, and walked away towards the Lions Gate Hotel.

✼✼✼

The sweet but bitter aroma of spilled beer, hours old and stuck to the tiled floor of the old pub, filled Frank's nostrils as he mopped the public bar area. He had started work after he had greeted the silver-haired manager Bob Bailey, who lived upstairs with his ageing wife. They maintained the pub during its dormant hours and looked after the occasional guest in the run-down rooms upstairs. Their constant presence also helped deter anyone stupid enough to rob Ned Farnsworth.

Was old Bobby Cliff's other informant? Nah, maybe, who-cares, Frank began to chide himself. *Keep your mind on what you're doing*

Frankie-boy. The satchel's interesting though, he added, while he danced silently with his mop.

The preceding weeks had taken a certain amount of discipline from Frank. Tired after a long week on Cockatoo Island, Frank would reluctantly wake at seven a.m. to be at The Lion's Gate by nine o'clock. Plenty of time, his mother would say as she cooked him breakfast. Grace was happy her son was trying to make extra money, and relieved he had put his troubles behind him. 'Don't want to be late because of a delayed tram,' he would say, to hide his real reason for the early departures—his meetings with Cliff Ryan.

Cliff had not let on much at each of their meetings. He had quietly listened to Frank's reports on the comings and goings of people, and put together the pieces of information from the young man before he asked a question, blunt and direct. The reluctant groomsman had been frustrated at times by the seemingly never-ending Sundays, but Frank's intuitive mind had been roused by the introduction of Cliff and the whiff of criminality that floated through every room and darkened corridor of the brick building that was the Lions Gate. To his immense satisfaction, his intuition had once again proven to be on-song. Cliff had revealed the Sunday before, that Charlie Watt and Tiger Black were the foot-soldiers who planted the bomb that killed his brother Don. Ned Farnsworth was the Sydney crime boss who had ordered it.

He stored his mop and bucket in the shed at the rear of the pub, and made his way into the cellar. The anticipation of revenge against those who had almost killed him had aroused his senses. His lust for vengeance grew as the hour drew near and flowed through his veins like a torrent. Almost sexual in its possessiveness, it augmented his feeling of strength and standing as a man.

Frank carried two at a time, and stacked the last of the empty timber beer crates neatly in the alley against the moss-streaked wall of the pub. He looked to his right and saw the crate with the blue tarpaulin on top of it, well hidden in plain view.

A quick glance down the alley towards Pitt Street told him there were no pedestrians, normal for a Sunday morning. He stepped back into the pub and was pleased to see that neither Bob, nor his wife, or anyone else was nearby, and the trolley that he used to carry cleaning equipment was unmoved from where he had left it. Frank moved calmly but with purpose and stepped back into the shaded, damp lane. He picked up the tarp-covered crate carefully, with his elbows splayed outward as shock absorbers.

Frank Miller placed the crate with its leather satchel on the bottom shelf of the trolley. He remembered Cliff's warning and wheeled the rickety vehicle steadily. He had deduced what the satchel was likely to contain, so he lifted the rear wheels when he crossed a threshold or change in flooring, to avoid any concussion.

When he reached the long table in the dining room, he transferred the crate as it was, not willing to risk contact with its contents. Frank sank to his hands and knees and gently pushed the package against the wall, safe from discovery by a polished leather shoe. He rose to his feet, wiped a bead of sweat on his forehead, and went about cleaning the dining room as normal for the congregation of shifty businessmen. He continued about his work and kept one eye on the clock that rested on the mantle of the fireplace. Frank felt everything was on track, but he was alarmed by the sudden appearance of Bob's wife Agnes with a large tray of sandwiches.

'Hello, Frank,' said Agnes. She was dressed in a long navy-blue dress and walked briskly with her platter of food and cutlery. 'Mr Farnsworth has requested some food for his meeting today.'

For reasons mostly to do with chance detection, Frank casually closed the distance between him and the elderly lady. He used a small brush and pan to pick up phantom pieces of dirt from the thick carpet.

'Now, Frank,' Agnes continued, as she placed the tray of sandwiches on the long table that hid his secret, 'I understand you have to leave early today.'

'Yes, Mrs Bailey.'

'Before you go, could you carry the large urn from the kitchen and place it on the table next to the sandwiches? Thank you.'

Agnes turned to leave and brushed against a knife that protruded from the tray upon the table. Caught in the fabric of her dress, the utensil spun from the tray to hit the carpet on its point. It was propelled under the table and lay hidden from view by the white cloth.

'Oh my,' exclaimed Mrs Agnes, 'how clumsy of me.'

Frank reacted quickly, and in a way expected of an employee or a young man in the presence of a lady. He bent on one knee and gently probed for the offending knife. Frank smiled and maintained eye contact with Agnes while he searched with an outstretched hand. Only marginally did he lift the hem of the linen, afraid his secret may be discovered.

'There you go, Mrs Bailey,' said Frank, as he produced the silver knife. 'Should I replace it with one from the kitchen?'

'No need, Frank, what they don't know won't hurt them,' she said with a smile and a pat on the hand; the irony of her comment was not missed by the masquerading groom.

Frank breathed a sigh of relief as Mrs Bailey left the room, and for a moment he allowed himself to consider her innocence or entanglement.

***

Men in groups of twos and threes filed down the hallway and into the dining room, while Frank, rag in-hand, leaned against the main bar. His hands were clammy with sweat as he wiped the dust from bottles of spirits that were displayed on shelving for customers.

Placing a bottle of Irish whiskey back on the shelf, Frank noted the time as 10.57 a.m. He removed his apron and placed it under the timber counter. He saw a pencil alongside a notebook and impulsively tore a page from it. He wrote down three words and folded the page twice, before he placed it in his pocket. Frank left the bar area and turned left down the hallway for the main doors.

'Hey, kid!' barked a voice from his right.

Frank stopped, his shoulders hunched.

'Yeh you, leaving eh?' asked Charlie Watt, already on guard at the closed dining room door, their meeting underway.

Frank turned slowly and swallowed in an attempt to contain his nerves. He tried to hide any visible eagerness, while his inner voice reminded him of Cliff's instructions.

'Knocking off,' said Frank quietly.

'And Bobby knows about this?' replied Watt. The hired muscle attempted to sound important. He was a bully and enjoyed the opportunity to assert some authority.

Eager to avoid any sort of confrontation that may delay his departure, Frank nodded meekly in the affirmative and allowed the moronic thug his moment. Frank was content with the knowledge of his imminent demise.

Happy with his little show of force, Watt returned to his position by the door without speaking to Frank. With indifference, he instructed the boy that he was free to go by a jerk of his head to one side. Frank turned on his heel to walk towards the front door and then against all reasonable judgement, he stopped. His ego took hold of him and unleashed his recklessness.

'I almost forgot,' said Frank as he strode towards the thug. 'Charlie, isn't it?'

'What… yeah, what's it to you, you little prick?' snarled Watt, his insecurities confronted and stroked at the same time. Pleased to be recognised, he thought the kid obviously admired him, but he was slightly alarmed at the boy's manner. It was completely at odds with the timid character who had nodded his head a few moments before.

Frank looked Charlie Watt straight in the eye. 'Mrs Bailey said this needed to be passed onto Mr Farnsworth.'

'Mr Farnsworth doesn't like to be interrupted early in his meetings,' replied Charlie, confused.

'That's what Mrs Bailey said.'

'Where's Mrs Bailey then?'

'How should I know, I'm just the groom.'

'That's right,' snapped Watt, 'a useless groom, I'll give it to Tiger in a minute.'

'You're the boss,' said Frank with a smile.

Frank turned and headed for the double doors that opened onto Pitt Street. He passed a cabinet on his left, full of sporting trophies and decorated with an oval shaped mirror. Frank saw Charlie Watt casually unfold the piece of paper to take a sly look, his forehead turned to rows of creased skin as the words—Don Hammer Ryan—created the tiniest of sparks in his inert mind.

***

Frank Miller left the pub without acknowledging the man on the front door and walked directly across Pitt Street and towards Belmore Park. He passed a man and woman with a suitcase atop a pram. The former Lions Gate Hotel groom failed to notice Detective William Tyrell as he strode by. The policeman stopped mid-stride and turned to watch the young man he once questioned.

Men mingled around the long table, adorned with sandwiches and fine china cups that waited to be filled with tea. They stood and made small talk and manoeuvred for their opportunity to impress their boss Farnsworth after his opening speech. Under the tablecloth and beneath a cloak of blue canvas, a metal frame sat snugly inside a brown leather satchel. Attached to the purposely built frame were two separate bundles of dynamite, five sticks in each, with fuses that protruded from each stack. Attached to the fuses was a cylindrical piece of lead pipe, its ends were sealed with thick wax plugs. Inside the lead tube cavity was a soldered piece of copper, it separated two substances from each other.

Tiger Black entered the room and handed a note to Ned Farnsworth. The crime boss excused himself from his associate and stepped to one side to ask Tiger where the note had come from. As he spoke, the sulphuric acid on one side of the copper disc continued its role and eroded the soft, thin metal barrier. Its demise would see the sulphuric acid meet and mix with the picric acid in the other chamber.

'Charlie just handed it to me, Mr Farnsworth,' said Tiger. 'I didn't ask him.'

'Well go and get Charlie and bring him to me, you dim-witted fool,' barked Farnsworth. His outburst turned a few heads, but they quickly returned to their original positions after they realised where the bellowing came from.

Ned Farnsworth unfolded the small piece of paper. The sulphuric acid had finished its work, and violated the copper's integrity. The sulphuric acid began to mix with picric acid and the reaction caused a silent but intense flame to develop that melted the wax ends of the lead tube. The flame escaped from its chamber and ignited the lacquer covered fuse connected to the dynamite.

Don Hammer Ryan. The sound passed Farnsworth's lips as a whisper; the name lingered in the forefront of his mind while its significance was considered. Black and Watts approached Farnsworth, but stopped abruptly as their boss's eyes turned bloodshot with rage. His mouth was a yawning cavity, with saliva that spray from his lips. A long and tortured sound emanated from his lungs that sounded like 'Symonds'. Confused, each man in the room focused his attention on an irate Farnsworth. The flame had now devoured the last of the water-proofed fuse and kissed the caked nitro-glycerine. The dining room was suddenly enveloped in a heat so intense that all Farnsworth saw was a white flash.

***

The roar of the explosion arrived at the head of a gusting breeze. Detective Tyrell instinctively clutched for his wife and baby boy, as pieces of brick and timber landed on the grass that surrounded them. Tyrell threw his wife to the ground and lay over her with their baby pressed between them. He tried to form a barrier between his family and the falling debris, almost one hundred and fifty yards from the brown leather satchel.

From the second floor of a terrace house on the opposite side of Belmore Park, Cliff Ryan smiled while he watched a dark grey cloud of smoke climb into the air. Underneath the dark column, flames leapt from the shattered remains of the Lions Gate Hotel. He picked up his coat and hat and exited the terrace building to turn north along Elizabeth Street and blend with the crowd.

Frank walked at an increased tempo since the sound of the explosion had reached his ears. He gasped when he looked over his shoulder to view the enormity of the blast, and a tingle ran down the back of his legs with the realisation of his proximity to catastrophe. The reality of the situation was driven home by the distant screams of innocent pedestrians, injured and maimed, caught up in the horrendous blast that he had helped facilitate. Frank crossed Elizabeth Street, and with no set destination—a detail he had overlooked—he rubbed the back of his hand where Mrs Bailey had touched him. But the cold and methodical voice that sometimes spoke to him from deep inside his mind quelled any misgivings that may have entered his mind.

Outside the hotel's burnt remains, a horse lay trapped by its harness. It was on its side and in agony. The poor animal kicked and thrashed against the leather straps of its harness. The carriage trace— shattered by the explosion—had pierced its flank and tore a gaping hole in its lung. It was allowed one last tortured whinny before it lay still. Detective Tyrell saw to the health of his wife and child before he moved closer to the blast site. His progress was halted by the intense flames that burnt what was left of the old pub and its neighbouring buildings.

William Tyrell's detective's instincts kicked in. He scanned the scene; his thought process continued to be interrupted by the vision of the young Miller boy in the park. *Was that a coincidence?* Good detectives never ruled anything out. He moved to the left, and was forced to wheel in a widening arc, as the heat intensified. Tyrell heard the bell of the horse-drawn fire brigade as it approached. It took on a more ominous sound as a dismembered arm caught his eye, scorched with tatted pieces of fine blue material fused to the burnt flesh. The question of how many bodies lay amongst the burning rubble sprang to the detective's mind. Small explosions that led to fires occurred in inner-city businesses regularly, especially those with kitchens. But Detective William Tyrell, as he stood amongst falling ash and thick smoke that burnt his eyes, was willing to stake his badge and occupation on the carnage spread before him being planned and calculated.

NINETEEN

Sydney, April 1917

With the assistance of a cane, Clarence limped down the gangway towards the same wharf he had departed from eighteen months ago, only now, he was laden with the guilt of returning home. The memories of his mates and their tortured ends carried on in his imprisoned thoughts.

He paused before he stepped onto the wharf. The temperate Sydney autumn sun provided a pleasant change from what he had been used to in England; it made the water appear to dance as he looked at familiar surroundings.

There wasn't a large crowd of people on the dock; the ship had transported mostly cargo. Any people on board were sailors, or like Clarence, unfit for active service. He spotted his wife before she saw him. Ruth stood by an empty pram and looked towards the stern of the ship. She pointed to the big steel object and explained what it was to the beautiful little boy she held in her arms. Mopped with dark wavy hair, his health shone through plump cheeks and eyes that sparkled; his grin revealed a solitary tooth.

Clarence stood for a moment to take in the most beautiful of scenes, a mother and her child, their interactions so in sync as to display nature in balance. The horrific events on the other side of the world so conflicted with the view before him as to make him question his own sense of reality. Clarence took a few steps towards her; he stopped as she turned. Their eyes met, there was a pause, and a moment's silence to give thanks for his return home before Ruth shuffled in her long skirt and closed the distance between them. She embraced Clarence and then pressed her face to his chest. Baby Reginald burst into tears at the sight of the stranger with the unfamiliar face shaded by a slouch hat.

'Hello, dear,' said Clarence warmly. He placed his hands on either side of Ruth's face and studied every feature. 'I've scared the poor little fella.'

'No, you didn't, that was my fault,' replied Ruth. She had rehearsed their reunion over and over while she lay awake at night. She had wanted Clarence's introduction to his son to be perfect. 'Reggie darling, this is your Daddy.' Ruth held the precious little boy out for Clarence to hold. The returned father was a little apprehensive at first but caved in after a little encouragement from Ruth.

Clarence dropped his kit bag to the ground and rested his cane against his waist before he took his son in his arms. Ruth's eyes looked down to settle on his walking aide, a pointed reminder of that day beside the rose bushes and all the emotions that had come, gone, and revisited since. She watched Clarence hold their child, and felt a happiness that had eluded her from the time he had boarded the transport for Egypt.

As Clarence smiled and played with their son, she noticed he had aged more than the time that had separated them. There was a more defined look to his features; maybe it was just loss of weight, but she thought not. It was more than that. His eyes, although happy, seemed to bear a heavy weight, but she pushed that from her mind and refocused on what was before her. She kissed her husband on the cheek. She was pleased they were together again. She had never been so naive as to think it would be the same as before—how could it? They were a family now, and that's all that mattered to Ruth.

'Clarence,' said Ruth, reluctant to interrupt the male bonding.

'Ruth! Sorry.'

'Don't be silly, I am so happy to see you with Reggie. I thought, seeing as it is still mid-morning, maybe we could sit in the park and take a moment before we head home.'

'Whatever you want.'

'I know you would love to see your parents, but I thought it would be nice to spend some time as a family, I've waited for this day for so long.'

'So have I,' replied Clarence. He passed his boy back to Ruth and his hip stiffened as he picked up his bag from the ground, it caused him to shuffle slightly.

The young family moved off to reclaim the baby's pram, which looked out of place by itself beneath the shadow of a large vessel. Her attention with Clarence, Ruth stopped suddenly as she bumped into another returned serviceman. She noticed the folded sleeve of his tunic and made a hurried apology.

For reasons he found hard to understand, Clarence would, without warning, experience a debilitating lapse of consciousness, when he would be momentarily transported back to the horrors of Fleurbaix. There was no structure to how it arrived; it was random and unforseen, but when it did strike—as it had in hospital and now on the wharf—it stiffened his body and left his thoughts in a whirlpool of darkness. Clarence had also seen the armless sleeve of a fellow Digger, and it took all his strength to rid his mind of the tormented images that flooded into his mind.

'Clarence, are you okay?' asked Ruth, confused at first and then concerned. 'Clarence darling.'

'Fine,' said Clarence startled, 'yes absolutely. Shall we?'

***

The Millers sat on a park bench and enjoyed the gentle sun. Baby Reginald tried his best to stand while he held his mother's knee, but he faltered and fell to the grassy earth with a thud. A quartet of seagulls, who spied a possible picnic, hovered above; they seemed to enjoy the entertainment provided by the young boy, while they waited to swoop.

On advice from Albert, Ruth did her best not to ask too many questions that related to Clarence's time overseas. Instead, she used the time to fill Clarence in on her own life: the pregnancy, her family, their baby's first twelve months, all of which Clarence was eager to hear. Clarence had not mentioned Archie, so she skirted the subject. Ruth admitted to herself silently that she wouldn't know what to say if Clarence was to mention his elder brother.

Alone with her husband and child, she took pleasure from the setting that had been present only in dreams. But Ruth knew—however uncomfortable it would be—that she must prepare Clarence for the house he would return to. For just as she had been mature enough to realise that her husband would be affected by his experiences, 96 Beattie Street had mutated with the forces applied by the world around them.

Ruth watched her husband and son play, and her mind drifted back to some of things she must now confront.

The impact of the telegram that informed the Millers that Archie was *missing in action* had been devastating. Grace had withdrawn somewhat; still the kind and loving mother, but mechanical in ways. Her eyes conveyed the realisation that she had lost her son. Her body language suggested that she would never come to terms with her loss. Albert had held on to hope as tight as his own nerves would allow. He wrote a letter a week to the Red Cross to search for information; a suppressed part of him dreaded a reply.

In October 1916, Albert Miller had answered a determined knock to the front door of his home. Confronted by the presence of Detective William Tyrell, Albert was asked to step to one side while two uniformed constables entered the house. A commotion followed, and Grace was left pleading, as Frank made a run for the backyard.

The scene ended in restrained convulsions from the youngest of the Miller men, under arrest for the planning and execution of the Lions Gate Bombing. Frank's face was crimson. Pinned to the ground by an unforgiving knee, it revealed panicked eyes that stared helplessly at a beaten figure—a mother collapsed under the weight of suffering.

The subsequent trial, where Frank, Ron Symonds, and Cliff Ryan, had stood accused of the murder of sixteen people, had tipped Grace Miller over the edge.

Against the wishes of her husband, Grace had attended the first day of Frank's trial in November of that year, and under immense stress, had taken a turn outside the courthouse. She had become disoriented and incoherent, and began to mutter at length; the only discernible sound was the name of her eldest son Archie.

Grace was admitted to the Sydney Sanitarium at Wahroonga and spent the best part of eight weeks as a patient in the private hospital. Ruth became little Alice's de facto mother during that time and continued in that role for all sense and purposes after her return. Both Albert and Ruth recognised Grace as a shell of her former self.

Ruth forced herself from her recollections, as her little boy warmed to the strange man in uniform. He took his hand off Ruth's leg and contemplated independence. 'Clarrie,' she said softly.

'Hang on, luv,' replied Clarrie enthusiastically. 'He's trying to walk.'

Ruth gasped, thrilled that her son might take his first steps in life in front of his father. Her joyous moment was interrupted by a pang of immature jealousy. *Luv? I don't recall being called luv before*, she said to herself. *Is that what the French women say or the English nurses?*

'Oh, almost mate,' exclaimed Clarence, proud of his son, even though his nappy-padded backside dropped to the grass after a few short seconds with no steps taken.

'Almost, little man,' cheered Ruth. She smiled at her two boys and internally wrapped herself over the knuckles for her petty thoughts;

she noticed that a vulnerability had crept into her life the more she loved.

'Sorry, Ruth, you were about to ask me something?'

Ruth sat upright, her eyes widened while she regathered her train of thought. 'Ah yes… letters. Did you get my letters?'

'Yes, of course, well some I suppose, depends on how many you wrote,' said Clarence with a smile.

'Hundreds.'

'Well, not all of them, but enough to keep me entertained. And you… did you receive mine?'

'Yes, I could recite most of them,' replied Ruth with a slight smile, Her recollections of Clarrie's letters summoned a question, hastily and thankfully retrieved before uttered, an enquiry about his much written-about friend, Sticks. For a man she had never met, the news of his death had brought on a surprised reaction when she had read the terrible words in a letter from Clarence while he recuperated at Harefield.

'That was one of the worst things you know… the mail,' Clarence offered, unwittingly understating his experiences abroad.

Ruth smiled, and then breathed deeply in preparation for the question she would ask next. 'Did you receive a letter from your father recently?' She knew by his lack of enquiry in certain matters that he hadn't, but she had to ask.

'No,' he replied. Clarence clapped his hands together in an effort to entice movement from Reginald, but the baby now played with dirt and had lost interest in the conquest of mobility. 'Don't worry; I'll remind the lazy bugger when we get home.'

'I don't know how to say this Clarrie… it's not easy. Your father tried to write, but obviously…'

'What is it Ruth?' said Clarence with sad calmness. 'Have you had word from Archie?'

That single sentence itself, along with a look, the desperate combination of a voice that yearned and eyes that longed, was enough to overcome Ruth with emotion. But she bit her lip, composed herself and continued.

'No, your father writes to the Red Cross weekly. It's...'

'So do I.'

'It's Frank, Clarence. Your brother Frank got mixed up with the wrong crowd,' Ruth paused for breath, and to gather her courage. Her speech gathered speed in its urgency to be done with the matter. This had flustered her, and alarmed Clarence. Ruth moved closer to her husband and then looked nervously away. Her anxious state had arisen from her desire to withhold the information and spare her husband the shock that the news would bring after so long away.

Ruth had watched Frank slowly change, and after what she had witnessed in the police station, she had received the revelation of the charges with dismay, but not complete surprise. His involvement was conceivable. She had glimpsed the sociopathic glare that he had worked so hard to conceal.

'Ruth,' said Clarence sharply. The tone of his voice drew her out of the silence that had grasped her. Her eyes were now watery and asked for forgiveness for the hurt she was about to impart.

'Frank's in prison,' she said.

Ruth looked at Clarence and watched the tide of confusion wash over him. She gently placed a hand on his cheek before she spoke again.

'This must come as a terrible shock and I dreaded telling you, but...'

'Prison, I don't understand Ruth,' said Clarrie. He appeared frailer than he had prior to the news, and Ruth watched a greyish pallour come over the returned soldier. A bubble of hatred for her incarcerated brother-in-law and the bane he had placed upon his family rose to the back of her throat.

Ruth held Clarence by the hand and hoped that her compassion could help Clarrie take in what would be unbelievable to a man whose last contact with his younger sibling was passing a football.

'Clarrie, this must seem like some sort of bad dream. I had hoped your father's letter had reached you and prepared you in some way, but I knew, almost as soon as I saw you, that it hadn't.'

'How could little Frank be in jail?' said Clarence in disbelief. 'He's a kid, what in God's name did he do?'

Ruth didn't answer the question directly; Clarence had dealt with enough loss of life, without hearing about his brother's contribution at the inner-city hotel.

'Frank,' Ruth sighed in exasperation. 'Frank got mixed-up... attracted to the wrong crowd. I don't know how, but he hid it well.'

'Hid it?'

'We… your mum and dad… me. We didn't know, or didn't notice until...'

'Until what?' shouted Clarence. He caught himself and turned slightly away and placed his head in his hands. Reginald added to the shift in mood by crying, startled by the harsh masculine voice that shattered the tranquil surrounds. 'I'm sorry, Ruth,' continued Clarence. 'I just can't believe what you have told me.'

'How could you? I didn't want this. I wanted our reunion to be for us—happy.' Tears forced their way from Ruth's eyes. 'And it was, but Frank, oh God,' Ruth held her own hands to her face. 'Your poor mother,' she said, and broke down. Clarence put his arm around her. He instantly felt hate for Frank, without learning of the depths to which his brother had sunk.

***

Re-adjustment to life as a civilian had come with its surprises during the first week home. On board ship, Clarence had imagined things would be as he had left them. He was the one that had undergone trauma, suffered loss and experienced hardship. But as he limped slowly along Darling Street, after meeting with his old boss, Mr

Blake, he realised the horrors in France had cast their shadow way beyond the battle field.

He was happy but saddened on the day of his return, when he had entered the kitchen and embraced his mother. Happy to be so blessed in being able to see her again, when so many he knew were deprived of the same joy, but saddened that he may have played some part in the tired and worn state in which she now appeared. Grace had become an old lady compared to the one he had left.

Albert had stood and shaken his hand when Clarence had released his mother. He was clearly grateful that he had made it home. Worry was etched across his forehead, and while he was the same Albert Miller, the fire that had shot from his eyes when Clarrie had announced he had enlisted was now extinguished.

He continued along the busy road and passed a middle-aged couple. The man noticed his cane and the returned from active service badge—issued by the Department of Defence—and nodded out of respect as they passed. Clarence had been advised to wear the badge, pinned to the lapel of his coat, after several returned Diggers had been accused of cowardice when they dressed in civilian clothes. Clarence stopped to admire some delicately crafted toys in a shop window just three doors down from the Reynolds bakery. He thought of Alice. He smiled and remembered how she had waited patiently in the corner of the kitchen to be greeted by her brother. She twisted back and forth to make her dress swirl, while she clutched the doll—held with love—which Ruth had given her almost two years ago. When Clarence had bent down, arms outstretched with a smile, Alice had hesitated a moment and then ran towards Clarrie to embrace him as children do, without restraint or embarrassment.

Although he had returned to shocking news, Clarence was glad to be home. The tale of Frank and his transformation was told in full by his father over several bottles of beer in the backyard of the Miller's home the night after he had returned. Clarence had sat in silence while his Dad relayed what he knew, right back to Frank's fight with Jimmy Taylor, which Albert surmised must have been the start of things. His father made a soft enquiry about his time overseas. He asked his second eldest son if they looked after him. The broadness of the question allowed Clarrie to give a quick nod, while he suppressed a vision of Joseph Finch, his face torn apart by a German bullet; the effect of the ale had helped the image fade away into the ground at Clarrie's feet. Albert poured another glass of beer for his son and changed the subject. He told tales of his little grandson and his temper tantrums, which brought smiles to both of their faces.

Clarrie realised he had been staring through the same window for some time now, so he turned to move. A motor vehicle passed and then suddenly backfired. Clarrie's expression turned from a dazed smile to one of complete shock, as he drew himself quickly against the wall of the toyshop; its brick and mortared face felt a lot like mud-encrusted hessian. As the echo of the bang subsided, Clarrie regained his thoughts. He limped away hurriedly with his head down and teeth clenched, amongst sly stares and whispers. A knot that tasted like Flanders' clay seemed wedged in his throat. From the window of his bakery, Harry Reynolds watched the sorry scene unfold, and wondered what the future held for his daughter and her husband.

Part Two

TWENTY

Denman Hill, Gilmurra, February 1922
Ruth wiped the last of the plates dry. She stopped to scratch a small piece of egg yolk that she had missed with her fingernail, before she placed the plate in the cupboard. She looked out the kitchen window, and her spirits were raised as a dark bank of cloud, thick like a puffed-out chest, formed in the west. It rolled east, towards the tree-lined ridge that rose above the paddocks to the rear of their home, and the property they had named Denman Hill, after Ruth's mother's hometown. *The rain will be welcomed*, she thought. The paddocks, although there was some feed, were scorched yellow-brown by the intense January and February sun. A gentle fall of life-giving water would bring that invigorating smell of moisture on dry grass that gave Ruth comfort.

She watched the hens scratch for whatever they could in the dusty yard, and she felt happy. Ruth had begun to feel at home on the three-hundred-acre farm, with all its trials and hardships, entwined with reward and satisfaction. Maybe it was her mother's country roots, but the fresh air and its contrasts of brisk winter mornings and hot summer evenings, painted with breathtaking sunsets of rich and ever-changing colours, appealed to her nature.

Ruth heard the baby stir, so she moved quietly to poke her head around the bedroom door. Summer days were not conducive for baby's naps, but little Emily had a pleasant nature and could handle the irritation. She was mellower than her abrasive older brother Reggie, who, at five years of age, had started school, much to his annoyance. Clarence worked hard to make the best of things, and he dealt the best he could with his family's tragedies. He was embarrassed by being forced to receive help from Ruth's parents during the drought. The small block and their lack of capital brought them to the brink of ruin during that time, but some fortunate decisions he had made in the purchase and sale of stock when the drought had finally broken in 1921 had seen them keep their heads above water.

Determined to repay every penny he had borrowed from the in-laws, Clarence devoted his energies to the farm. There were moments where he would be lost from Ruth and his surrounds and stare into oblivion, entranced and immobilised by the horrors of war. There was even the odd occasion when a whiskey bottle would be found drained of its comfort, but they were becoming less of an issue, or less noticeable. Ruth had hoped the addition to the family of a little girl would re-ignite some of the spontaneous and dreamy moments that Clarence had once enjoyed.

Change and uncertainty were not things that had ever scared Ruth. But she could admit it had not been easy to move from suburban Sydney to rural New South Wales, leaving friends and family and the security of what she knew. It was a move that was forced upon them. The familiarities that one may think would help repatriate a returned serviceman: job, family, acquaintances, had all conspired to work against Clarence and his efforts to put the war behind him.

Occurrences, like the day when he had looked for cover after the motor vehicle had backfired in Darling Street, had left him mortified. He had become withdrawn; his reactions to mundane questions by co-workers at *The Observer* and family alike were abrupt and dismissive at times. So unlike the person his associates remembered and cared for. They would replace their look of shock with one of pity and turn to walk away, the question left for another time. Their benevolence after his release of frustration deepened his insecurities and his fragile state. The tentacles of his most dreadful experiences anchored themselves to become part of who he now was. Without a way of shifting the feelings that plagued his existence, Clarence was trapped between conflicted emotions.

Ruth supported him by being there when she was needed. When she knew, by instinct, that words couldn't remedy, only space, she would melt into the background to observe from a distance. She would follow with a gesture to comfort; her timing with such things was almost always perfect.

Her devotion was never tested, but her understanding of her husband was sometimes blurred when she witnessed him turn from the son she knew he adored. The little boy would be crest-fallen. Innocent of his father's troubles, he would grasp for the trouser leg he relied on for balance as it moved away.

While they lived in Balmain, evenings at the Imperial had become more frequent for Clarence. More frequent because they had never happened prior to the war, more telling, not because he frequented the hotel nightly, but because his visits were more about expunging memory than socialising. The alcohol only proved to weaken resolve—not cure trauma.

Ruth's experience with drunken men was non-existent, and the obnoxious and mumbling mess that would present itself at the front door added to the pressures that had built around them. She did not want to burden her parents or Clarence's, and often vented her frustrations by writing in her journal; the faintly lined sheets of paper provided a form of counsel without imparting judgement.

Her love for Clarence was unshakeable. She thought constantly of a way to bring balance back to their life, and was open and willing to look at anything. Ruth remembered how a possible solution arose one Sunday morning, as the rare sound of large raindrops rang against the corrugated iron roof of Denman Hill, slowly at first and then with a nice constant rhythm. The hens scurried for cover and their frantic sprint brought a smile to Ruth's face.

Ruth's father and mother had suggested it. They showed her a full-page advertisement in the newspaper that related to the Soldier Settlement Scheme. Ruth was at first against the idea, but as her father spoke over Sunday tea, she had warmed to it. The town of Gilmurra had sounded very familiar, as Mr Reynolds had read the notice from the Minister for Lands, Mr W.G. Ashford.

Mr and Mrs Reynolds had discussed the opportunity and had no doubt planned how they would approach Ruth with the idea. They were desperate not to offend Clarence with the idea, and wanted to avoid any suggestion that he wasn't assimilating to civilian life, but they were also aware that a continuation of things as they were would eventually erode what he and Ruth had.

Ruth had been struck with the obvious hurdles of how they would afford the five percent deposit and subsequent instalments that attracted five percent interest per annum. There was also the fact that neither of them was skilled in farming. But Ruth was satisfied when her parents said they would back them financially while they got established. Ruth's mother also added that on top of the scheme's training program, she thought it would be wise if Clarrie spent time on a relative's property at Merriwa, near her hometown of Denman.

Roused by Emily's cries, Ruth made her way to the baby's bedroom and picked her up. She cradled the six-week-old baby against her chest and gently rocked her back and forth.

'It is only rain, little one,' said Ruth softly. 'It's a strange sound but very welcome.'

Sitting in the wooden rocking chair by the window, Ruth un-buttoned her blouse and removed her breast to feed and calm her beautiful little girl. She sang to her child softly when a thought occurred.

'I just realised, Emily,' she said while she gently stroked the baby's forehead. 'You're a country girl, born and bred.'

As the baby lay content in her arms, Ruth was hypnotised by the continuing sound of rain. She drifted back to Balmain; the excavation of memories gave her strength as they reminded her of how far they had come.

Clarence had greeted Ruth's proposal with little enthusiasm, and while he was dissatisfied, and hamstrung by meaningless assignments at the job he once loved, his response sounded like a man who would prefer to suffer what he knew rather than take a chance on fulfilment. It was unlike the Clarence that had ordered bread with Keats tucked under his arm.

Ruth had tried to add weight to her idea but got the opposite result when she had mentioned that the properties in question were near the town of Gilmurra. She told Clarence that she remembered Gilmurra from mentions in his letters of the hometown of a man in his section. Ruth was disappointed and deflated when her husband sank into the ugly hole which left his body devoid of warmth when she mentioned the man's name. When he returned from the Imperial Hotel incapable of speech, she remembered how she had cried into her pillow and felt almost as alone as those nights when Clarrie was overseas. With the flannel pillow case clenched inside her fist, she had vowed not to give up on her husband. She whispered *How do I love thee, let me count the ways*, and cried some more.

Several weeks later, Clarence returned home from work as normal, and unexpectedly, while he made a pot of tea, announced that they should apply for the block of land she had mentioned. A change would do them good, he said. A short time after, Ruth had learnt of the real motivation behind Clarrie's change of heart. He had been fired by his boss. Clarrie had struck a fellow journalist in full view of the office staff, something Mr Blake had said he couldn't tolerate, not on top of Clarrie's continual anti-social behaviour. Ruth began to ask Clarence why he hit the man, but stopped short. She told herself that it didn't really matter. She had got the change she was looking for, and maybe it was meant to happen this way.

Clarence was relieved Ruth hadn't pushed the subject. She had accepted his brief statement of what *had* occurred in a calm manner. Clarrie didn't want to lie to his wife; she had a broad and accepting mind and he held her on a pedestal. But no one, not even Ruth, would accept that Lieutenant Sharp, the man who had pushed Clarence into battle at gunpoint, had shouted and yelled at him until he obeyed his order to hit his fellow journalist.

As Ruth placed Emily back in her cot, she heard the door to the side of the house bang shut. She walked out to investigate, and was greeted by Alice, her wet hair in tangled strands over her forehead. She stood in the centre of the kitchen and smiled cheekily before she produced two loaves of bread from under her coat that she had somehow kept dry all the way from her job at the Gilmurra Bakery.

'Well done, Ally.'

'Mr Duncan said I could bring them home.'

'He's a nice man, your boss,' replied Ruth. 'You're early, even for a Saturday?'

'Got a lift with Mr Adler in his lorry.'

'I thought you liked riding your bike in the rain,' teased Ruth.

'Is M awake?' said Alice. She referred to her niece, who she had tagged with 'M', short for Emily.

'Just gone to sleep, but you'll see her soon enough,' said Ruth. She knew how much Alice looked on her baby as a little sister.

'What about Reggie, is he with Clarence?'

'Little Reginald is playing over at the Donagheys'.'

Ruth smiled, and suggested to Alice that she take a seat while she dried her hair with a towel produced from a stack in the walk-in closet that adjoined the kitchen. She stood behind her husband's youngest sibling and gently massaged her hair; Ruth felt pride and admiration for the young lady who had lost so much, but remained so full of life. She had left school before Christmas and got a full-time job at the Gilmurra Bakery. She had told Ruth that she wanted to pay her way. Ruth felt she understood why.

From the time Grace was admitted to the private hospital during Frank's court-case, Ruth had been Ally's mother in everything but name. When Clarrie and Ruth had announced they had been successful in securing a Soldier Settlers' block, Albert had approached Ruth a day or so later, and asked if they would take Alice with them.

Ruth remembered Albert looking at the ground, as he explained how he thought it would be in Alice's best interest. 'A chance,' he had said, 'with my wife not well, for my little girl to have the guidance of a strong and loving woman in her life.' That compliment floated into Ruth's mind every now and then, never more so than on the train to Sydney for Albert's funeral in the summer of 1920. Tears streamed down her face as she rocked with the motion of the locomotive, her thoughts with her father-in-law, who had been through so much. His life had ended with a sudden and massive heart attack; his selfless request had reminded her of how complete the love of a parent for their child could be. Willing to forgo his own emotional needs, he sought a better life for his daughter. He knew that although he loved his children without question, he couldn't, through the demands of his own work and caring for Grace, provide the attention a young child needed.

Ruth cut Ally a slice of bread from one of the loaves she brought home and smeared it with butter and a generous amount of blackberry jam.

'There you go, Ally,' said Ruth, 'eat that, while I get a brush to attack these knots in your hair.'

Ally picked up the large slice of bread and watched Ruth as she disappeared down the hall. She savoured the sweet tasting jam but looked towards the hallway long after Ruth had disappeared. The image of the striking woman with dark-wavy hair had replaced that of her own mother a long time ago, even before they had boarded the train for Gilmurra when she was only twelve.

***

The perfume of peaches, mixed with lemons and a hint of oranges, carried on the light breeze from the small orchard at Denman Hill. The scent relaxed Clarrie as he worked. He was mindful of keeping busy, and felt physical work provided him with the best defence against bad memories. They were mostly suppressed, but always capable of ambush.

The sense of smell can be a powerful conjurer, and although he passed through the fragrant yard daily to enter the shed that sheltered his flat-bed truck, the scent of lemon—the fruit having its origins in grafts taken from the family home—had transported him back to Beattie Street on this particular day, suddenly and without warning.

When his mother died, a week exactly after Albert passed, it seemed almost surreal for Clarence and Ruth. They had received the news via a constable who had knocked on the front door of the family's Beattie Street home. Clarence hadn't known this, but the constable was one of the men who had wrestled his younger brother to the ground in the back yard when he had attempted to evade arrest. The constable had looked even more contrite than a deliverer of bad news might, aware of the troubles this ordinary suburban family had been through. He solemnly passed on the news that a woman who bore his mother's likeness had been found in Mort Bay, unconscious, and later to be pronounced dead. A photo of a man in uniform was found in her clothing.

Clarence had scoffed at first and told the constable that his mother was sound asleep in her bedroom. But when the constable had produced a photo of Archie in front of a pyramid in Egypt, he had collapsed. At some time during the night, Grace Miller had quietly left a sleeping house. She walked the considerable distance to the water's edge, and calmly stepped into Mort Bay as if she was strolling into the arms of her husband.

Clarence and Ruth had told Alice that her mother had drowned in an accident. She had slipped on the timbers of the wharf and struck her head. Then, through whatever money they could muster and the charity of St John's, they buried Grace Miller next to Albert.

Clarrie felt a deep sadness at the death and sad end of such a wonderful woman. He remembered how he had sat in the kitchen of 96 Beattie Street, feeling cold in a house that was once radiant with the love and happiness created by his deceased mother. In all his grief, Clarence realised that it was no longer the home it had been. His young sister ratified his feelings when she entered the kitchen from the backyard and said that she would like to go home now.

Clarence had put his wife, son, and young sister on a train for Gilmurra the next day, while he stayed to meet with a solicitor and estate agent. He had decided to put the Beattie Street home up for sale, but before he left for Gilmurra himself, Clarence had one more thing he needed to do. With the assistance of Detective Tyrell, Clarence visited his brother Frank in jail.

Owing to the severity of his crime, Frank had not been allowed to attend his father's funeral, so when Clarence sat down on a wooden stool in front of a steel mesh grille, they were laying eyes on each other for the first time in five years. Clarence did not recognise the man that sat on the other side of the cage. Some people say that, regardless of physical change, the eyes usually give a clue to the person's identity after long absences, a glint or a look, something to spark a forgotten memory, but for Clarence Miller—there was nothing.

He looked at Frank, and dark emotionless eyes stared back at him. He realised he felt intimidated and uncomfortable in his presence. The dislike that he felt towards his brother was allowed to rise and form as anger, with the security of the steel screen between them. The animosity that passed from Clarence was reciprocated by Frank. His brother had not seen fit to contact him since his return from France.

Dressed in trousers and a singlet, Clarence could see how his body had been affected by five years in prison. Frank's muscles were tight and lean from hard work, but lacked mass from the poor prison diet. His shoulders carried several criss-crossed welts, probably the result of prison guard discipline, or territorial struggles with inmates.

How do I look to him, Clarence thought before he passed on the news of his mother's death. The words became a lump that formed in his throat. His emotions were still so raw, so he paused before he continued. His brother lit a smoke—his face did not show a trace of feeling or emotion. Frank took a long drag on his cigarette and then stared at Clarence while he exhaled. He pinched the smouldering end of his smoke between thumb and forefinger—for use a later time—and then stood and turned from Clarence, without a word uttered. He took the few short paces to bang on the steel door that had kept him secure in his cubicle while he received his visitor. Within seconds, a guard unlatched the heavy bolt that barred the door, opened it, and held Frank at gun point, while another guard shackled his hands and feet.

Clarence had witnessed horrors in France he hadn't thought possible, but he was left aghast by the demeaning way in which Frank was handled by the guards. Within the dark and damp walls of the penitentiary, Clarence's brother, whom he had last seen as a boy, was being restrained like an animal. All Clarence wanted to do was leave Sydney and get back to Ruth and his home near Gilmurra. *But Frank is an animal*, he thought, as the guard finished his job with the chains—to society, and uncomfortably, to him. Whether in a gesture to confirm his brother's opinion, or through an expression of violent grief, Frank unleashed a vicious head-butt to the unarmed guard's nose. Almost instantly Frank received a powerful blow to the abdomen with the stock of the armed guard's shotgun, it was followed by a jab with the same weapon to the side of the head as he doubled over in pain.

Knowing it was likely he would never see Frank again; Clarence left his brother as ashamed as when he last saw Archie, only this time he felt a sense of anger that he had been burdened by Frank's choices. He reassured himself that he didn't have anything to do with his brother's derailment. Maybe that was what made him feel guilty. He walked away from the menacing building with its high-bricked walls, thinking at the time he had left the worst behind him. Clarence had failed, and would continue to fail, to acknowledge the one thing that would affect him the most.

Now, Clarence leaned against the bonnet of his truck and waded through his reflections, while he slowly turned a hammer in his hands. His thoughts laboured under the weight of regret and pulled at his being like mud in a murky swamp. Hoisted from the past by a cockatoo's screech, Clarrie left the shed through the front door. It brought him into open air at the side of the house, and left the spellbinding lemon trees to themselves.

***

Ruth and Clarence had decided to take Emily into town the following Friday. Clarence needed to pick up some fence wire for the creek paddock, and Ruth wanted to show off her baby girl while she got a few items for the kitchen. Her visits to Gilmurra were less frequent since the birth of their second child, so Ruth suggested to Clarrie that they take the chance to have a counter meal at the Royal Hotel. They could fill the afternoon with a stroll before they picked up little Reg from school and Ally from work.

Clarence and Ruth entered the lounge of the hotel with their cumbersome pram and selected a table in the corner.

'This will be nice, Clarrie,' said Ruth. 'We haven't done this for a long time.'

'A long time,' agreed Clarrie. 'You wouldn't have fitted through that door before Emily was born.'

'Thanks very much,' whispered Ruth. She feigned offence but was happy to see her husband in a playful mood.

'I saw George Phillips up the street while you were in the store,' continued Clarrie.

'The school principal?'

'Yes, he had a word to me about Reggie.'

Ruth sighed. 'What's he done now?'

'Nothing serious really,' replied Clarence with a grin. 'Being disruptive… pulled a girl's pig-tails. Do you think I'm tough enough on him?'

'I'm not sure,' said Ruth. She looked perplexed, as if the thought of disciplining her child had never crossed her mind. 'He has a short fuse, I'll admit that, but isn't he just like most other boys?'

'He takes after you in that department, my dear,' said Clarrie. An accusation made with fondness.

'Hardly. I never got into trouble.'

'Exactly. I will go up and order, shall I?'

'Excellent. Roast lamb for me please, Clarence.'

Clarence waited behind another customer at the small counter that separated the public bar from the lounge area. The barrier allowed Jack Drummond to take meal orders while he kept an eye on the main bar and the impatient drinkers. An unsatisfied thirst was enough reason to tempt the patron to try his luck up the road at the Orient Hotel.

While he waited patiently, Clarrie looked through to the public bar and saw lawyer and returned serviceman, Arthur Atkins. Atkins enjoyed a glass of ale on a Friday afternoon before he sat down to a counter meal with his father James, also a lawyer, and head of their burgeoning law firm. The father and son met every Friday to go over their business, and Clarrie cursed that he had forgotten that fact before he had agreed to Ruth's request.

Clarence decided to look at the chalkboard menu to avoid contact, but Arthur had already spotted him. The fellow veteran smiled warmly and raised his glass to greet Clarrie, but the former private felt anxious, and returned an inadequate nod and a grin that looked more like a grimace. Not perturbed by the awkward response, Atkins handled the rebuff with grace, as he always had since Clarence and his family had been gladly received into the small community, almost four years ago.

Despite his impoliteness, there was no dislike on Clarence's part towards the former Lance Corporal. A lesser man than Arthur would be forgiven if he had taken offence and given up on Clarrie long ago, but Atkins had remained compassionate to what he saw in Clarence, solid and unwavering in his politeness. The irony was that Clarence held Atkins in the highest of regard. He had saved Clarence's life after all, an act that allowed him to return to Australia and reunite with his family. But instead of humbling gratitude, Clarence was beset with guilt each time he laid eyes on Arthur. The charge which Clarrie laid upon himself was never clearly defined, for to assign his reactions to Arthur to a particular event would in turn, make that event real. And there was an understanding deep in Private Miller's sub-conscious that couldn't allow that to happen.

Clarence placed his order and sat back at the table with Ruth; he did his best to resist a strong urge to make up an excuse and leave. Ruth noticed the difference in his complexion, and the stiffness to his posture as soon as he sat down. She chose to avoid confrontation and talked merrily about any and every topic she could think of until Clarence rode out whatever had taken hold of him.

***

After a pleasant meal, Clarence and Ruth took a walk, with Emily sound asleep in the pram. They left the main street and walked through the park to the Tilcan River. Its waters glistened under sunlight, filtered through a canopy of majestic gum trees, silky oaks and willows. Dollar birds and Rainbow Bee Eaters called from the safety of the lofty branches; their songs blended with the relaxing sound of the water that raced over ancient rounded stones. Ruth smiled, and thought it the perfect place to be on a warm summer's afternoon. It was moments like this that gave Ruth confidence in a bright future.

'Clarrie,' said Ruth as she reached into a canvas pouch at the rear of the pram to produce a large wrapped parcel.

'What's that Ruth?'

'A present for Reggie.'

'Do you think he deserves one after what Mr Phillips said?' replied Clarence.

'It was a bit of an impulse, and I know we can't afford impulses,' confessed Ruth, as she held up her hand in defence, 'but I haven't bought him anything in ages, and… well, I thought it would be nice if you gave it to him.'

Clarence didn't speak at first. He was struck by the truth in his wife's statement, and it made his mind trek over images of the last two years. They hadn't bought him anything; things were tight, but maybe he had been too frugal with his money.

'Yes, that would be nice, Ruthy. I will give it to him when we get home.'

Clarence gently placed Emily back into her pram, and suggested to Ruth that they should make their way to Reggie's school if they wanted to be there when classes ended.

***

Young Mathew Adler leapt from the back of the Millers' truck before it had come to a complete stop outside his family's front gate, the farm being the one that neighboured the Millers to the north. The energetic lad waved to Reggie and Alice, and then thanked Mr and Mrs Miller, as he began to jog up the road that led to his home.

'That boy never stops running,' remarked Ruth to Clarrie. 'Bye,

Mathew, say hello to your mother,' she shouted after him. But the lad was too far away to hear.

Clarence turned his truck around and headed south back to Denman Hill, having made the last of the drop-offs for the afternoon. They had already dropped off Wally Tunstill and his sister Anne, as well as Peter Donaghey, who was in the same grade as Reggie; the Donaghey's property bordered their own to the south. It was Peter's father Bill who had taught Ruth to ride when they first arrived. Clarence had been introduced to horses when he was young, but was given a much-needed refresher course while living with Ruth's relatives in Merriwaa. Bill never said anything to Clarence, but he was in no doubt who was the better rider. 'Maybe it was my skill as a teacher,' he would joke with Ruth.

After they cleared the truck of all the purchases made in Gilmurra, Clarence joined his son at the kitchen table. He watched the little boy as he drank a glass of milk; he had the dark hair of his mother but features and eyes like his own. Clarence smiled as the lad swung his legs back and forth; they weren't quite long enough to reach the floor.

'Reg,' said Clarence.

'Yes, Daddy.'

'Come with me, mate, I have a surprise.'

Clarence stood up and waited for Reggie to follow.

'What's a surprise?'

'You'll see,' laughed Clarrie. 'It's in your bedroom.'

Clarrie was aware that Reggie was like him in many ways; he could be quite soft and would often need to be cajoled into trying something new or comforted back to sleep after a nightmare. Ruth had bought the present to help alleviate his broken slumber. But Reg also had splashes of his mother in him; sometimes restless, he found it difficult to sit still for periods of time, which regularly saw him get into trouble in class. He also possessed a temper.

Clarence swooped Reggie up into his arms as they entered the bedroom and sat his son on the bed. He turned to hand him the wrapped package from its hiding spot on top of Reggie's dresser.

'A present!' exclaimed Reg.

'Yes, mate, open it.'

Reggie tore at the wrapping and pulled out a light brown fluffy bear, with dark brown beady eyes and floppy ears.

'It's a grizzly bear,' said Reg.

'No, not a grizzly bear,' laughed his father. 'This is a very special bear… a happy bear, with magical powers.'

Reggie looked at the bear, then up at his father and back to the bear. He pulled the soft toy close to his own face to peer deeply into its eyes. Clarence responded and put his arm around Reggie's shoulder.

'You see, Reggie,' said Clarence softly. He gently took the bear from his son and placed it on his own lap. He turned to face the intrigued little boy. 'This bear… his name is Harvey. Harvey the Happy Bear.'

Reggie looked at his father with eyes wide open.

'Harvey has magical powers,' continued Clarrie, 'to make you feel happy when you get a little sad or frightened.'

Ruth watched from the hallway and smiled as her husband mesmerised Reggie with his tale, so much like the man she first saw in her family's bakery.

'Do you like him?' asked Clarrie.

Reggie nodded his head and stretched out his arms; Clarrie held the bear out and then withdrew it again.

'There is a trick though, Reggie,' said Clarence. 'Harvey's magic only works if you hug him. Do you think you can make his magic work?'

'Yes, Daddy,' whispered Reg. He took the bear from his father and held it close to his chest. His dad was right, thought the little man, as dads always are. Harvey was magic.

'Daddy,' said Reg as his father rose to leave the room.

'Yes mate.'

'Does Peter have a bear?'

'I'm not sure, Reg, maybe,' said Clarence. His heart broke for his son. *Does it start this early, when kids worry what other people think*? he wondered. Clarence knelt down in front of the boy and said calmly. 'Do you like the bear?'

'Yes, Daddy.'

'Well, I won't tell Peter or anyone else that you have a bear called Harvey, if you don't. How's that sound?'

Reggie smiled in acceptance of his father's solution, and they went back into the kitchen with Harvey on the pillow at the head of Reginald's bed.

TWENTY ONE

Denman Hill, March 1924

Clarence and his guest shuffled through the kitchen door; both men were pleased to escape the cold, wind-whipped rain. They removed their oilskin coats and felt hats and placed them on the rack just inside the door. As they chatted away, Clarence and his young companion received a penetrating glance from Ruth; she drew attention to the mud-covered boots still on their feet.

'Sorry, Ruth, said Clarence, 'I was just taking them off.'

'I'm sure you were, Clarrie,' Ruth replied sarcastically, with a hint of a smile.

'Sorry, Mrs Miller,' said the nervous young man, doubled over as he tried to remove his footwear.

Ruth glared at her husband; she tried to remind him of the common courtesy of introducing a person that your wife has never met.

'Oh,' said Clarrie, startled. 'Ruth, this is Norman Clark. Norman, this is my wife Ruth.'

'Hello, Norman, it's a pleasure to meet you… and I was only joking about the boots.'

'No, she wasn't,' whispered Clarrie.

Norman smiled at Mr Miller's joke but felt a flush of warmth run to his cheeks. Mrs Miller's attractive features caught him off-guard.

Norman was only twenty years old, and he saw Clarence as being a fair bit older than the eight years that separated them. Norman was naive about what the strain of war and drink can do to a man's appearance. 'Hello, Mrs Miller.'

'That little fellow stuck to his mother's leg is Reggie,' continued Clarrie, 'and the little one on the rug is our Emily, or M, as we call her.'

Norman stood humbly at the door, his hair slightly wet on the ends. It gave him a sort of schoolboy look, and Ruth surmised that he was a decent young man.

'Come in, Norman, sit down,' said Ruth warmly. 'I will make a fresh pot of tea. It looks like you both need it.'

'Thank you, Mrs Miller, that would be nice, 'said the young man. 'The rain is needed, but it is unseasonably cold out.'

Ruth began to suggest to Norman that he call her Ruth instead of Mrs Miller, but she stopped herself. She realised that the soothing sound of Mrs, spoken by a visitor, was agreeable; it gave life order and made their house feel like a home.

'Clark …' said Ruth slowly, which hinted at the question to come. 'We are only relatively new here, Norman, so I don't think I know your family.'

'Norm's from Albury, Ruth,' blurted Clarrie.

'Really? I've never been to Albury but I have heard it is very nice.'

'In between Albury and Howlong actually,' said Norman, 'but I always say Albury, it's easier.'

'So, your family has a property?' asked Ruth while she placed a steaming pot of tea on the table. 'Milk?'

'Yes please, no sugar thanks. My family has a property, but I am the second youngest of eight, so...'

'My goodness, eight,' gasped Ruth.

'Yes, six boys and two girls,' replied Norman. He smiled broadly at the recollection of his family, and thought how at home he felt, in conversation around a kitchen table with the Miller family.

'Norman came out to give some advice on cropping,' said Clarrie. 'Thinks we might be able to increase our yield and have a bit left over to sell after we've baled hay and kept some grain to sow.'

'Sounds interesting,' said Ruth. She was enjoying the company of the polite young visitor and the positive effect he seemed to have on Clarence. It was a welcome change from the cantankerous person that had moped around the farm for the last few days, after he had spent a whole day and part of the night at the Royal.

With beer and whiskey in him, Clarence's manner had been cold and stern when he arrived home. The coldness had quickly turned to heat when he slapped Reg across the back of the ear for the most trivial of matters—an uneaten crust. Young Reggie—hurt and afraid—ran, while his mother remained shamefully silent. The boy's room had become a refuge. He would hide beneath the cover on his bed and quietly talk to Harvey the bear, a habit that also irritated Clarrie. He now thought his son was too old for soft toys.

'I am not sure how much help I will be,' replied Norman modestly.

'Are you joking, Norm, you've been great,' said Clarrie enthusiastically. 'I'm glad you persuaded Thomas to let you come out. He'll have to watch himself, old Tom. Young Norm might take over,' finished Clarrie, with a prod and a wink to his young friend.

Ruth lifted the teacup to her mouth and paused. A thought occurred to her, and she smiled. 'I am sure Norman will be of great help to you Clarence,' said Ruth. Her smile was directed at her husband's harmless ignorance; the smile became a broad grin.

'Yes, Ruth, I agree.'

A pause in conversation was interrupted by the sound of Norman standing abruptly. Ruth laughed silently at her husband's inability to see the real motivation for Norman's visit on a Saturday afternoon. Ruth looked to her right; she could see Alice in one of her best dresses at the end of the hall. Her intuition proven correct, Ruth watched the captivated young gentleman, flushed red in the cheeks.

'Ah, here she is,' began Clarrie. 'Norman, this is my sis...'

'Hello, Alice,' said the young man, as if no one else was in the room.

'Oh, you know each other,' said Clarence, still oblivious to the chemistry in the room.

'Yes, Mr Miller,' replied Norman. He sounded formal and slightly nervous. 'I met Alice at the bakery, several weeks ago.'

'Oh, very well then.'

'Hello, Norman,' said Alice, as entranced as her male friend. 'How are you?'

'How ironic,' whispered Ruth.

Norman turned quickly towards Mrs Miller, thinking he had heard something, but quickly turned his gaze back to Alice.

'Clarence, I almost forgot!' exclaimed Ruth. 'Will you come and have a look at my pony? He has the most terrible rash behind its fetlock.'

'It's probably just greasy heel, I'll look at it later.'

'It's much worse than that!' exclaimed Ruth, further fabricating her story, while she moved around to Clarrie's chair to assist him out of it. 'I need you to look at it now.'

'All right, all right, I'll do it now. Sorry about this, Norm. Alice, would you keep Mr Clark company for a moment? I'll be back as soon as I tend to my wife's request.' Before he got a reply, Clarence suddenly remembered his youth, and realised that his little sister had grown from a young girl into a woman. He turned sheepish and hurriedly exited the kitchen door for the now fatally ill pony.

***

The brakes shuddered as Clarence parked his truck outside Peades' Stock and Station Agency. Norman had taken up residence in a one-room flat above the store in which he worked. The two men stood beside the truck and discussed farm related topics for a while. Clarrie thanked the young man for his time and then shook his hand.

Clarrie turned to step into his vehicle and stopped. The large sign, which read *Royal Hotel*, had caught his eye.

'Tell Thomas I will call in during the week,' said Clarence in an effort to shake of the call of his nemesis. He tried hard not to look in the pub's direction. 'And thanks again for your advice, Norm.'

Clarrie moved behind the wheel of the truck and gripped the steering wheel hard when a nervous voice broke his private struggle against temptation.

'Mr Miller.'

'Yes, Norm,' replied Clarrie as he leaned out the window, grateful for the distraction.

Norm looked at the ground and twisted his hat in his hands. He chided himself because he realised that if he was going to say what he was going to say, he needed to do it as a man. Norm stood to his full six feet and one inch, straightened his broad shoulders and began again.

'Mr Miller, I would like—with your permission—to ask Alice to the Autumn Ball in two weeks time.'

Clarence had never given a thought to the likelihood of having to deal with such matters on behalf of his sister. He wasn't even used to the idea of his little sister being romantically interested in someone. Clarrie took a moment, one that did no favours for a nervous Norm, smiled, and then gave his approval. He thought of the day—all those years ago—on the doorstep of Ruth's parent's house.

Relieved and pleased, Norm stepped forward and shook Clarrie's hand enthusiastically. Abruptly, but with a smile, he turned to walk away, with the intent of someone who had urgent news to deliver. Clarrie felt at peace after the manly exchange with Norm. He looked towards the Royal Hotel, and decided he no longer required the comfort of the amber fluid; he thought of his sister instead.

Tragically, for reasons he couldn't hope to try and explain, he opened the truck door and began to walk. A soft voice urged him back to the truck; a louder one propelled him forward. His hand rose to push on the timber doors, each fitted with glass panels and emblazoned with bold gold letters. With his shoulders rounded slightly, a physical sign that he had succumbed, Clarrie stepped into the pub.

***

The vehicle repeatedly surged forward and then jolted. Clarence overcompensated with the brake, as his drunken condition allowed his foot to apply too much, then not enough, throttle. The headlamps swayed from side to side on the winding road and illuminated the wet green grass of Denman Hills' front paddock. The rain had made a difficult job even more difficult for a boozed driver.

Clarence stopped the vehicle outside the shed. He realised—as drunk as he was—that the narrow opening of the corrugated iron out-building was too big a challenge for him. Pleased to be home, hungry and worn out, Clarence opened the door to the truck and stumbled into the rain. His trailing leg caught on the bench seat of the vehicle and sent him crashing, face first, to the muddied driveway.

The alcohol prevented the feeling of any real pain. Clarence's only source of anger stemmed from the mud and grit he had to remove from his mouth and eyes. He struggled to his knees and cursed his misfortune, when a sudden and intrusive voice sent him back against his vehicle.

'Miller!' barked Lieutenant Sharp. 'A deserter as well are we?'

Clarence spun his head to the left to see Lieutenant Sharp, who stood over him. His face was a contorted with rage and his tunic was covered in blood. Startled, Clarence cowered as the rain drops increased in their intensity; they cracked like rifle fire as they hit his sodden head. Clarence looked to his right and recoiled at the sight of a German soldier that scampered through the darkness. He overbalanced from shock and landed on his backside, which brought another tirade from his tormentor.

'Shoot, for Christ's sake, Private,' screamed Sharp, his unholstered revolver pointed outwards into the darkness. 'Shoot before they reach Corporal Conner's position.'

Clarence looked left at a maddened lieutenant and then right as the Germans approached. Engulfed by adrenalin, he stood up and sprinted. From the window of his bedroom, eight-year-old Reginald Miller stood on his mattress and looked out into the darkness. He watched his father act in a terrified and possessed way, and was unable to make sense of his dad's actions. The little boy became scared by the crazed look on his father's face; the frenzied figure ran towards the side of the house as though something chased him. Anxious, Reginald clutched his toy bear, dropped to his bed and pulled the covers over his head in an attempt to disappear. Reggie heard a dull thud as Clarence crashed over the waist-high fence that separated the driveway from the house yard.

Clarence rolled onto his back and his head spun with intoxication and phantasm. Rain pelted his face as he struggled with images he couldn't reconcile. 'Corporal Conner,' he mumbled. He spat water from his lips. 'Alf,' he cried, as the side of his house, huge in size from his position on the ground, added to his confusion. Clarence strained to sit upright. He looked right and recognised his vehicle, its door still open. It seemed to extend like a dark hand of recollection. He jerked his head in violent movements and saw the silhouettes of gumtrees instead of soldiers—and silence instead of Lieutenant Sharp. Clarence felt utterly helpless, but that emotion turned quickly into frustrated anger. The former soldier, now husband and father, fell to the ground and grunted cries of resentment.

TWENTY TWO

Ruth sat straight-backed in a cushioned chair. Her hands were clasped across her lap, while she stared with detachment at an oil painting on the opposite wall. To one side a young lady sat behind a desk and sorted through documents that needed to be filed. She had paid no further attention to Mrs Miller after she had politely told her that Mr Atkins would be with her as soon as possible.

While feeling out-of-place and somewhat vulnerable, Ruth had decided to take a step that she considered to be absolutely necessary, but would no doubt be construed by others, in a conservative society, as inappropriate.

After the pleasant day with Norman Clark, Clarrie had been in high spirits. The discovery of Alice and Norman's feelings towards each other gave Ruth and Clarrie much to talk about while they went about their mock treatment of the perfectly healthy gelding. When Clarence had left the farm to drive Norman back into town, Ruth had playfully admonished Alice for keeping her blossoming romance from her and began to probe her for more details. She enjoyed the added dimension to their household.

As things seemed to now happen, more regularly than ever, joy was countered by despair. Clarence returned home later that evening drunk and obnoxious, and strangely splattered with mud. He seemed eager to engage in one form of confrontation or another. Maybe he hoped that a verbal tirade, or possibly more, would help purge the conflict that had taken control of his life.

Ruth had manoeuvred around her love like she was housed with a creature of unpredictable qualities. She attempted by instinct and increased experience to control the environment with passive and non-confronting actions—the correct actions had become harder to discern. With a bowl of soup and a towel to dry, Ruth chose wisely. She had kept her family detached—on this occasion—from their father's alternative personality, an illness as Ruth saw it. As each episode became more difficult, she wondered, despite all her concessions and encouragements, if it would ever heal.

An opened door broke Ruth from her thoughts and pretended appraisal of the oil painting. Her attention was seized by the voice of Arthur Atkins.

'Do come in, Mrs Miller,' said Arthur, with his arm outstretched to guide the way.

Ruth stood quickly and moved towards Arthur. She nodded to the clerical worker out of politeness as she passed, but the young lady remained focused on her work.

'How can I help you today?' asked Arthur as he closed the office door behind him. He noted the conspicuous absence of Clarrie.

'Thank you for seeing me on short notice, Mr Atkins.'

'Please, call me Arthur, and it is no problem, honestly.'

'Well,' said Ruth as she looked into her lap. 'I hope you don't see this as being inappropriate,' she paused under emotional strain. 'Well I know it probably is, but I didn't know what else to do. I told your secretary that I would like to alter my will… but that is not why I am here.'

'Take your time, Ruth,' said Arthur quietly. 'Would you like some tea?'

Ruth shook her head to say no. She wanted to move on now that she had put her toe in the water. 'I don't know how else to say this and please forgive me, but what happened to Clarence while he was in France?'

Arthur was slightly stunned, but not offended at the directness of the question. He took a moment to answer. He admired the courage of the women who sat across from him. Her beauty was obvious to any man; the depths of her strength shown through her eyes that simmered with emotion.

'That is a hard question to answer, Ruth,' replied Arthur. He stood to pace slowly away from his desk; thoughts that he would rather forget had suddenly replayed in his mind.

'I am sorry, Arthur, I should leave,' said Ruth. She rose quickly from the leather chair she sat in.

'No, Ruth, please, sit… please. I didn't mean it that way.' Arthur poured himself a whiskey, he thought to offer Ruth a glass but realised the absurdity and took a sip from the crystal tumbler instead. 'You know that Clarence and I were in the same section overseas?'

'No… well I knew you were in the same battalion. I'm sorry I really don't understand how the army is structured. He mentioned you in a letter and I gathered you must have been close.'

'We were in many ways, but that was over there and… I can still remember the first day I saw him,' said Arthur while he looked towards the window of his office to hold himself together.

Ruth cleared her throat, not sure if she wanted to laugh or cry at the vision Arthur's statement conjured. The noise snatched Arthur away from his own dream.

'I can appreciate what it took for you to come here today, Ruth,' continued Arthur. 'I understand how difficult it must have been, I really do. Margaret has never asked me about my experiences abroad, she would… Sorry, that was appallingly ill-mannered of me, Margaret is wonderful. Please forgive me.'

Ruth smiled to pardon Arthur as he resumed his seat behind the large mahogany desk. She felt sympathy for Arthur. She had met his well-maintained, but cold and conceited wife.

'I know the war is long over,' said Ruth, 'and we are supposed to forget and move on, but it has become impossible, and with

Clarence's...' Ruth stopped herself from discussing his alcohol dependence. 'I just want to help him, Arthur, to talk to him,' she said. A tear rolled down her beautifully formed cheek.

Arthur reached for his breast pocket and produced a clean handkerchief for Ruth to take.

'I boarded the troopship, Ruth,' said Arthur, in a calm and contained voice, 'like most men, enthusiastic about defending the Empire. I returned to Australia glad that I had survived. I knew, however, that while I had no doubt changed as a person, I had done what I had to do in order to get myself, and the men around me from one point to the next.' Arthur sipped from his tumbler while Ruth sat quietly. She felt relief as the world she knew nothing of partially opened. It was somewhat overwhelming after years of speculation and assumption.

'You have to realise, Ruth, that some of things I will say, I would not care to relate to most men, let alone a respectable woman such as yourself.'

Ruth began to reassure Arthur but was stopped by a delicate movement of his hand.

'But, I understand, or should I say, I can appreciate what you may have experienced, so I would like to respect the courage you have shown by being as frank and open with you, as you have with me.'

'Thank you, Arthur,' replied Ruth with sincerity.

'Clarence was involved in a battle in the northeast of France, near a place held by the Germans, called Fromelles, near Fleubaix. Our battalion, the 53rd, one of four in the 14th Brigade, belonged to the newly formed 5th Division and was made up of Gallipoli veterans—such as myself—the other half being men like Clarence, who were reinforcements.'

'We trained in Egypt, as you know, and were sent to the so-called quiet sector of Armientères.' Arthur paused once again; this time he opened the top draw of his desk to remove an unopened letter. He placed it to his right and then ignored it, as if it had no relevance to the current topic.

Ruth looked towards the envelope and then returned her gaze to Arthur as he began to speak.

'I do not profess to be an expert in military planning or tactics Ruth. But I will say, that while we were a division of committed soldiers, determined to display all the courageous and selfless qualities expected of us. I believed then, as I do now—with the added knowledge of hindsight—that we were hastily engaged into a poorly planned operation, that was under-equipped and doomed before it began.'

'I spent months on the Gallipoli Peninsula; I saw and experienced things that, before my embarkation, were beyond my imagination. The action…' Arthur covered his mouth with a clenched fist to clear his throat and his head. 'The action near Fromelles was… something entirely different.'

Arthur stood from his desk and walked over to the far side of his office. He removed a book from a heavily laden shelf, for no other reason than to compose his suddenly shaken emotions. Ruth had the commonsense or awareness not to follow his path with a curious look. She respected the exposed position this courageous and forward-thinking man had placed himself in.

'I don't think I would relay to you, even if I could with my limited means, what happened during that afternoon and night of senseless slaughter; the lack of regard for human life which saw more than seven thousand Australian and British casualties. I don't know if it would help…' said Arthur as he trailed off, a smile etched with pain and remembrance forced to his lips. It revealed, through its sudden collapse, a battle of his own.

Arthur sat back at his desk, drained of colour. He placed a finger on the letter that rested to his right and dragged it towards him.

'I have often wondered what I would say, having to admit to you, however it may appear, that I have envisaged this meeting taking place. After I returned home and resumed my pre-war life, I became increasingly aware that the war did not in fact end in 1918. It continued on through memories that lingered; too ghastly and horrific for many men's minds to digest. Their illness remains untreated, because, to put it simply, it is not visible.

'I noticed the change in Clarence almost immediately,' said Ruth. She remembered the post-war years in Balmain, 'but I expected it—to a certain extent. I just thought we would work through it. Maybe I was naive.'

'May I ask,' said Arthur cautiously, 'does Clarence talk of his brother at all?'

Ruth shook her head quickly and allowed her face to drop so she could hide the newly formed tears. She dabbed her eyes with Arthur's handkerchief and then lifted her face to make eye contact again. 'No, Arthur, he never speaks of Archie, never,' Ruth raised the white embroidered cotton to her cheek.

Arthur Atkins paused before he replied. He felt embarrassment at his arousal towards Ruth while she was visibly distressed. Her strength of character and freedom of emotion was displayed through her willingness to look him in the eye, while tears filled with devotion to her husband followed the lines of her captivating features. The delicate and feminine way in which she applied the square piece of cloth to her face made him long for something as potent in his life.

'Ruth,' said Arthur, 'I have tentatively expressed my views in regard to the effects of mental strain caused by battle with government officials. My hope was to initiate a program of sorts to be used at our Returned Soldiers and Sailors meetings, but the responses I have received,' sighed Arthur, 'well, let me just say that they are not worth repeating.'

Arthur lifted the envelope onto its edge and stared blankly, as he considered past decisions.

'This is a letter from me to your husband while he was recuperating in England.'

Ruth lifted her chin slightly, a reflex action, defensive in its nature, aimed to absorb any previously unimagined news that may be about to surface.

'It was marked return to sender, and eventually found its way to Gilmurra amongst other mail for returned servicemen in this district. I will leave it to your discretion if and when you give it to Clarence. It may go some way,' suggested Arthur, 'in helping him.'

'May I ask why you have held it so long?'

Arthur blinked at the direct but fair question. 'As I hinted before,' replied Arthur, 'you could have called Clarence and I mates when we were overseas. But since your arrival in Gilmurra, my attempts to socialise with your husband have not been received well.'

'I have seen that,' said Ruth apologetically, 'and his behaviour towards you has always confused me, so I am sorry Arthur, whatever his reasons may be.'

A knock on the heavy timber doors interrupted the conversation. The secretary entered the room seconds later.

'Yes, Anne?' said Arthur, while he stayed seated.

'Your wife is here to see you, Mr Atkins.'

'Thank you, Anne, tell Mrs Atkins that I will be finished with my appointment shortly.'

'Yes, Mr Atkins,' replied the secretary obediently.

'I will leave, Arthur, so you can continue with your day,' said Ruth, as she rose from her seat.

Arthur stood to shake Ruth's hand.

'I feel humbled, Ruth,' said Arthur, a slight quake in his voice, 'that you have approached me today. You have shown great courage to pursue the concerns you have for Clarence. You have my word that this discussion will remain private.'

'Thank you, Arthur,' replied Ruth, 'for your kindness and understanding. It has helped me.'

'I will make a few innocuous changes to your last will and testament,' said Arthur with a smile, as he escorted Ruth to the door— 'for my secretary's sake.'

Ruth looked at Arthur Atkins, and smiled in recognition of his discretion. As she passed through the reception, Ruth smiled at Anne and said a friendly hello to Mrs Atkins. Margaret Atkins had to repress her rage when she noticed the embroidered 'A A' on the corner of a handkerchief Mrs Miller clasped in her hands.

TWENTY THREE

Denman Hill June 1924

The sound of a vehicle took Ruth's attention away from her inspection of ripening navel oranges; the full and rounded fruit contrasted with the greenness that surrounded her on a bright but cool winter's afternoon.

She recognised the vehicle and she smiled at love—young and energised—once matched, yielding to no other force on earth. Norman's punctuality was testimony to it. Ruth bent down to lift the bucket at her feet and selected three of the heavier oranges, and moved on to the lemon tree.

The kitchen door slammed in the distance; it told Ruth there would be no need to call for Alice to greet her visitor. A figure adorned in a long white dress—previously kept for special occasions—floated past Ruth. Alice's gait flowed with elegance and suggested that this was such an occasion. Her controlled manner hid a desire to break into a run, reducing the time spent apart.

Ruth made her way back to the kitchen. She enjoyed the light that Norman and Alice's courtship had brought to Denman Hill. It was a brightness that was needed to counter the ashen clouds of Clarence's woe. It rolled across the paddocks and touched everyone who could lay claim to being a part of his life.

At times, Ruth had felt nauseous since she had met with Arthur

Atkins. She had taken Arthur's letter home and hid it in a drawer until the right time came to pass it on. That moment had become harder to recognise with each day that passed, and her stalling had brought on waves of anxiousness that were now more prevalent in her demeanour. Eventually and ashamedly, out of a desire to avoid conflict, Ruth decided to read the letter herself rather than give it to her husband. Her conscience rationalised the decision by suggesting he would only throw it away.

The contents of the letter had enlightened Ruth in many ways, but also posed other questions that could only be answered by Clarence. Why was Arthur saying that Clarrie should not feel responsible for Archie's fate? What were 'the orders' that Clarence was obliged to follow?

There was a brief mention of Arthur and Clarence being together when her husband was wounded; Arthur had also sustained a wound to his leg. Did this provide a clue to Clarence's rudeness towards Mr Atkins?

The letter had helped her. She could now understand why he wouldn't want to talk about such horrendous things. Why he would not want to be reminded that of the 850 of his 53rd Battalion that went into battle, only 227 answered the roll call on the morning of the 21st of July?

With the exception of his older brother, Ruth had never heard Clarence talk about anyone like he spoke of his friend Sticks. With excruciating pain, Ruth recalled the letter that informed her of his death, and with empathy clouded by despondency, she realised why he never mentioned either name.

Tired from the emotional peaks and troughs, Ruth stared out the kitchen window. An altar of sorts, were she could cast her thoughts, and piece together images that floated back and forth. Gradually she allowed—or weakened to—slivers of doubt. The unwavering and self-motivating ideal that love would overcome any obstacle was threatened by uncertainty. It crept through her defences, while a bizarre image of Arthur Atkins holding her hand shamed her into looking towards the ground. The kitchen door opened with a creak, and joyful laughter brought a wave of cheerfulness into the room. It pulled Ruth away from annulling fantasy and reminded her of a solemn promise.

***

'Good afternoon, Mrs Miller,' said Norm. He held documents folded in half; the papers caught Ruth's eye.

'Hello, Norman,' Replied Ruth, 'how was work this week?'

'Busy, with Mr Peade away.'

'Ruth,' said Alice eagerly, 'is Clarence nearby? Norman would like to speak with him.'

'He is over at the shearing shed with Reginald,' replied Ruth, curious, but slightly alarmed at why Alice would interject on Norman's behalf. *Obviously not work related*, she thought. 'I think he said he needed to repair one of the holding yards.'

'Oh,' said Alice. She looked impatient. 'You could walk over and give him a hand, Norman.'

'He should be home any minute,' said Ruth, 'have you had lunch?'

'Yes, I have, Mrs Miller, thank you.'

'You might catch him on the way back,' suggested Alice, determined to get her way. 'I will stay here with Ruth and Emily.'

Ruth could see that although Norman stood at well over six foot and looked as strong as an ox, he was as pliable as wet clay in the presence of Alice.

***

Clarence and Norm walked with heavy feet and were deep in concentrated, but amiable conversation. They strode into the kitchen with Reggie, who carried a jawbone from a long-deceased sheep.

'Reginald, what is that in your hand?' cried his mother, revealing her city upbringing.

'A dinosaur bone,' replied the young man proudly. 'Norm helped me finded it.'

'Aren't you lucky,' replied Ruth, recovered from her shock. 'I have a sandwich ready for you, so put your fossil away and wash up.'

'It's a dinosaur, Mum.'

'You're right, sorry, now go and wash.'

'Ruth,' said Clarence, 'Could Alice sit with Reg while he has his lunch? Norman has something he would like to share with us.'

Alice stood on the far side of the table and looked offended at being excluded. She was still the baby sister in Clarence's eyes. Ruth wiped her hands on her apron and tried to think what Norman would want to talk about, apart from the obvious and uncomfortable discussion that sometimes arose between unmarried couples and parents. Ruth nodded and smiled like you do when someone serves you an unappealing meal; she removed her apron and gestured down the hall towards the sitting room. Alice took a seat at the kitchen table and withheld any eye contact from an apologetic Norman.

Ruth walked with a fluency that could suggest grace or caution in the anticipation of upheaval. She led the men into the large room at the front of the house and wondered if Norman had already asked for Alice's hand in marriage. *Too soon*, she thought. *But okay for you and Clarence*, came a reply from deeper within her consciousness.

'Why don't we sit at the dining table?' suggested Clarence.

Norman and Ruth took a seat at the polished dining table that was another gift from Ruth's mother. It was kept for entertaining, which was rare in their situation, and was guarded by a matching cabinet.

'While we were in the shearing shed,' said Clarence, 'young Norm put forward a business proposition that I think is worth listening to.'

'Business proposition?' stated Ruth. Her tone came across as incredulous, when what she was feeling was relief. That reaction brought on guilt. *Why would I feel apprehensive about Alice being married?* she thought.

'Yes, dear, listen to what Norman has to say. Norm, tell Mrs Miller what you told me.'

'Well,' started Norman, nervously. 'As you know things haven't turned out the way Bill Donaghey and his wife Mary had planned, and they have decided to pack up and leave their property Annondale, and return to Newcastle.'

'I will miss them,' said Ruth, 'they have become good friends of ours.'

'Yes, they are very nice people, Mrs Miller,' replied Norman sincerely.

'My whole life,' continued Norm, 'has revolved around farming. The decision to leave my family's property stemmed from the fact that I was the second youngest. The size of our place and lack of local opportunities restricted my choices, hence my relocation to Gilmurra. The land is in my blood, and I have been looking for an opportunity to run my own place... and I believe I have found it.'

With the anxiousness about nuptials gone, Ruth listened to Norman Clark speak. She was captivated by the easy, yet commanding way in which he discussed matters of business. He showed a maturity and level-headedness that had seen him do so well with Thomas Peade.

Norman, while sympathetic to the Donagheys' plight, told the Millers how it was a common occurrence within the Soldier Settlers Scheme. Many men had descended into ruin after enduring poor returns brought about by lack of knowledge, harsh conditions, and lack of capital. Ruth said a silent prayer for her parents who had seen them through tough times.

While they asked the occasional question, Clarence and Ruth listened as Norman outlined his proposal. He stated that he felt the size of the blocks had a lot to do with the inadequacy of return. His recent studies suggested to him that new practices could also increase productivity; it convinced him that what he had in mind would be a success.

'My plan, Mrs Miller, which I hope to be our plan, is that we form a partnership and combine two farms to run them together as one. The benefits will be a joint labour force with increased buying power when low prices present opportunities, and a rise in production through better farming. We could introduce crop and stock rotation, made available by the larger acreage, techniques most people on the land dismiss—to their disadvantage. In time,' Norman paused as he drew near the end of his presentation, 'with our position strengthened through the implementation of these practices, and others,' he held up the papers he had brought, 'we will be in a position to expand and secure our families' future.' The use of the word families stuck Ruth as more than coincidental.

Ruth stayed silent for a moment, while she attempted to digest what was a well-considered and put-forward plan. She looked Norman directly in the eye before she spoke, while Clarence looked on eagerly.

'Norman, what you have said sounds very interesting, but as you could appreciate, there would be many things for our family to consider. I would like to take some time to discuss it with Mr Miller before we give you an answer.'

'Naturally, Mrs Miller,' replied Norman, still full of enthusiasm, 'everything related to my plan is in here,' he continued. He held out the documents and hesitated about whom to hand them to. Common practice was that it should be Mr Miller, but the mood around the table suggested it would be Ruth. Not wanting to upset the balance, Ruth gave an imperceptible shift of her eyes that instructed Clarence to accept the bundle of papers from Norman.

The meeting over, Ruth stood, and Norman rose quickly to stand. Clarence sat to flick through the documents, and missed the opportunity to show the etiquette expected of a gentleman on the land.

TWENTY FOUR

Gilmurra, September 1924

Spring was Ruth's favourite time of year; the temperature was warm but not hot. The grass was green, and blossoms varied in colour and brilliance; it made the main street of Gilmurra appear as a playground.

Ruth walked slowly past the bakery. She stopped and turned to wait for Emily. She was good on her feet for a two-year old, but readily distracted by anything that passed her line of sight. She bent down to pick her daughter up and then waved enthusiastically towards the bakery window where Ally was trying to get M's attention. Emily squealed with excitement when she saw her aunt, which caused an elderly couple to jump with fright as they walked with rounded shoulders past Ruth and her excited daughter. Not one to stay still for long, Emily squirmed in Ruth's arms until she was placed on the ground. She let out another squeal as Reggie ran past her.

'Quiet, Emily, or people will think I have raised unruly children,' whispered the proud mother, not in the least embarrassed by her daughter's enthusiasm. She looked back towards the bakery and glowed with pride at the woman Alice had become. The business proposition put forward to the Miller's by Norman Clark had been accepted after careful consideration and advice from Arthur Atkins. The meetings that Clarence was required to attend were strained at times, but at no time through the fault of Mr Atkins.

Once Ruth's parents—as creditors of the Millers—had agreed, the deal was finalised. This was followed promptly by a proposal of marriage from Norman to Alice. Ruth smiled while she watched her children and remembered how she had remarked to Norman quietly, that she hadn't recalled the tabling of a marriage proposal while reading his business plan. Norman blushed at Ruth's suggestion, but took the joke in good humour.

The new partnership, had in fact, brought a sense of security to Ruth. Her husband, while energised at times by his business partner's implementations, slipped with regularity into moments of melancholy. Sometimes solemn in its affliction, in other instances irritable and aggressive, it was always treated—whether at the Royal or at home—with debilitating alcohol.

Ruth's smile, while she watched over her children, was replaced by a tightening of her jaw, induced by thoughts of her husband's drunken actions. As was her way, Ruth was bound by loyalty and the determination to be a light for her family to follow, so she turned her considerations back to Alice and the children.

In a casual way, Ruth took in the surrounds of the busy street and noticed Arthur and Margaret Atkins as they approached.

'Hello, Mrs Miller,' said Arthur. He tipped his hat and hid his feelings for Ruth by being as formal as expected when greeting a married woman.

'Good morning, Mr Atkins.'

'You remember my wife, Margaret.'

'Of course, how do you do?'

'I'm very well,' replied Mrs Atkins haughtily. The clenched handkerchief—its story not pursued and so unexplained—still burned in her mind. 'My, what playful children you have,' she continued. The comment was deliberately meant to condescend.

'Young Emily certainly has a lot of energy,' replied Ruth.

'She is very pretty, and grown so quickly,' stated Arthur. He did his best to make up for his wife's rudeness. 'How is Clarence?'

The question could be taken as polite conversation or an offer of assistance.

'He is well, thank you, Arthur. Working hard with young Norman,' replied Ruth. She wanted to ask Albert for advice or possibly intervention but was prevented from doing through politeness. Ruth was unwilling to embarrass Mr Atkins in front of his wife. The woman had an air of superiority that she found hard—or didn't try— to conceal.

'Glad to hear it,' replied Arthur, but he took note of Ruth's eyes as they darted away. 'We've had some good rain over the winter, so we should be able to make use of a productive spring.'

'We all hope so,' replied Ruth. She knew Arthur was being polite to make up for his wife, and she suddenly wished the conversation would end. 'It is nice to see you both, but I think I should grab young Emily before she wanders off,' said Ruth, in an attempt to bring an easy close to the conversation.

'Certainly, Ruth. Maybe Clarence will join us in the march next April.'

'I hope so, Arthur,' replied Ruth, but the subject would not be raised with her husband.

Ruth gathered her two children and gave a cursory glance towards the bakery. She hoped to catch Ally's eye before they moved off. The shop was now devoid of customers, and Ruth noticed Alice deep in conversation with her husband. The young couple, who had exchanged vows in St Andrew's in early August, were oblivious to the world around them. Ruth remembered times when she was encased in the same cocoon.

'Your aunty has gone and grown up on us, Emily,' she said with fondness and recognition of change.

She took Reggie by the hand and started to walk towards Peades' Stock & Station Agents, where Clarence had called in earlier. The Millers had purchased everything from seed and fertiliser, to fencing-wire and farming equipment from Thomas Peade over the years. Clarrie would often visit Tom to glean whatever he could about the latest farming innovations, as well as advice on local tried-and-trusted farming methods. Tom had been very good to the Millers. Early on, he had generously walked over their property with Clarrie and made suggestions on what could and what wouldn't work. Tom gave Clarence encouragement when needed, and a pat on the back when he made some good decisions of his own.

Although Norman had a background in agriculture, Thomas had played a big role in his development. The Millers, through their new partnership, were benefiting from that tutelage. Thomas had never mentioned it, nor had anyone else, but Clarrie had eventually learned that Thomas had lost his only son, Lachlan, at Passchendaele. Clarrie understood the Peades' desire to forget, and he never raised the subject.

'Daddy,' yelled Emily, as she spotted her father coming out of the Royal Hotel.

He held a package of assorted items bound with twine and waved towards his family as if surprised to see them. It was like the double timber doors with glass panels and the word *Bar* written on them had somehow transported him to another place, far away from families, acquaintances and horse-drawn carts. The few ales that he had consumed, had allowed him—for a moment—to forget.

'Ruth… baby M,' said Clarrie with a soft glow to his cheeks. 'G'day, Reggie,' he continued, as he rustled his son's hair. Reggie looked up at his father strangely. The enthusiastic greeting was welcomed, but at odds with the sharp order he had received when he climbed out of the truck too slowly for his father's liking upon arrival in town. 'Ducked in to the Royal for a minute, Tom was busy with customers.'

'Oh… seems like you accomplished a bit in that minute, Clarence.'

'Don't be like that, Ruth,' replied Clarrie, while he placed his arm on her shoulder, 'it's not often I have a quiet beer.' The absurdity of the statement—even in his intoxicated state—made him cringe a little.

'It's eleven in the morning,' she said quietly, turned on an angle to shield Reg from the conversation.

Clarence looked dazed, as his mind processed her statement. Ruth decided to change the subject, while Arthur Atkins's casual query over Clarence's wellbeing rang in her ears.

'Alice will be finished work soon,' Ruth said. 'Let's walk up to the truck and wait for her. I will invite her over for lunch. Norm won't be home until later; he has a meeting with a man about some machinery.'

Suddenly conscious of his inebriated condition among an alert public, Clarence straightened his shoulders and lifted his chin in an attempt to look sober; it only made his condition more obvious.

'What is that under your arm, Clarrie?' asked Ruth, while she walked.

Clarence stopped and reverted to a more relaxed pose. He held the bundle in front of him and studied it intently. 'Looks like a heap of your letters you must have sent,' he said. The beer had dulled his senses. There was no adverse reaction to the letters that represented his time in France. 'Don't know what this other thing is,' he continued. Clarrie looked at what appeared to be some sort of box, neatly wrapped and about six by six inches and an inch deep.

'Oh, my goodness, Clarrie,' said Ruth, shocked and excited by the unexpected find. 'There is a whole pile of them. Who gave them to you?'

'The pub,' said Clarrie. 'Joseph Tunks from the Post Office left 'em there. Had them for a while, said I was more likely to get...' Clarence stopped before he incriminated himself any further.

'May I?' said Ruth. She held out her free hand and ignored Clarrie's accidental admission.

Clarence took one last look at the package that emitted ill-will, and handed it to Ruth.

'There's so many here, darling, one from Christmas,' said Ruth. She was excited by the letters, but then felt sadness. Ruth remembered the anguish and the distance that separated them at that time. Clarence was swept from his previous thoughts and stared blankly at the pavement while he watched his mate Sticks sing *Come Oh Ye*

Faithful during Christmas eve on board the *Warilda*. The performance had ended after howls of protests, and Clarence smiled for a split second as he remembered with fondness his mate's idiocy. The smile was replaced by clenched teeth and narrowed eyes.

Ruth watched Clarrie's facial contortions and placed her arm through his and kissed him on the cheek. 'I will go and get Alice and we'll head home; Mr Duncan won't mind.'

***

Alice helped unpack the last of things purchased in town and then, without fuss, after she had caught a subtle gesture from Ruth, quietly escorted the children outside. She promised them a special reward if they helped her with grooming their mum's pony.

Ruth placed the kettle on the stove top and then moved back to the sink. She took a deep breath to steady herself while she watched Reggie sprint ahead of Alice towards the horse stables, with Emily close behind.

Ruth smiled to the view outside her window and looked to the tree-lined ridge for strength, as she heard Clarence's footsteps approach from along the hallway. With her eyes closed briefly, Ruth held the vision of a brilliant blue sky that dominated the corrugated hills and the greyish green foliage of the native trees. Determined to take advantage of the situation that presented itself, she turned and retrieved two cups and saucers from the cupboard.

'Cup of tea, Clarrie?' she said to her husband as he entered the kitchen. He looked more sober, but was tired from his quick-fire session at the Royal.

'Thanks, Ruth, nice and strong please,' he replied. Clarence took a seat at the far end of the kitchen table; the pile of letters atop the wrapped box grabbed his attention. 'Any chance of a sandwich?' he added. He turned his gaze quickly from the bundle to look at the wall when Ruth placed teacups on the table. His clumsy effort drew more attention towards the box.

'Cold lamb and chutney?' replied Ruth.

'Lovely.'

'Why don't we take a look at a couple of my letters?' said Ruth, as she removed the bread from the keeper. 'I probably wrote some silly things, it might be fun.'

'If you like, dear,' replied Clarence. He swallowed as he forced out the words.

'Just one or two,' said Ruth casually. She talked and moved fluently between bench and table, as if the letters were insignificant and not her main focus. Ruth filled their cups with tea and handed him the sandwich.

Ruth allowed her tea to cool a little and slid the package towards her from her seat at the side of the table. She loosened the twine and slid the top letter out with an efficiency that left no time for protest.

'Oh,' she said with a slight giggle. 'It's dated the 30th of November, Clarence, you would have been in the middle of the ocean.' Ruth looked sideways to see Clarrie give a forced smile as he chewed mechanically on the lamb sandwich. She turned her eyes back to the letter, ignoring her husband's mood, and ploughed on.

Ruth covered her mouth with embarrassment while she scanned the script. 'Clarrie, you must hear this, I can't believe I wrote it.' After a pause she began to read aloud, the smile on her face reached Clarrie, and slackened the shackles of apprehension that gripped him.

> *"Our love is like spring,*
> *When the birds sing,*

'Oh, how awful,' she remarked. Ruth allowed a brief but warm smile that contradicted her statement.

Our love is pure,
Too bright to stare

'I'll never make a poet.' Ruth was embarrassed at her emotional verse. 'It's really bad, isn't it?' she continued with a look of horror on her face, 'I mean adorable. Oh, I don't know, Clarrie.' She breathed out to compose herself. 'I'll try to continue.' Ruth sipped her tea and looked up to see her husband's outstretched hand.

Ruth placed the cup awkwardly back on its saucer. The scrape of the cup against the saucer gained an unusual prominence amongst the other homely noises. The sound was enhanced by the once familiar look that would project from Clarrie's dark eyes. It held Ruth in suspension as she remembered moments long ago in Birchgrove Park.

She handed over the letter to Clarence and wiped the trace of tears that lined her eyes. Brought on by self-mocking and bashfulness, they were now replaced by fuller drops summoned by happiness.

Clarence smiled as he read in silence, his grin emphasised the creases that had developed in his skin over the years; the 'crow's feet' around his eyes that had extended their reach—aided by his time overseas and the hot Gilmurra sun. Ruth took the time to study Clarence and enjoy the lightness that had found its way to the surface.

'Okay,' said Clarence, 'here I go.' He held a semi-clenched fist to his mouth while he cleared his throat. His veined and bony hand, tanned by the sun, was unable to hide an ever-widening smirk.

A star, bright with fire
Clouded and greyed when placed
*Alongside my des_r_*

'Stop, Clarrie,' screamed Ruth. She squirmed with embarrassment; her delicate hands covered her mouth and nose. 'Please stop.'
'Not on your life, this is incredible, you can really write!'

Ruth leapt from her chair and darted around the corner of the table; she attempted to snatch the letter from Clarrie's grasp.

'Uh-uh,' exclaimed Clarence, as he withdrew the note from his wife's grasp. 'What was that word, darling, what were the deleted letters, I couldn't quite make it out? De-si-re, oh I couldn't repeat such a word.' Clarence acted as if shocked.

After she recovered her balance, Ruth stood with hands on hips, her cheeks flushed. .

'Please, Clarrie, I feel foolish.'

Clarrie realised he had taken the torment far enough and handed over the letter, only to catch his wife's wrist as she grasped it. He drew her gently in to sit on his lap. The impulsive action took Ruth completely by surprise.

As she eased herself into the comfort of her husband's arms, she marvelled at what time meant. Countless hours of struggles erased, or maybe camouflaged, with a moment of emotional contact.

'Mummy! Mummy!' Came the scream. It increased in volume as it reached the side of the house; quickly and cruelly it broke the married couple's affectionate embrace.

Ruth turned slowly at first, and then jumped off Clarrie's lap when she saw young Reggie in the kitchen doorway, his face covered in blood.

'Oh, my goodness Reggie, what happened?' Ruth knelt down to inspect her son. Reggie was now overcome with the sight of the blood and was unable to speak. He took short sharp breaths, in between sobs that were interrupted by the need to remove the blood that filled his mouth and his smashed nose.

'He fell off the fence,' came the shout from Ally, 'is he alright?' She carried Emily and looked distraught when she reached the kitchen door. The tea towel that Clarence had thrown to his wife after he saw Reg was now soaked in blood; it answered Alice's question.

Clarence knelt beside Ruth and looked closely at Reginald's face. The young boy tried to pull away, as the shock of his own blood was replaced by the blinding pain. The anticipation of more pain from his father's hands made Reggie even more upset.

'Hold on son, let me have a look,' said Clarence. The blood brought unwelcome flashes of soldiers in agony to Clarence.

Reggie wailed and tried to pull away again, but Clarrie stared at his boy and gripped him firmly by his shoulders. The young boy was caught between a desire to run and the fear of what would be delivered if he did; he had caught the all-too-familiar look in his father's eyes.

'Reggie darling, hold still for Daddy,' pleaded Ruth. Clarence breathed deeply to regain control of his emotions and focused on his son.

'He was on the top rail of the horse yard,' explained Ally, still teary and upset, 'and then he just fell, straight on the ground. He didn't attempt to break his fall. I'm so sorry Ruth, he sits there all the time, I didn't...'

'It's not your fault, Ally,' interjected Ruth.

'It's broken, smashed in fact,' stated Clarence calmly. He released his hold on Reggie and the boy turned towards his mother. 'We'll have to take him to Doctor Bainbridge's.'

While concerned for her son, Ruth paused for a second to curse God, Father Time, or whoever was responsible for the interruption to her moment with Clarrie.

'I'll take him, Clarrie,' said Ruth. 'You stay here with Emily.'

Clarence began to speak, but stopped after a look from his wife. He realised it wouldn't be a good idea if he drove Reg to Dr Bainbridge's house; the doctor and his wife were strong supporters of the Temperance Movement. Clarence picked Reg up in his arms to carry him to their truck, while Ruth hurried towards the hallway cupboard for clean towels and handkerchiefs to stem the blood.

'Alice,' said Ruth, as she walked briskly through the kitchen, 'come with me will you please? Reg will need to be comforted while I drive. Put M in her cot with her bear; she's due for a sleep anyway.'

Alice nodded and did as she was asked; Ruth took one last glance around the kitchen before she snatched her bag.

Ruth arrived at the truck and saw Reg already propped up on the bench seat with a towel under his nose. His face, where not marked with blood, was pale from the loss of it.

'Emily is in the cot, Clarrie,' said Ruth. She tried to remain calm, but her anxiety came through in her voice. 'She will be fine but stay close to the house to listen for her.'

'I have some literature to read on contagious cattle diseases.'

'Sounds like fun.'

'Norm gave it to me; I'll try not to fall asleep.'

'We will be back soon,' said Ruth before she climbed into the well-used lorry.

Clarence stood to the side as Ruth reversed the vehicle from its garage. She stopped suddenly, took a few attempts to select first gear, and then made a wide arc in the gravelled yard, gathering speed to the front gate and Tully road.

Like Ruth, Clarence lamented over the interruption to their special moment. He consoled himself with the warm feeling that still lingered from the exchange. Clarrie stopped at the water tank to wash the blood from his hands and heard a faint cry that came from the house. He wiped his hands on his trousers and then entered the kitchen through the side door. His eyes were drawn to the neatly wrapped box as he stepped quietly around the blotches of blood that had already dried. He stopped and stared and hoped little Emily would calm of her own accord.

He paused in the centre of the kitchen, but the sound of Emily's cries grew in intensity. Frozen to the spot, Clarrie continued to stare at the package. All the feelings of happiness—aroused by the banter with Ruth—were replaced with trepidation; the spirit of joy that had danced was scorched by the fires of a tortured soul.

Clarrie wrenched his mind free and walked towards Emily's bedroom. He hoped his daughter, and then some reading, would occupy his thoughts enough to forget about the package.

Clarence rocked his daughter in rigid arms. He breathed deeply and began to relax; the tension that he had felt faded, drawn away as Emily softened in his embrace.

He quietly left Emily in her cot and turned towards the lounge room, where he would read the literature on cattle provided by Norman.

Relaxed in a leather armchair, Clarence gazed out through the windows of the large room that looked out towards the east. The flat stretch of ground that led to Tully Road became undulating, with small outcrops of rock. The sand-coloured grass was bleached from the searing sun; it swayed rhythmically, only interrupted by the occasional eucalypt, with trunk and branches twisted from biting winter winds. Beyond the rise, content in its own valley, weaved the Tilcan River; clear and cool, it was an oasis to the land that lay baked around it.

He thumbed the bound folder of documents to delay pulling on the twine that secured the weighty clump. His mind was engaged in a conflict that grew in strength the longer he remained inactive.

Get the package from the kitchen, Clarence, whispered a voice from inside his head. The murmur that had haunted him for so long grew in confidence. It filled the room and seemed to press at Clarence from all angles.

I'm going to read.

Cattle diseases! You can do that anytime and you know it.

It's not often I get a chance to sit in peace and quiet, the more information I can learn the better.

You don't like peace and quiet, Clarrie, who are you trying to fool? Get the package and open it!

Clarence placed his right forefinger on his cheek and pressed as his cheek muscles tightened. His neck and shoulders tensed. With an effort that caused his hand to shake, Clarence Miller drew his hand away from his face and pulled on the neatly tied twine. The bundle of papers, now released from their shackles, grew in size slightly, as if they had exhaled.

Clarence peeled away the cover-sheet and studied the title. His eyes focused on the bold-type to make clear and precise shapes, but the process was being sabotaged; the passage of clear and articulate thought was blocked by noises that insisted on being heard.

Why force yourself to sit here, when you know exactly what you want to do.

'Cattle and Infectious Disease' by H.R. McMurray, read Clarence, slowly and purposefully.

You are pathetic, Miller, Lieutenant Sharp should have put a bullet in you.

'Chapter One, the...'

Clarence scattered the educational sheets as he stood abruptly from the armchair and marched towards the hallway. He paused for a moment at the kitchen table, and then snatched at the package; he pulled it towards him.

He stared at the package with widened eyes. A grimace formed on his lips. Clarence dropped to the closest chair and tasted the bitterness of his own sweat as he struggled for breath. The beads formed on his forehead, releasing the heat from within his fear-stricken body.

Clarence worked slowly at the wrapping. A part of him suggested that a gentle hand might soothe what he felt to be a volatile force that lay trapped within the confines of the box he held. He pulled the paper away and then twitched. A letter, neatly folded, sat on top of a flat box, black and with no markings.

For no reason, Clarence pushed to one side the letter that had the words Australian Imperial Force emblazoned across its top, and proceeded to lift the lid on the six by six-inch container. He saw a brown leather pouch, partially hidden by a pinkish sheet of paper folded exactly in half. His mind was full of thoughts, not one of them discernible. The voice that had goaded him was now cruel in its silence.

A dull ache formed behind his eyes as he lifted the folded paper with his right hand and the leather pouch with his left. He noted the weight of the pouch and solid object within.

He unfolded the sheet of paper roughly with one hand. Clarence was struck by a feeling of misery, and a loathing for diligent postal workers. The Coat of Arms and the words *Buckingham Palace* seared Clarence's eyes, and melted the chains of imprisoned memories.

> *I join with my grateful people*
> *In sending you this memorial*
> *of a brave life given for others*
> *in the Great War.*

Hope, hope that can send you mad with torment or preserve an idea that is more palatable than the acceptance of what is likely, had held Clarence Miller in a state of unnatural conflict.

It tore at his soul's delicate fibres. The partially healed remnants, calcified and scarred, had not allowed freedom within a spirit that had graced the earth without concern—until men had ordered other men to kill.

The pink sheet was released from his grip and floated slowly to the timber floor of the kitchen. Its descent held him captive while liberated memories, horrible and vivid, played out before him.

Clarence remained motionless; his skin was washed pale by the scenes that raced in front of his wide-open eyes. His mouth filled with the bitter taste of cordite. He swallowed hard and tried to rid himself of the memories, but the effort only brought a worse sensation, putrid and evil in smell. The mud of Flanders made him gag as a flare blossomed against the black sky above him. It illuminated his brother's face, brave and unyielding, alone and ready to meet his fate.

With his right arm lifted, Clarence twisted and contorted his fingers in an effort to reach his brother, while an unseen force held him securely to the chair in which he sat. The voice of Arthur Atkins suddenly blared in his ears, and his stomach turned at the sound of machine gun fire; the humiliating feel of a weakened bladder revisited him.

The muscles in his gnarled hand relaxed. He watched Archie fade into nothing, while sickening feelings of cowardice and impotence washed over him as they had on that night many years ago. The stark realisation of what he had been asked to do, and what he had done under orders, struck without pity or compassion. He remembered the small but definite flicker of relief when they began the retreat, knowing that he might get the chance to live. That feeling had been buried inside him and could never be admitted.

Clarence bowed his head and clenched his eyes shut as he fought with the voice that persecuted his existence. The concussion of Mills bombs that exploded was followed by several rifle shots, which tensed his body again. The sounds chilled Clarrie's blood with their clarity. Like a fence wire strained too tight, Clarence felt a part of his mind snap. The kitchen instantly converted from blackness to blinding light. He lifted his head and opened his eyes to the recognition of the German Mauser rifle that killed his brother.

The tortured man screamed Archie's name and then moaned in terror as the image of his older brother, wounded and bloodied, rolled off the kitchen table into his lap. The soldier's face projected a look of ghastly shock and his eyes portrayed dismay after his life had ended. Clarence reeled and sobbed. He pushed frantically at the kitchen floor with his feet and tipped the chair backwards. He fell and lay sprawled on the floor. Clarence rolled away from the table and scrambled to his feet, to run for the kitchen door, maddened with fear and stricken with guilt.

Driven by the past and the sights and sounds that sped through his field of vision, he attempted to out-run his mate Sticks, while a triumphant German soldier stood over a lifeless Archie. A Red Cross letter appeared, perched on the mantle of his Beattie Street home—ignored and forgotten. He saw a woman, overcome by misery, floating on a rising tide.

Spittle dripped from his chin; he panted and coughed in fits, and then he ran for the ridge that lined the western sky.

TWENTY FIVE

Alerted by Emily's cry, Ruth opened the screen door to the kitchen and ushered Reggie inside. She called out to Clarence and looked quizzically at the overturned chair and the mess of letters scattered across the table, moved from its normal position.

'Alice, would you put Reggie in his bed?' asked Ruth, as she walked towards Emily's room. 'Prop him up with pillows, like the doctor said.'

'Yes, Ruth,' replied Alice. She too had glanced at the disturbed furniture.

Ruth opened the door to her daughter's room and was annoyed to find M totally distressed and wet with sweat. *Where on earth can Clarence be?* she said, while she tried to calm Emily.

'Clarrie!' she yelled. Emily responded with louder cries at the raised voice. 'I could strangle your father, M,' she whispered. She stopped calling for Clarence; his immediate appearance wouldn't help her calm the baby.

She poured milk into a teacup for Emily and held it while the little girl drank eagerly. Ruth cuddled her baby and took a seat at the table, still annoyed with Clarence. She ignored the mess and left the fallen chair where it was, only to have her attention drawn to the leather pouch that sat on the edge of the table.

Ruth reached for the pouch and slid it towards her. The object aroused her curiosity, so she placed a much calmer Emily in the chair next to her and quickly opened the pouch. Ruth saw part of a metal disc, and immediately removed it from the protective case and began to study the strange item.

With the disc in her outstretched right hand, Ruth could make out a lady in robes. The woman held a trident and stood behind a Lion. 'Odd,' she remarked, as she turned the medallion clock-wise to read the inscription on the outer edge.

'HE DIED FOR FREEDOM AND HONOUR.' Ruth whispered the words and then covered her mouth. She moved her right hand and revealed another inscription.

'ARCHIBALD ALBERT MILLER'

Ruth's thoughts turned immediately to her husband. The loyal and loving wife stood and called out her husband's name, but her voice trailed off as she realised the futility of it. Her eyes caught a solemn figure in the doorway to the hall.

'Is that Archie's?' said the soft voice.

Unable to speak, Ruth nodded. Her eyes met Alice's, and then returned to the bronze medallion. The token invoked sadness for a young woman, who, although loved and cherished by Ruth as her own, had watched her family almost vanish before her eyes. Her sister-in-law's needs, Ruth thought with shame, not always at the forefront of people's minds; like a child, Alice was seen as one who needed protection from the truth. Ruth wondered if that had been wise. Would she take that approach with her own children?

'Yes, Alice,' said Ruth softly. She held out the medallion for Alice to take. 'It is Archie's, and I am so very sorry.'

The words, when they were said, sounded bizarre to Ruth. Not because of the sentiment, but because of the time, almost eight years after Archie had been killed in action. Ruth had held out hope, like everyone, that Archie had been taken prisoner after Fromelles. But she had accepted Archie's death long ago. Long before she had spoken to Arthur, even before the letter had arrived all those years ago from the

Red Cross. The letter had informed Albert that there was no record of an Archibald Albert Miller in any of the German prisoner-of-war camps. It had confirmed what Grace Miller had already known.

Through blind stubbornness, or devoted brotherly love, Ruth was not sure which, Clarence had not come to terms with the fact that Archie had not returned. Clarrie had made the issue almost unresolvable, with barely a mention of his brother's name. People in general did not talk about the war, which she could understand, but Ruth felt that there was more to her husband's behaviour than a willingness to forget and move on. Arthur Atkins's face, and the true intention of his enquiries, leapt into Ruth's consciousness, as she handed the medallion to Alice.

Alice took the Dead Man's Penny from Ruth and walked towards the table and sat down. She stroked the face of the object in one slow movement, before she held it to her chest.

'Sometimes I find it hard to remember his face,' said Alice, as she placed the memorial plaque on the table.

Ruth moved quietly to sit beside Alice. She placed a hand on her shoulder to comfort her, and once again Ruth felt shame at not having addressed the subject.

'I remember some things,' continued Alice. 'He always used to pick me up and toss me in the air.' She paused, smiling faintly as she re-lived the moment. 'But his face, well I don't know if the one I see is his, or...' a tear slid from her eyes. 'I was only little when he died, Ruth.'

Alice's cry came from deep inside her; the medallion made Archie's death strangely official but left a feeling of inadequacy. A metal disc as a memorial for a brother's life—a life Alice never got to appreciate—seemed insultingly insufficient.

***

The air was like fire as it passed through his windpipe into his tormented lungs. The rocky incline was sparsely covered with dry grass and stunted gums, and his vision was blurred by tears and sweat that ran across his eyes. Clarence faltered on the uneven surface, and then continued on in a frenzy, desperate to outrun the pack of wild dogs that was his past. He stumbled and skinned his knees on the jagged rocks, then bruised and gouged the palms of his hands as he fought to right himself.

Clarence reached the ridge of the hill and then stopped; he turned in circles and tried to get his bearings. The thirsty gum trees spun as he revolved, their dull green leaves and dark stringy bark replaced by mud-encrusted sandbags and water-logged craters. He caught the sound of movement to his right and ran again; he leapt over a large flat boulder that marked the peak of the ridge, and rolled onto his side as the hill fell away beneath him to the valley below.

Trousers torn, the blood from cuts and abrasions seeped into his boots after his frantic descent. Clarence spotted a depression in the earth far off in the distance. It snaked its way from left to right, and Clarence recognised it as the Australian trench. He increased his efforts to outrun his pursuers. He strode with determination past the cattle yards, and across the paddock towards the creek and the twisted branches of the willow tree.

The sun was pushed from the Denman Hill sky by a frenzied mind. Darkness enveloped Clarence's surrounds, heightening his sense of vulnerability and danger. In the distance, he heard Alf Connor scream for more ammunition. Clarence turned his head, his face a mask of panic. A sense of dread propelled him forward, as Alf's voice receded in the spatter of machine gun fire.

With the safety of the trench in sight, Clarence tripped over a half-buried log that sent him face-first to the ground. Dazed from the impact, he brushed dried grass and dirt from his face, and tasted the Flanders mud as he spat. He saw shadows lurking in the darkness as he battled to regain his feet. He looked towards the object that had taken his feet from under him, and withdrew in fright at the image of

Birdie Finch in an unnatural and terrible pose. The bullet wound to his face was covered with feasting maggots.

Clarence scrambled across the ground and rolled into the trench. He thrashed in the icy water of the creek, and then pulled his body towards the dirt wall, to huddle behind its shelter. Terrified, he tried to raise the courage to look over the lip and across open ground.

'What in God's name are you doing here, Miller?'

The voice was familiar. It seared his awareness and startled him. It forced him to look left. Dressed in a blood-splattered tunic with the epaulettes of a lieutenant, there stood a man with a pistol. He stood, defiant and enraged, among the commotion. Clarrie strained his eyes and squinted to make out the face beneath the peaked cap.

'Lieutenant Sharp,' whispered Clarence.

'Why aren't you with your section, soldier?'

Confused, Clarence looked to his right and away from the lieutenant; he jumped at the sight of two soldiers, their bodies entwined with barbed wire. The head of one of the men—disconnected from its rightful place—lay cradled in his arms, a stupefied smile frozen on its face.

'What's the problem, Miller, never seen a dead man before? You probably got him killed with your cowardice. Look at me when I'm talking to you,' screamed Lieutenant Sharp.

He spun his head around to look at the maddened officer. Clarence breathed frantically and then covered his head with his hands.

'Don't you go soft on me again, Miller,' hissed the lieutenant. 'The Germans are everywhere, show some backbone and be ready to fight when they come.'

***

The bay gelding weaved its way up the slope of the hill under the urgings of its rider. The horse placed his hooves between scattered rocks and camouflaged rabbit holes. Ruth was more than worried at what had become of Clarence; she slapped the horse on each shoulder with her reins and dug her heels into his flank to push him on.

After she had comforted Alice and ensured she was all right, Ruth had made her a cup of tea and put Emily down to sleep again. She checked on Reggie, who was asleep, and then left Alice to watch after the children while she searched for Clarence.

She had checked all the sheds close to the house, along with the orchard, before she saddled and mounted Chester to check the shearing shed and beyond. There had been no trace of Clarence, so she decided to climb the hill to the west and look in the creek paddock, and possibly beyond. *But how far could he get on foot?*

Horse and rider crested the ridge and descended the slope toward the valley below; her trusted gelding negotiated the outcrops of stone and eucalypts deftly. The horse remained steady when soft spring ground gave way under its hooves; it allowed Ruth to scan the paddock for any sign of Clarence. Her eyes squinted as she broke from the shade of trees and into open pasture; a movement of her wrists—delicate yet definite—told the gelding to halt. Ruth took time to think. She looked for a moment at the cattleyards and wondered where on earth she should go next. Cattle that grazed on winter grass, and a creek shaded by a willow tree, were all she could see before the land rose again to be covered with more gum trees. Ruth gave her mount a gentle dig with her heels and continued her search.

***

His knees tucked to his chest, Clarence clenched his eyes shut. The incessant voice of Lieutenant Sharp, the sound of shells that whistled as they approached, and the death rattle of countless machine guns all seared his brain and constricted his movement.

'Stand to, Miller, here they come,' screamed Sharp. 'Stand to Miller, do you hear me man? Fritz is out there; protect your brother for the love of God!'

Clarence opened his eyes to darkened shapes and shadows that came and went. The soldiers, entangled in wire next to him—one decapitated—were now bony skeletons; pieces of woollen cloth, rotted and stained, hung like medals from their rib cages. Clarence breathed heavily, then let out a loud sob as he turned to grasp the trench wall. The lieutenant's face was only inches from Clarrie's, and it made him shrink in horror. Sharp's breath was putrid with death and decay and his voice shrilled with an intensity that maddened.

Against every sinew in his body that wished to stay still, Clarence took a foothold, and inched his way up the gully, which was gouged by the constant flow of the creek. Its dry orange dirt was scattered with tufts of grass but was wet and slimy to Clarence's touch. Just like the unforgettable Flanders clay, it seemed to ooze through his tightened fingers.

'Get on that parapet, Miller, and cut those bastard Germans down.'

Clarence looked across at the frenzied lieutenant. The willow tree swayed behind him. Suddenly the branches appeared to the traumatised private as impaled corpses; his good friend Jack dropped from high above to fall at the lieutenant's feet.

'See what happens when you don't act, Miller, people die!'

Clarence buried his head into the wall of the trench; he screamed, as he was—a madman.

***

The gelding pricked his ears and propped; the unusual sound flooded the horse's senses with alarm and tensed every muscle in his body. Ruth calmed Chester with a soft voice and gentle pat, while she stared intently towards the creek. The sound, though human, was tortured and crazed. She dug the heels of her boots into the gelding's flanks, driven by fear. Ruth galloped her charge across the paddock and towards the willow. She spotted movement in the gully. She reined in

Chester, roughly and without concern, and then dismounted while his head was still held aloft.

'Clarence!' Ruth brushed the hair from her face and strode towards the creek.

'This is it, Miller,' yelled Lieutenant Sharp. He produced his revolver and pointed it at Private Miller. 'Fritz is upon us, defend our position or I will shoot you where you lie.'

Clarence pulled his wretched body up the slope to peer over the parapet. To his horror he saw what the lieutenant had proclaimed. A German was striding like a conqueror intent on killing him.

Clarence felt the presence of the dark barrel near his temple and then heard the metallic sound of the revolver, cocked and ready to fire. The smell of his nemesis's rotted breath lay over him like a disease; it compelled Clarence to rip at his skin while he sobbed. He wanted it all to end. Desiring to be freed from bondage more than he feared death, he hoped the German would save him from another day of suffering. Clarence leapt from the trench as the soldier, dressed in the steely grey of his Bavarian regiment, appeared at its edge.

'Clarence, I'm...' started Ruth, before she gasped in shock.

Clarence grabbed the German by the tunic and used its oncoming momentum to roll backwards. The two bodies were thrown back into the trench; the enemy combatant frantically threw its arms about and ripped at Private Miller's hair. They plunged to the bottom of the gully. The Bavarian landed first, submerged in the cold waters of the creek. The branches of the willow waved over the scene below.

Deranged and beyond appeasing, Clarence lunged for the throat of his enemy after the fall had broken them apart. He held his captive submerged, locked in a murderous stare, screams of wounded men and futile charges against unrelenting guns rang in his ears, as the goading of Lieutenant Sharp thumped like a drum behind his feverish eyes. Desperate, the German clawed at his face; his trapped legs lifted and straightened violently to unseat the weight that held them.

Emboldened, Private Miller's underlying cowardice was replaced by uncommon bravado in the face of victory. He thrust harder and downward with his contracted hands, as bubbles of escaped air rose through the muddied pool of water that lay at the trench floor. The weakened fight from below him told his corrupted mind that all would be healed. Everything that had pained him would be at an end, and he would live in peace, the way Ruth and he had planned.

Ruth's face flashed into Clarence's conscience as the soldier went limp against the trench floor. He was relieved to have seen off his attacker but startled by the sudden feeling of cold water and the intrusion of bright sunlight.

***

With a forearm over his eyes to block out the sun, Clarence staggered through water that varied from knee to waist deep. He coughed and spluttered with exhaustion, and then stepped into a larger hole that caused him to fall headlong into the cold water. The icy stream stung his face as if it had been raked with a hot iron. The water entered the gouges dug by sharp nails and made him flinch.

Clarence wrestled with body and mind and brought himself to his knees. He was still in the creek, up to his waist in water, but with his back to the corpse. A breeze gusted and extended the reach of the willow tree; leaves from a low branch flicked Clarence across the face. He swung violently at the foliage. The sudden recognition of where he was brought the world around him to a standstill. He turned his head slowly, and acknowledged that day had turned to night and back to sparkling sunlight. Silence had replaced the concussion of noise. Lieutenant Sharp and other ghastly visions had vanished, replaced by the dejected self-pity that he always felt after his demons had surfaced.

Confused, he lifted a hand to touch his wounded face, and remembered the soldier he had fought. The reality of the struggle alarmed him. He had felt the body beneath him and felt the struggle, and then the submission that came with the life being taken.

'How could I feel that?' he asked. A foreboding made him turn his body.

Clarence froze at the sight. His wife floated in the cool waters only yards away. Her dark hair flowed, drawn by the current, like the olive-green reeds that surrounded her. It exposed her face, which was now white as snow and devoid of life. Her eyelids were closed and expressed peace, a falsehood to her violent and unforeseen end.

Clarence dropped to the water beside Ruth, and lifted her limp body out of the creek. Streams of water rushed from her clothes and hair; a shower of unrevealed traumas and mind-altering pain that Clarence had turned from. It had built up to wash over his life, killing—in the end—the one person that could have freed him.

He staggered out of the gully with the body of his wife and coughed at the taste of his own bile. A tiny part of his mind hoped he was irrevocably mad, and this was a nightmare. But wasn't he already there? Already finished, long ago? Why hadn't he killed himself like he wanted to when he lay prone beside the house on that rainy night? Why hadn't he stayed in Archie's place with Louth, and all would have been well. Why?

Clarence lifted his head skyward and let out a scream. It tore at his lungs and caused birds to fly from the crowns of trees. He put his lips to the ear of the only person he could love, and he spoke quietly. With guilt beyond redemption, he cursed the fate that he had once rejoiced in and felt without hope—at an end.

From the corner of his eye, Clarence saw Ruth's much-loved gelding, the horse staying near—waiting. In slow and even movements Clarence stood, and quietly approached the horse. He patted him on the neck and asked for forgiveness, and then removed the leather bridle and long reins attached to it.

TWENTY SIX

Gilmurra, September 1924

The small gathering broke away from the twin grave site, leaving Harry and Mary Reynolds standing side by side. They stared motionless, as if they too were made of marble or granite. Their inscriptions, not of gold lettering, but of immeasurable pain, were permanently etched on their features. They looked towards a single headstone that read:

In Loving Memory of
Clarence Miller 1-3-1896 – 3-9-1924
Ruth Miller 14-4-1897 – 3-9-1924
Accidentally killed

The block of granite stood between mounds of earth, scrutinised without tear or cry by a small, slender figure. Arthur Atkins stood to the side and watched Reginald.

Norman picked Emily up, while he put his other arm around Alice, overcome with grief. They stepped forward, one slow pace at a time. Alice had felt the finality that came with the lowering of the caskets into the ground. Each painful step away from the grave was a step away from her brother and sister-in-law. It closed a chapter, and confined them to memory.

The direction she had taken in life, the beliefs that she held, and freedom she had known as she grew up, could be attributed to her beloved Ruth. The memories of her own parents, while pleasant and warm, were more like the fond recollections of grandparents. Ruth had been the beacon that shone; she had stepped to the fore and guided her through her formative years.

Sent by a concerned Alice, Norman had not known why he acted the way he did after he had found Ruth on that terrible day. Naturally shocked and devastated when he found Ruth dead, he had come to the conclusion—with Chester nearby—that a fall from the usually even-tempered mount had been the cause. He had not noticed—in the confusion—her wet clothing or her bruised throat.

His thoughts had turned to Clarence; he made a quick search of the area and had found disturbed ground in the creek bed. Not long after, Norman made the horrendous discovery. Clarence, still and extinct, was suspended from a branch of a large tree by leather reins. The sight, which had kept Norman awake at nights, dropped him to his knees beneath the willow. He vomited on the ground, his senses overcome with tragedy and waste. A family—his family—whom he loved, shattered to the core.

For reasons of reputation, or to avoid shame for his wife and for Reggie, as well as out of concern for Emily's sanity, Norman made a snap decision. After he composed himself, he released Clarence from the tree branch and brought him to rest near his wife. He looked at them both, brought to an end by circumstances too sinister in their truth. He remembered Alice's stories about the two people who raised her. He decided, at that moment, to give his version of what was likely to the authorities. *Their bodies found within yards of each other, a horse found with its saddle hanging due to a loose girth, a tragic and probably avoidable accident.*

Norman squeezed the bridge of his nose as he tried to purge the terrible images in his mind. He stopped to look for Reggie, glad that the funeral was over. Oddly, through his wrong but necessary interference, there was one to have. A burden to carry, he realised, but one worth carrying, for the sake of what was left of his wife's family.

Whether through reluctance to stir up trouble or promote scandal in a small country town, Ruth's and Clarence's deaths were never investigated by the authorities, beyond an interview with Norman. As he watched Arthur Atkins at the grave site, bending down to talk to a rigid Reginald, Norman waited, and wondered what the coming years would hold for the young lad, now robbed of his parents.

With an arm around the young boy's shoulders, Arthur paused to speak with Mr and Mrs Reynolds. Harry broke from his static pose to tilt his head. His action acknowledged Arthur's presence, but his eyes said something else. Arthur spoke again to Reginald, and convinced the young lad to walk away from the cold headstone and join his aunty and uncle, as Thomas Reynolds approached from a distance to assist his mother to a motor vehicle.

'Mrs Clark,' said Arthur, 'please accept my sincere condolences. Clarence and Ruth will be missed by all in the community.'

Alice nodded a silent but genuine thank you, and turned her attention to Reggie.

'Norman,' said Arthur, 'may I have a word?'

'Of course, Mr Atkins,' replied Norm. He placed Emily at Alice's feet and moved several yards from his wife and the children.

'I know you have things to attend to,' said Arthur, 'so I will be brief. I wanted to expand on what I said before to Alice and possibly make it more official.'

Norm looked at Arthur, not exactly sure what the solicitor and war veteran meant.

'In the aftermath of this tragedy, Norman,' said Arthur, 'you will be faced with many obstacles. Some of them legal, in relation to your partnership with the Millers; others involve the children. We can talk on this later, but I would like to offer you my services at no charge for anything regarding the Miller's estate.'

Slightly taken aback by Arthur's offer, Norman had to admit to himself that he hadn't thought of such things.

'That is very generous of you, Mr Atkins, but...'

'I must insist, at the risk of seeming rude,' interrupted Atkins. 'It would bring some comfort to assist Clarence's children, having served with him.' Arthur offered his hand, and excused himself before Norman could argue.

***

Arthur Atkins stood in his office, his right arm rested against the mantle of the fireplace. His thoughts were far away as he swirled untouched whiskey in the bottom of a tumbler. When the news had reached him—through his father—that Clarence and Ruth Miller had been killed, he was blind-sided by emotion. His father saw his response as a sense of loss at another comrade taken from this world. In reality, Arthur had a suppressed need to release anger driven by admiration that was, in truth, love. Love for a soul that he saw as beautiful and inspiring, taken without warning.

Either through morbid curiosity to question what was stated, or a desire to somehow lay a portion of the blame on himself through inaction, Arthur pondered the circumstances that led to the Miller's demise. *But it was a fall from a horse, a married couple riding together*, he said to himself.

Regardless, the tragedy inspired him to go further and do more for people like Clarence and their families. He felt a dull but corroding shame that he had missed such an opportunity, which had presented itself through a brave woman.

He decided that if his theories were not taken seriously by his local member, he would have to find a bigger voice. He would stand for the federal seat of Colston in the next election.

The door to his office was flung open, no less violently than if he was being raided by the police. It startled Arthur from his thoughts.

'You went to the funeral, I see,' said Margaret Atkins in a raised and strangely accusing voice.

Arthur turned from the mantle, surprised but also annoyed at the intrusion and the aggressiveness of it.

'Of course, I attended the funeral,' replied Arthur, bewildered by his wife's statement. 'In case it has slipped from your memory, I served with Mr Miller in France.'

'Mr Miller,' replied Mrs Atkins condescendingly, as she pretended to take interest in a vase filled with roses.' 'He was a drunk, propped up by his in-laws.'

Arthur stared at his wife, stunned for a moment into silence. He placed the tumbler, with whiskey still in it, on the mahogany desk. He withdrew both of his hands and clasped them behind his back to release the tension that he felt. He opened and closed one of his hands before he spoke. 'I am fully aware, Margaret,' said Arthur, emphasising her name, 'that you have lived, with all your family's wealth...'

'I beg your pardon, I...'

'... In somewhat of a cocoon, never really appreciating, or wanting to for that matter, what people have gone through in recent times.'

'I won't be lectured to like a child, Arthur,' hissed Mrs Atkins, unused to having her thoughtless comments challenged.

Arthur stood as he had on many occasions, while serving King and Country, not speaking but looking, getting stronger people than Margaret Atkins to do as they were told.

'Clarence Miller,' said Arthur firmly, 'however he may have appeared to you, experienced things overseas that you could not even begin to imagine. I know, because I saw them with him. When you are in my presence,' continued Arthur, his voice raised, not in volume but in intensity, 'you will speak of him and his family with respect.'

Margaret Atkins stared at her husband as he breathed a little heavier. She watched him drink the contents of the crystal tumbler on his desk in one mouthful. She stayed motionless, stung by the tirade, but she recovered quickly. It allowed her own issues to boil to the surface, not aggressively, but coldly and callously. Margaret was not deluded—regardless of what Arthur thought of her—that she could intimidate her husband. Arthur's monogrammed handkerchief, clutched tightly in Mrs Miller's hand, flashed before her eyes.

'You loved her, didn't you?' said Margaret. She delivered the words like she had fired an arrow.

The words reached Arthur as they were intended; they pierced his heart. The flicker in Arthur's eye told Margaret what she had suspected, and she was hurt. Her temples burned, but outwardly she remained composed—years of being trained in the discipline of polite society.

'You loved that little tart,' she hissed with the venom of a serpent, 'but you weren't enough to drag her away from her pathetic husband.'

A white sheet blanketed Arthur's vision. All the restraint and discipline that he displayed in times of life threatening peril dissolved. He reacted, and with his right hand, he hurled the drained tumbler at his wife. The crystal shattered in a hundred pieces against the panelled wall next to the double timber doors. Arthur stepped from behind his desk, his eyes splintered with rage. He strode towards his wife and then stopped a few feet short of her while he pointed a clenched fist.

'Love,' roared Arthur in a voice that carried resentment and loneliness. 'Love... you wretched and disgusting woman. How does a person like you, who has never felt love, talk of it?' Arthur paused to look at someone he didn't recognise. 'Get out of my office, Margaret... and get out of my life.'

She barely flinched from the tirade, but was internally scarred. Margaret Atkins—nee Hamilton—turned and exited Arthur's office, while his rage and fire slowly faded. Arthur slumped where he stood.

A slight sound told him the door to the adjoining office had opened—the office of James Atkins.

'Son,' said Atkins senior, 'come inside for a moment.'

Part Three

TWENTY SEVEN

Denman Hill, June 1938

Alice handed Reginald a fresh cup of tea, while her nephew, with newspaper in hand, kept his eyes concentrated on the opposite wall. A notice board covered with pamphlets from different charitable organisations gave a welcome distraction from what was happening down the sterile corridor.

'Won't be much longer, Reg,' said Alice. She ignored the rebuff and then took a seat next to him with her own cup. She sipped the hot brew and allowed it to warm her as the rain, driven by a cold winter wind, splattered on the hospital windows.

'Huh?' grunted Reg, his eyes fixed on the notice board.

'It won't be long, dear,' repeated Alice, 'Judith will be fine.'

Reginald appeared not to have heard what Alice had said, and he looked down towards his newspaper. Alice wanted to attribute his behaviour to nerves at the impending birth of their first child, but she knew better.

'That Chamberlain will lead us all to war if he hasn't already,' said Reg.

'Sorry, dear?' replied Alice.

'Neville Chamberlain, the British Prime Minister. He is as weak a politician as you could find; Hitler will have him jumping through hoops draped in a Nazi flag soon.'

'I don't like to think about it Reg, really.'

'Well you must, Alice,' said Reg. He was suddenly animated, the most energised he had been all day. 'They have walked into Austria, which wasn't surprising, and now Hitler has beaten his chest about the Sudetenland in western Czechoslovakia. Meanwhile all Chamberlain does is try to pacify him. He has handed him treats like you would a spoilt child.'

'No one wants war,' said Alice quietly. Talk of violent conflict stirred memories that she would rather to keep to one side. Reg's ardent views surprised Alice, for her nephew had never struck her as the courageous type.

'Hitler wants it,' replied Reginald. He placed his cup on a small table next to his chair and covered his mouth to suppress a cough that had lingered recently. 'Mark my words, Alice; they will hand the Nazis the Sudetenland and then Hitler will take the whole of Czechoslovakia, and he won't stop there.'

Alice didn't answer for a moment; she had learnt to let Reginald's opinionated beliefs—be they right or wrong—fizzle out of their own accord; it made life more harmonious. Reg stared at her and waited for a comment, but Alice was saved by the matron who was walking towards them.

'Ah—looks like we have some news,' smiled Alice.

Reginald turned, and seemed almost disappointed to be interrupted in the midst of airing his position on world events.

'Mr Miller?' asked the matron with a pleasant smile on her face.

'Yes?' said Reg as he slowly stood up. Alice looked on with a glow to her cheeks. She took a moment to wonder how her brave nephew would conduct himself in the presence of Herr Hitler. She then cautioned herself against such childish thoughts.

'I am pleased to inform you that you are the proud father of a baby boy,' said the matron, 'seven pound, ten ounces.'

'Oh, isn't that wonderful Reg,' exclaimed Alice, truly delighted. 'I am so pleased for you.' She stepped forward to embrace the new dad.

Reginald exhaled quickly, a short huff laced with a faint smile. He was overwhelmed, caught somewhere between his own emotions and the self-doubt that came with sudden and undeniable responsibility.

'If you care to follow me, Mr Miller, said the Matron, I will take you to your wife and son.'

Alice didn't think and took a step forward to join them. The Matron turned and raised a hand to stop her. The act was not intended to offend, but delivered in the same way a ticket collector might stop a child from stepping onto the Ferris wheel at a fairground when the ride was full. Abruptly—in a moment of joy—it reminded Alice that she was unable to bear children. A hurt, amongst many in her life, that ached in the most indescribable way.

'Just the parents for the moment, I'm sorry.'

'Of course,' replied Alice.

Without a consoling touch or gentle word Reginald moved down the corridor, escorted by the matron; once again Alice was not surprised.

***

Emily busied herself about the house in anticipation of the arrival of Judith and little baby David. She cleaned the mess that her brother had allowed to accumulate in his wife's absence. Home from Saint Catherine's while on school holidays, she mentally ran through her list of friends at boarding school who could boast to having a nephew at the age of sixteen, and found there to be none. It brought a smile to her face.

In an attempt to avoid confrontations with her brother, she had elected to stay with Aunt Alice and Uncle Norm at Avondale while on holidays. Although Reg was now married, the clashes of personalities that had existed between brother and sister since Emily was able to speak had not lessened, despite the accommodations of her lovely sister-in-law Judith. If she were to answer directly—which she never had a problem with doing—Emily would say that the thought of Judith's comfort was the reason she had cleaned so vigorously, not any overbearing sense of sisterly duty.

Energetic and independent when a young girl, Emily had grown into a passionate and idealistic young lady. She had often been told—particularly by her aunt—that she was a lot like her mother, with her father's eyes, which always brought a feeling of warmth, closely followed by regret.

Her only attachments to her deceased parents were photographs, relayed stories and the unique spiritual bond that exists between mother and child. She had always, even more so of late, shown a desire to know her parents, and Alice had done her best to satisfy Emily's curiosity. She told Emily of her own feelings towards Ruth, and the mystical spell that she had captivated her with while a young girl. Alice relived the almost fairy-tale like memories of Emily's parents' wedding, the times when she would secretly watch Ruth read letters from Clarence who was serving overseas. She relayed, with sadness, the misunderstood tear that she would watch roll down the cheek of the mother, that would in turn roll down the cheek of the daughter as she listened.

For his own reasons, Reginald wasn't as welcoming when Emily had approached him one evening to talk of their parents. He brushed her off the instant she mentioned their names; one of the reasons, among many, why Emily saw her brother as weak.

Emily possessed a sharp intellect and had been sent to board at the prestigious Saint Catherine's in Melbourne to further her education. She had repaid Alice's and Norm's faith in her and their investment by studying diligently. She topped her class in everything but religion, much to the displeasure of the nuns. Emily's questions—which were dismissed and then eventually ignored—were too frequent and disruptive for their liking. A conversation with a conciliatory Aunt Alice was needed to alleviate any tensions and avert the installation of obstacles to her advancement.

She dusted the skirting boards in the lounge room, and then stood upright abruptly. Her ears picked up the sound of the Ford coupe utility as it made its way sedately along the driveway. Emily looked out the window to confirm what she heard, and glimpsed the dark blue vehicle before it disappeared into a slight depression. Excited, Emily scurried down the hall for the back door.

Emily negotiated the path around the house, and waited impatiently for the vehicle to appear. She raised her arms above her head as the vehicle pulled out of the gully and came into view. She smiled and waved happily at Reginald as he stepped out of the car. Her brother tipped his hat and then gave a warm smile in return. The deed signified the magnitude of the event—the moment not lost on Emily.

Reg walked around the vehicle and opened the passenger side door to allow his wife to step out. Judith looked radiant as she moved into the winter sunshine with her baby held securely in her arms.

Emily approached Judith and kissed her on the cheek; cautiously, she placed an arm around her, terrified of hurting little David.

'I'm so excited, Jude,' said Emily, as Reg removed Judith's bags and the baby's bassinet from the tray of the vehicle. 'You look wonderful.'

'Thank you, Emily,' replied Judith proudly, 'let's go inside and you can hold him.'

Emily's eyes widened, and she turned quickly to make for the house, only to be stopped by the sound of another vehicle—a Ford exactly like Reg's, but white.

'Aunt Alice, Uncle Norm, Judith is home,' exclaimed Emily as the Clarks stepped out of their vehicle. Both the blue and the white Fords had been astute purchases by Norman. The vehicle's load-carrying capacity classed it as a work truck, so it allowed the Miller-Clark partnership to obtain a loan to buy them. Norm negotiated a good price from a depression-hit dealer.

'Yes, M,' said Alice with a smile, 'what wonderful timing.'

'Congratulations Judith… Reg,' said Norm, as he reached out to shake Reginald's hand firmly.

'Thank you, Norm,' replied Reg. 'Should we get the little fella inside?'

'Certainly, Reg,' said Alice.

'Let me help you with the bags, mate,' offered Norm.

'Thanks.'

Norm and Alice stood back to allow Reg the honour of leading his family into the house. Norm felt a pang of discomfort while he witnessed the pleasant scene. The ache was lessened by the knowledge that they had been able to nurture two children into or near adulthood, giving all the parental love that they possessed. Unable to raise a family as nature intended, they gave Reg and Emily all the devotion, tenderness and kindness that nature would want.

***

Norman and Reg stepped out of the house and walked towards the milking shed, while Judith fed baby David. Alice and Emily remained inside to prepare lunch in the kitchen. Both of them were full of the unbridled joy that comes with a baby's first day at home. Pleased to be back at Denman Hill after ten days in Gilmurra Hospital, Judith sat quietly in an armchair and stared in wonder at her son.

'What made you choose David as a name?' asked Emily. The question came out more intrusive than she intended. 'It's a lovely name,' she continued quickly, 'I was just curious.'

Judith paused for a moment to think and then looked up from her infant son. Although shy and reserved, Judith gave Alice the impression that she had a strength that lay well covered by her outward appearance. Brought up in a family of ten, her parents were hard workers and honest members of the community. Unskilled, Mr Pratt would do his best to provide in any way he could. Judith learnt early in life that not to expect helped to avoid disappointment. Maybe that was why she was drawn to Reginald. While undoubtedly self-centred, he had a certain arrogance around women, which could be construed as charm. He had shown interest in her, where others had not, and as sad as it may sound, that was a reason in itself. Judith's domestic situation had not provided for nice dresses and attendance at social functions.

'I had a few in mind, Emily,' replied Judith, 'but David just came to me. I suppose I should have consulted Reginald, but it just felt right.'

'Good for you,' stated Alice, pleased to jump into Judith's corner and support her.

'It means "beloved" or "friend", and it may sound odd, but that is what I thought when I first looked at his little face. He will be a friend to all.'

'How lovely,' said Alice as she wiped a tear from her eye with a handkerchief.

***

'I was thinking, Reg,' said Norm while he propped himself against the milking shed, 'we should look to put on one, possibly two men in the future.'

'Do you think we need it?' replied Reg. 'I thought we were on top of things, and we are still recovering from the Depression.'

'It's probably a bad day to bring this up,' said Norm. He knew Reg's resistance to change, 'with the baby coming home and everything.'

'No, it's fine,' said Reg.

'I just think it could be a good time to look at expanding. There's a block of about one thousand acres with frontage to the Tilcan coming up for sale.'

'Whereabouts?'

'Sid Mortimer's place.'

'Oh,' replied Reg. A feeling of inadequacy came over him. He couldn't help it, but he was often consumed with jealousy when he was unable to see what other people could. There was no need for it. *Different people have different strengths,* Norm would tell him while he was growing up. Norm had learnt to interpret his behaviour over the years, and had decided not to impart too many truths, now that Reg was a married man. 'If you think it is a good move, Norm, but...'

'What's on your mind Reg?'

'Well, Europe, the Japanese, don't you think we are headed for conflict in one way or another?'

'Yes, more than likely,' replied Norm in a confident voice. 'But strange as it may seem, Reg, it may be all the more reason. We should go into town together next week and have a chat with the accountant. What do you say?'

'Sure, Norm,' replied Reg, annoyed that he somehow felt less in control than when he had stepped out of his vehicle to meet Emily.

'Good, now let's go and see this son of yours again, and toast his health,' said Norm while he placed his arm, as thick as an oak branch, around Reg's shoulders. The act unintentionally belittled the newly made father. It caused the cold iron doors that restricted Reg's personality to contract a little more.

The afternoon passed quickly and turned to evening. The small gathering of Millers and Clarks had enjoyed the food prepared by Alice and Emily, with compliments given by all. Reg, who was now on the slide—after celebratory ales—was also unusually open with praise. As he moved from tipsy cheerfulness to objectionable drunk, the issue of world peace and his view on it found its way into the conversations.

Early in their courtship, Judith had noticed Reg's lack of resistance to the effects of alcohol. At the time she had not read much into it, but now, perhaps with the protectiveness that comes with motherhood, she found it distasteful. She stood up in the middle of her husband's lecture and moved to the stove to boil the kettle. Alice noticed Judith's annoyance, and casually retrieved an unfinished platter of sandwiches. She offered the food to the distracted men and removed the beer glasses, to be replaced by cups of hot tea. She nudged Norm as she did and gave the much soberer man a wink and a nod in Reginald's direction.

TWENTY EIGHT

Gilmurra, 3 September 1939

Through the open wrought iron gates supported by sandstone pillars, Alice walked along the gravel pathway that meandered through the Gilmurra cemetery. With a bouquet of flowers in her hand, she looked up through the canopy of pine branches and nettles. The light, warm in its touch, dazzled as it brushed her face, and flooded her mind with thoughts of Ruth and Clarence. Their death, fifteen years ago on this day, was still so raw and painful.

Alice noticed a figure approach from further along the path; she recognised the man and made eye contact.

'Good morning, Mrs Clark,' said Arthur. He had visited the Millers grave and was on his way to the train station.

'Good morning, Mr Atkins,' replied Alice politely. Neither person paused for small talk; both were there for the same reason, but with emotions that would not relate.

After a few minutes, Alice found herself at the headstone. A small bunch of flowers lay against the slightly weather-worn granite. She wiped a tear from her eye with a delicately made handkerchief, and placed her bouquet down, while she stared at the gold lettering that told the world that the couple that lay here once existed. It didn't mention: that they were once very much in love, as much in love as any two people could be.

'Your grandson is beautiful, and growing every day,' said Alice in a whisper while she wiped her eyes again. 'Judith is a wonderful mother. Reggie has a lovely little family. Emily… ' Alice released a restrained cry as she thought of the young girl who had become a young lady, never knowing her parents. 'Emily is a very bright young lady… you would be so proud. Like you, Clarrie, but so much like you Ruthy—independent and cheeky. She told me that she will study law at Sydney University, and I believe her. She gives those teachers in Melbourne a terrible time.' Alice let out a laugh that turned into a cry, and she tucked her chin to her chest and covered her eyes with one hand in an effort to control it.

In the distance, the grind of a steam locomotive's wheels, which had gripped and then slipped on the cold steel tracks, made its way to Alice on a light breeze. The clearer sound of its whistle confirmed the trains arrival in Gilmurra.

'Speaking of M,' said Alice quietly, 'there she is… back from school. I will go and meet her, I'm sure she will want to come back up and visit. She loves you both.' Alice kissed her own hand and then placed that hand gently on the headstone before she walked away.

On the platform of Gilmurra train station, Alice greeted a bubbly, slightly dishevelled Emily, who had sat up through the overnight journey from Melbourne. They embraced, exchanged pleasantries and then hugged again before they walked arm-in-arm to the cafe for tea and toast and a long talk. After they finished their pot of tea, they walked arm-in-arm again, through the wrought iron gates to Emily's parents' headstone. They talked some more, and then together in a moment of silence, they stared at the bleak headstone. Alice offered her embrace as comfort and held Emily while the young lady had her turn to cry.

***

The sight of Alice hugging the very grown-up Emily Miller on the train station platform gave Arthur Atkins mixed feelings of familiarity and detachment. He held an opened newspaper and looked out the window of his first-class compartment. He recalled how involved he had been with Reginald and Emily after the death of their parents. He had ensured all the legal requirements were in place for a smooth transition into guardianship for Norm and Alice, and he had re-worked the Miller and Clark partnership without interruption. Arthur's work was meticulous and had satisfied Mr and Mrs Reynolds as to their grandchildren's share in the pastoral enterprise. Now, with work and other commitments, and after fifteen long years, he would be surprised if Emily was able to recognise him should they cross paths in the street; *would she have to ask his name when selling him a raffle ticket for the CWA? More than likely*, he thought.

It had not been an easy time for Arthur after Clarence and Ruth had passed away. There were still times, not often—but often enough—when Arthur would allow questions to enter his mind in regard to the circumstances of their death. The period of examination would always be short lived; Arthur inevitably would chastise himself, he doubted if he or anyone had a right to question such things.

He had an undergone a period of separation from his wife after their heated exchange. It was declared—by both families—as an extended holiday for Margaret, its aim being to prevent gossip and damage to reputation. After an eventual reconciliation, motivated, not by love, but by considerations for their future, Arthur and Margaret lived the unhappy life of practicality—smiling in public, polite but mostly avoiding each other at home.

Arthur had engrossed himself in work and juggled his hours between the law practice and his entry into public life. After long consideration, he had decided his conscience and his community would be best served if he were affiliated with the Country Party. He did not believe in a Socialist Australia, as hard-line Labor people did, and he didn't feel comfortable with joining the Nationalist Party, with their ties to pro-conscription men such as Billy Hughes. The irony—as Arthur would have to confront—was in the compromises of politics that lay around every corner. The coalition between the Nationalists and Country Party would see him eventually co-exist with people he had tried to avoid. Arthur consoled himself in his devotion to winning his seat and serving his electorate.

After being introduced to the leader of the Country Party, Sir Earl Page, by a former University colleague, Arthur was put forward as the Country Party candidate for the seat of Colston in the 1925 federal election. Arthur had worked tirelessly within his electorate in the months that led up to the ballot. Supported by his wife at public engagements and his father's office with day-to-day administration, he defeated John Higgins of Labor and the Independent candidate, James O'Donnell, in what could be described as a narrow margin.

Arthur's hard work within his own electorate, and the perception of his constituents that he was an honest, reliable man, saw him re-elected at the next five consecutive federal elections. Each time, he increased his majority, even when in opposition to Scullin's Labor government. This in turn increased his stature within the party, until the last election in 1937, when Gordon Higgins, a protégé of the current Labor leader John Curtin, and the son of Arthur's former rival John Higgins, made a stunning debut. Higgins pulled thirty-eight per cent of the vote to Arthur's forty-six, an increase to Labor from the previous election in 1934 of over eleven percent.

That last election had been a wake-up call for the member for Colston. Arthur wondered what he had done differently to cause the swing among his loyal voters. *Maybe that was the problem*, he thought, as a group of late-comers scurried onto the train bound for Canberra and then Sydney. A man in black uniform with a whistle held between his lips urged them over the gap that separated station from carriage.

He had ridden the wave when the Nationalists had lost fifteen seats and government, including the seat of Stanley Bruce, the coalition leader and Prime Minister. He had prevailed when Bruce's men—in opposition—had been absorbed into the United Australia Party led by former Labor man, Joseph Lyons, to become the new coalition partner of the Country Party. The new political force had defeated Scullin in a landslide, and he had held the party line right through the 1930s; when not once—much to Margaret's chagrin—was he offered a front bench position.

All through this time, he thought, as the train's whistle blew, he had stayed true to his beliefs. And now, as the train jolted into motion, he realised he felt tired. Arthur looked down at the paper he held—a day old—and was struck by the headline and the irony it held. For the majority of his political life, he had fought, not only for his electorate, but for the rights of returned service men, and now he saw the words: *'Germany Invades Poland.'*

Deep in thought, Arthur didn't hear the door to the compartment slide open. He pondered, without hope of an easy answer, how the world had come to this again.

'Tickets please, sir,' said an elderly conductor.

Arthur lifted his head to smile at the man.

'Oh, it's you, Mr Atkins,' said the conductor, 'I didn't realise you were back home.'

'Hello, Bill,' replied Arthur. The elderly man's face showed that he was chuffed to be recognised by a sitting member of parliament, regardless of the fact that he had known Arthur since he was a little boy. 'Just a quick visit this time, Bill.'

'Horrible business that, isn't it,' said Bill. He pointed to the newspaper and then punched Arthur's ticket.

Arthur stared at the newspaper but didn't answer. He had spent the most recent years of his life making speeches and putting his point forward, but now he was suddenly unable to speak. He was struck by the simplicity of the man's statement and its truth. *A horrible business it is*, he said silently, *the most horrible of any kind.*

Bill felt uncomfortable in the silence and excused himself with a tip of his hat.

***

Alice removed the roast lamb from the stove, just as Reginald, Judith and little David pulled up to the front of the house. Emily walked quickly down the hall towards the front door after she had heard the vehicle. She had come back to Avondale with Alice as usual for her school holiday stay, but that morning she had told Alice that she would like to spend a few nights at her brother's house. The desire to spend time with her little nephew outweighed any argument she might have with Reginald.

The aroma of a traditional Sunday roast greeted the Millers as they entered the house. Emily fussed over Judith and David. She walked backwards down the hallway and stayed as close to the little baby as possible.

'Emily,' cried Alice in a motherly way, 'give your sister-in-law some room.'

'Sorry,' said Emily as she stepped to one side.

'Hello Judith, Reg,' said Norm, before he stepped through the lounge room doorway. He held a folded newspaper in his hand. Its contents had not altogether surprised him, but it was still being digested; the unacceptable aggression by Germany had brought to an almost certain reality what many had foreseen. It brought into action a decision Norm had already made.

'Hello, Norman,' replied Judith with a smile, 'thank you for inviting us over.'

'Our pleasure; would you like to put that in the spare room?' said Norm, pointing to the bassinet that Reg held.

'If it's not too much trouble Norm, thank you,' said Judith.

'Follow me, Reg.'

'The lamb's ready,' said Alice, 'come and have a seat while I get Norm to carve.'

'I think Hitler has finally prodded the old Lion into action,' said Reg.

'Certainly looks that way,' replied Norman while he took the bassinet from Reg.

'It will if England and France stand true to their word,' replied Reg in an excited voice, 'and not hang the Poles out to dry like they did the poor old Czechs!'

'Reg,' said Norm quietly but firmly, while he turned to face the younger man. Norm realised that even though one of Reg's sermons was most likely unavoidable, he had probably reacted too early to reign him in, and adjusted his approach accordingly. 'Whatever happens will happen in due course.' Norm tried to make a point without the appearance of a lecture; he paused for a moment. 'I have the radio on in the lounge-room, I...'

His blood still up, Reginald took that as an invitation to move to the room where the radio sat but was halted by Norm's voice.

'I am sure you and I think the same... we would like to protect the ladies from as much of this as possible... tough times lie ahead.'

'Of course, Norm,' said Reg. He knew he was being instructed, but to keep the perception of his own manhood, he went along with Norm.

'Alice has cooked a roast,' said Norm. 'Why don't we enjoy that, and then we can retire to the lounge,' continued Norman. He had other things on his mind. He used the pretence of calmness as a way to divert his own misgivings as to how he would best tell Alice that he had decided to enlist, should war be declared.

***

With baby David content and asleep, the Millers decided to stay for supper. The huge lunch that Alice prepared earlier made the evening meal a light one, and after Emily had cleared the table, they moved onto the verandah to enjoy a crystal-clear spring evening. The ladies wore cardigans, and they all sipped tea to keep the cool but pleasant air at bay. The near full moon stood like a sentry and guarded the property, casting a soft light over the surrounding paddocks.

'Isn't the moon lovely?' said Emily, as she leaned over the balustrade and stared into the sky.

'It's a waning gibbous,' commented Reginald.

'Oh, really, Reggie,' mocked Emily in an aristocratic voice.

'Yes, it is,' replied Reg matter-of-factly, 'I thought they may have taught you that at school.'

'Now, now you two,' interjected Alice, 'it's been a lovely evening, let us not spoil it.'

'What time did they say the Prime Minister will speak on the radio, Uncle Norm? said Emily, changing the subject. She smiled as she watched her older brother brood over their exchange.

'9.15, M,' replied Norm. He smiled at his niece's cheek and her ability to rile her brother.

'Do you think there will be war?' continued Emily.

'Of course there will be,' blurted Reg. 'the Nazis have gone too far this time, even for an appeaser like Chamberlain.'

Emily looked towards her brother without a word, and then directed her gaze back to Norm, which irked Reginald even more.

Norm, like Alice, wanted the night to pass peacefully, so he chose to answer in a way that would keep Reginald's temper from getting the better of him.

'I have to agree with your brother, M, war does look likely.' Emily gasped as her trusted uncle spoke the words. 'But I pray, like everyone, that Germany will back down.'

Reg went to speak, not satisfied with Norm's olive branch, but desisted. Norman's stern look reminded Reg of their earlier conversation.

'I pray that they find a peaceful solution,' said Judith. 'What good comes of war?'

'Indeed,' said Alice, seated in her favourite rocking chair. She stared blindly into the night. 'What good?' she said again before she sipped on her tea. Her mind was with Archie and Clarence, her mother and father, Frank—who she sometimes forgot existed. 'War... war destroyed my family,' she stated. She stood and entered the house. Her departure left a chill that swept like a ghost along the verandah. It touched each person and affected them in their own way.

'I will go and speak to her,' said Norm quietly. His wife's release of her innermost thoughts, like a dagger to his guilt-ridden heart. The magnitude of the decision he had made struck him with a realism that left him with a desire for atonement, even before he enacted the hurt.

***

Sorry, not for what she had said, nor for when she said it; for she felt it needed to be said. She was just sorry—as she always was—for causing any form of upset. Alice placed a tray, with a fresh pot of tea and biscuits, on a small table in the centre of the lounge room and refilled everyone's cup. As they gathered around the radio and waited for the address from the Prime Minister, each person gave Alice a reassuring smile and a thank you. Each let her know that they were all family, there for her when she needed them.

Norman adjusted the volume and then stood back to receive suggestions, before he resumed his seat in a large leather armchair. Alice moved alongside him and sat on the chair arm; she took Norm's hand in hers. Reg sat forward slightly on the two-seater with Judith, while Emily stood behind her with one hand on Judith's shoulder; the other nervously straightened her dress.

A moment's silence came over the radio, followed by some background noise, and then a voice.

'Here is the Prime Minister of Australia, the right honourable R.G. Menzies.'

'Fellow Australians, it is my melancholy duty to inform you officially that in consequence of a persistence by Germany in her invasion of Poland, Great Britain has declared war upon her and that, as a result, Australia is also at war.'

Judith gasped as Alice squeezed Norm's hand hard, while she raised her other hand to her mouth. Reg slumped back in his seat, numb, now that what he had spoken of so vigorously had arrived in a sentence. Emily slowly removed her hand from Judith's shoulder and moved to sit by her brother's feet.

'No harder task can fall to the lot of a democratic leader than to make such an announcement...'

Only Norman stayed seated to hear the Prime Minister's full speech; Judith, summoned by a baby's cry, excused herself and hurried down the hall. With the status quo disrupted, there was a gradual departure of people from the lounge room; Reginald was the first to leave, followed by Alice.

Emily sat with her uncle for a few minutes, and then rose to her feet. She realised that Norm was engrossed in the radio, not her presence, which made it easier for her to depart. She made her way to the verandah, where she found her brother. He leaned against one of the many timber posts that supported the porch roof. His face and body were softly lit by the calm light of the moon. Emily thought it made him look younger—more composed. Reg lifted his head slightly and blew a cloud of tobacco smoke into the air. The habit of cigarettes had recently become part of his life.

'Hello, Reg,' said Emily; it sounded odd to her once it was said.

Reg nodded towards her, but didn't speak. He looked back towards the open space in front of the house. The dark and twisted gum trees, which had survived indiscriminate clearing many years ago, appeared to Reg as disgruntled custodians of a sacred but disturbed place. Emily allowed him his space, and moved towards the rail directly in front of her. She contemplated what she had just heard on the radio.

'Some time back, a year perhaps' said Reginald suddenly, 'while you were home from school, you asked me about our parents.'

Emily turned to face her brother, but remained where she was, surprised at the topic Reg had raised.

'I didn't answer you,' continued Reg, 'and I suppose, you would probably wonder why I would act in that way.' Reg paused to draw back on his smoke. He still stared intently at the eucalypt guardsmen. 'I think of our mother a lot, though it's getting harder, more of a feeling than a recollection of events. She was beautiful and loving, I can remember that.'

A tear rolled down Emily's face and rested on her upper lip. She raised her hand to wipe it. In the strange light, the figure on the verandah seemed more like an apparition than her brother; his mood and countenance were at odds with what Emily had come to expect. Reg's voice carried words and thoughts that were precious beyond belief, like hot sands that had known the caressing effect of water, but were tortured by its limited supply.

'My father… our father, he was different.' Like he was in confession, Reg paused, while he considered how much to say. His options were limited. 'I remember him giving me a teddy bear as a present; in my mind I cannot see his face, but I know he is there handing it to me. I called it Harvey.'

Emily lifted her hand once again to her mouth and pushed her lips together, a reaction to the image of a little boy, feet dangling off a bed, innocent and impressionable.

'But I remember being scared of him. I remember running after he would hit me and hiding, and I remember my mother crying.'

The metallic sound of a door handle being turned caused Emily to turn away from her brother. She looked towards the front door of the house and saw her Aunt Alice step past the threshold.

'Emily,' said Alice, 'I thought I heard someone out here.'

Emily looked back towards her brother and lamented her Aunt's timing. She felt despondent, for, like the apparition she had seen him to be, her brother—speaking to her as he never had—was gone.

'Are you alright, dear?' asked Alice, as she noticed Emily's tear-filled eyes. 'It's upsetting, the thought of war, but you have us, dear; you will always have us.'

Emily leaned into Alice's hug, her thoughts with Reg. Alice's last words rung in her ears. *My mother probably promised us the same thing*, she thought, *you will always have us.*

TWENTY NINE

Avondale, 5 September, 1939

'Why, Norman, why?' cried Alice, as she broke away from her husband. Norman, who stood on the lawn at the rear of their house, watched Alice. He had prepared himself for a reaction. He stood motionless as Alice walked a few paces to stand beside an immature elm tree. One arm was folded to her chest, the other supported the hand that clasped her face.

Norman took a step towards his wife, but she spun violently. She took her hand from her face and thrust it towards him.

'Stop, Norman,' yelled Alice. Her heart screamed with fear and abandonment. 'Why would you do this to me!' The 'you' was not Norman, but her life. Norman would bear the brunt though, for he had delivered life's most recent blow.

'Ally!'

'Why, Norman?' continued Alice. She cried hysterically before she ran and left Norm alone where he stood. Norm's shoulders were hunched, his face lined with despair for the hurt he had caused, but his resolve was shamefully unmoved. That feeling caused Norm to ask questions that had never previously risen.

***

Several hours passed before Alice returned to the house. She entered through the back door that led into an annex and found her husband at the kitchen table with a newspaper in hand. A tea cup—long since emptied—sat close to his right hand.

Norm stood and moved towards Alice, who rushed forward to embrace the man she loved.

'I know it's hard to understand, Ally,' said Norm, as he held Alice's head to his chest, 'but it is something I feel I must do.'

Alice listened to Norm speak and knew that no matter what they said to each other, things wouldn't change. She knew her husband to be a thoughtful and intelligent man, who wasn't prone to making rash decisions. It was likely that he had thought of this for some time, well before the Prime Minister's speech. But it didn't stop her asking herself—*why?*

'You are all I have, Norman,' said Alice as she lifted her head to reveal eyes that glistened with tears. 'If I could stop you, I would, a thousand times over. I don't care that tyrants need to be stood up to and stopped, I honestly don't—not when it's thousands of miles away. I just want you by my side forever. But... ' Alice paused to sit at the table. Norm did the same while he held his wife's hand. 'But—the crazy thing is—and I thought of this while I cried my eyes out and wondered who or what I was upset with. I knew, as I always have, that I love you, more than anything, I love you, Norman, and I could never ask you to be anyone other than you.'

Humbled by Alice's honesty and selflessness, Norm leant over and kissed his wife. He gently wiped away a tear that slid down her cheek. He followed—with his lips—the path of his own hand, not touching but near. He caught the familiar scent of his wife's skin, soft and pure; the pleasure from this simple act forced him to close his eyes. He allowed his hand to fall over her shoulder and down to her waist, and he felt the surge of desire that always had bewitched him. Norm opened his eyes to see the lady he had married fifteen years ago, and contemplations of what he would expose to chance entered his mind.

'You know that I am sorry, don't you Norm?'

'Don't be silly, Ally,' replied Norm as he returned to his seat. He squeezed the hand that he had held all this time. 'I would be concerned if you didn't get upset,' he added, and then laughed a little. He admired his wife's courage.

'Not that,' replied Alice, 'I was angry in the backyard, I am still angry, just not at you.' Alice shifted in her seat and looked at the timber floor; the seriousness of Norm's announcement had drawn her to address something that had always remained unsaid. 'I am sorry, Norman,' continued Alice. She no longer looked at the floor but directly into her husband's eyes, 'I am sorry that I have never been able to give you a child.'

Norman opened his mouth, but no words came. He was shocked, but also heartbroken that Alice, the woman he loved, could think that what she confessed to being a sorrowful regret, was a burden she should carry alone.

'I know you love me, Norman, and I feel loved, but I wanted that so badly for you—for us.'

He searched for words that could give any comfort at all to Ally, however small; he felt overwhelmed and reached out once more to hug his wife. 'I love you, Alice. You have done nothing but bring happiness to my life. It has always been you, and you alone, that feeds my every want in this world.' He held his wife's shoulders in his powerful hands. The scene may have appeared aggressive to a person who stumbled into the room, but this was Norm's best known way of conveying his deepest, most sincere feelings. His arms, as he held Alice tightly, relayed all the emotion he had coiled up in his masculine frame. 'Alice, I would be just another farmer's son if I hadn't met you; working and resting, never knowing, let alone feeling, what it is to be someone's love, their friend and companion.'

Alice moved towards her husband and felt a need to possess him. Her want was a composite of love, frailty, and the fear of loss. Her energies simmered beneath the surface, her skin responsive to the most delicate touch or imperceptible breeze. Gently but persuasively, Alice placed her hands on Norman's chest. She brushed them lightly against the fabric of his shirt, before she removed them to unbuttoning her floral dress. Alice allowed it to fall to the timber boards. The cotton garment floating down, taking inhibitions and shyness with it. She kissed the man she loved gently on the neck and unbuckled his belt. The tempo of their movements increased as the strained emotions of the last few hours reformed into unrestrained passion. Norm frantically removed Alice's undergarments, and then picked up his wife in one fluid movement. Alice wrapped her slender legs around his waist, while her hands were clasped around his neck. They kissed roughly. Alice's intensity drove Norman to a frenzy of lust that craved release. They stumbled towards the kitchen wall. Alice sighed as she felt the coldness of the plaster on her back, and moaned in complete submission as her husband entered her. His hips pushed harder as Alice clawed her nails along his shoulder blades. The low rumblings that came from deep within him developed into a ravenous cry as Alice used her entwined legs to meet his every thrust. Alice's body became rigid, frozen in place at the height of her excitement. She pressed her body closer against his, as every muscle in her body tightened and then shuddered, driving her husband over the edge. He was rendered helpless and under her complete control in one blinding flash of pleasure.

***

'Oh, hello,' said Judith sharply. She placed one hand to her chest while the other clasped the clothes line. The peg that she was about to place fell from her grasp. 'You gave me a fright.'

'Sorry,' said Norm, 'didn't mean to sneak up on you.'

'No, no, not your fault, I was a million miles away… shopping in one of those big stores in Sydney,' she said with a giggle.

Norm smiled, but didn't reply immediately His morning had

been unscripted, to say the least, and he was not sure how the next scene would play out. 'Is Reg about?'

'Yes,' replied Judith. She noted Norman's mood. 'He is over in the shed... doing some work on a plough, I think. Is everything alright?'

'Yes Jude, I won't keep him long,' said Norman as he made his way directly to the structure that housed the machinery, alongside the stable and milking shed.

Reg cursed as the spanner he was using slipped off the nut. It propelled his hand into the solid steel of the plough and skinned his knuckles.

'Useless prick of a thing,' yelled Reg.

'Having some trouble?' asked Norm from just outside the shed.

Reg kissed his knuckles, thought of something to say and then decided against it. 'Hello, Norm. Bastard nuts are rusted on.'

'Try giving it a whack.'

'Already have. What brings you over this way Norm; I thought you were going over to see Richard and Paul?'

'I am... eventually. Couple of things came up this morning.' Norm took a casual look around the shed to give himself the time to gather his thoughts. 'I've got something to tell you, Reg, or ask you, is probably the better way of saying it,' Norm felt the contradiction in that his wife was not given the same option. 'So I might as well just come out and say it. How do you feel about running the three places? I want to enlist.'

Reg rose from where he was crouched beside the plough. A range of thoughts passed through his mind. The most prominent being how Norm had been able to get under his guard and declare his intention to fight for his country. The feeling of jealousy that often weakened him crept into his veins.

The sensation had no real right to project itself, for Reg—since the Prime Minister's speech—had discovered he had no desire to enlist. His energetic assessment of world politics, he realised, was about as far as he wanted to go. The declaration of war had softened his aggressiveness, and led him to his moment with Emily, where he had opened up and revealed some family history she was not aware of. It had felt good at the time—in that moment—but Reg had instantly regretted his actions, and berated himself while he had escaped down one side of the house. The divulging of closely held memories and emotions brought a sense of emasculation. That sensation brought forward a different type of aggressiveness, one of bitterness and malice, which would strive to take hold of the young father.

Confused by his own inadequacies, Reg focused his energies into not being manipulated by his uncle's steadfast persona. A shrewder person may have welcomed Norm's announcement, as it tied him to the farm and provided an excuse not to enlist. But Reg was more insidious than clever or intelligent, and he spoke before he collected his thoughts. 'What about the new block?'

'I have thought about that,' replied Norm. He attempted to work on Reg's ego. 'But I think the McMillan boys will handle it under your supervision.'

'I suppose so...' said Reg. The idea of being in complete charge and out of his uncle's shadow gave him a thrill that made him feel oddly excited after his initial resentment. 'Have you said anything to the McMillans?'

'Of course not, Reg, Alice and you are the only people who know, and Judith, once you speak to her. Richard and Paul are employees, good ones at that, but employees all the same.'

'How did Aunt Alice take the news?'

'Upset—at first,' said Norm humbly, 'but she is understanding and supportive.'

'I thought of joining myself,' said Reg, confident Norm would be resolute in his decision.

'I didn't realise...'

'But then, what would we do with the property?' asked Reg.

Norm pretended to inspect the plough. He ran his hand along it and allowed Reg's question to hang in the air for a moment.

'We...' started Norm.

'If you think the McMillans are up to it, I think I could run the farms,' interjected Reg. 'We can't let the place go backwards after we have worked so hard.'

'That's what I thought,' replied Norm innocently. 'Well, it's settled then, you're the boss now, mate,' added Norm with an awkward smile, as he reached out to shake Reg's tentative hand.

'When will you leave?'

'Not for a bit. I have to be in Sydney in a few weeks, but if it is alright with you, I would like to go a bit earlier and have a few days with Alice, a sort of holiday before I depart.'

'Certainly, Norm, whatever you like,' replied Reg. The enormity of what had just unfolded started to sink in.

'It will give us a chance to go and see the solicitor and make sure everything is in order.'

'In order?' quizzed Reg, without thought.

'Well... yes, mate,' replied Norm. He had tried to imply what he would prefer not to say out loud. 'Just to cover ourselves...'

'Yes, yes, Norm, sorry,' said Reg, flustered, 'you just tell me when.'

'You have made this easy for me Reg, thanks' said Norm. 'I appreciate it.' The two men shook hands, and then Norm left the shed and passed through the backyard towards the clothesline. The white sheets and pillow cases that Judith had hung out swayed gently in the light breeze, while Judith stood at the kitchen window and watched. Norm passed behind the sheets like an actor may step behind a curtain on stage. Judith was struck by the fluid and almost spiritual transition, and it caused her to pause and think. She craned her neck to catch another glimpse of Norm—but he was gone.

***

'Hello, dear,' said Judith, as Reg stormed into the kitchen, chest puffed out and full of bravado. He stopped suddenly near the kitchen table, as if he had forgotten why he had entered in the first place. 'Have you misplaced something Reg?'

'Misplaced?' questioned Reg. He didn't understand what his wife had said. He looked around the room with a half-smile on his face and then wiped his forehead with the back of hand.

'You look a little lost, dear,' enquired Judith.

'What on earth are you talking about woman!' exclaimed Reg. 'Would you mind making some tea?'

Judith moved towards the stove and thought of asking her husband if he was all right, but decided against it; she chose to remain quiet.

Several minutes of awkward silence passed before Reg suddenly decided to speak.

'Norm is going to enlist.'

'Oh, my goodness,' said Judith. 'Is that what he came to see you about?'

'Yes, it was in fact,' replied Reg, full of self-importance. 'He feels I can run all three properties. Which, I must say,' continued Reginald, while he stirred his tea that Judith had placed in front of him, 'is fateful in its timing, seeing that I was planning to propose a few changes to how things were run anyway.'

'Oh,' replied Judith, not sounding as convinced of her husband's ability as he was . 'How is Alice?' she asked.

'You know he had to talk me around,' said Reg, completely oblivious to his wife's question. 'Not in the question of whether I could handle the role,' he boasted, while he sipped his tea. 'Actually, I feel sometimes Norm has tried to hold me back intentionally, worried I might show him up.'

Judith looked at her husband quizzically, and asked her self quickly if he had been drinking, such was his behaviour. But she realised her husband was intoxicated by something else: egotism.

'No, what I mean is,' continued Reg—his answer had become a rant—'he had to convince me not to enlist myself. Norm made a compelling argument that my knowledge and youth would be far better put to use in running the three farms, advancing both our families' interests.'

'You were going to enlist Reg?' asked Judith, 'I wasn't aware.'

'Well of course I was going to enlist and defend my country, Judith,' exclaimed Reg in a raised voice. 'Really, woman,' he scoffed, before he gulped the last of his tea.

From down the hall the baby began to cry. Judith looked in the direction of the sound.

'Does that baby ever stop crying?' said Reg. He stood and exited the house without another word.

THIRTY

Margaret Atkins lay in her large bed and stared at the ceiling. With the sheets and quilt pushed to one end, she felt a devilish sense of invigoration, laced with defiance. She rolled onto her side and was captured by the site of the lavender plants in full bloom that grew just outside the bedroom window; the open windows carried their scent along with the already warm air.

While the summers were unbearably hot, and the winters frigid, Margaret had taken to life in Canberra relatively well. Spring and autumn were pleasant, and overall the seasons were not unlike those in her home town of Gilmurra. The attraction of the fledgling national capital was that she wasn't under the intense scrutiny of the established and prying social clique of Gilmurra. Ironically, she had been a most enthusiastic member of that group, until she had experienced for herself the gavel of country social justice. The withdrawn glances and hurried whispers were her sentence, after stories of her row with Arthur grew their own legs.

New faces, and more importantly to Margaret, more influential faces, meant a fresh start while still having the stability—as artificial as it was—of marriage to a respected member of parliament. Arthur had recently bought a house in the suburb of Manuka, and Margaret had engaged herself in various social and charitable organisations. She had become acquainted with all the right people, and had plenty to keep her busy while her husband fulfilled his duties within his electorate.

Arthur had held his reservations as to her true motivations for joining such organisations. To his eye, Margaret had only ever shown interest in the advancement of one woman, and that was her. If Arthur had cared enough to air his thoughts with Margaret, she would probably even admit it to him, but only him; how her new friends perceived her was far more important than the revelation of hidden traits.

The door to the en-suite slid open. Margaret turned away from the window and faced the figure that stood at the edge of the bed.

'Do you always have such long showers?' asked Margaret as she grinned cheekily, while draped over one of the many pillows on the bed.

'No, my dear, I don't,' smiled the young political correspondent, who moonlighted as a tennis instructor, 'but I needed a moment to regain my strength.'

'Come back to bed, Lachlan,' purred Margaret, 'I haven't finished with you yet.'

Lachlan Campbell wrote for *The Argus* in Melbourne, and had developed a reputation for getting scoops in the political arena. His employees on La Trobe Street marvelled at his assumed, but of course unnamed, pool of sources, Margaret Atkins being one.

'You know, Lachy,' said Margaret, as she ran a hand over his body, 'one of the benefits of living in Canberra is that my husband's electorate is hundreds of miles away, and he loves nothing more than keeping in touch with his loyal voters. It allows me to be with you.'

'You are a fiend, aren't you, Margaret?' said Lachlan playfully, but really believing she was.

'A desirable one though?' she suggested.

'I can't stay much longer,' said Lachlan, changing the subject. 'I have a meeting with Arthur Fadden.'

'Oh, spare me Lachlan; another boring man on the long and painful list of my husband's boring friends.'

'Is your husband close with Fadden?' asked Lachlan in search of a story; he felt something was amiss within the party that could destabilise and hurt the coalition and help Labor; Campbell's admiration for Curtin always came through in his articles.

'You could say...'

'Did you hear that?' said Lachlan.

'Here what?'

'Sounded like a door.'

'Nonsense, Lachy,' said Margaret as she leaned over to kiss his chest, 'probably the...'

'Now isn't this delightful?' said a calm and measured voice.

'Oh, my God,' cried Lachlan. He sat bolt upright while he attempted to gather up the sheets.

'Arthur!' cried Margaret, 'you're supposed to be...'

'In my electorate,' said Arthur helpfully. 'Hello, Lachlan, fancy seeing you here. *The Argus* not paying well, or is this research?' Lachlan Campbell sat beetroot-red, knowing that he would be on the next train to Melbourne. If he was lucky he would retain a job at the paper covering the social pages. Arthur Atkins was a respected man; even his adversaries liked him. Lachlan Campbell wouldn't get a hello out of a politician now—let alone a comment. 'No, Margaret, unfortunately for you,' continued Arthur, 'the whole team came down with a stomach bug, so we turned around.'

Margaret, also beetroot-red, not from embarrassment, but with fury at being caught out by her publicly adored husband, lay marooned on the little white island of crumpled sheets and pillows, without hope of rescue. 'Don't think you will get a divorce, you smug bastard!' she screamed. Her voice made Lachlan shrink further into the bed. The once cocky journalist wished the mattress would swallow him up before things got worse.

'Courts don't look too favourably on adultery, dear.'

'You might think I am stupid, Arthur, but you need to prove it, and I am sure neither one of us will say anything,' taunted Margaret.

Arthur stared back calmly; he had seen that look in her eye before.

'So, try if you will, Arthur.'

'My dear, you remember Stanton, don't you, from my office?' said Arthur. The Member for Colston looked casually out into the living area and gestured in a hurried and encouraging manner to his staffer. The need to maintain dignity—after years of play-acting—left Arthur at that moment, and was replaced by a desire to be in his father's company, where he could enjoy a quiet beer. Arthur had acknowledged, through his unorthodox act, that his marriage needed to come to an end. 'Stanton was kind enough to help me with my luggage, Margaret. Now Stanton, you've met Mrs Atkins, haven't you?'

'Yes, sir,' said the embarrassed clerk.

'And our friend Campbell?' asked Arthur.

'Hello, Lachlan.'

'Well, I am glad that's settled,' said Arthur. He smiled at his wife like a man who has been cleared of debt.

'Get out, get out of this house!' screamed Margaret. The shrill of her voice caused the journalist to tumble out of bed with fright. He scrambled to his feet, his garments clutched to his chest. Arthur and Stanton stepped politely to one side for the flustered escapee.

'No, Margaret,' said Arthur. He resumed his previous position and allowed the uncomfortable Stanton to withdraw. 'I will take a stroll, not a terribly long one, and when I return, you and whatever you can carry will no longer be here.'

'What about money?' cried Margaret pathetically, as Arthur turned and left the room.

'Telephone your father.'

***

Denman Hill, October 1940

'I'm in charge of running the properties now,' barked Reginald. He rose from the lounge and paced towards the windows that overlooked the front paddocks of *Denman Hill*, 'or have you forgotten that Alice?'

'You may be—while Norm is away,' retorted Alice. A self-assured emphasis on her husband's name hit Reg as it intended. Her nephew looked down, the grimace ever so slight, but noticeable. Alice felt she had let her emotions get the better of her, something that was easily done in Reg's presence, and she attempted to brush over her comment. 'Regardless of who is in charge,' she said calmly, 'we are in partnership, and in my role as book-keeper; I need to be able to discuss things with you.'

'And I,' exclaimed Reg, with his confidence returned, 'need to be able to purchase things for the farms, on account—when I need them!'

'Accounts from the Royal Hotel, overdue, mind you, for five pound three and sixpence, does not,' shouted Alice, 'constitute needs for the farm.' She lowered her voice, but her blood still raced. 'It should be a personal expense taken from the wage you draw.'

Annoyed that his authority—so important to how he viewed himself—had been undermined in successive blows, he stewed in silence, and thrust out his hand for the statement that detailed his spending; Alice obliged.

'How did the total get so high, Reg?'

'Mind your own business!'

The spring-hinged door to the kitchen banged. It announced that Judith had returned from her walk with little David, and caused Alice to turn her head towards the back of the house.

'Well,' replied Alice, as she shifted from businesswoman to de-facto mother, a reaction she couldn't help sometimes, even when her nephew was being such a pig. 'If you need some assistance, let me know.'

Reg grunted and then roughly forced the bill into his trouser pocket. He slumped to resume his seat on the lounge, cross-legged, and with his chin cradled in thumb and forefinger. He stared blankly through the timber-sashed windows for as long as it took for Alice to leave the room.

'Hello, Jude,' said Alice as she stepped from the hall into the kitchen. 'Good morning, little man,' she said to the little toddler who clung to his mother's leg.

'Alice, what a nice surprise.'

'Just popped over to go through the accounts with Reg; boring but has to be done.'

'Better you than me,' replied Judith, 'It would give me a headache. Are you staying for tea and a fresh scone?'

'How could I resist, Jude, thank you. Did you enjoy your walk with Mummy, King David?'

'He did,' replied Judith for her son, 'but Mummy got tired of battling the bumpy road with that rigid pram. Have a seat, Alice, and I'll go and ask Reg if he would like to join us.' Judith picked David up and then passed him to his great-aunt before she walked down the hallway.

Alice placed the adorable little boy on her knee. She stroked his straight brown hair and gazed into his round brown eyes—full of warmth and willingness to love. Alice kissed his forehead; it felt the most natural and perfect thing to do. 'My, you have grown David,' said Alice, 'can you still ride a horse?'

David nodded yes and said a soft 'gee-up', and then held on for dear life. He laughed with his head thrown back and mouth wide open, as Alice began to bounce him every which way; it made Alice smile. She glanced down and noticed a bruise on David's leg, part way up his thigh. She stopped her horse games and had a closer look.

'Is that sore, Davey?' asked Alice in a soft voice. She pointed to the discoloured patch, which was not round, as most bruises were, but long and thin. 'Does that "ouch"?' repeated Alice to the toddler.

David nodded yes, and then yelled, 'Horsey,' not ready to finish the game.

'He's not there,' remarked Judith, as she re-entered the kitchen, 'must have gone out the front door.'

'Probably out in the front paddock,' said Alice offhandedly before she placed a jovial David on the floor next to her. The young boy scurried away as soon as his feet touched the timber boards. 'Have you seen that mark on David's leg, Jude?'

'Yes, poor little thing,' replied Judith, 'Reg said he fell off the back of the Ford when they were carting wood.'

'Oh,' replied Alice, not sure what to think.

'Have you had a letter from Norman, if you don't mind me asking?'

'Not at all, Judith, I appreciate you asking; it helps to talk, I think it does anyway,' said Alice. She moved her eyes to stare at the teacup Judith filled. A vision of Norman dressed in uniform entered her mind. It pushed to the side—for the time being—her concerns over David. Alice pictured her husband, tall and handsome, in front of the Queen Victoria building in Sydney. He had marvelled at the impressive structure on their short but enjoyable stay in the bustling city, and the thought made her smile. 'I received a letter two days ago, actually… and I've been a bit selfish, I kept it to myself. I have read it over and over; stared at the photo he included, and then read the letter again.'

Judith smiled and placed her hand on Alice's as she took a seat across from her.

'It sounds funny,' continued Alice, 'but it has been exhilarating in a way when I have held his letter and photograph at night; no one in the whole world except the two of us, a moment shared.' Alice sighed. 'It surprised me what can be extracted through words on a page.'

Judith took a sip of her tea to allow Alice a moment. It made her think of things herself. Judith wondered for a moment, as she looked at Alice, had her husband Reginald experienced moments of solitude where he thought about her in the way that Alice obviously thought of Norm?

'Did he mention where he was?'

'He did, but it was crossed out. The photograph looked to be taken in some sort of studio with a backdrop, so I'm not exactly sure Jude. I bumped into James Atkins, and he seemed to think Arthur was in the Middle East, but I'm not sure how he would know that,' said Alice. She paused to sample a scone. 'Maybe captain's letters don't get censored as much.'

'I forgot Arthur Atkins had joined up,' said Judith, 'terrible business with his wife: he was a fine local member.'

'He was… and a great friend to this family.' replied Alice. 'But I guess the embarrassment of his wife's infidelity was too much, especially being a public figure. Whatever the reasons, his contribution to the community and representation in parliament will be sorely missed in this area… I can't, unfortunately, say the same for his wife.'

'Living in Sydney with an aunt, I heard,' said Judith, 'but enough of that. You haven't mentioned Emily in over two weeks.'

'I haven't heard from her in over three weeks, the little devil,' replied Alice. 'I wrote to her after her last letter and again yesterday. I suppose she is busy with her studies… well, I hope it is her studies she is busy with.'

Both women looked at each other and laughed. They always enjoyed each other's company and they could both imagine—without saying—what Emily might be getting up to.

'Judith, you make the most delicious scones!' exclaimed Alice, as she eyed the plate in the centre of the kitchen table. 'I shouldn't, but I will have just one more.'

'I'm glad you like them Alice,' replied Judith, 'but they are not as good as yours, the blue ribbons from the show prove it.'

'I pay the judges,' giggled Alice, 'yours are the best.'

THIRTY ONE

The door of the rail car compartment grated as it opened; it caused the elderly man seated opposite Emily to stir slightly, but not wake. A neatly dressed gentleman, he had fallen asleep while the train sat motionless at the Central Station platform. The young doctor who entered paused to tilt his hat towards the two occupants before he lifted his suitcase into the racks above the dark green upholstered seats. The soles of his fine leather shoes—wet from the rain outside—squeaked as he pivoted on the linoleum floor.

'Excuse me, Miss, is this seat taken?' asked the tall, slender man. He removed his hat from his head and held it over his chest, lightly clasped by fingers that would suit a pianist. His smile was enhanced by soft blue eyes that radiated humility with enough self-confidence to make the man sure of himself, without being arrogant.

'No, sir,' replied Emily, as she picked up the hard-covered book she had put down on the seat next to her.

'No need Miss, there is quite enough room for your book; study or pleasure?' asked the man, as he glanced at the title.

'A bit of both,' replied Emily with a blush, 'a little more study to be done though.'

'*Australia and Federation*,' he said out loud, while he took a seat at a respectable distance, but close enough to engage in conversation.

'My first year at Sydney University,' said Emily with a smile.

'Really?' replied the man. He sat straighter. His enthusiastic response drew a confused and incoherent babble from the elderly man who slept. Emily hid a devilish grin with her hand; the sparkle in her eye revealed a mischievous thought she had attempted to conceal.

Emily's new travelling companion was entranced at once. The corner of his mouth turned upwards, and he stopped breathing for a moment. His eyes had witnessed something beyond the visual sense, something he hadn't felt before.

'Emily Miller,' she said holding out her hand, breaking the silence.

'I'm sorry, how rude of me. Robert Anderson, pleasure to meet you, Miss Miller,' said Dr Anderson, his composure regained. Modesty prevented him from giving his proper title. 'You mentioned your studies. I was fortunate enough to obtain a degree while I resided at St John's.'

'My type are not allowed within those walls, Mr Anderson,' remarked Emily in protest. Her dark brown eyes that had previously sparkled, transformed to a smouldering cinnamon shade, sedate but ready to ignite, given the right fuel.

'Wouldn't a lady prefer the Women's College?' replied Robert. He immediately wished he hadn't, and then desperately tried to make amends, 'I mean… '

'I would prefer—a choice, like most other women. But I suppose, Mr Anderson, we should be grateful that we are allowed the privilege to develop our obviously under-developed brains… and therefore, display the courtesy that men require for their world to function.' Emily opened her book and began to read, or at least, pretended to.

'I apologise if I offended you, Miss Miller, it wasn't my intention.'

Emily had not intended to spend her train journey home to Gilmurra crusading for women's rights, nor did she want to sit in uncomfortable silence. She closed her book and faced Mr Anderson. 'Do you know something, Mr Anderson?'

Robert shrugged in a way that said he was unwilling to answer, but ready to listen.

'I have found,' continued Emily, 'that men in general, never "mean to offend", but have the almost instinctive ability to do so when it comes to offering their advice on how women would, or perhaps—should feel.'

'You are absolutely right. I have worked alongside many gifted and talented women in my field. I have seen them come up against barriers that simply,' said Robert, interlocking his hands and then spreading them, maybe to emphasise his point or maybe in a reaction to his uneasiness, 'are not placed in front of their male counterparts. I hope, Miss Miller, that will change with time.'

Emily paused to look closely at the man now she had vented her frustrations. He hadn't surprised her with his response to her previous statement. It was in line with the impression she received when he first nodded hello—the eyes had said it. His comment about her college— to which she had bristled too quickly—was merely thoughtless, idle chat. He had not reverted to labels and assigned her a name, or declared her crazy, as some men did when confronted on campus with her zeal and determination. He had listened, and then spoken from his own experience, and acknowledged the faults that society as a whole preferred not to confront. There was something about him, something that she liked very much.

'Not too much time, I hope,' said Emily.

Robert nodded with a smile that signalled the end of the discussion. He eased back in his seat and unfolded a newspaper and began to read. It left Emily slightly lost and completely disarmed. After her rebuke of Mr Anderson, she was—in an instant—left stranded, as if she should make some further comment to prolong the conversation. Her position of ascendency had been eroded by Mr Anderson's simple action. An intentional ploy? She could not tell, but she felt a sudden pang of annoyance that was complicated by an undoubted attraction.

Engrossed in his paper, Robert turned the page of the broadsheet. He had not even glanced at the young lady who sat next to him since their discussion. Driven by curiosity, Emily's eyes darted in the direction of the paper. Her attention was caught by the front-page headline: **Italians Invade Egypt**. Her thoughts immediately shifted to her Uncle Norman; *would he be preparing to fight the Italians?* Emily was abruptly overtaken with a desire to be with her family. She wished she hadn't waited so long to reply to her Aunt Alice's letters.

***

Alice waited on the platform of the train station, dressed in her Sunday best on a warm Saturday afternoon in the middle of a Gilmurra spring. She had brought Judith and young David along for the drive to meet Emily. Judith had been pleasantly surprised at how much she had missed her sister-in-law's energy since her last visit; it was a healthy tonic from the rigidity of their household.

Although Judith tried not to upset Reginald, the task was becoming ever more difficult. Judith felt that her husband had grown more detached as time went on. She would ask him—bravely in light of his quick temper—if he was all right, but he would shoot her down condescendingly. He would tell her that she was stupid and she wouldn't understand the pressures of running a farm—let alone three. Judith dropped the subject.

Judith would acknowledge to anyone that she was a woman of limited education. Her father thought it was more important to work for pay than to attend school; but as humble as she was, she didn't consider herself stupid. It was her suspicion that Reginald was not totally at ease with being at home while Norm was away. It was a very strange thing for a man's wife to think, and she had questioned her own reasoning. But if her theory was correct, and Reg's lack of contentment was over him not enlisting, then the irony to Judith was that she believed her husband would not join up if given the choice. Judith felt that Reg just wanted the townsfolk to understand he couldn't; he had been prevented by the burden of responsibility—that would be enough to satisfy him.

'David, here comes your Aunt M,' said Alice excitedly as the train from Sydney rolled at walking pace towards the platform. David showed more interest in the pendant that dangled from his mother's neck than the train that approached.

'Look Davey,' said Judith while she tried to break her son's grip, 'the big train is here.'

Two men in uniform passed in front of Alice and Judith, and blocked their view for a moment. Each woman had different thoughts enter their mind with the blur of khaki that passed between them and the first carriages of the train. The buoyant, proud men exchanged words as casually as if they might drop towels at their feet at any minute and dive into the Tilcan River. Their strong young faces, shaded by slouch hats, filled Alice with trepidation over Norman's whereabouts, and Judith with an unavoidable pity for her Reginald.

'Oh, sorry, Dr Bainbridge' said Alice as she bumped into the local GP in an effort to catch sight of Emily.

Dr Bainbridge smiled and tilted his hat at Alice. The elderly man raised his arm slowly in the air and attempted to catch a passenger's attention.

'There she is Jude, I can see her,' said Alice, as she waved frantically. 'She can see us.' *Oh my, she looks so beautiful.* Alice raised her hand to her mouth. Alice felt as if she was being sucked backwards in time. The excitement of the crowded platform went eerily silent, as she suddenly found herself on the kitchen floor of number 96 Beattie Street. She gazed in wonder at a beautiful lady with a smile that beamed like ones she had only seen in films. The graceful figure with dark wavy hair and eyes that penetrated deep into your soul bent towards her to say her name and wrap her in a lifelong spell.

'Aunt Ally!'

The sound of the train whistle snapped Alice back into reality, and a cacophony of sound. The colours of the rainbow flowed by as people exited and boarded the train.

'Aunty Alice, are you alright?' asked a concerned Emily, while Judith looked on. She waited for Alice to respond before she greeted Judith.

'Certainly, Ruth,' replied Alice quietly, 'you look lovely. How was the trip?'

'You called me Ruth,' said Emily with half a smile.

Tempted to make an excuse, she decided against it. 'For a moment, I thought you were, my dear M. I am so glad to have you home,' she continued, and wrapped her arms around the young lady. Emily sank into the arms of the only mother she had known.

'Welcome home, Emily,' said Judith, as she moved forward to kiss her cheek. David pushed his head closer into his mother's chest as the two women exchanged greetings.

'Hello, Jude, and how are you little David, who's not so little anymore?'

'Pleasure to see you again, Doctor Bainbridge,' said a voice from behind and to the side of Emily; its familiarity made her turn.

'Welcome to Gilmurra, Dr Anderson,' replied Doctor Bainbridge, 'a pleasant trip, I hope.'

'That must be the new doctor,' whispered Judith. She nudged Alice with her elbow, while Emily stared at her former travelling companion.

'Very enjoyable, thank you, Doctor.'

'You never mentioned you were a Doctor,' blurted Emily.

The directness of Emily's accusation made Doctor Bainbridge recoil slightly. His conservative and elderly mind wondered—dreaded—what the young Miller girl could possibly mean.

'Emily!' said Alice, chastising her niece. She also wondered what she could possibly mean.

'Ah, Miss Miller, ladies,' said Robert Anderson, as he turned to face Emily. He gave a warm smile and tipped his hat.

'Mrs Clark, Mrs Miller,' said Doctor Bainbridge, recovered from his initial shock. 'May I present Dr Robert Anderson; our new general practitioner.'

'Lovely to meet you, Doctor Anderson,' said Alice. Both women nodded with a smile, and then turned their attention to Emily.

'No, I don't believe I did, Miss Miller,' replied Doctor Anderson. He paused to smirk at his sparring partner, and continued. 'My apologies... Miss Miller and I met on the train, Dr Bainbridge.' The elderly Doctor smiled towards Emily politely, but mostly in relief. Any anxiety Alice felt had not quite been relieved as yet. Her glances back and forth between the young doctor and her niece quickened. 'Would you have gone a little easier on me during our discussion Miss Miller... had you known my profession?'

'Emily,' said Alice, in a barely audible whisper while she shook her head.

Emily cheeks flushed a little, partly with anger, and partly in wounded pride. She raised her chin and said, 'Probably not.'

'I thought that might be the case,' replied Doctor Anderson, 'and I am pleased you didn't say otherwise. I enjoyed our conversation and your company, Miss Miller.'

'I have a car in the driveway, Doctor Anderson,' said Doctor Bainbridge politely. Robert Anderson held eye contact with Emily to the brink of what would be considered courteous, before he acknowledged the older Doctor.

'Certainly Doctor, Mrs Clark, Mrs Miller... Miss Miller.'

'Welcome to Gilmurra, Doctor Anderson,' said Alice with a smile. 'If we can help you at all settling in, we would be more than pleased to do so.'

'How very nice of you, Mrs Clark, thank you.'

'What a lovely man,' said Judith, as the two doctors walked away.

'Yes, he did seem nice, Jude,' said Alice before she turned to face Emily. 'My question, Judith, would be how our lovely Emily would manage to get into a disagreement with such a nice person.'

'What makes you think I had an argument with the lovely Doctor,' replied Emily, her smile as sarcastic as it was dismissive.

'Oh—just one of those funny feelings you get, dear, when you have known someone their whole lives… I'm glad you're home M, let's grab your luggage.'

***

'Was that Miss Miller's family—her mother?' asked Doctor Anderson as he joined Doctor Bainbridge in the back seat of the Dodge sedan. The young driver started the vehicle after he received a nod.

'No Doctor, her sister-in-law and aunt; both her parents were tragically killed when she was but a toddler.'

Robert sat silent for a moment, blindsided by the answer to a question he thought was slightly snoopy, but natural enough. 'How sad,' he said. He meant the latter word in its truest form.

'Incredibly,' replied the older man. Doctor Bainbridge was struck with a vision of two children seated on the kitchen floor at Denman Hill on that most terrible of days. The Doctor had arrived to the Miller home after a call from the police sergeant. The youngsters were mostly oblivious to the scene of shock and disbelief, the tears and suppressed moans while Alice was sedated. The doctor recalled feelings of confusion and disorientation when he was eventually led over the ridge to look at the deceased couple. The image of them side by side in the paddock grass still haunted him.

Robert noticed Bainbridge's ashen pallor, and wished he had refrained from asking questions on his first day in the small town.

***

'Robert is a lovely young man, Gordon,' said Eliza Bainbridge, while she knitted beside the soft light of a lamp. Her hands were stiff with arthritis and worked slowly but steadily. Any discomfort she felt was not revealed through her countenance, a lifetime of hard work had overcome life's difficulties and instilled resilience in her. 'You did very well in selecting him.'

'Thank you, Eliza,' replied Gordon as he took a seat in the armchair opposite his wife, 'and thank you for the lovely meal. If Robert had any reservations about his decision while on his journey from Sydney, your cooking sealed the contract.' Gordon Bainbridge smiled towards Eliza and then let out a bronchial cough that had become chronic over the last six months; it had forced—along with age and wearied bones—the decision to retire. 'I saw the young Miller girl today,' said Doctor Bainbridge suddenly, in a slightly different tone. 'She arrived on the train; I believe she studies at Sydney University. Who would have thought?'

'Times have changed,' replied Eliza without interruption to her work. 'I heard she is a very intelligent young lady, excelled at Saint Catherine's.'

'Yes,' said the Doctor, his mind somewhere else. 'I believe she is… the image of her mother, apart from her hair being brown.'

'Mrs Clark has done a terrific job raising both of them,' said Eliza, still concentrated on the tips of her needles. 'What that woman has endured beggars belief.'

Doctor Bainbridge didn't reply. His mind slipped a little further away, while his conscience dredged the deep recesses that harboured unwanted memories. He reached for a book that lay on the table beside him—the words encased in it had shaped his life. He ran his finger along its leather spine, with horizontal ridges an inch apart. The movement sounded to the old man like a cogwheel that turned slowly to raise the hidden sediment from the past. 'He killed her, you know.'

'Excuse me, Gordon?' said Eliza. She looked up from her knitting for the first time.

'Clarence Miller,' said the doctor with a dull even tone. 'He killed his wife.'

'Gordon,' said Eliza, 'it was an accident, a terrible accident—you said so yourself. What would make you say such a thing now?'

The elderly doctor breathed in deeply while he slowly shook his head. He hoped to clear his mind and his shame. 'I know now what I knew then Eliza; the convenience of a plausible account delivered by a respected and trustworthy man, itself accepted anxiously by the sergeant, allowed me to come to the conclusion everyone wanted.' Doctor Bainbridge paused to clear his throat; the tremor in his hand revealed his inner turmoil. 'It was a difficult... a most appalling situation.'

Shocked, Mrs Bainbridge stared at her husband. The pain on his face was vivid and real. It told her that—whatever the facts—her husband believed his words to be true. 'My dear, what use is there in dragging this up? Why punish yourself for something that happened so long ago, the events distorted by time and age? What could needless speculation do to young Emily, or the family of Sergeant Thomas, now deceased?'

'I saw the bruises on her throat, Eliza,' said the doctor, his voice not raised, but more intense.

Her composure became disjointed and Eliza shifted in her seat. 'Bruising, dear, why are you doing this to yourself? From my elderly and faded memory, the Millers fell from a horse—together—while at full gallop. What part of their body wouldn't be bruised?'

'I took the path presented by the sergeant and did not fulfil the oath I was bound by.'

'Please, Gordon; you are a doctor of medicine and a fine one at that. Never once from where I sat did you act unprofessionally or improperly. If you choose to spend your retirement dissecting every decision you made while you practised, you will only achieve insanity—not absolution or enlightenment.'

Doctor Bainbridge raised the sacred book to his chest and praised God for his loyal wife. He then asked for forgiveness. 'It is my one regret, Elisa, and I am resigned to being held accountable for it when my worthiness is ultimately questioned.'

THIRTY TWO

Bardia, Libya, 6 January 1941

The cold desert wind blew without pause, and caused the canvas of Captain Arthur Atkins's tent to flap. The pile of papers on his makeshift desk required weights to keep them in place, so the captain chose captured bottles of Italian liquor to thwart the determined gusts. The previous three days fighting had been intense in parts, but had gone the way of the Australians. Arthur's 16th Brigade had attacked the Italian defensive perimeter near Bardia, a seaside village on the Libyan coast, on the morning of the 3rd of January. The initial success of the 16th allowed them to push forward to the town of Bardia itself, which they captured on the afternoon of the 4th. The 17th Brigade had found stronger resistance in the south, which they were able to overcome on the morning of the 5th of January.

Arthur picked up an already opened bottle of wine that he had placed at his feet to avoid detection. He was aware that his fellow officers followed protocols more strictly than he. Arthur didn't flaunt army regulations regularly; he had just seen it all before. What most of his men had witnessed for the first time in their lives that day, the dead and the dying, the scared and the brave—he had seen before. Arthur placed the cork between his teeth and jerked the bottle back violently while he looked at reports and casualty lists that had begun to arrive at his tent.

'Knock, knock,' said a voice, for want of a door to tap on.

'Enter,' said Atkins, while he looked down at some notes. 'Secure the blasted flap,' yelled the captain.

'I have the latest casualty lists for you, Captain,' said the young man sheepishly, before he saluted and stood to attention.

'At ease, Lance Corporal,' said Atkins. He stopped work and casually leaned back in his chair. 'What's your name, soldier? I don't believe I know you.'

'The name's Conner, Captain Atkins: Christopher Conner, transferred from the 2/5th of the 17th Brigade today Captain.'

'Welcome to C Company of the 2/2nd, Lance Corporal Conner,' said Arthur, as he held out his hand to receive the papers. Whose platoon have you been assigned too?'

'13 Platoon, Lieutenant Calder.'

Arthur raised his eyebrows without comment, as he took the papers from the young lance corporal. Lieutenant Lawrence David Calder, a product of The King's School Parramatta, while capable as both a soldier and officer, was less than popular with his men. His abrupt and condescending manner had sent a tingle through Arthur's fingers as he added the new documents to a pile already held prisoner by a bottle of Italian red.

Arthur reverted to what he was studying earlier, but noticed the lance corporal still inside the tent. 'Dismissed, Corporal.'

Conner shifted from one foot to the other and then came to attention, before he saluted sharply. 'It's an honour and privilege to serve under you, Captain Atkins.'

'Pleased to have you, Conner,' replied Arthur a little amused by the lance corporal's behaviour. *This man is serious about being a soldier*, Arthur thought to himself. He watched the lad with puffed out chest and steely eyes.

'You served with my father, sir, in the Great War. Alfred Conner.'

While Arthur had always been a steady character, reliable and honest, good in a crisis, he had changed slightly since his divorce from his wife and retirement from politics. The return to life in the armed forces had also brought changes—as they had in 1915. He had become a little more open in relaying his thoughts. The structured life of private school, University, and law practice, followed by public life, had encouraged measured and emotionless responses—barring his outburst with Margaret in his Gilmurra office.

Captain Atkins rose from his chair. He felt a mixture of shock and elation, as though he was about to greet a long lost and loved kinsman. He strode towards the lance corporal with his hand outstretched, while his face glowed. 'I can see it, damned if I can't,' exclaimed Arthur.

He shook the young man's hand firmly. 'I can tell you right now, young Christopher, the honour is all mine. Your father was a great man and a true friend.' Arthur stared at Christopher Conner. Flashes of Alf Conner's cheeky smile darted through his mind. The son that stood in front of him seemed like a visitor from another world.

'I don't remember Dad.'

'My apologies, Christopher,' said Arthur quickly, 'I didn't show much tact.'

'Don't apologise, Captain,' replied Christopher. 'I am chuffed that you hold my father in such high regard. My mother still has the kind letter you wrote her from France. It meant a lot to her... and me, sir.'

Arthur looked at the ground for a moment and clenched his teeth. His toes curled inside his boots as he remembered the hellish night at Fromelles. 'Well, Chris,' said Arthur quietly. 'It's not hard to write nice things about good men.' Arthur gave the young man a nod that made his eyebrows pull closer together. He conveyed a message that he couldn't have hoped to voice at that moment. Arthur glanced to his left and caught site of some boxes—half a dozen in all—lazily hidden behind a greatcoat. Captain Atkins reached under the coat and took a box of cigars from the pile and presented it to the son of his mate. 'Courtesy of the Dagos, Chris, share them with your mates, but don't wave them about,' suggested Arthur with a wink. 'A real pleasure to meet you, Chris,' said Arthur, as he offered his hand once more, 'once we slow down a bit, I will shout you a beer and we'll have a good chat about your father.'

'I'd like that, Captain,' said Lance Corporal Conner. He saluted and then turned on his heel to exit the tent and face the stiff desert breeze. As he bent into the wind, he thought to himself that his mates were right. *Arthur Atkins is a top bloke.*

Arthur turned back to his desk, invigorated by his meeting with Christopher. His light mood suddenly challenged by another blast of desert air from an open tent flap.

'Christ,' yelled Arthur, as loose papers that were not secured danced about like dried leaves.

'Sorry to bother you Captain Atkins,' said a rigid and moustached Lieutenant Calder, 'but it is a matter of some urgency. I apprehended the Corporal outside with this box of cigars.'

Lance Corporal Conner looked straight ahead without speaking, while Calder continued his rant. Arthur was flabbergasted at the lieutenant's fastidiousness, and ran his fingers through his hair as he attempted to relieve the sudden onset of tension.

'I gave them to him, Lieutenant, said Arthur, 'to give to Lieutenant Colonel Lambert, our Commanding Officer, as a gift.' Captain Atkins reached forward to take the box from the lieutenant in the process.

'Oh,' replied Calder, halted for a moment, but not entirely happy with the answer. His elitist nature got the better of him, and he decided to pursue the matter further. 'Captain, forgive me, but do you think it is wise to encourage the movement of captured goods among the men?'

Arthur felt as though the blood vessel, or whatever it was that pulsed near his temple, might split. He took a deep breath before he spoke. 'That will be all thank you, Corporal, be sure the CO receives these,' he said. Arthur passed the box to Christopher, who stood behind Calder. The lance corporal winked at the captain as he took back his cigars.

Captain Atkins paced away from the statue-like Lieutenant Calder while he waited for Conner to exit the tent.

'Captain, I find...'

'Lieutenant Calder!' shouted Arthur, as he spun to face his subordinate in a roar that seemed to quieten the desert gale and make limp the ends of Calder's manicured moustache. 'May I remind you, Lieutenant, that not only am I your Commanding Officer,' continued Arthur with menace that matched his bulging eyes, 'but I have also seen more battles and encountered more enemy combatants than you have had tailored suits, and I will not tolerate...'

'But, Captain… ' said Lieutenant Calder, shocked by Arthur's intensity.

'I will not tolerate!' blasted Captain Atkins, 'you or anyone else questioning me in front of my men, or so help me, I will take one of those boxes and shove it right up your fucking arse! Do you hear me, Calder!'

Having absorbed Atkins's tirade, Calder pulled the hem of his tunic to not only straighten it, but to recalibrate his composure. 'If that will be all, Captain,' said the lieutenant while he saluted.

'Dismissed,' said Captain Atkins without a salute. As Calder turned to leave the tent, Arthur knew he had made an enemy of a well-connected young officer.

Pissed off, Arthur sat back down at his desk—wearier than before. He took another mouthful of Italian wine and picked up the pages that Conner had brought him. Arthur scanned the typed reports. He balked before he read through the casualty list. The task was never pleasant, but he was relieved at the low number of dead and wounded. He read the names quickly and felt a pang of grief for the fallen men, and decided to take one more drink; a quiet toast to the men who had given their lives. Before the bottle reached his lips, Arthur froze. The letters typed on paper were now deciphered into words. His mind had held the cipher key that unlocked what his subconscious was happy to leave scrambled. Arthur Atkins hurled the wine bottle across the tent and then stood. He struck out with his boot, not only in frustration and anger, but in confusion. How does this supposedly beautiful universe work? He felt overwhelmed with pity and sorrow for a family who had seen too much pain. He smashed the remaining cigar boxes with his heavy boot, and looked once more at the page that read: *VX 11891- SGT. Clark. Norman. E. Killed In Action.*

THIRTY THREE

Gilmurra, January 1949

Emily negotiated the small flight of steps that led out onto the green lawn at the rear of the Gilmurra Hall. The stillness and quiet of the evening's summer air contrasted with the lively, fast tempo music played by the band inside. She clasped her long white dress with both hands to keep the lovely gown from being damaged; this job had been performed for most of the day by her matron of honour, Helen Winter. She turned slowly and looked to see the sky gradually change; streaks of amber and grey hovered above brown scorched hills. Only the Tilcan, faintly heard in the distance, provided a vein of growth. The willows, elms and silky oaks that relied on its waters cut a path between the hills that held Gilmurra safely in seclusion.

Emily had only been Mrs Anderson for a few short hours, but she already felt different. The vibrant colour of a sky in sunset acknowledged to her the sanctity of what she had undertaken. When Emily had graduated from Sydney University in the previous year with a law degree, she had felt a surge of pride after almost eight years of hard work. A sense of personal achievement at overcoming a difficult task, made arduous by discriminatory views, and even love. Robert, with his open mind, had made the latter as uncomplicated as a long-distance relationship could be.

The pair continued their romance, which had begun with a dinner invitation in 1941; its true origins had begun the previous year on the train from Sydney to Gilmurra. What Emily knew now was something she couldn't possibly have known or learnt before this day; the idea of self had taken a subordinate place to the harmonious uniting of two souls.

On the same stairs that Emily had negotiated a moment before, Doctor Robert Anderson gazed at his wife. He was torn between the passionate need to dash across the lawn and embrace the woman he loved, and a peaceful contented feeling. His eyes poured over her perfect image, the scene almost abstract in its potency.

He decided to savour the moment. Robert stood and watched as Emily turned in a slow and intoxicating circle. Her face caught the last rays of a dying but resplendent sun, as her hypnotic dance to the gods of marriage was halted by the sight of her husband.

'It didn't take long for you to find me,' said Emily, her hands clasped behind her back, one shoulder turned towards Robert, while her face—tilted slightly down—remained further adrift. Eye contact was made with a seductive shift of her dark eyes.

'Couldn't bear to be without you,' replied Robert dramatically. His smile showed to the surrounding trees—still in the calm air—that he was truly besotted by the lady almost ten years his junior.

'Come and join your wife for a dance, before our guests send out a search party.'

Robert walked towards his wife and then jogged the final steps to take her outstretched hand. He allowed her to twirl sedately before he placed his hand around her slender waist. They began a close and intimate sway that was now watched by a small crowd of women detached from the reception, each with a tissue raised to their eyes. Robert and Emily Anderson, with eyes only for each other, were oblivious to their presence.

***

The ground that surrounded the rose bushes was hard and compacted.

It made it difficult for Alice to extract the weeds from around the base of the thorny plants that she had put so much work into of late. It was January, so Alice had begun work early; she hoped to finish before the summer sun rose high in the sky and made work unbearable. The sound of a motorcar was a welcome distraction from her chore, and from her thoughts about the letter she had received in the lead-up to the wedding. Alice removed her gloves, stood, and then walked to the side of the house. Her spirits lifted immediately when she realised it was Emily who stepped out of the cream coloured vehicle.

'Hello, dear,' said Alice warmly, 'I didn't expect to see you the day after your wedding.'

'I wanted to come out and thank you for all the work you did,' replied Emily. She walked towards Alice, radiant and full of energy. 'Robert and I have been up before the sun; walked along the river, had breakfast, read the paper. You're gardening I see.'

Alice gave a resigned shrug with a forced smile. The gesture said, without trying to dampen the mood, *what else would a widowed lady do*? But she pushed any negative thoughts aside. 'I see you still have use of that lovely car you used in the wedding,' said Alice cheerily, 'I love that colour.'

'Yes… well, Robert has been a bit of a devil,' said Emily. She made an effort to sound offended. 'It's mine.'

'Oh, my goodness M, it is lovely.'

'A new Holden 48-215, something or other,' explained Emily. She babbled like she was a teenager. 'I said to Robert: when do we take this car back, and he said—rather cheekily I might add—"why would you take it back, don't you like it?" I was so angry Alice.'

Alice turned to smile at Emily. She remembered the little girl who would often try to pull the wool over her eyes, and was glad that some things hadn't changed.

'Robert said people call it the FX, but I couldn't tell you what that means.'

'It really is beautiful, M; you'll be the talk of the town. Well, you already are; now they will just be jealous. Come inside and have a quick cuppa with your old Aunty.'

'Lead the way, Aunty,' replied Emily. As she followed, Emily suddenly realised that the years had made her loved aunt or step-mother older than she should be. The death of her adored husband Norman had taken a part of her that could never be replaced. Her caring and loving nature was still to the fore, but certain energies that had withered over time. Her body had become fuller, and flecks of grey in her hair were now streaks.

They entered the house through the annex and moved into the kitchen. Emily took a seat at the table and noticed a letter, opened and propped against a vase. Emily did not want to seem rude, so she looked away quickly, but Alice had seen her inquisitive expression, and instead of saying something, she turned to the stove.

'It was such a memorable day, M,' remarked Alice, still at the stove. 'So much happiness, it was truly wonderful.'

'It was, wasn't it, but to tell you the truth, Aunt Alice, it was all a bit of a blur.'

'I bet it was,' replied Alice. She turned from the stove and laughed. Emily smiled at the sight. 'Forgive me Emily, but I had to laugh. I just remembered your brother. He was walking around with this concerned look on his face all night... he looked—' Alice began to laugh again, which made Emily chuckle harder. 'He looked like he was tallying the bill every time someone placed a morsel of food in their mouth. It was so funny.'

Emily laughed heartily, while she imitated her older brother, 'He is different. Maybe we should hide the bill from him.'

'Maybe... but we shouldn't tease,' said Alice feeling guilty.

'Yes we should, Aunty, he deserves it.'

'So, when are you off on your honeymoon to the coast, dear?'

'Wednesday; I know it is not the convention, but the Doctor filling in for Robert doesn't arrive until Tuesday, so he will be working tomorrow.'

'Do you have to work, dear?'

'No, Mr Atkins has been so good,' replied Emily with genuine appreciation, 'not only did he allow me time off before the wedding, but he has given me another full two weeks, with pay!' added Emily.

Alice tilted her head slightly, like she had said a prayer in thanks of good people. 'He is a good man, that Arthur Atkins. I have told you, haven't I,' continued Alice, 'how good he was to you and your brother—to us.'

Emily reached over and placed a hand on her Auntie's arm. She knew the word 'us' had such a different emotional meaning for the two women.

'I miss Uncle Norm very much,' said Emily with tenderness, while tears welled in her eyes, 'so I cannot begin to know how you feel.'

Alice retrieved a tissue from her apron pocket and dabbed her own eyes, moist with memories and the ache of loss. 'It's no easier now than it was then, dear, the pain I mean. Just more spaced apart; I still look for him at times, and then depending on my mood or the circumstance, I smile or cry.' Alice lifted her cup and sipped the strong brew, before she placed it back on its saucer gently—respectfully—while she thought of her husband. 'After Norman was killed, Arthur wrote me a most thoughtful and comforting letter. It was some relief to know Norman didn't suffer.'

'We were all so proud of him Alice… very proud.'

Alice looked at the beautiful young lady in front of her—the image of her mother—and she was reminded of why people battled on after tragedy. Family; it was family, in any form that kept you going, and she felt blessed, even when besieged, that she had the will and the want to keep her family together and functioning. 'He loved you very much, Emily, very much.' Alice glanced at the envelope against the vase and decided to confide in her niece. She reached to her right and picked up the envelope to stare at it momentarily. 'I received this letter last week,' said Alice in a measured voice.

Emily smiled at Alice, but didn't speak, confused as to what serious business the envelope might contain. The recently married woman—instinctively—knew it was of that nature, and not general correspondence.

'My brother died two weeks ago,' said Alice bluntly.

Emily leaned forward with her eyebrows narrowed. She tried to understand what her Aunty had just said, but her mind was clouded by unfamiliarity made strong by isolation and the lack of reference to a subject willed into disassociation.

'My brother Frank, passed away alone,' Alice sobbed deeply and then held a tissue to her nose, 'and in prison and…'

Emily leapt from her chair to hug Alice, as she cried uncontrollably. She held her Aunty tightly but did not speak. She felt ill-equipped to source the appropriate words to soothe and calm. The verbalising of Frank's name had a strange effect on Emily; it was like the discovery of a chest that revealed incriminating documents a family thought destroyed.

Alice cried for a considerable time. Her emotion revealed itself as having as much to do with shame as it had to do with grief or regret; shame in the evil of Frank's act, shame in the disowning of a sibling; regret and resentment for events that conspired to destroy a family.

Alice's sobs began to fade as Emily left for the bathroom and returned with fresh tissue paper.

'Thank you, dear,' said Alice… 'and sorry for my outburst.'

'Don't be silly,' replied Emily, concerned for her Aunt. 'Why did you keep this to yourself until now?'

'I didn't want to disrupt the organising of the wedding.' replied Alice, surprised at her own reasoning. 'I suppose that seems a bit ridiculous, but to be perfectly honest, M, the reality of it didn't really strike me until just now, when I said it out loud—to you.'

'When is the funeral?' asked Emily.

'Done,' replied Alice. She looked down at her apron.

'What!'

'He was buried within the grounds of the prison the day after he was pronounced dead—complications after he contracted pneumonia.'

'Can they do that,' exclaimed Emily, 'surely not, I…'

'M,' said Alice with a raised hand that was meant to placate.

'Sorry, I just…'

'Want to help,' interjected Alice. 'I know you do and I appreciate it, but I am under no illusions about the unspeakable act my brother committed. The effect it had on innocent people, and where that placed him in the eyes of the authorities.' Alice stood to walk to the stove and retrieve the kettle from the hotplate. She returned to the table, and poured a little hot water into their half empty cups to freshen the cooled tea. 'I remember telling you that your Uncle Frank was in jail when you were young, maybe eleven. You had asked me who he was when looking at a photo.'

'I remember.'

'And, probably wrongly, I brushed over it… but how do you tell a little girl of the crime Frank had committed? And then, in shame, I moved on. Well actually, I am not sure if I am ashamed of moving on, or ashamed of him—perhaps a little of both.'

'The University library maintains an extensive archive of newspapers,' said Emily as respectfully as she could.

'So, you know the details,' replied Alice, 'what a fool to think I could hide something from you Emily.'

'How old were you?'

'Ten, I think. That is what is so strange for me, M, and perhaps a reason why I acted the way I did when I received the news. Because… in many ways, it is like I never had a brother called Frank or Archie. Though both were different, and for different reasons, neither of them was spoken of. Archie was first missing and then maybe a prisoner. We didn't… well, my parents didn't know. She was never the same, my mother. Over time—through pain of loss—Archie wasn't mentioned, and Frank… what is there to say that you don't know?'

Typical of her personality, Emily asked what she didn't know: 'Do you remember him?'

'Apart from the two photos I possess of him, yes, in glimpses. Or more like I see a figure at play, while I follow him around. He was five years older than me. With Archie it was different, I have fewer memories of him but he shines like a light in my mind—a hero.' Alice glanced around the room, and then gave her attention back to Emily. She needed to talk. The heavily weighted memories were too much. 'There were times when I would speak to your mother about my family, and it is from those chats that I have some knowledge of who they were.' Alice was lulled into silence for a moment by her recollections.

For a confident young woman, Emily was suddenly nervous; she had spoken to her Aunt before about her family, and she had relished every conversation, but this seemed different, it had sprung out of nowhere, and she felt willing but unprepared. The randomness of her visit now seemed fated.

'I have told you before, M, how your mother practically raised me, even before we moved to Denman Hill. My mother Grace was a loving mother, kind and calm; they were great friends, Ruth and my mum, great friends—your mother told me that often.' Alice stood up and walked over to a shelf beside the kitchen window. She took a photo framed in silver from it. 'But... she changed, I was told, on the day the telegram came about Archie being missing in action.'

Emily turned to take the photo of her Aunt as she walked behind her. She held the picture of Grace Miller in both hands and studied it closely, even though she had seen it many times before.

'And when Frank was arrested,' continued Alice, 'it was the last straw, so to speak. She collapsed outside the courthouse and was taken to hospital. Eventually she returned home, but it was your mother who cared for me.' Alice sniffed, and thought to share something else with Emily, something about her mother's passing, but she decided against it.

Emily went to speak, but stopped, and then squinted as she drew a breath. 'From what you have told me over the years,' said Emily, 'you always said that you remembered your father as a big, strong man, who worked hard and loved his children,'

'Yes, he was, but again, my memories have faded, and I relied on your mother to pass on stories, but I still have visions of him that I cling to.'

'Why then… or how… was Frank so different? How did he become the person who did what he did?' continued Emily.

'There was the one night that your mother said stood out beyond all others and gave her the clearest indication to Frank's state of mind. He had been injured by an explosion; this is well before the *Lion's Gate*, and taken to hospital. My parents were shocked and worried, naturally, but not as much as when a detective had asked to question Frank after he had recovered. My parents, Ruth told me, were convinced that he was in the wrong place, at the wrong time, but the detective had his suspicions.

'For one reason or another, after they had got nowhere with Frank themselves, he asked your mum to talk to him—see if he would loosen up.' Alice took one last mouthful of tea and emptied the cup. Emily left hers, and continued to gaze at her aunt. 'I will never forget,' said Alice, 'when your mother relayed this story to me, how sad she was. She maintained that she felt that Frank was a normal kid, who, through vulnerability and circumstances, got mixed up with the wrong people. But that night at the police station she saw something that chilled her to the bone. It intimidated her like nothing had before, and she knew—right then—that he was gone.'

'Gone?' said Emily.

'The person she looked at, the boy she knew, had vanished, replaced by someone she did not want to be around. Your mother wasn't prone to making silly statements Emily. She was an intelligent woman, and I suppose after I heard her speak of my brother, and knowing what he did, I never felt the desire to visit him. Your father did—once—and I never heard him utter his name after that, never.'

'I can understand that, I think,' replied Emily, 'It would be awkward to say the very least.'

'He blamed Frank… apart from everything he had done, for destroying your grandmother's health. It was your mother's opinion that it was the war, not just Frank, but everything. "The war changed everything," she would say, and I believe she was right.'

Emily paused before she asked her next question, both to compose herself, and to admire the courage and determination that Alice had shown through unimaginable hardship. 'What are your memories of my father?'

'When I was a child?'

Emily shrugged; she did not want to commit to a definite answer. She would be happy to hear anything about the parent she had no recollection of.

Alice noticed the look of longing in her niece's eye, a sad look; for while Alice had experienced loss at a young age, she, at the very least had some memory of her mother and father—Emily had nothing except a notion.

'Clarence was ten years older than me, always caring in nature from what I remember, talkative and happy.' Alice breathed deeply and looked across to see Emily eyes, wet with tears, attentive as anyone could be, so she made a decision to focus on positive memories. 'My most vivid recollection of your father from my time in Balmain was the day he brought your mother home for the first time. I have told you this story many times before,' smiled Alice, 'but allow me to tell it again, as it is my most cherished childhood memory, apart from their wedding day.'

Alice was happy to move away from discussing Frank, and told Emily every detail she could recall of the happy young couple. The stories—as they always did—became stories about Ruth, and Alice was unable and unwilling to hide her admiration for Emily's mother.

'Can I ask you another question Aunty?'

'Of course,' replied Alice, 'after what we have discussed, I don't think any topic would be considered intrusive.'

Both ladies laughed; they revelled in the relationship that they had developed. The closeness and honesty was met with compassion and, above all, humour.'

'Are you happy here at Avondale?, asked Emily.

'Now that Norman is dead, you mean.'

'Yes.'

'Well, I have managed for almost eight years now,' replied Alice. She stood to clear the tea cups, a little bristled but not angry, more surprised by the question and her niece's perception.

'The house looks wonderful,' replied Emily quickly, 'and of course you have… managed, that's not what I mean. Are you happy living here—by yourself?' Emily re-asked the question with her familiar directness.

Alice looked uncomfortable all of a sudden, which was not what Emily intended, so she spoke again before Alice could answer. 'I am sorry, Aunty, forget I asked, I just had a thought the other day that maybe… and it is really none of my business,' continued Emily apologetically, 'that it might be nice for you to be around Judith and the children. She could probably do with the help, now she has three.'

'I don't think Reg would like that, dear, the house is full now.'

'I was going to persuade him to build you a cottage. But forget I mentioned it, or maybe think about it?' said Emily with a playful smile.

'You are incorrigible,' joked Alice, 'you need to get back to your husband. I have kept you too long. Give me a hug before you fly off in your new car.'

Emily walked over to Alice and gave her a warm hug. 'I will say a prayer for your brother Frank tonight.'

'Thank you, dear, and thank you for listening.'

'Thank you, Aunty, I cherish our talks,' replied Emily as she kissed Alice on the cheek.

Emily turned and picked up her handbag, which she had left beside her chair. She had a strong urge to say something she had wanted to speak of for a long time.

'Alice,' said Emily. She looked through the kitchen window, before she gathered the strength to turn and look directly at her Aunt.

'Yes M.'

'You know that when I call you Aunty, it is something that I have just gotten used to, a habit. And while I love—in fact crave—hearing stories of my mother, it is you that I consider to be my mum, and always have.'

Alice stared at Emily with a humble expression that displayed happiness that was beyond wilful exuberance. The glint in her eye and the upturned corner of her mouth revealed a joy that comes with being called by the name that Emily had said with such affection.

'I have always loved you, and considered you to be my daughter,' whispered Alice softly, as tears streamed down her face, 'but to hear you say those words, Emily, fills my heart with happiness. I am so very proud of you, so very proud.'

Emily rushed across the kitchen floor and hugged Alice with love and happiness. 'I love you, Mum,' she said.

THIRTY FOUR

'Can I have a quick word?' yelled Emily. She stepped backwards a few paces to avoid a bale of hay that Reginald had thrown from the top of the stack. The sweet smell of lucerne filled Emily's senses and invoked childhood memories.

Reg stood with hands on hips to exaggerate his annoyance. 'You can see I'm busy, Emily, can't it wait?'

'I leave for the coast tomorrow, so no, it can't,' shouted Emily. Her annoyance was not exaggerated. 'It won't take long,' she continued as she stepped out of the way of Paul McMillan, who collected the bales and placed them on the tray of the Ford. What were once the McMIllan brothers at work on the properties was now just the one, the older brother Richard was killed fighting the Japanese at Milne Bay.

'Hold on then. Bloody hell, you can be a pain,' moaned Reg as he made his descent on the bales. The haphazard way in which they were removed from the stack formed a sort of staircase which made Reg's task easier. 'Paul, take a smoko, I won't be long.'

'Okay, boss,' said Paul, before he moved politely away.

'Did he just call you boss?' asked Emily, mildly amused.

'Yes,' replied Reg indignantly, 'why wouldn't he? What is it you need to talk so urgently about? God knows I can't afford to stop work. That wedding cost me a fortune.'

Emily rolled her eyes instead of answering; she waited a moment to allow Reg to feel foolish before she broached what she came to talk about. 'I have been thinking it would be a good idea for Alice to come and live at Denman Hill.'

'Have you,' scoffed Reg. 'why would she want to do that? She has her own place.'

'It is terribly lonely for her over there; it's not good for her.'

'She can visit whenever she wants. Why must you meddle, Emily?' said Reg quickly. He started to sound panicked. 'Everyone is happy where they are.'

'She's not happy, Reg, I can tell.'

'Well move her in with you and Robert, if you're so concerned.'

'I wouldn't hesitate,' said Emily sharply, before she quietened her voice for the labourer's sake, 'but she loves being around your children, and she would be a help for Jude.'

'We haven't got the room.'

'Well make it then… build a cottage for her; it is the least you could do!' Barked Mrs Anderson, her blood now up.

'Least I could do… what in Christ's name is that supposed to mean?'

'What is it supposed to mean?' shouted Emily, as she took a step forward, no longer worried about Paul's proximity. Reg involuntarily took half a step back as he saw his sister's eyes. He instantly hated himself for it. 'It means that you should show a little more gratitude, a little more compassion and some semblance of love for the women who raised you. Do I actually have to spell it out for you, Reg?'

'Now listen here, Emily, I… '

'Oh, shut up! Do the right thing and build the damn cottage. You can even have the honour of acting chivalrously and telling her yourself.'

Reg's face was red with anger and embarrassment, but he chose not to speak. He didn't have the courage to get into a protracted argument with his sister or anyone else with substance. He found it easier to domineer over the more timid people within his circle.

'I am going home to pack,' said Emily firmly, fed up with her brother's attitude, 'I'll leave it with you.'

***

The bottle cap bounced off the table and fell to the timber floorboards on the Denman Hill verandah. Reg poured the pilsener into his froth-marked glass, and gazed groggily over his front paddocks. Seated in a comfortable cane chair, he used his right forearm to push the four empty bottles huddled on the table next to him. It made room for the freshly opened one, already half empty.

Reg brooded while he sat; his pride was wounded from the exchange with his sister. 'Smart bitch,' he mumbled under his breath as he took a long mouthful of beer from his glass. The more intoxicated he became, the more confident he was in what he should have said. Reg had relived the argument many times in his mind, until, in a bout of fantasy, Emily had eventually apologised for her disrespectful attitude.

The screen door at the front of the house creaked. Judith stepped onto the verandah slowly. .

'Dinner will be about ten minutes, Reg,' said Judith quietly, while she glanced at the five bottles on the table.

'Is it on the table?' barked Reg.

'No, dear, about ten minutes.'

'Well call me in ten minutes,' replied Reg dismissively. Judith noted the unusual contortions her husband's facial features took on when drunk. One of his eyes seemed larger than the other, and his cheeks looked like they had lost all elasticity. She thought it made him look sad—pathetic.

'Yes, Reg,' said Judith before she withdrew down the hall.

'David,' she said, as she entered the kitchen.

'Yes, Mum.'

'I am so sorry to do this to you,' said the concerned mother. Judith did her best to appear calm, although her stomach churned with anxiousness. 'But I promised Aunt Alice that you would do a couple of chores for her this afternoon, and I totally forgot. I am so silly.'

'But we are about to eat, Mum.'

'I know, darling… and that is why I feel so silly, because Aunt Alice wanted you to eat with her. Apple pie, I think,' added Judith desperately.'

'I love apple pie,' said David excitedly.

'Yes, I know, said Judith quickly. She removed the boy's place settings as she spoke. 'Take William with you, Alice would love to see him; quick-sticks.'

'Ride or walk?'

'Ride I think, darling, it will be quicker… but no galloping with William, and sit him in front of you—not behind.'

Judith ushered the boys out the kitchen door and then made her way to the telephone in the hallway. She picked up the receiver and asked the operator for Avondale. After a period of time, Judith heard Alice's voice.

'Alice, its Judith.'

'Hello, Jude.'

Judith turned to face the front door, ready to sight Reginald should he suddenly decide to enter the house. 'Alice,' said Judith, in a calm voice. 'I have sent the boys over to your house for dinner. Reg… isn't feeling well,' offered Judith. She was mindful of switchboard operators who listened in on private calls and then gossiped.

'That's no good, Jude, what's wrong with him… oh,' exclaimed Alice, as she caught on. 'Yes of course, of course; are you all right, my dear?' asked Alice uneasily.

'Perfectly; I told David to do some chores for you.'

'I can always find some of those,' replied Alice. She did her best to be cheerful, but there was angst in her voice. 'Now you are certain you don't need any help?'

'Absolutely,' replied Judith. She took a sharp breath as she heard the screen door open. 'Thank you, Alice, the boys love your cooking,' said Judith loudly, for Reg's sake. 'I must go now, thanks again.'

'Who was that?' said Reg, as he trudged down the hall, his supply of pilsener exhausted. 'Thought you said dinner was ten minutes away, I'm starved.'

Judith didn't reply to Reg's question or his statement. She knew there to be no correct one. Instead she turned and walked peacefully towards the kitchen to serve the two meals.

'Where are David and William,' slurred Reg, 'and the baby?'

'Elizabeth is asleep, Reg,' said Alice, while she placed carrots, peas, and potatoes on the plate alongside slices of corned beef, 'and the boys are at Alice's. David is doing a couple of jobs.'

'Wish he would do a few around here,' mumbled Reg before he belched.

'Alice needs the help, dear,' replied Judith as she placed Reg's meal in front of him, 'and the boys enjoy the time with her.'

'Alice, bloody Alice,' mumbled Reg, as though he was under attack.

'Excuse me, dear?'

'Nothin',' grunted Reg. He sliced a portion of corned beef, pushed some peas onto his fork and then devoured it. He cut some more meat as he chewed and then looked up at Judith as she sat at the opposite end of the table. 'That sister of mine wants me... no, demanded, that I build Alice a cottage at the back of this house, so she can move from Avondale.'

Judith cut small morsels of food and then placed the tip of the fork in her mouth.

'It wasn't enough that I spent a fortune on her wedding, now this,' complained Reg. He stabbed at the vegetables on his plate while he held his knife pointed to the ceiling. 'Did you actually cook these potatoes?' he hissed. Uncouthly he removed a piece from his mouth with his fingers, stared at it and then dropped it on his plate. Reg wiped what remained on his hand against his trousers. 'How hard is it to get a good meal after a hard day's work?'

Judith looked at her plate and absorbed the insult. She gave thanks that she had sent her boys to the sanctuary of Alice's house. Judith had been excited at first when Reg had announced Emily's plan, but had suddenly experienced misgivings. The scheme she had quickly devised and executed that day would not be possible if Alice came to live with them.

Only days before, David had been hit repeatedly across the back of his legs with his father's belt for forgetting to wash his hands before dinner; Judith had felt ashamed of herself as she watched her eldest son try to hold back tears while he sat—hands cleaned—chewing slowly on his food. She had done nothing to intervene, and reasoned or made the excuse that intervention may have prolonged the ordeal.

'Why should I build Alice a cottage?'

Trapped, Judith knew she had stayed silent for as long as Reg would tolerate. Although he would never concede to her opinion, he needed affirmation from her. It reinforced his notion that he was the respected and needed man of the house; correct in his thoughts, able to make decisions that his wife could not make. Judith's very real dilemma lay in what she chose to say.

'It would probably be lonely over there, dear.'

Reg looked up from his meal. The very thin veil which held all his insecurities was drawn back by Judith's comment, to reveal in full his violent temper. 'So, you're behind this!' roared Reg. 'You?' he said more quietly. 'You deceitful woman, going behind my back...'

'Reg, what are you talking about,' replied Judith, her voice panicky, 'behind what?'

'In cahoots with my smart-arse sister,' snarled Reg. He stood and walked towards his wife. Judith was genuinely scared. 'Think you can get your stupid fucking husband to do what you want!' he yelled as he stood over Judith. Reg placed one hand on the table and one on the back of her chair, while the frightened woman, cowered under the coward.

'No, Reg, I don't know what you are talking about, please,' she cried. Judith's face was directed to the ground. Her eyes angled up defensively, anticipating what she once thought unthinkable.

'Oh, yes you do,' growled Reg. He lifted his hand up high. The sight of the frightened woman—subject to his whim— brought on an erection, and a strange smirk appeared on his face. A flashback of himself as a child, in the same position his wife now took, instantly deflated his bizarre arousal. It made his frame limp, and the squeal Judith made in terror, as she waited to be struck, brought bile to the back of his throat.

In a spasm of shame-riddled anger, Reg, with his whole palm, flicked her plate off the table. Judith screamed as she caught the movement of his hand from the corner of her eye; the desperate cry muffled the sound of shattered china against the kitchen wall.

Reginald Miller grimaced while he paced backwards—his drunkenness still evident in his movement. He looked around the kitchen like he had scanned the scene for witnesses, while the temperature of his blood dropped steadily. He wiped his hands down the length of his shirt, unconsciously desiring to scrape the film of self loathing from his skin. Reg's head ached with the awareness of what he had been prepared to do.

'Jude,' he said, pitifully.

Judith's sudden movement filled the kitchen with a sound that grated and then ended with a screech, as the chair legs scraped along the timber floor boards. The noise made Reg breath in, nervously, as if he were the victim.

'It was just the drink... I worked all day... and Emily. I'd never... you know that.' Reg stared at his wife as she backed towards the sink. Not once did she make eye-contact with him. 'Are you going to say something?' asked Reg. He sounded deflated but surprised that she hadn't cheerfully accepted his mumbled justifications.

'I am fine, thank you, Reg,' replied Judith, while she stood straight-backed with her hands clasped in front. Her gaze was angled to the floor at Reg's feet. 'I would like to clean the floor, if you don't mind.'

'Sure, luv,' said Reg, with a note of hope and some certainty in his voice. 'You're a good wife,' he continued to Judith's unresponsive, crouched body. He turned suddenly and walked down the hallway and out the front door. When Judith heard the front screen door bang shut, she dropped the pieces of broken plate and collapsed. She moaned a sorrowful cry. She had been relieved from danger, but was resigned to captivity.

Part Four

THIRTY FIVE

Denman Hill, July 1953

'Now, Mrs Miller,' said Sergeant Smyth sternly. The sergeant considered Judith's state and eased his tone. 'Mrs Miller, could you please, for the sake of clarity, go over what you have just said to Constable Bolton?'

'I am not sure she has to say anything, Sergeant,' interjected Alice, who stood behind the seated mother. She had tried to support Judith, but sounded panicked.

'That is true, Mrs Clark,' replied the Sergeant, 'but then I would have to take Mrs Miller into the station, and that is not something I want to do.'

Judith opened a conciliatory hand towards Alice while she nodded towards the sergeant to confirm she was happy to speak. 'I will tell you everything that has happened tonight,' said Judith, 'but I should be… we all should be looking for my son. He is hurt.' Judith fell silent as images of her husband beating her son flashed before her eyes. It brought a terrible feeling of sadness and then anger to every part of her body.

'I know it must be hard, Mrs Miller,' replied Sergeant Smyth, 'I have several men on the job right at this moment, all of them experienced. Mr Adler and his sons are also out with them; we will find your boy.' The sergeant stopped for a moment. He was also a father, and knew how futile his words would sound to a worried mother whose only concern was for her child.

Judith clasped Alice's hand for comfort and then released it to give her full attention to Sergeant Smyth. 'My husband came home drunk from the hotel,' said Judith calmly, her hands were clasped in her lap as she sat straight-backed in an upholstered chair. 'He had been there all day.'

'Approximately at what time did he return home?' asked Sergeant Smyth.

'It was dark… about seven o'clock.'

'The hotels close at six; any idea where your husband may have been in the time between the pub closing and arriving home? It's only a ten-minute trip.'

Judith stared blankly at the sergeant and the look ridiculed him. Every man and woman in the district knew that the publicans flaunted with the closing hours and provided grog on the sly. It was worth the risk for the few extra quid they reasoned.

'Yes—well, never mind that, seven o'clock you say,' stated Smyth, he realised the stupidity of the question. 'What happened after he arrived home?'

'I heard a loud bang,' replied Judith. 'He had crashed the vehicle into the shed. I was in the front room reading and I got up and moved into the kitchen. My children were with Alice in the cottage. I heard a second loud noise, minutes later; Reg had fallen over a wheelbarrow in the darkness—that's when he became aggressive.'

'I had an exchange with him prior to that, Sergeant,' added Alice.

'An argument?'

'Yes,' replied Alice, 'he made quite a raucous… I asked him to think of the children. He swore at me, told me to go inside, and that's when I heard the second noise.'

'Thank you, Mrs Clark,' said the Sergeant. 'Mrs Miller, what happened from there?'

Judith hesitated before she replied; the visions of her crazed husband—manic like a wild boar—revisited her once more. Her stomach tightened as she recalled how her David had stood defiant and brave in front of the cowardly thug that she was bound by law to call her husband. 'He began to scream for my son…'

'David?' interrupted the sergeant.

'No, William, he blamed William for his accident. He screamed and roared little Will's name,' cried Judith, 'I prayed that he would climb out a window and run, run anywhere. I was so scared Sergeant,' added Judith, and began to cry.

Take your time, Mrs Miller,' said Smyth. 'Constable, go to the kitchen and fix Mrs Miller and Mrs Clark a cup of tea.' The constable stood immediately and followed his superior's orders; the Sergeant's reputation, along with his six foot, two-hundred-and-twenty-pound frame, was enough to engage the respect of his men.

Sergeant Smyth watched the constable leave the room before he leaned in closer to Judith. 'Mrs Miller,' began the policeman… 'Mrs Clark. I believe, well I think I know what sort of a man your husband is. I keep a good eye on the town and its goings on. Whatever happened, he wasn't in good shape when we sent him off to the hospital, and he probably…' The Sergeant paused, in search for the right words as Judith and Alice stared at him, unsure of what to make of the sudden change in atmosphere. 'I have sons myself, Mrs Miller… I …'

'Sergeant,' shouted a voice from down the hall followed by heavy footsteps. 'Sir,' said the young constable as he entered the room, 'they found the lad, he's a bit knocked about, but Cummings and Ryan found the boy, sir.'

The sergeant stood and politely made way for Judith, who rushed down the hall, followed closely by Alice. Judith burst into the kitchen and threw her arms around her son. The teenager was wrapped in one of the constable's coats. His hair and body were soaked, and he shuddered from the cold and the shock of his ordeal.

'Oh, my David,' said Judith softly, 'I am so sorry… so sorry, darling.'

David said nothing but leaned into his mother as she cried. Alice moved around behind him, relieved to see him safe, but concerned for his immediate health.'

'We found him over the ridge sergeant, beneath the willow beside the creek; he was soaking wet.'

'Well done, boys,' replied the sergeant, 'it couldn't have been easy.'

'Blind luck really, sir... '

'Sergeant,' snapped Alice, breaking into the exchange. 'We need to get David to a hospital immediately.' Alice didn't wait for the sergeant to reply, but moved to remove David's clothing while she issued instructions. 'Judith, dry clothing, dear, lots of layers and blankets; young man, under the sink there is a hot water bottle, maybe two,' she said with authority. 'Fill them with hot but not boiling water—as quick as you can.'

Alice clasped the boy to her own body for warmth as his mother arrived with dry clothing and blankets. The two of them wrestled with David's increasingly lethargic body, as the effects of the icy water coupled with frigid air started to take hold. Alice gasped, and Judith felt hatred when they saw the open wounds and raised reddened welts across the boy's back from the beating at the hands of his father.

'Sergeant,' said Alice firmly, 'have one of your men bring a car up to the side gate. We must get David to hospital.' She placed the hot water bottles in between layers of David's clothing as she spoke.

Smyth could see the urgency of the situation, but he desperately wanted Judith Miller to be able to give a good account of what had happened; for more than one reason, he hated the likes of Reg Miller. A weak man. Smythe had watched him spend more time in the pub than a family man should, a spruiker who babbled when drunk, but was nowhere to be seen when his country needed him. He sat back and allowed people like Norman Clark and Sergeant Smyth's son Peter—killed within months of each other—to plug the gap for him. He wanted Miller to do time for what he had done to David; he didn't want a fancy lawyer to exploit holes in their police work.

'Cummings,' barked Smyth, 'bring the car up. Mrs Miller, make your way to the car please, we will take care of your son.'

'Go, Jude,' said Alice. She moved to hand Judith a coat from the stand in the corner, while Smythe ushered her towards the door, 'I will stay with William and Elizabeth.'

'Ryan, help me get the lad to the car,' ordered Smyth, 'when we get to the hospital you are to stand guard beside Reg Miller's bed.'

'Worried his missus might try and finish him off, Sarge,' said the young constable who felt cocky after being the one to find the young Miller boy.'

'I'll finish you off if you open your trap again, you useless little prick.'

'Yes, sir, sorry, sir.'

***

Judith Miller walked slowly down the half-lit hall of the Gilmurra Hospital towards the white double doors of Ward B, where her husband lay. She placed both hands on the doors and stood motionless. Deliberately, Judith rested her face to against the painted timber rectangles. From afar, she appeared like a woman who paid homage to a shrine, not a mentally and physically exhausted mother whose world had been turned upside down in a moment. But that was a lie. If she was honest with herself, the events of that evening had hinted at their coming on many occasions. Those hints had been too hastily disregarded.

Judith pushed on the timber doors, where the paint had been worn away in two rough circles by the countless comings and goings during the hospital's existence. She slid quietly through the small opening and into the ward without any emotion, and stared at the only patient in the room; a dim light came from a small lamp that sat beside Reginald's bed. The soft glow gave Reginald a look of virtue, and his blood-stained and bandaged head the appearance of a victim.

The constable, seated beside him, had drifted to sleep while on duty. His presence suggested the man may have endured persecution and needed protection; the falsity of the scene made Judith sick to the stomach.

'Why did I put up with you for so long,' Judith whispered. Her husband stirred in his bed. Maybe he felt the pure hatred that emanated from his wife's pores. 'You never loved me. Never. But I could have lived with that, if only you loved my children—but you wouldn't.' Judith paused; her hands were interlocked in front, with her handbag slung midway up her left forearm. 'Your son David fights for his life down the hall, and I blame myself. I blame myself for not protecting him, but I always thought that the father… the husband, did the protecting; not the beating or the threatening.' Judith moved to the side of the bed that was opposite to the lamp. The shaded light only just touched her and it gave her a ghostly appearance. 'I remember, many years ago, when you would yell and scream at me. Stand over me. Bully me. Leave me without breath while I waited for the blow. I would cry, when you lost your nerve, and you would smash something else instead.' Judith glanced at the sleeping constable and then back at her husband. 'But that all changed didn't it, and I didn't have to wait or wonder after that.' Judith placed her free hand to her face in remembrance of the injuries, and then into her handbag. She clasped at something inside, and the sound roused the derelict policeman. His thoughts were groggy until he saw a figure beside his charge's bed.

'I loathe you, Reginald Miller,' said Judith quietly, while Constable Ryan sat frozen to his seat, all his self-assuredness from Denman Hill gone. 'Not for what you did to me, but what you did to David… and what you would do to William and Elizabeth.'

'Mrs Miller,' said the constable in a whisper. The intentions of the woman who stood before him were calm and composed, but her eyes showed a steely resolve. It aroused his worst fears; there was already an acceptance that his career may be over because of his ineptitude. 'Mrs Miller,' he said again. Ryan noticed her hand hidden inside her handbag. 'Please step away from the bed and your husband. You... no one is supposed to be here.'

Judith looked at the young constable and stared like a lord would at a servant, and then, as if he weren't there, she resumed her hateful gaze at the helpless, soul-less figure in the bed. 'My only blessing,' she said, 'is the knowledge that you will never harm my children again.'

'No!' shouted the constable as he watched Judith withdraw her hand from the bag she carried. The constable slipped and fell onto the smooth vinyl floor as he attempted to restrain Mrs Miller. He scrambled and lifted himself to his knees, and then clasped Mrs Miller's wrist as it moved towards the unconscious patient. The dumbfounded policeman gasped for breath and let out a childish but relieved giggle, as he noticed the shiny gold band held between Judith's thumb and forefinger.

'Forgive me, Mrs Miller,' said Constable Ryan. He felt foolish and released his grip on Judith's wrist. 'I thought...'

'You thought?' replied Judith coldly. 'It would be interesting to hear what a young man who can't keep his eyes open to carry out a task would think—wouldn't it?'

'Yes, ma'am.'

Judith held her wedding band in the light and looked at it. She contemplated things that the constable, in his young and immature years, wouldn't or couldn't understand. She lowered the ring that had bound their marriage towards Reginald's chest and paused. For no particular reason, Judith raised her hand and placed the gold band on his bandaged forehead. She held it in place for a moment like she had conducted a ritual and then let it—and him—go.

'Tell Sergeant Smyth,' said Judith, 'that provided my son has improved during the night, I will be at the police station by nine in the morning to give a statement in regard to Reginald Miller's assault on my son.' Judith turned and left the ward to be by David's side.

THIRTY SIX

Denman Hill, August 1953

Emily handed William a biscuit of hay over the door of Blackie's stable. Her nephew received it in one hand and placed it in the feeder while he continued to brush the bay gelding's coat. He worked furiously to impress his much-loved aunt. She had given the horse to William as a gift before she moved to Sydney.

'He looks fantastic, Will,' said Emily. She smiled at her nephew; the smile he returned gave her a wonderful feeling, but that joy was instantly challenged by sadness. Emily was unable to comprehend the circumstances that would allow a grown man to beat his son in the way her brother had beaten David; the thought ripped at her heart.

'Thanks, Aunty M,' replied William, engaged in his work, 'he's my best mate.'

'And you're his by the look of it,' said Emily with sincerity.

While she watched the young lad, thoughts swirled inside her mind. One in particular forced its way to the front—not in defence of her brother—that was not possible. It was more like a clue as to who he was. It was her conversation with Reginald on the verandah during that eventful September evening in 1939 that she thought of. Reginald had revealed vague parts of his childhood; his memories and fears that he carried like wounds, which were never allowed to heal.

Snatched from her thoughts by a snort from Blackie, Emily sighted a large chest that showed only one studded edge underneath a pile of unfolded horse rugs.

She walked towards the wall that was the home to various pieces of tack, and shelter to a mysterious and intriguing case. Bending over, Emily stared at the object without touching the canvas that mostly hid it from view. She realised that in all the many times she had visited the stables, she couldn't recall seeing it.'

'Aunty M,' said William quietly. He surprised Emily by appearing at her side. He had stopped his work, unsettled by emotions he had tried to ignore.

'Oh! William,' said Emily with a jump, 'I was in another world What is it, dear?'

William stared at the compacted dirt floor of the stables; pieces of scattered straw gave him something to focus on while he steadied himself. 'Is Davo going to be alright?' he asked. William looked up, to reveal eyes washed with tears, and a face etched with concern. His lips were tightly pressed together and showed a hint of anger.

'My darling boy,' said Emily. She dropped to one knee to embrace her nephew and hold him close to her chest. 'He will be home before you know it, Will,' she continued. Emily gently withdrew from her hug to hold the boy with both hands; her arms were bent at the elbow to give her grasp softness. 'He will want to ride with you all over the hills, I promise. He just needs to rest in hospital for a bit to regain his strength,' finished Emily.

William nodded his head, pleased with the reassurance; his trust in his aunt was absolute. There was silence for a moment while Emily waited for the "and" to come from William's mouth. The "and" that would lead to the enquiry of his father's condition. But it never came; the young boy didn't care and didn't want to know, and sadly—or not—neither did she.

Emily poked William playfully in the stomach with her finger. Her love for her nephew undiminished after her move away from

Gilmurra to Sydney, the birth of her daughter had enhanced, not lessened the bonds of affection. 'You know what?'

'What?' replied William with a smirk.

'Little Ruth will wake up soon and she is always hungry after a sleep.'

'She eats more than me,' remarked William of his little cousin.

'If you mash up her vegetables once I have cooked them,' said Emily, 'nice and smooth so she can eat them… there may, or may not,' she teased, 'be a box of chocolates in my suitcase for a good little helper.'

William turned and ran for the kitchen, before Emily could rise from her crouched position to follow him. Casually she looked back at the chest against the stable wall.

***

With her one-year-old daughter down for her afternoon sleep, Emily asked William—rewarded and satisfied after his assistance that morning—to play with Elizabeth and listen for baby Ruth while she attended to a job in the back-yard. She went out the kitchen door and moved steadily across the lawn, which was green but short in the winter months. Emily stopped suddenly as she breached the gap in between Alice's cottage to the left and the chook pen on the right. The horse stables in front of her seemed to assume the venerable qualities of a church that guarded sacred relics.

Motivated by a need to satisfy her curiosity, she was at a loss to explain why a chest in a stable had affected her in such away. It had taken hold of her and occupied her thoughts to the point where she could not ignore its silent but incessant call.

Emily walked slowly towards the stable door and then hesitated at its entrance. She craned her neck to look down the length of the stable, and inspected the area as if it were foreign to her. Immediately she felt foolish and checked her actions. She admonished her childishness and walked with purpose towards the chest, and removed the horse rugs in one determined effort. The disturbance filled the air with dust that made her cough and squint.

Emily knelt down before the timber crate and its domed top. The dark panelled finish with pressed-tin strips, each bordered with evenly spaced nails, added to the mystique that had captured her at first sight.

Emily lifted the latch that lay against a lock, broken long ago. She raised the lid and allowed it to rest against the stable wall. A rectangular piece of canvas had been placed on top, probably to protect or shield the items that lay beneath. A faded piece of paper inscribed with neat handwriting rested on top of that.

Albums, books and souvenirs

Whose writing is that? questioned Emily.

She pocketed the note and removed the canvas. Emily smiled. Two photo albums were the first thing to catch her eye; their unfamiliarity had immediately increased her interest. Gently she removed the leather covered albums and moved back towards the stable entrance where there was more light. Emily sat down on a bale of hay and breathed in deeply. She had already anticipated the contents of the albums that she held. On the first page she saw and recognised her parents. They stood on a flight of small stairs in front of a church; the handsome couple looked as happy and in love as any couple could be. As she brushed her hand over the photo, a tear fell to rest on her knuckles. Emily reacted and quickly lifted her arm to protect the preserved image. There was a group photo of the same day; the woman who raised her was just a little girl. Alice stood at the feet of the married couple; the smile and glint in her eyes, said everything. Emily recalled the stories Alice had told her. That single photo now revealed the past to her, like an affidavit to that history.

Emily closed the second album; she felt drained but exalted by her discovery. She was happy to have new memories, but sad that they were ever lost. Emily walked back to the opened chest and set aside the albums, while she inspected what lay beneath. Books on agricultural practices, a shoebox full of letters, and a satchel that held a rather large medallion were some of things Emily removed before she uncovered what looked like a journal. *Maybe it's a hand-written cookbook, like the one Alice keeps,* she thought. There were some loose bits of paper that protruded from the side to give strength to that notion.

Black underneath a floral pattern, the diary or notebook was definitely feminine, and Emily knew without a doubt that it had once belonged to her mother. She turned away from the chest and sank to sit on the dusty floor with her back rested against the box. Emily closed her eyes and said a silent prayer. She asked for permission, and then forgiveness; forgiveness for having opened something once and forever private.

Emily removed the journal and resumed her seat on the bale of hay. She opened the cover, and was struck by five words written boldly on a forty-five-degree angle: *How Do I love thee.* Emily recognised the poem from school, but wondered why it was penned so prominently in her mother's book. She contemplated for a moment, and then began to read. She read of love, spontaneous and true; her pondering over the five words was answered almost immediately. She read of her mother's joy in being accepted so easily into a family, whose parents, burdened with the worry of a serving son, continued to love and care for the siblings that remained. She cried with Ruth when her father enlisted, and felt her anger rise at the cowardly girl who delivered the shameful package. She thought of her own wedding day, and lifted her tear-filled eyes to the stable ceiling as she imagined her parent's ceremony. She tried, but didn't want to know, what it would be like to watch Robert leave for war, as her mother had watched her father; the strength of the woman lost to memory, but held within her heart, admired through the words on brownish paper.

Emily was startled back to reality by the sight of William at the stable doorway. He held her daughter Ruth as best he could; Elizabeth stood partially hidden to one side of her brother.

'Oh my, what time is it?'

'Ruthy is hungry, Aunty M,' said William quietly He appeared repentant for having disturbed his Aunt.

'I am so sorry, William,' cried Emily, 'I lost track of time.'

'I gave Lizbeth some milk,' replied William, getting his tongue around his sister's name, 'but I don't know what Ruth has besides vegetables.'

'You did very well William, I am so sorry,' repeated Emily. She scurried back to the chest to replace the albums, but she kept hold of the journal; her nephew's eyes followed her movements.

'Father said we couldn't touch that,' said William dryly. It left Emily a little lost for words while she replaced the rugs.

'Well...' started Emily

'So, I'm glad you did,' stated the lad, his tone still dry.

***

The Ford powered steadily along the Tully Road towards town. Its driver—with the window down—used the cool crisp air to clear her mind of the many thoughts she had had since reading her mother's entire journal. She had stayed up after the rest of the house had gone to bed, and read the diary by the fire in the lounge room.

Emily had risen early after an interrupted sleep. She had been restless throughout the night, and had made the decision to drive into Gilmurra. The pages in the diary that Emily had devoured increased in their potency as they moved from Balmain and onto Denman Hill. The words hit her hard; the happenings that she read about, the challenges that her mother had faced in the post-war years, had largely taken place within the walls that surrounded her that night.

Parts of her mother's writings were hard to read, and Emily

had found it difficult to understand how her mother had endured. How had she dealt with what was left of her father Clarrie when he returned home from overseas. It was love, that she knew. Love and devotion; but the doubt that was allowed to express itself—briefly, occasionally—on the lined pages of her diary must not have been allowed to reveal itself in her daily life. Emily gained a sense of her mother's strength from the pages as she turned them. The paradoxical feelings of joy and heartache intertwined, always allowing the idea of hope without being able to dispel gloom.

She thought of her father; the man he was and the man he became; what war had done to a beautiful soul. She wondered—feeling guilt and unworthiness—if her uncle Archie, killed in a faraway land, mourned and revered as a hero, his image forever cast in sparkling youth, had been handed the more humane ending. Her father Clarence had returned home to loved ones alive, with his heart beating and limbs moving, but with a soul that had perished; extinguished not by bullet or shell, a bayonet or bomb, but by horror—unrelenting horror.

Emily cried as she steered the farm vehicle along the undulating road. The release of emotion weakened her resolve, and she began to sob uncontrollably as the thought of a particular entry in the diary came back to her. At first she had turned away from it, but the need for truth within her family history had forced her to read on. What made it hard for Emily was that it was the first time that she had cause to reproach her mother's actions. It gave her mother's memory a human frailty, when she had always thought of her as a saint.

It read: *Today is the first time I can honestly say that I felt ashamed of myself. I fool myself by thinking that writing it down will absolve me but I am sincere in my sorrow, my little boy being the only one, besides God himself, who can ultimately forgive me.*

Emily cried harder as she remembered the blurred ink that marked the page, the pain that lay in those tears—hard to imagine.

I stood and did nothing while Clarence, smelling of alcohol, hit Reggie continually because he had mud on his boots inside the house. I screamed but he wouldn't stop. He screamed that men need discipline, which made no sense. I will never forget the look on my little boy's face, so frightened, confused, and I fear—I know—it has happened before. I will never forgive myself. I worry endlessly for Clarence, but not today.

Emily gripped the steering wheel with white knuckled hands, and let out a painful moan. The image of her own daughter danced behind her eyes. She forced the gear stick into position and pulled back on to the road. She no longer thought, she was just intent to arrive at her destination.

***

She dabbed and wiped around her eyes with a tissue to hide the signs of tears, and applied some makeup. There was little movement around the hospital, as it was so early, but Emily was not concerned. She knew where her brother was. She would not pause and ask for directions. The guard placed on her brother was no longer an obstacle, as Sergeant Smyth had removed the constable, embarrassed; a replacement seemed, in the circumstances, ridiculous.

Emily made her way through the corridors, and entered the ward, where she saw Reginald in bed motionless. His eyes were open, but his face had no expression. Without delay, she moved to his bedside and drew up a chair to sit directly in the view that he held.

'Good morning, Reginald.'

Only his eyes moved towards her: she noticed his bandaged head, sullen look, and pale complexion, which made him appear many years older. *Maybe the strain of guilt has taken its toll as well*, she thought.

'I won't keep you long,' stated Emily. 'How are you? She asked begrudgingly.

Her brother looked at her with his greyish eyes but did not respond. He held her gaze for a moment, before he shifted his stare to one side of her.

'I brought you something to read,' she eased her tone slightly. Emily wanted above all else to get her message across. 'And I strongly urge you to read it. Maybe you have already; I'm not sure.'

Emily held the journal up for her brother to see, and then placed it on the movable table that lay across his torso. Reginald gave it a quick glance through eye-lids that flickered, something Emily was not able to interpret; was it recognition of something known?

Emily looked around the empty ward, and took in its sterile environment. She looked back towards her brother. The word that suggested a bond, stung her. She decided that she did not want to be there, and she knew—from his countenance—he was aware of her feelings.

'Reg, you are my brother… but I will never forgive you for what you did to David… what you had already done; a boy, your son, who only ever aimed to please you.'

Emily saw a tear roll down Reg's cheek while he lay motionless. She paused for a moment, and then decided to press on. Emily realised that this moment was the only moment in which she could make some difference.

'Our lives were not easy, yours was harder than mine. But we were loved by our aunt and uncle—our adopted mother and father. I am not sure what lies ahead for you, but if you do one thing, Reg,' appealed Emily, 'read what I gave you.' She looked down at her lap and then at her brother, who met her stare. 'It may help you.'

Emily stood to leave; she turned, but stopped at the sound of a frail voice.

'How is David?'

Emily closed her eyes and clenched her teeth. She fought back tears, the tragedy of everything, the nurturing of pain over years and generations, feeling as if it had become too much. She knew, as she stood with hunched shoulders, that she was in the presence of a man who placated his demons through violence. He had been the subject of such himself, and was now left with a ruined life—if he looked at it that way. She answered his question, but took liberties that she wasn't sure were hers to take.

'Physically he is seriously hurt, but in recovery; mentally, I don't know. I feel he will grow into a fine young man, if allowed to… with his mother and those that love him.'

Reg took Emily's message as it was intended and sank into his pillows. He now knew the only course for him to take. Emily left the hospital quickly; she wanted the embrace of her husband and daughter.

***

Arthur Atkins and his secretary made their way to Gilmurra Hospital. Arthur had received the strange request to visit Reginald Miller; strange because he represented his wife. That reason alone had caused him to refuse the request at first. Subsequent messages and sentiments of good will—if Reg's character possessed that—had finally persuaded the ageing lawyer.

Arthur and his secretary sat next to Reg's bed on chairs provided by an orderly. They exchanged a curious glance with one another, and then both declined offers of tea from the matron on duty.

'How may we help you, Mr Miller,' asked Arthur, shocked by Reginald's aged look. His eyes reminded him of Clarence's, well after the war.

Reg attempted to sit a little straighter. He winced at the pain he felt in his head, but neither Arthur nor his secretary moved to assist him.

'Thank you for coming, Arthur,' said Reg. His voice matched his appearance, 'I know it was an unusual and unwanted request.'

Arthur nodded in acceptance of the thanks.

'I am uncertain as to my future…'

'Mr Miller,' interjected Arthur,' you know I cannot speak of the allegations against you, I… '

Reginald raised his open palm to relieve Mr Atkins of the need to explain himself.

'I would like your secretary to pen a letter for me, and for you to deliver it to David.' Reg felt weak. He paused to take a breath before he continued. 'If you could do me that service, I would then ask you to draw up the necessary documents that would enable me to transfer what I own, under Judith's direction, to my son…' Reg stopped, overcome by the word that represented what he had never seen himself as. He looked towards an open window. He could hear the cries of his first-born son all those years ago. David's life had begun only a matter of yards from where he lay. He envisaged, his mother and father.

'Equally,' he continued quietly, 'with William and Elizabeth.'

Mr Atkins's secretary looked towards her boss for direction; Arthur looked at Reg for a moment. His mind drifted and he pictured Archie Miller with a fresh-faced Clarence in the Egyptian desert. He clenched his teeth in remembrance of Ruth. The thought of Alice and all she had suffered caused Arthur to look towards the ceiling. *It's over now. All the recurring pain that tore this family apart will end.* Arthur exhaled and felt some relief. He signalled his approval to his secretary. She removed a notepad and pencil from a leather satchel and waited for Reginald to speak.

Epilogue

The geldings walked calmly along the creek that glistened in the sunlight. The two brothers chatted freely; the younger boy pleased to be in the company of his big brother again. David reached out with his left hand and offered William a stick of gum from the packet he held, while he rolled with his mount's gait. William took one, and then a second. He gave his sibling and friend a loving smile and then casually plucked the whole packet from his hand.

They laughed together as they approached the large willow that spread its roots beside the creek, its branches devoid of leaves. Slowly the horses ambled past the gnarled and twisted tree; its wooded arms reached like they yearned to reveal a story. The horses snorted and David felt a tingle run down his spine, as he remembered where he hid on that cold and dark night. He was tempted to reach for the scars across his back, but he resisted. He pushed the thought of his father from his mind and stroked his mount's neck instead.

The horses calmed, and David gave a slight nod to William. With kindness, the Miller boys turned their mounts east for the ridge and home, where their mother, sister and Aunt Alice waited in peaceful surrounds.

They rode side by side, and casually but purposefully glanced at each Hereford cow to score their condition. Winter rains had made the ground soft, and David was conscious of footrot within the herd.

Patiently he spoke to his younger brother about the cattle that surrounded them. They were his future, and he was confident that he would step to the fore and shape the Miller family destiny.